Translating the Literatures
of Small European Nations

Translating the Literatures of Small European Nations

Edited by
Rajendra Chitnis,
Jakob Stougaard-Nielsen, Rhian Atkin
and Zoran Milutinović

Liverpool University Press

First published 2020 by
Liverpool University Press
4 Cambridge Street
Liverpool
L69 7ZU

This paperback edition published 2022

Copyright © 2022 Liverpool University Press

The right of Rajendra Chitnis, Jakob Stougaard-Nielsen, Rhian Atkin and Zoran Milutinović to be identified as the editors of this work has been asserted by them in accordance with the Copyright, Designs and Patents Act 1988.

All rights reserved. No part of this book may be reproduced, stored in a retrieval system, or transmitted, in any form or by any means, electronic, mechanical, photocopying, recording, or otherwise, without the prior written permission of the publisher.

British Library Cataloguing-in-Publication data
A British Library CIP record is available

ISBN 978-1-78962-052-8 cased
ISBN 978-1-80207-739-1 paperback

Cover image designed by Daniel Šticha.

Typeset by Carnegie Book Production, Lancaster
Printed and bound by CPI Group (UK) Ltd, Croydon CR0 4YY

Contents

Acknowledgements   vii

Introduction   1
   Rajendra Chitnis and Jakob Stougaard-Nielsen

1. The Global Presentation of Small National Literatures: South Slavs in Literary History and Theory   9
   David Norris

2. Translators as Ambassadors and Gatekeepers: The Case of South Slav Literature   27
   Zoran Milutinović

3. Supply-driven Translation: Compensating for Lack of Demand   48
   Ondřej Vimr

4. Literature as Cultural Diplomacy: Czech Literature in Great Britain, 1918–38   69
   Rajendra Chitnis

5. Exporting the Canon: The Mixed Experience of the Dutch *Bibliotheca Neerlandica*   91
   Irvin Wolters

6. Creative Autonomy and Institutional Support in Contemporary Slovene Literature   109
   Olivia Hellewell

Contents

    7. Strategies for Success? Evaluating the Rise of Catalan Literature   126
        Richard M. Mansell

    8. Gender, Genre and Nation: Nineteenth-century Swedish Women Writers on Export   145
        Gunilla Hermansson and Yvonne Leffler

    9. Translating as Re-telling: On the English Proliferation of C.P. Cavafy   165
        Paschalis Nikolaou

   10. Criminal Peripheries: The Globalization of Scandinavian Crime Fiction and Its Agents   184
        Jakob Stougaard-Nielsen

   11. Literary Translation and Digital Culture: The Transmedial Breakthrough of Poland's *The Witcher*   205
        Paulina Drewniak

   12. Towards a Multilingual Poetics: Self-translation, Translingualism and Maltese Literature   227
        Josianne Mamo

   13. Does Size Matter? Questioning Methods for the Study of 'Small'   247
        Rhian Atkin

Coda: When Small is Big and Big is Small   267
        Svend Erik Larsen

Index   273

Acknowledgements

This volume arises from a two-year Research Innovations project funded by the UK's Arts and Humanities Research Council (AHRC) under its Translating Cultures theme. The project team would like to thank the AHRC for their support, and the theme fellow, Charles Forsdick, for his sustained interest in our work in progress. We are also extremely grateful to our advisory board – Alexandra Büchler (Literature across Frontiers, Mercator Institute for Media, Languages and Culture, University of Aberystwyth), Sarah Death (translator and editor), Alex Drace-Francis (University of Amsterdam), Svend Erik Larsen (University of Aarhus) and Carol O'Sullivan (University of Bristol) – for all their time, ideas, encouragement and participation. The principal investigator, Rajendra Chitnis, would also like to thank colleagues in the School of Modern Languages and throughout the University of Bristol for their professional and personal support over the lifetime of the project, especially Hannah Blackman, Charles Burdett and Derek Offord.

Arts & Humanities Research Council

The AHRC funds world-class, independent researchers in a wide range of subjects: history, archaeology, digital content, philosophy, languages, design, heritage, area studies, the creative and performing arts, and much more. In the financial year 2018–19, the AHRC will spend approximately £98 million on research and postgraduate training, in collaboration with a number of partners. The quality and range of research supported by this investment of

Acknowledgements

public funds not only provides social and cultural benefits and contributes to the economic success of the UK but also to the culture and welfare of societies around the globe.

Introduction

*Rajendra Chitnis (University of Bristol)
and Jakob Stougaard-Nielsen (UCL)*

In his essay 'Die Weltliteratur', Milan Kundera (2013 [2005], 292–93) identifies 'provincialism', defined as 'the inability (or the refusal) to see one's own culture in the *large context*', in both large and small nations. While the latter may hold 'world culture in high esteem but feel it to be something alien' and 'inaccessible', with 'little connection to their national literature', the former, by contrast, may appear provincial in their resistance to the Goethean idea of world literature because their own literature seems to them sufficiently rich that they need take no interest in what people write elsewhere. This book explores how 'small-nation' European literatures, written in less commonly spoken languages or from less familiar traditions and ostensibly dependent on translation to reach the wider world, negotiate and seek to overcome the inequality born of these mutual 'provincialisms', as expressed in theory, reception and industry practice.

As this book documents, we can easily discern these contrasting provincialisms in the ways in which translated literatures cross European borders and languages. Translations flow predominantly from the 'Greenwich Meridian of Literature', today mainly anglophone markets, to the rest of Europe, and only rarely and fleetingly does the tide change (Casanova, 2004, 90). Lawrence Venuti (2008, 13) memorably describes the complacency, or provincialism, of Anglo-American publishing as 'imperialistic abroad and xenophobic at home'. The unequal dynamics of the transnational publishing market are felt especially in smaller European nations, since their literatures rarely find their way to readers in larger nations, while most translations into their own languages have an English source. Although there are regional variations within Europe, according to Miha Kovač (2002, 49–51), 'almost 50 percent of all translations in the world are made from English into various languages,

Introduction

but only six percent of all translations are made into English'. An increasingly unequal transnational market for literature, marked by increasing lack of diversity, makes it ever more difficult for authors from small nations to reach international audiences.

The consequence of hegemonic inequalities between global and European centres and their peripheries is not only small-nation authors' exclusion from the European mainstream, but also the declining diversity of voices accessible to the centre. Claire Squires (2009, 408) writes: 'European nations typically have access to a large number of books translated from English, but also a percentage from other languages that is at least equivalent to, and often more than, that to which British and American readers typically have access.' British and American readers are, therefore, comparatively 'culturally impoverished', while 'their publishing industries derive financial benefit from foreign and translation rights'. In their quantitative study for Literature across Frontiers of translations in the British Isles between 1990 and 2012, however, Alexandra Büchler and Giulia Trentacosti (2015) contest the veracity of the often-quoted but never statistically documented 3 per cent share of translations in English-language publishing, demonstrating that the share in the UK and Ireland is consistently above 4 per cent, and that between 2000 and 2012 there was a 69 per cent growth in the number of titles in translation, dominated by works in French, with the second most prominent language, German, far behind, followed by Spanish, Russian, Italian, Swedish, Norwegian, Dutch, Portuguese and Danish. The challenge facing literatures from small European nations was, however, reflected in the publication of fewer than ten translations in the entire period from Armenian, Belarusian, Georgian, Latvian, Lithuanian, Macedonian, Slovak, Slovenian and Ukrainian. Our own 2017 industry-focused report, arising from extensive, AHRC-funded engagement with professional intermediaries including translators, large and small publishers, agents and state and third-sector promoters, captured similar cautious optimism about quantity and concern about diversity (Chitnis et al., 2017).

In classifying certain national literatures as 'small', we place them firmly in cultural, economic and geographical peripheries. This identity between peripheral literatures and smaller nations is noted by Itamar Even-Zohar (1990, 48) who argues that, 'as unpalatable as this idea may seem to us', 'we have no choice but to admit that within a group of relatable national literatures, such as the literatures of Europe, hierarchical relations have been established since the very beginnings of these literatures'. Differently defined but overlapping labels like 'minor', 'dominated', 'peripheral', 'marginal' or 'less

Introduction

diffused' reflect a scholarly consensus about the unequal international context in which literatures circulate, to which the leading Danish comparatist, Svend Erik Larsen, returns in his concluding response to our volume. Our use here of the less theoretically established and marked term 'small' relates less to the size of the nation or historical subservience to empire than to the hegemonies of transnational publishing in which these literatures operate, and finds a parallel in the work of Mette Hjort (2005, 31), who writes of Danish cinema in a global context:

> *Small* points at least as much to the dynamics of recognition, indifference, and participation, nationally and transnationally, as it does to various forms of *mathesis* or quantification. What the concept of small nation acknowledges is that the game of culture, be it film culture or some other form of cultural articulation, is more accessible to some groups than others, more hospitable to some aspirations than others, and, in the long run a process involving winners and losers.

All chapters here are underpinned by a perception that prevailing approaches do not provide an adequate understanding of how literatures from small European nations gain access to this 'game', learn and shape its rules and become players. The design of this volume reflects Casanova's assertion that our 'literary unconscious' and our organization of literary production, promotion and reception remain stubbornly 'national', especially for smaller European literatures, for which notions of 'world literature' can constitute an existential threat. At the same time, however, nationally centred approaches produce illusions of exceptionality, when, as this volume demonstrates, in the context of translation, these literatures lie on a shared spectrum of opportunities, motivations, strategies, obstacles and reception that must be examined comparatively. By contrast, scholars inspired by Goethe's multiply interpreted vision of *Weltliteratur*, who seek to study literature as a single corpus, separate from its 'extra-literary' national contexts, seek to move beyond the past politicized, nationalist division of literature to more fluid models like Irina Neupokoyeva's 'literary zones' (Neupokoyeva, 2013), Pascale Casanova's *World Republic of Letters* (Casanova, 2004) or Franco Moretti's maps, trees and waves (Moretti, 2013). These models aspire to overcoming the implicit hierarchy of national literatures, notionally facilitating the inclusion of works written in less widely known languages from less familiar traditions, whether from the periphery of Europe or from postcolonial and non-European cultures, but their proponents are more interested in works that have already entered supranational literary systems than in how this does (or does not)

Introduction

occur. Roig Sanz and Meylaerts (2018, 3) note that 'it has been assumed that minor literatures play a marginal role in the global literary system' and in this volume, as in their eclectic collection of case studies of cultural mediators, we 'abandon the focus on "innovative" centres and "imitative peripheries" and [...] follow processes of cultural exchange as they develop'.

Both Damrosch's notion of 'world literature' and Casanova's 'world republic' promise integration based on disregard for geopolitical and power relations, but as soon as they venture into integration projects, as David Norris shows in Chapter One, they cannot but replicate and perpetuate stereotypes from popular cultural geography and geopolitical imagination. Most notably, theorists writing from the perspective of the centre, inspired perhaps by Deleuze and Guattari's 1975 account of Franz Kafka (1883–1924) and sometimes encouraged by narratives emanating from particular small nations or individual authors, have grown accustomed to perceiving small-nation literatures as irredeemably sad and unfortunate; Casanova (2004, 181), for instance, writes with unwitting condescension about the 'unequal structure that [...] opposes large literary spaces to small ones and often places writers from small countries in situations that are both tragic and unbearable'. In this volume, readers will encounter literary contexts where smallness is not only lamented, but also celebrated (even fetishized), accepted, denied, ignored, or dependent on perspective. By analysing case studies of concrete practice, this book presents these literatures not as self-absorbed victims of systemic neglect and dominance, but as active, imaginative, practical and astute, often seeking to perform like 'big' literatures as much as they define themselves in opposition to them.

In this volume, we, like Hjort, seek to draw out the connections between small-nation contexts, and, to use Cairns Craig's phrase, to 'centre on the peripheries', to achieve a deeper understanding of how small nations variously negotiate structural constraints and opportunities. We have become accustomed to study the centre and the margin, as Françoise Lionnet and Shu-Mei Shih (2005, 2) remind us, but we 'rarely examine the relationships among different margins'. By continually considering small-nation literatures within a dominant centre–periphery model, we run the risk of confirming the exclusivity of that very relationship and the inevitable hegemony of the centre. To achieve diversity, also in our critical approach to an unequal market for translations, we must go beyond this dyad, without underestimating ever-present power relations and peripheral desires for the centre. To centre on the peripheries, Craig (2007, 32) proposes, 'is to refuse to write our cultural histories on the model of nineteenth-century railways that run from the centre to the periphery and back again on a single track'. Instead, we must 'trace the ways in which the peripheries appropriate from each other the tools of cultural resistance, copy forms by which they can adapt to the pressures of outside forces, and remake the differences by which they can continue to live within their own value systems'. Galin Tihanov (2014, 186) goes further in asserting that 'a clear distinction between centre and periphery, between "minor" and "major" literary texts [has] become highly suspect. In the age of incessant transnational information flows literature no longer has fixed abode or audience, nor does it any longer come with secure value markers attached to it.' His notion of 'marginocentricity', in which 'centre and periphery become fluid, mobile, and provisional, prone to swapping their places and exchanging cultural valences', invites a concomitantly flexible, porous method of characterizing these literatures' interaction with the surrounding world.

Translating the Literature of Small European Nations thus ultimately constitutes an exploration of the inequalities of globalization, strategies for engaging with them and methods of studying and understanding them. It advocates and models a comparative, transnational approach, juxtaposing a previously unparalleled number and range of case studies written by specialists in given national literatures from Scandinavia to the Mediterranean and the Low Countries to the Balkans, and including such diverse linguistic, cultural and political contexts as Catalan, Maltese, Polish and Portuguese. These examples highlight the variety encompassed by our definition of 'small' and marginalized by existing industry structures and scholarly approaches, and authors regularly address the extent to which these literatures and given writers within them accept, embrace or struggle with this type of designation. The studies here consistently test the theoretical against the practical and, taken together, combine literary studies, historiography and sociological translation studies to produce a comprehensive analytical account of the opportunities and obstacles that arise, the strategies and mechanisms exploited, their underlying motivations and outcomes, and how success and failure may be defined as these literatures endeavour to reach the international mainstream. These studies, moreover, repeatedly bring to the fore less familiar voices from within small-nation scholarship, whose work is set alongside internationally established figures in comparative literary and descriptive translation studies. By studying how the contemporary circulation of literature works both in and between the peripheries and centres of Europe, the book reveals how far the literatures of small European nations constitute a distinct system in their interaction with the European imagination and market.

Introduction

The chapters presented here were selected from over 60 papers offered and 24 delivered at an AHRC-funded project conference and postgraduate workshop held in Bristol in September 2015, based on how well the case study illuminated a more general aspect of the international circulation of these literatures, while including the maximum possible diversity of literatures represented. The shape of the volume was finalized at a workshop attended by all contributors in Cardiff in 2016. As a UK-based project team, we particularly regret that we failed to secure a suitable chapter on Celtic-language literature, but have designed the volume to encourage multi-faceted comparison both across the different chapters and with other contexts not explicitly discussed.

The chapters form a narrative arc that moves from the prevailing stereotyping of these literatures in hierarchical, 'centre–periphery' frameworks, through evaluations of historical and contemporary attempts to overcome this marginalization, to chapters drawing on transmedia, creative writing, translingual and gender studies approaches that posit more radical ways of rethinking the international circulation of these literatures by identifying and subvert underlying power structures and *idées fixes* in both theory and practice. The reader may also follow key threads throughout the chapters, including repeated examination of the term 'small', the interaction between national literatures' self-perception and their international reception, notably in text selection and canon formation, and the consecrating function of the international 'centre', gender and genre imbalance and exploitation, the notion of supply- rather than demand-led translation, the role of literature in cultural diplomacy, the relationship between state or third-sector institutions and individual advocates and gatekeepers ('agents of translation' (Milton and Bandia, 2009), 'customs-officers and smugglers' (Roig Sanz and Meylaerts, 2019)), and the changing role of literature in conceptions of national identity.

As world literary and translation studies scholars increasingly prioritize the claims of non-European literatures to equal exposure alongside European literatures, this volume serves as a reminder that the label 'European' has really referred to only a very few 'major' European literatures, of which others are implicitly presented as shadows or imitators. In June 2017, the Danish foreign minister, Kristian Jensen, declared: 'There are two kinds of European nations. There are small nations and there are countries that have not yet realized they are small nations' (Murphy, 2017). During our research, our interactions with translators, publishers and promoters of literary translation revealed that, as the gaze of the world moves, it is not only the peripheral European literatures

Introduction

that are struggling to be heard. For both small literatures beyond Europe and European literatures that are yet to realize their smallness, then, this volume serves also as a record of the thought-processes and innovative actions that the literatures of small European nations have pioneered.

Bibliography

Büchler, Alexandra and Giulia Trentacosti. 2015. Publishing Translated Literature in the United Kingdom and Ireland 1990–2012: Statistical Report. Available from: https://www.lit-across-frontiers.org/wp-content/uploads/2013/03/Translation-Statistics-Study_Update_May2015.pdf [accessed 18 January 2018].

Casanova, Pascale. 2004. *The World Republic of Letters*. Trans. M.B. DeBevoise (Cambridge, MA: Harvard University Press).

Chitnis, Rajendra, Jakob Stougaard-Nielsen, Rhian Atkin and Zoran Milutinović. 2017. Translating the Literatures of Smaller European Nations: A Picture from the UK, 2014–16. Available from: https://www.bristol.ac.uk/media-library/sites/arts/research/translating-lits-of-small-nations/Translating%20Smaller%20European%20Literatures%20Report(3).pdf [accessed 18 January 2018].

Craig, Cairns. 2007. Centring on the Peripheries. In Thomsen, Bjarne Thorup (ed.). *Centring on the Peripheries: Studies in Scandinavian, Scottish, Gaelic and Greenlandic Literature* (Norwich: Norvik Press), 13–38.

Damrosch, David. 2013 [2003]. What is World Literature? In D'Haen, Theo, Domínguez, César and Thomsen, Mads Rosendahl (eds), *World Literature: A Reader* (London and New York: Routledge), 198–206.

Even-Zohar, Itamar. 1990. The Position of Translated Literature within the Literary Polysystem. *Poetics Today*, 11, 45–51.

Hjort, Mette. 2005. *Small Nation, Global Cinema: The New Danish Cinema* (Minneapolis, MN: University of Minnesota Press).

Kovač, Miha. 2002. The State of Affairs in Post-communist Central and Eastern European Book Industries. *Publishing Research Quarterly*, 18, 43–53.

Kundera, Milan. 2013 [2005]. Die Weltliteratur. In D'Haen, Theo, César Domínguez and Mads Rosendahl Thomsen (eds), *World Literature: A Reader* (London and New York: Routledge), 289–300.

Lionnet, Françoise and Shu-mei Shih (eds). 2005. *Minor Transnationalism* (Durham, NC: Duke University Press).

Milton, John and Paul Bandia. 2009. *Agents of Translation* (Amsterdam: Benjamins).

Moretti, Franco. 2013 [2000]. Conjectures on World Literature. In D'Haen, Theo, César Domínguez and Mads Rosendahl Thomsen (eds), *World Literature: A Reader* (London and New York: Routledge), 160–75.

Introduction

Murphy, Connor. Brits Angry at Dane's 'Small Nation' Jibe. Available from: https://www.politico.eu/article/kristian-jensen-brits-angry-at-danes-small-nation-jibe/ [accessed 17 December 2018].

Neupokoyeva, Irina. 2013 [1973]. Dialectics of Historical Development of National and World Literature. In D'Haen, Theo, César Domínguez and Mads Rosendahl Thomsen (eds). *World Literature: A Reader* (London and New York: Routledge), 104–13.

Roig Sanz, Diana and Reine Meylaerts. 2018. General Introduction. Literary Translation and Cultural Mediators. Toward an Agent and Process-Oriented Approach. In Roig Sanz, Diana and Reine Meylaerts (eds), *Literary Translation and Cultural Mediators in 'Peripheral' Cultures: Customs Officers or Smugglers?* (London: Palgrave Macmillan), 1–40.

Squires, Claire. 2009. The Global Market, 1970–2000: Consumers. In Eliot, Simon and Jonathan Rose (eds). *A Companion to the History of the Book* (Oxford: Wiley-Blackwell), 406–18.

Tihanov, Galin. 2014. Do 'Minor Literatures' Still Exist? The Fortunes of a Concept in the Changing Frameworks of Literary History. In Biti, Vladimir (ed.). *Reexamining the National-Philological Legacy: Quest for a New Paradigm?* (Amsterdam: Rodopi), 169–90.

Venuti, Lawrence. 2008. *The Translator's Invisibility: A History of Translation*, 2nd edn (Milton Park: Routledge).

Chapter One

The Global Presentation of Small National Literatures: South Slavs in Literary History and Theory

David Norris (University of Nottingham)

The literatures of small European nations are dependent on their larger and more visible neighbours to facilitate their introduction and acceptance in an international literary context, as this volume will repeatedly show. They are therefore in meaningful ways subordinate to their more significant others. Dominant nations offer two types of model for others to follow: first, they exert an influence by exporting new stylistic features that are then received abroad and emulated as signs of poetic novelty and experiment; second, their literary histories offer a system of periodization and classificatory terms which smaller nations are compelled to adopt to realize themselves within recognized historical patterns. The unidirectional system of exchange offers a vital channel of communication for subordinate literatures, bestowing some degree of recognition on a particular author or on a body of cultural products and granting a degree of cultural legitimacy. In this chapter, I shall examine this international context by addressing first what has been said by representatives from dominant literary and linguistic cultures about the status of the literatures of small nations, and then what has been said by representatives from small nations about their own cultural status and literary histories. In both sections, literature figures as part of a relational structure combining a sliding scale of large and small literatures stretching across Europe, from those considered the most prestigious to those considered the most peripheral. My case study of Serbia as a small nation in this respect also includes reference to Serbian literature within the regional network of other Yugoslav cultures.

Serbian and other Yugoslav literatures are considered small, minor or dominated because of the low numbers of those who would lay claim to them as part of their cultural heritage. The relatively low number of speakers of a

David Norris

common language or inhabitants in a particular culture space are not the only criteria for considering a literature to be small. Their lack of 'literary resources' is a more significant factor (Casanova, 2004, 15). These resources are indicators of prestige and allow a national cultural space the ability to grant recognition even beyond its own borders via its powerful combination of an influential reading public, a language with many active users who are not native speakers, an institutional infrastructure encompassing academic, publishing and other specialized sectors able to disseminate judgements for domestic and foreign consumption. These attributes differentiate the dominant centres, which influence others, from the dominated periphery, which is influenced by trends from those centres. The relationship is variable over time since once major centres may decline and minor literatures assume more dominant roles.

What Dominant Literatures Say About Themselves and Others

My examples of approaches taken to the relational structure between major and minor literatures as discussed in leading international centres are drawn mainly from critical writings by Linda Hutcheon, Pascale Casanova and David Damrosch. They might not necessarily regard themselves as representatives of globally dominant cultures, and prefer to be seen as academics with a sense of engagement whose enquiries and arguments in this field are the results of their research. The importance and rigour of their scholarship is not in question; however, some of their underlying assumptions and views overlap significantly, and contrast with the approaches to this subject taken by scholars from Serbia and former Yugoslavia. Linda Hutcheon, in her essay 'Rethinking the National Model', is mostly concerned about general principles governing the writing of literary history among small nations. She begins with a telling remark about the influence of non-literary matters that shaped her approach to writing about the issue:

> This chapter was researched and written in the final moments of the twentieth century, when various nations around the world re-erupted into their pattern of sectarian violence in the name of ethnic or religious identity. The conflict in Kosovo happened to be the one that coincided with my final rewriting, but all these eruptions have inevitably conditioned my response to the subject at hand: the need to rethink the dominance of the national model of literary history, a model that has always been

premised on ethnic and often linguistic singularity, not to say purity. (Hutcheon, 2002, 3)

Hutcheon sees traditional literary histories as products of an interventionist political agenda aimed at creating a sense of the nation as an organic body, based on ethnic and linguistic purity. She criticizes the persistence of such writing because of its implicit parallel between national and literary progress: 'And it persists not so much in the form of a simple explanatory or causal narrative (although that too continues), but most obviously in a teleological narrative of continuous evolution' (Hutcheon, 2002, 5).

The main point of Hutcheon's essay is to consider alternatives to the national model of literary history, including regional literary histories that emphasize 'certain nodal points at which different cultures have met and merged' (2002, 8). There have been other trends in scholarly and academic projects in recent years that have influenced ways in which literary history may be written, including the development of comparative or world literature, postcolonial studies, cultural studies and mobility studies. These projects have encouraged a greater pluralism in thinking about literary history, without eradicating its political agenda; indeed, on the contrary, they intentionally bring it to the surface and reveal the links between literary and other types of discourse. Hutcheon also indicates that her critical approach to national literary histories and her preference for plurality and hybridity in literature in the context of a globalized network of interlocking cultural experience may appear threatening to small or newly emergent literatures. Her underlying assumption is that traditional practices of literary history, in particular the reliance on a national frame or even nationalist paradigm, persist among smaller or newly emergent national groups. Her references to alternatives appear to demonstrate that the demand to move away from this model is strongest in academic circles from large and powerful national communities with an established international presence in all spheres of economic, political and cultural life. Her awareness of the point prompts the remark, early in her essay: 'Dismantling is the luxury of the already established and the already articulated' (Hutcheon, 2002, 9). Europe's small nations are destined to follow the same path marked out by established literary cultures.

Hutcheon's argument contains two features that immediately signal the danger of a new kind of hegemony among the academic community from dominant cultural systems. The first element of her argument arises from the need to consider regional rather than national paradigms, without detailing whose narrative frame is to determine the borders of these regional units for writing literary history. Her suggestion does not eradicate the danger of established literary cultures imposing new models or criteria for writing new literary histories. The second element is her comment that the luxury of dismantling the national framework belongs only to those who have an established sense of their origin and rise within such a framework. The assumption is that small literatures are in the business only of promoting the progression of their own national narrative through the writing of literary history, whereas even a brief examination of the concerns of critics and literary historians from small nations reveals that they have a far more complex perspective on their place in the global literary system. Some of these critics and historians pre-empt what appear to be the new approaches promoted by Hutcheon and others.

Given events in southeastern Europe during the 1990s, to which Hutcheon refers in her discussion, the region has developed a reputation that has led to generalized judgements about its cultural politics based on, among other things, assumptions about the role of the national frame in the literary histories of small nations as a part of their struggle to gain political legitimacy. Cultural critics abroad consequently tend to give cursory attention to details from easily available studies that would cast greater light on the complexity of each case. In the same volume as Hutcheon's essay, Stephen Greenblatt published his contribution to the debate on alternative models for writing literary history. In his view, literary history needs to adopt a completely different approach and to replace its narratives of origins and evolution by an emphasis on forces of disruption, change and migration as they have had the greatest impact on shaping the world's literary histories. This approach is preferred to the nationalist reliance on creating a narrative that is based on 'a rooted sense of cultural legitimacy' (Greenblatt, 2002, 61). In his carefully crafted argument, Greenblatt (2002, 57) also includes a comment on the teaching of history in contemporary Bosnia grounded on the evidence of an article published in the *New York Times*:

> Where students in Sarajevo were formerly taught out of a single textbook, no doubt full of Titoist lies, they are now asked to declare whether they are Serb, Muslim, or Croat, and are then divided into separate ethnic classes, each of which is taught a radically different version of history out of different textbooks.

He bewails the lack of regard for children from mixed marriages and the absence of attempts to teach a more integrated and complex version of the culture of the region. While it is safe to assume that the educational system of the Socialist Federal Republic of Yugoslavia was not perfect, Greenblatt goes further in his estimation that pupils were taught falsehoods. His remarks on the schooling system in Bosnia today are too simplistic, and jar with his more nuanced approach to other matters. Today's schooling system in Bosnia is based on three different linguistic communities, each of which has the right to be taught in their native language and the right to separate teaching of geography, history and literature. The languages in question, Bosnian, Croatian and Serbian, are mutually comprehensible and until the civil war were regarded as a single linguistic unit, termed Serbo-Croatian. Their division into three languages is the result of their recognition ratified by the Dayton peace negotiations brokered under the auspices of the United States of America at the end of 1995. Information about the complex overlap of linguistic, cultural and political questions in the former Yugoslavia is readily available, as is the role of the world's dominant powers in agreeing the linguistic and cultural dissection of Bosnia.

Hutcheon's views on the central place of national questions in small literatures are supported by Pascale Casanova. The debates about differences and connections between large and small literatures use a variety of terms to refer to their relational structure: great and small, dominant and dominated, major and minor. Discussing these terms, Casanova (2011, 133) comes to another distinction: 'On consideration, however, perhaps the most important opposition is between combative literatures and pacified or non-engaged ones.' Casanova's choice of combative literatures arises from the view that small nations exploit the national frame of literary production and literary history, even exploiting the literary context to promote a national frame of identity politics, unlike the literatures of their larger neighbours who have outgrown this stage of development. She says, '"Small" literatures have generally had a very strong link with anything that touches on national definition, history or honour. Yet this link has become attenuated or forgotten in the oldest and richest national literatures, which have seen a progressive separation between the literary and political orders' (Casanova, 2011, 129). Her opinion that in established national literatures there is a separation of the literary and political orders is not convincing.

In *The World Republic of Letters*, Pascale Casanova makes a case for examining literature in its international context as world literature. Turning to the Serbian and Yugoslav writer Danilo Kiš (1935–89), she draws a picture of him as a writer with an international literary career whose reputation as a cosmopolitan figure led to his being shunned in his own country.[1] Although well known and lauded among literary circles in Belgrade, it was only when his works were translated into French and English, crowning them with a stamp of approval from prestigious literary centres, that he achieved international literary success. Writers like Kiš clearly can attract a global readership only through translation into more widely spoken languages. However, explaining the process which led to his success, Casanova immediately sees the overlap between Kiš's situation and her understanding of the difference between combative and non-engaged literatures of the 'oldest and richest' cultural centres. She declares, 'In adopting the "European and American novel" as an aesthetic norm, Kiš broke with the "anachronistic" literary practices of his country and appealed to the international present' (2004, 113). There is no disguising her view that only by becoming 'more like us' can a writer from a small literature free himself from its narrow national concerns.

Using selected quotations from Kiš's essays published abroad in translation, Casanova arrives at some general statements about the literary scene in the country when he left to pursue his ambitions abroad. She says that Yugoslavia in the 1970s represented 'a closed literary world that had not yet been touched by any of the great literary, aesthetic, and formal revolutions of the twentieth century', adding in brackets that Western literary innovations were 'an epithet that invariably carried a pejorative sense in Belgrade' (Casanova, 2004, 114). Her remarks, based on an uncritical evaluation of some of Kiš's essays, are not supported by decades of critical writing about Yugoslav literature, especially about its openness to Western influences after the split between Yugoslavia and the Soviet Union in 1948. The political break between Tito and Stalin was the crucial event that shaped the future development of Yugoslav self-managing socialism and its rapprochement with the West. The Communist Party of Yugoslavia formally surrendered its adherence to the principles of Socialist Realism and adopted a much more liberal and open cultural policy, publishing Western authors in translation and returning the country to its place within the European sphere of influence from which it had emerged at the beginning of the twentieth century. Her passing reference to 'the political influence of the Soviet Union' on Yugoslavia during Kiš's lifetime is entirely out of place (Casanova, 2004, 198). On the basis of evidence from a single source, employing an uncritical approach to her material, Casanova creates a context for the reception of Yugoslav literature among readers who also probably have no access

[1] For more on Casanova's treatment of Kiš see Milutinović, 2014.

The Global Presentation of Small National Literatures

to material in the source language. She supplies a horizon of literary and historical expectations that are incompatible with the major part of critical work on this topic. The relationship of literary production to the mono-party system governing Yugoslavia was complex, but was also very different from the centralized control exercised elsewhere in the Eastern Bloc. Literary critics from smaller European nations would find themselves in a far less forgiving environment were they to make unsubstantiated generalizations about their more visible neighbours, including comments from other critics in their home institutions.

It is not difficult to find examples that question the alacrity with which she asserts the emerging internationalism of established literary traditions. F.R. Leavis (1983, 9) reveals another side to the oldest and richest national literatures in the audacious opening sentence to his 1948 book *The Great Tradition*. He writes: 'The great English novelists are Jane Austen, George Eliot, Henry James and Joseph Conrad – to stop for the moment at that comparatively safe point in history.' Very few would support Leavis's hierarchical list of great English novelists today, not least because of his somewhat cavalier adoption of writers whose origins lie outside England. His criteria for defining their literary stature are based on an ethical rather than ethnic imperative in their writing which marks out their place in the English tradition since 'they are all distinguished by a vital capacity for experience, a kind of reverent openness before life, and a marked moral intensity' (Leavis, 1983, 18). According to his theoretical model, Flaubert and Goethe may be great writers, but they are not great English writers because they do not articulate those qualities of character and human potential that are essentially English. Criticizing such conservative literary histories in his 1983 book *Literary Theory: An Introduction*, Terry Eagleton (1983, 28) writes: 'What was at stake in English studies was less English *literature* than *English* literature: our great "national poets" Shakespeare and Milton, the sense of an "organic" national tradition and identity to which new recruits could be admitted by the study of humane letters.' Eagleton attacks the traditional approach to writing literary history without disturbing the power relations that legitimize Leavis's cooption of literary figures from outside, continuing to retain the adjective 'English' when more recent developments prefer to avoid the national framework altogether. The practices of literary criticism and literary history in the second half of the twentieth century compromise Casanova's confident assertion that major literatures evolve away from the national paradigm. What has happened, however, is that a certain proportion of the academic community in dominant cultural centres, scholars like

David Norris

Hutcheon and Casanova, have in recent years seriously questioned the validity of literature's national classificatory system.

David Damrosch, in his book *What is World Literature?*, discusses diverse works in order to demonstrate how they can be read outside their national context and be adopted as texts in translation within the framework of world literary studies; in his words, his book is intended 'to clarify the ways in which works of world literature can best be read' (Damrosch, 2003, 5). He assumes the role of a mediator, introducing literary works into the orbit of international attention for which he has been recognized as an authority by his appointment in America as a Professor of English and Comparative Literature. His opinions are part of the literary resources of a large and financially well endowed institutional infrastructure. He finishes his introductory chapter to his study with a qualifying phrase regarding his aims: 'What follows is an essay in definition, a celebration of new opportunities, and a gallery of cautionary tales' (Damrosch, 2003, 36). In *What is World Literature?* he takes the novel *Hazarski rečnik* (Dictionary of the Khazars) by the Serbian author Milorad Pavić (1929–2009) as one of his examples.[2] The *Dictionary* is written as three parts assembled by Jewish, Moslem and Christian representatives, each telling the story of the Khazars' conversion to their faith. Each part is presented as a series of encyclopaedia entries in alphabetical order.

In Damrosch's argument, Pavić's novel contains a nationalist undercurrent embedded in allegorical elements of the stories missed by readers abroad but immediately understood by local readers. Turning to Pavić's statements about Serbs and the Serbian language, he searches for evidence of the author's nationalist message in this and other outputs that he links to cultural and linguistic circumstances in Serbian society of the 1980s and 1990s. Damrosch takes up the point of the source language of the novel as described in two different translated editions in which the English version remains unaltered. The 1988 English translation of the *Dictionary* states that it was translated from Serbo-Croatian, while a later 1996 English translation states that it was translated from Serbian. Serbo-Croatian was the name given to the language spoken across Serbia, Croatia, Bosnia and Montenegro in Yugoslavia. Since the disappearance of the country, its successor states insist that their local usage, with no substantive syntactic or morphological changes, is now a distinct language called Serbian, Croatian, Bosnian or Montenegrin. Pointing to a close relationship between Serbian and Croatian,

---

[2] For more on Damrosch's treatment of Pavić see Ribnikar, 2016.

The Global Presentation of Small National Literatures

Damrosch emphasizes the difference in script as the distinguishing factor between the two variants of the language, with the Cyrillic alphabet used in Serbian and the Roman or Latin alphabet in Croatian: 'Formerly virtually indistinguishable from Croatian except in script (Cyrillic versus Roman), Serbian now became a distinct language, and Pavić took the opportunity to have his book "translated" *into* Serbian' (Damrosch, 2003, 272). Damrosch conflates the publication of the two English translations with that of two different editions of the novel in Serbia; the earlier edition was printed in the Cyrillic alphabet and the later one in the Latin script. Damrosch would appear to be saying that this later edition is Pavić's novel 'translated' into Serbian. His view of the differences between Serbian and Croatian would indicate that the later edition should be in the Cyrillic and not in the Latin script. But the language used in Serbia for over 100 years, whether called Serbo-Croatian or Serbian, has been an example of synchronic digraphia. In other words, both writing systems are in regular use, each containing the same number of letters denoting the same phonemes, but in a different alphabetical order. Thus, the two editions of the novel are distinguished by their arrangement of entries, and as such the later version has all the appearances of a translation.

Damrosch (2003, 268) refers to the Serbian Academy of Sciences and Arts and Pavić's association with it: 'Language was a crucial area for the nationalist programme of resurgence, spearheaded by activities of the Serbian Academy of Sciences and Arts, to which Pavić was elected in 1991.' Pavić and some members of the Academy were supporters of the Serbian nationalist programme, which included an attack on the common language identified as Serbo-Croatian. However, the situation was not as simple as Damrosch wishes. Danilo Kiš, described by Casanova as a writer who freed himself from the nationalist framework, was also a member of the Serbian Academy. The same institution today continues to produce Serbia's definitive dictionary called, as before, *Rečnik srpskohrvatskog književnog i narodnog jezika* (*Dictionary of the Serbo-Croatian Literary and Popular Language*). In a telling remark about the status of translated literature in the United States, Damrosch (2003, 18) writes: 'Even today, foreign works will rarely be translated at all in the United States, much less widely distributed, unless they reflect American concerns and fit comfortably with American images of the foreign culture in question.' Damrosch's investigation regarding Pavić's *Dictionary* in its wider social and political context may not be the only image of this foreign culture produced in America. However, coming from such a prominent mediator, his discussion on this topic might be classified as one of his 'cautionary tales' of what may happen in international cultural exchange between those holding vastly unequal literary and linguistic resources.

The relational structure between the literatures of small nations and their more powerful neighbours presented by Hutcheon, Casanova and Damrosch is a form of historical narrative, examining textual developments and interpretive frameworks used to evaluate literary evolutions, individual writers, their works and their reception at home and abroad. They throw light on neglected writers and traditions, judging what should be valued in those traditions, showing how literary works from lesser known cultural spaces written in languages rarely spoken outside their home territory can be translated and become accessible to an international and not just national reading public. In their references to literature in Serbia and former Yugoslavia, the complexity of the linguistic, historical and cultural relationships that have determined the shifting plates of identity in the region are ignored in favour of simplified and sometimes mistaken evidence to support the image of a cultural mentality driven by the necessities of chauvinist demands. Their oversights and under-researched arguments would not be made about a literature with a greater international presence; as Casanova (2011, 131) observes, 'Inequality between literatures is of course a fact of structure and not of value.' The inhospitable environment created for small literatures exposes more about the horizons of expectations of those who dictate the agenda of international literary exchange. In this world of cultural translation, the reception of works from minor literatures among their larger and more powerful neighbours is a vital issue that influences the definition of the function of literature, the shape of the canon and ultimately the politics of literary culture in small European nations.

What Small Literatures Say About Themselves

Some literary critics and historians writing in English and French seem to assume that the history of the literatures of small nations is preoccupied only with the abuse of literature as a means to establish an agenda to maintain linguistic or ethnic purity. However, the work of intellectuals from small nations reveals more complex concerns, which demonstrate that the field of literary history is one of unresolved tensions, much as in any other cultural setting. In the remainder of this chapter, I shall turn to the work of three scholars from Serbian and Yugoslav literatures. The critic and literary historian, Jovan Skerlić (1877–1914), published his important work *Istorija nove srpske književnosti* (History of Modern Serbian Literature) just prior to the First World War in 1914. Pavle Popović (1868–1939) worked in the very different atmosphere after the First World War when the Kingdom of Serbia was subsumed within the larger Yugoslav state. Svetozar Petrović (1931–2005), writing during the period of socialist Yugoslavia, also turned his attention to the very specific place of the literature of a small European nation in its wider cultural context.

In the introduction to his *History of Modern Serbian Literature*, Skerlić discusses a shorter version of his book that appeared two years earlier as a textbook for use in Serbian schools. He points to a significant difference between the two editions, saying: 'The cultural historical moments which condition the development of literature are here given greater space than in the school edition' (Skerlić, 1921, viii). True to his aims, Skerlić introduces each of his significant periods of Serbian literary history with a section on 'Cultural and Literary Circumstances'. Turning his attention to modern literature, he links change in literary expression with the political climate of those years. In particular, he emphasizes the changes that followed the assassination in Belgrade of King Alexander and Queen Draga in 1903 and the enthronement of a new dynasty in Serbia. The new king, Peter, confirmed constitutional government and his reign represented an opening of Serbian society to modern, European intellectual currents. Skerlić's construction of Serbian cultural identity is closely linked to these internal political changes. It falls within the characteristic exposition of literary history in a small European nation as described by Hutcheon, subsuming literary history within the greater national narrative.

On another level, Skerlić (1921, vii–viii) extends literary identity to a regional level uniting both Serbian and Croatian traditions: 'Croatian and Serbian literatures are the literature of one nation and one language, but they are still two literatures. This is a paradox, an anachronism, evidence of our cultural national backwardness, but it is so.' Having established that significant point, Skerlić later emphasizes both 'Serbo-Croatian literary unification' and 'foreign influences in Serbian literature' with slightly more attention devoted to the latter (1921, 448–51). He proposes a classification of Serbian literature shaped as a series of expanding circles: first, Serbian literature in Serbia; then, expanding out in the surrounding region, linked to neighbouring cultures and in particular to recent developments in Croatia; and finally, as one of the independent and associated national communities within a modern European network. His approach to Serbian literary history at the beginning of the twentieth century is characterized by a classificatory system that is at once national, regional and international; in contrast to Leavis's insistence on identifying the uniqueness of English literature as the product of a specific moral imperative embedded in the literary text of an author. For Skerlić, literary production unfolds in a national frame, but any assessment of its cultural value is reckoned in its relationship to other literatures and intellectual traditions. He pre-empts later attempts in literary history to produce a literature of the region through the gradual merger of communities linked by linguistic and cultural similarities.

Popović's major study of Yugoslav literary history, *Jugoslovenska književnost* (Yugoslav Literature), was published in 1918 in Cambridge in the UK, where he spent much of the First World War while Serbia was occupied by enemy forces. The creation of a Yugoslav state uniting the South Slav nations was one of the war aims among intellectuals from the region. Popović's underlying political aim in writing his new literary history was, as Predrag Palavestra (2008, 468) outlines, 'in order to serve as evidence of the cultural unity of all the peoples encompassed and moved by the same political idea for unification'. In his narrative, Popović formulates a literary history for the Serbs, Croats and Slovenes that promotes the cultural background of the three constituent communities in a collective framework. He regards their literary history as a series of largely parallel developments, the consequence of their historical division under the rule of foreign powers, until able to claim a common Yugoslav identity. After the war, he elaborated in more detail on the nature of the literary and cultural connections uniting the main groups within the Kingdom of Serbs, Croats and Slovenes, formed in 1918 and later renamed the Kingdom of Yugoslavia. He delivered a paper on the subject as his inaugural lecture to the Serbian Academy of Sciences and Arts in 1922 with the title 'Jugoslovenska književnost kao celina' ('Yugoslav Literature as a Whole'). In his lecture he challenges the production of individual national literary histories for Serbs, Croats and Slovenes, which he refers to as provincial histories, and builds a case for a Yugoslav literature. His approach resembles an early version of today's preferred attempts to seek unity in diversity across a region in which similarity of language was an important factor. The initial problem was to find a classificatory system that would encompass literary production across the whole territory of the kingdom. Recognizing that Yugoslav literature may not be considered in the same light as English or French literatures, he establishes an idealized perspective on the evolution of those national literatures, stating that in those examples 'literature was always the property of the whole country and all its regions'

The Global Presentation of Small National Literatures

(Popović, 1999, 106). Instead, he looks elsewhere in Europe for appropriate models and equates Yugoslav literature with Italian or German literatures in which uneven and inconsistent developments occurred at varied speeds in different parts of the territories divided for long periods of their histories in separate administrative units, until their eventual unification. Following their example, he sees no reason why it would not be possible to find common traits linking the different cultural regions that make up Yugoslavia as a first step in connecting them to broader, European cultural trends.

Popović's conclusion (1999, 108) regarding the enterprise facing Yugoslav literary historians reveals his perspective:

> I really believe that a better classification can be found for our literature, for the whole period of its existence from the beginning to today, and I shall present it to you now. We shall not find in it, really, a genuine and complete unity over a long period, but I hope that we shall 1) get close to an organic division into periods, and subsume our tribal and regional literatures under the large communal headings of the spiritual and intellectual trends, at home and abroad; and 2) find the tendencies and characteristics of unity, some in the older period and especially in more modern times.

His reasoning and wording exposes for him the limitations of what can be achieved in writing a unified literary history that is not the product of a long evolution of the nation. The clue for the enterprise is to find an adequate classificatory system that will facilitate the discovery of 'an organic division' into relevant periods, which in turn can be linked to other cultural developments on either a local or a global scale. His use of the term 'organic' is limited to the formulation of an adequate framework, an articulated historical motive that facilitates the production of a literary history. In these terms, Popović does not insist that what will be produced is anything more than an intellectual construction answering the needs of a broader contemporary agenda. He has not embarked on an analysis of literary trends and movements, or a romantic quest for the soul of the nation, but he has attempted to formulate a framework ultimately legitimized by its correspondence with the frameworks already established by larger cultural units. His work focuses on demonstrating how developments across the region were part of European trends. Often, a trend is particularly evident in only one part of the Yugoslav tradition; so, he writes of the strength of Renaissance influence in the urban areas on the Dalmatian coast, of the appearance of the Reformation in Slovenia, of the Enlightenment in the regions inhabited by Serbs in Austria-Hungary and of the influence of modern literary movements as a common Yugoslav feature. On the one hand, Skerlić insists that foreign literary influence is evidence that Serbian literature has a place in European literary space. On the other hand, Popović demonstrates that the historical process of literary unification, or merging of the regions, that happened among the South Slavs, happened elsewhere and is one of the general characteristics of European literatures to which England and France are the exceptions.

Fifty years after Popović's inaugural lecture to the Serbian Academy, Svetozar Petrović published three papers, which he delivered during the 1960s at conferences in a differently organized Yugoslavia and in a different intellectual climate. His work also reveals that the internal perspective from the small culture is a missing link in discussions to date on the status of small literatures and their production of literary histories. His work offers a different perspective on cultural transmission as it affects small literatures, on the construction of literary history and canon formation. He also draws attention to different reactions among writers from small nations in different historical periods. The three papers are published in his book *Priroda kritike* (The Nature of Criticism): 'Metodološka pitanja specifična za proučavanje naših nacionalnih književnosti' ('Methodological Issues Specific to the Study of Our National Literatures') delivered in Sarajevo in 1964; 'Stanovište sadašnjosti i stanovište prošlosti u historiji književnosti (Prilog utvrđivanju granice među filologijom i politikom)' ('The Perspective of Today and the Perspective of the Past in the History of Literature [A Contribution to Reinforce the Borders between Philology and Politics]'), Budva, 1969; 'Književnost malog naroda i strani utjecaj' ('The Literature of a Small Nation and Foreign Influence'), Titov Veles, 1970. Petrović, living in the Socialist Federal Republic of Yugoslavia, was writing in a context of literary history with both similarities and differences from the one faced by Popović. In Yugoslavia after the Second World War, the debate concerned whether the term Yugoslav literature or Yugoslav literatures was more appropriate. The use of the singular or plural form held significant political implications. Yugoslav literature was the favoured term in the years immediately after the Second World War, to be replaced by the plural form later in support of the claim that socialist Yugoslavia was a multinational state, comprising free and equal nations. Each nation had its own cultural background, including, therefore, its own literature. Petrović sees this as a significant factor in conditioning approaches to the writing of literary history and to literary study generally in Yugoslavia.

In the essay 'Methodological Issues Specific to the Study of Our National Literatures', he discusses the nature of the national communities in Yugoslavia.

Pointing out that the national community is not an organic unity, he presents the complexity of the histories of Yugoslav literature and of individual authors: 'The past of our literatures is full, therefore, of mutable national identities, to today there is a frequent incidence in them of writers who begin their literary career in one and finish it in another national literature' (Petrović, 1972, 206). Petrović emphasizes the need for literary study to take account of the plurality of contexts that inform the dynamic development of literary styles and trends, which is the product more of their diversity than their continuity. His approach focuses on issues of discontinuity and dislocation. As such, it overlaps with Greenblatt's insistence that the narrative of emergence of literary history be replaced by greater weight given to the forces of disruption that shape cultural and literary transformations.

In his third essay on this topic, 'The Literature of a Small Nation and Foreign Influence', Petrović brings out the most salient points that define a small literature, particularly with reference to what he calls the limitation of the 'power of transmission of the literature of a small nation' (Petrović, 1972, 260). A number of assumptions arise from this position that he addresses, formulating the basic problem as the following:

> the plight, for example, that the power of transmission of the literature of a small nation, its market value on an international level, will be generally less than its real artistic value, and that there will in still greater measure be a lack of proportion between the value of a good writer from a literature of a small nation and his influence on the wider literary community (European literature in our case) of which his nation is part. (Petrović, 1972, 260–61)

His formulation of the limited power of transmission is akin to Casanova's view on the lack of literary resources in a small literature. However, Petrović's perspective is internal to the small nation and he focuses on how such factors have a great influence on the status of the writer, on canon formation and on the function of literature in a given society. He differentiates the impact of this effect in the nineteenth and in the twentieth centuries. In the nineteenth century, when the writer of a small literature was unable to influence the direction of the greater literary trend, he was canonized as a national prophet, providing a model for national authenticity and resistance to direct political and economic submission. Literature became a symbolic site for resistance and the canon was seemingly constructed in an authentic national space. At the same time, the local literature's stylistic formations could be linked aesthetically to external stylistic formations and thus earn a recognized place in a larger tradition. In the twentieth century, Petrović suggests, the national frame is redundant and the small national literature responds quite differently to the literature of its dominant partners and its larger global context. Writers are now less likely to accept the role of prophet of the nation. The global rather than the national context takes priority and canon formation is constructed with an eye to the demand for translated literature among the dominant literatures. Petrović describes this as 'an exaggerated obsession with the pursuit of international affirmation', leading to a renunciation of the national or local context as an environment that is too small and limiting (1972, 266). The tendency towards rejecting foreign influence as inauthentic or uncritical acceptance of all foreign models is precisely the result of the minor literature's position in a power structure in which the domination of economic markets and the currency of political influence are confused with the legitimizing role of cultural production in authenticating the existence of the community responsible for its production. It is not a structure created by or managed for the benefit of small literatures. Petrović does not endorse the consequences of these activities for small literatures. Rather, he tries to contextualize the issue from the perspective of the small nation, aware of what is happening but unable to stop the mechanism that creates the problem.

Conclusion

In their writings on the problems of producing the literary history of a small nation, Popović and Petrović differ from the premises put forward in recent research published by international scholars in comparative and world literature. Their work pre-empts recent findings and reveals an awareness of the problems that mark such an environment. Popović's approach and classificatory system is based not on the production of a national narrative, but on the production of a larger development. His construction of Yugoslav literary history was a project aimed at producing a regional cultural community in response to the need in small literary environments to seek legitimacy not in the internal production of a national narrative, but to mediate that narrative through the already established frameworks of the narratives of significant others. Petrović proposes that writers in small literatures, rather than being actors in militant national narratives, shun their home environment in favour of success abroad. In this view, Kiš's work was not so much liberated from the limitations of a small literary environment, as assimilated by the power of greater literary resources in an unequal global structure. Their work contrasts with both Hutcheon's view that the literary histories of small nations are produced to demonstrate ethnic and linguistic singularity and Casanova's description of 'combative literatures'. Popović seeks out the nodal points of merger in the narratives of Yugoslav literary history, while Petrović focuses on the narratives of disjuncture and segregation.

Minor literatures remain subject to cycles of representations which to a greater or lesser extent vary from views at home. Translations of their works enter the wider market of the book trade in the context provided by such misrepresentations. Not only are writers from small literatures incapable of directing the larger world of which they are part, critics and historians from small literatures are also incapable of influencing the conditions for transnational exchange which determines the context of the reception of literary translations. The structural inequality in intercultural relations is the precondition which shapes the limited range of responses available to the literatures of small nations and defines their limited power of transmission. They do not have the visibility or the cultural capital on which to construct representations of themselves and do not possess the reach to influence the wider stylistic and aesthetic trends in which they recognize themselves. The literature of a small nation, from its point of view, is defined as one not in a position to influence the opinions expressed about them through activating their literary resources on an international scale and, at the same time, not able to ignore the models of dominant literary centres.

Bibliography

Casanova, Pascal. 2004. *The World Republic of Letters*. Trans. M.B. DeBevoise (Cambridge, MA: Harvard University Press, 2004).
Casanova, Pascale. 2011. Combative Literatures. *New Left Review*, 72, 123–34.
Damrosch, David. 2003. *What is World Literature?* (Princeton: Princeton University Press).
Eagleton, Terry. 1983. *Literary Theory: An Introduction* (Oxford: Blackwell).
Greenblatt, Stephen. 2002. Racial Memory and Literary History. In Mario J. Valdes and Linda Hutcheon (eds). *Rethinking Literary History: A Dialogue on Theory* (Oxford: Oxford University Press), 50–62.
Hutcheon, Linda. 2002. Rethinking the National Model. In Mario J. Valdes and Linda Hutcheon (eds). *Rethinking Literary History: A Dialogue on Theory* (Oxford: Oxford University Press), 3–49.

Leavis, Frank R. 1983. *The Great Tradition: George Eliot, Henry James, Joseph Conrad* (Harmondsworth: Penguin Books).
Milutinović, Zoran. 2014. Territorial Trap: Danilo Kiš, Cultural Geography, and Geopolitical Imagination. *East European Politics and Society*, 28, 715–38.
Palavestra, Predrag. 2008. Pavle Popović. In *Istorija srpske književne kritike 1768–2007*, vol. 2 (Novi Sad: Matica srpska), 457–73.
Petrović, Svetozar. 1972. *Priroda kritike* (Zagreb: Liber).
Popović, Pavle. 1999. Jugoslovenska književnost kao Celina. In Pavle Popović, Sabrana dela, *Jugoslovenska književnost*, vol. 9, edited by Nenad Ljubinković (Belgrade: Zavod za udžbenike i nastavna sredstva), 106–41.
Ribnikar, Vladislava. 2016. Između nacionalnog i svetskog: komparatistika i 'veliko nepročitano'. In Marčetić, Adrijana, Zorica Bečanović Nikolić and Vesna Elez (eds). *Komparativna književnost: teorija, tumačenja, perspektive* (Belgrade: Faculty of Philology), 49–62.
Skerlić, Jovan. 1921. *Istorija nove srpske književnosti* (Belgrade: Geca Kon).

Chapter Two

Translators as Ambassadors and Gatekeepers: The Case of South Slav Literature

Zoran Milutinović (UCL SSEES)

Like scholars and journalists, translators also struggle with notions of objectivity, impartiality, commitment and engagement. They are not merely humble language workers, some claim; their work involves them in conflicts of this world and makes them inevitably partial: 'engaged and committed, either implicitly or explicitly' (Tymoczko, 2000, 24). Mona Baker (2013, 24) believes that the inevitable partiality of translation is not to be bemoaned, but embraced and celebrated, and used 'as a tool for changing the world'. Translators never simply reproduce texts, but 'reframe aspects of political conflicts, and hence participate in the construction of social and political reality' (Baker, 2007, 151). Baker (2007, 154) rejects the notion of objectivity and notes that even 'uncritical fidelity to the source text or utterance has consequences that an informed translator or interpreter may not wish to be party to' (Baker, 2006, 128). Instead of a calm space in which notions of accuracy and faithfulness reign supreme, the translation space is a battlefield of partialities. How far can we go in being partial before we lose the trust readers grant our translations and the promotions we arrange for them? Is there still some space left for the outmoded notion of professional ethics in this world of conflicting partialities, or is professionalism always merely a cover-up for a partiality that is different from mine?

Francis R. Jones and the Ethics of the Translator-gatekeeper

A version of this stance can be found in Francis R. Jones's (2009) article 'Ethics, Aesthetics and *Décision*: Literary Translating in the Wars of the Yugoslav Succession', included in Baker's *Translation Studies*. Jones is not only

Zoran Milutinović

a translator of Bosniak, Croatian and Serbian literature, but also a translation studies scholar keenly aware of the ethical and political dimensions of his profession: in several publications he has thematized the problem of deciding what to translate – or not to translate – during the times when his source cultures were in conflict, and thus represents an ideal test-case for the principles discussed above. Jones (2001, 263) sees the translator as both ambassador and gatekeeper: 'I see part of the translator-as-ambassador's role as that of a gatekeeper: in other words, by translating or refusing to translate, she has the power to decide which writers and which ideas can be heard in the target culture.' This position begins to cause concern when Jones (2000, 66) pairs it with his view of the general tenability of objectivity and impartiality: 'any notion of academic impartiality is a dangerous fiction', and 'no neutral, objective stance is possible when describing recent and drastic events' (Jones and Arsenijević, 2005, 69). Even if possible, objectivity and impartiality are undesirable, for 'might an Olympian stance of pan-Yugoslav fairness not be an act of hypocrisy or blindness as reprehensible as my government's insistence that aggressor and victim were equal?' (Jones, 2009, 12). Those who still insist on objectivity as a valid academic position are actually unethical: 'the ethics of neutrality [...] may not always be the most appropriate ethic for the literary translator. Indeed, partiality might often be more appropriate' (Jones, 2009, 16). Objectivity and impartiality are both impossible and unethical; partiality is not only the sole position available, but also the only ethical one. Hence, Jones (2009, 7) frequently underlines his partiality: 'I am patently not neutral in my account of external events and social relations, nor can I be.'

All scholars find themselves in a hermeneutical situation: *absolute* objectivity and impartiality are impossible, as our understanding is always limited by the prior intelligibility with which we understand the issue we want to interpret, guided by a specific perspective or point of view, and shaped by a specific conceptuality, the vocabulary at our disposal. These are all good reasons for interpretative humility. Yet thousands of academics pursue what Jones dismisses as dangerous fiction and reprehensible hypocrisy; they believe that being in a hermeneutical situation does not mean that we can never overcome it through a revision of the prior intelligibility we brought to the process, by taking another perspective and by devising a new vocabulary. This guarantees, not absolute objectivity – hence our humility, a recognition that our truths are only human and subject to revision, reinterpretation and dispute – but that we have done everything in our power to propose what we see as truth beyond reasonable doubt. There is no reason for translators to be in a different position. Jones's reply to this objection is that his partisanship is

Translators as Ambassadors and Gatekeepers

justified because he chose to represent the cosmopolitan voices from within the source cultures in conflict, and to deny any presence in the lingua franca to what he sees as ethnonationalist views. 'This means that translation', maintains Jones (2005, 72), 'has the power to support, subvert or ignore the images created by nationalism or Balkanism. I can do so either by giving international voice to discourses supporting, subverting or ignoring these images; or by validating such discourses in the eyes of source readers.' Having been 'strongly committed to an anti-nationalist, civil-society agenda' (Jones, 2005, 69) and following his 'own cosmopolitanist views' (Jones, 2010, 233), he has 'felt the need to defend and promote the complexity and potential for tolerance in Bosnian culture, both via literary translation and the translation editing of works and discussions promoting inter-communal/non-particularistic dialogue' (2009, 11). He frames the war in Bosnia and Herzegovina (1992–95) as 'the political conflict between cosmopolitanism and ethnonationalism' (2010, 245), in which the Bosniak-dominated government led by Alija Izetbegović's Party of Democratic Action stood for cosmopolitanism, while Bosnian Serbs, and to lesser extent Bosnian Croats, stood for ethnonationalism. It is worth noting that Jones regularly qualifies the Bosniak government's cosmopolitan stance as ambiguous: it adhered to the cosmopolitan principle 'officially at least' (2011, 20; 2005, 75); it 'claimed to uphold a "multicultural" model of Bosnia (no matter how imperfectly it did so in practice)' (2014, 360). But even this merely official, only claimed and imperfect cosmopolitanism justifies the translator's bias: Jones's partisanship led him in the 1990s to promote, translate and edit translations of the Bosniak authors close to Izetbegović's government: Džemaludin Latić (b.1957), whose poetry he found 'rather sub-standard', but as his 'socio-political loyalty outweighed artistic judgment' he 'improved' it in his translation (Jones, 2009, 13); the essays of Rusmir Mahmutćehajić (b.1948), 'which promoted inter-ethnic tolerance rooted in a shared religiosity as the unifying Bosnian idea' (Jones, 2009, 10);[1] and also the poetry collection *Kameni spavač* (1966) by Mak Dizdar (1917–71), whose work in the 1990s 'became seen as an iconic symbol of Bosnian identity by those who supported Bosnian independence' (Jones, 2011, 47).

The gatekeeping part of the translator's work consisted in refraining from publishing translations of Serbian authors even when they were not

---

[1] Jones is listed as translator or co-translator of five of Mahmutćehajić's books: *Living Bosnia* (1996), *Bosnia the Good* (2000), *The Denial of Bosnia* (2000), *Sarajevo Essays* (2003) and *Learning from Bosnia* (2005).

ethnonationalists: he feared that publishing his translations of Serbian poets 'might be propagandized by the nationalist regime in Belgrade' (Jones, 2009, 12). This applied to the unnamed 'living writers of excellent texts (and/or personal friends) who supported or failed to oppose regimes which [he] felt to be hateful' (2009, 12), as well as to dead ones, such as Vasko Popa (1922–91). Popa's collection *Uspravna zemlja* (1972) explored some motives from the Kosovo myth, and although Jones (2009, 12) admits that while 'writing these poems, Popa was positively exploring his cultural roots, seeking pan-human archetypes through cultural particulars, in an age (the 1970s) when such explorations were relatively untainted', he feared that publishing translations of these poems might give credibility to Serbian nationalism. This is the ambassadorial-gatekeeping logic: the excellent texts are to be suppressed, and the sub-standard ones improved and published; of the two poetry collections, published at the same time and exploring the mediaeval motives in a similar way, the one that received an ideological and political reading would be promoted, and the other, which received no such reading, would be suppressed. Years after the war in Bosnia and Herzegovina ended, Jones (2010, 245) surveyed the field to assess who had translated Bosniak and Serbian poetry into English, and what was translated, and concluded that no translation projects of Bosniak poetry promoted ethnonationalism.

Ethnonationalism in Translated Bosniak Literature: Latić, Mahmutćehajić and Dizdar

There is, however, at least one ethnonationalist poet promoted by Jones himself: Džemaludin Latić (Ali and Lifschultz, 1993, 114–15), a professor at Sarajevo's Faculty of Islamic Studies, one of the accused in the 1983 trial of Bosnian pan-Islamists, one of Izetbegović's closest associates, a founder of the Party of Democratic Action (SDA), and the editor-in-chief of the Party's news magazine *Ljiljan* (1990–94). Judging by the following claim he can hardly be described as the promoter of cosmopolitan views:

> My religion prohibits a marriage between Muslim women and non-Muslim men. [...] In principle, a Muslim man can marry a monotheist woman. [...] However, this is only in principle. Most religious scholars, such as European Council for Fatwas, maintain that in the situations such as the Bosnian and Balkan ones, Muslim men should marry only Muslim women. (Arnautović, 2009)

John R. Schindler (2007, 142) noted several other similar claims made by Latić: he 'lashed out at "the apostate Salman Rushdie" [...] adding that "Imam Khomeini's fatwa [the death sentence against Rushdie] is a must for every Muslim to carry out"'. The list goes on: he also claimed:

> 'Jihad is our holy task' [...]. Citing a popular SDA view, Izetbegović's top propagandist denounced the Serbs as 'polytheists' (a common prejudice among devout Muslims, who consider that belief in the Holy Trinity removes Christians from the ranks of monotheist). (Schindler, 2007, 197)

Beganović (2011, 427) quotes Latić's claim that the Bosniak members of Sarajevo's *Club 99* – at the time an association of liberal intellectuals from all Bosnian ethnicities committed to the promotion of democracy and civil society, opposed to all ethnonational policies and thus closest to Jones's understanding of cosmopolitanism – will lead Muslims into a decaying civilization, and will 'turn them into a shapeless mass, a people in religious and political amnesia – because they think that the road to a free society goes via rejecting national, and especially religious specificities in Bosnia and Herzegovina'. These statements do not present Latić as a bearer of cosmopolitan views.

Jones's claim that the Bosniak-dominated government in Sarajevo advocated cosmopolitanism 'at least officially' attests that he is aware of the discrepancy between the declared political aims of Izetbegović's SDA and its activities during the war. 'SDA adopted an ambiguous stand and reiterated its commitment to a united and multi-ethnic Bosnia-Herzegovina while turning the territories held by the Bosnian army into a *de facto* Muslim entity', maintains Bougarel (1999, 9). 'Living together is a beautiful thing, but I think and I can freely say that it is a lie, that it is not that for which our soldiers are dying [...] [Our soldier] risks his life to defend his family, his land, his people', stated Izetbegović at the SDA convention in March 1994 (Bougarel, 1996, 94). Vjekoslav Perica (2002, 88), who studied the impact of religion on the wars of Yugoslav succession, concludes that 'Alija Izetbegović and the SDA pursued Bosnian nationalism with a strong religious dimension'. It was 'a nationalist party created by the representatives of a pan-Islamist stream that first appeared in the 1930s and reorganized in the 1970s'; thus in the first democratic election in 1990 a 'secularized Bosnian Muslim population brought to power the representatives of a small pan-Islamist minority' (Bougarel, 2007, 99, 117). Izetbegović's pan-Islamist ideology was explained in his *Islamic Declaration*, written in 1970 and published in 1990. There he clearly stated that 'once Muslims become a majority in one country (thanks to the relative high population growth) they should demand a state of their own, organized according to Islamic laws and norms because, in Izetbegović's words, "Islam and non-Islamic systems are incompatible"' (Perica, 2002, 77). In a recent publication Bougarel claims that 'most research published about Bosnia-Herzegovina has failed to take account of political Islam. This failure is attributable sometimes to simple ignorance, and sometimes to a well-intentioned form of self-censorship that is no longer necessary' (Bougarel, 2017, location 168). The Party's main goal was the 'greater Muslim' project: 'a state composed of Bosnia-Herzegovina and Sandžak [a part of Serbia], in which Muslims would be the majority, and the Serbs and Croats would be reduced to national minorities' (Bougarel, 1999, 7). Izetbegović was very explicit about this point: 'Serbs and Croats will have in Bosnia-Herzegovina the same rights as Arabs in France', he promised (Bougarel, 2007, 120). Nor were others ambiguous about their vision of Bosnia's future: Adnan Jahić, the Party's spokesperson and the president of its parliamentary group, wrote in 1993 that 'Islam is not primarily interested in formal democracy [...] but rather in its principles and positive ethical values that will contribute to the fulfilment of the Islamic idea within the community' (Bougarel, 2007, 112). Instead of 'formal democracy', '[t]he future Muslim state "will have a Muslim ideology based on Islam, on Islamic legal-religious and ethical-social principles, but also on elements of West European origin that are not in conflict with the former ones"' (Bougarel, 2007, 116).

As for non-Muslims, a 'complete equality of rights will be guaranteed to all citizens, yet the social achievement of each individual will depend not only on his own economic activity, but also on how much he will consciously accept and follow the principles and the spirit of the Muslim ideology' (Bougarel, 2007, 117). Bougarel (2007, 118, 120) concludes that Jahić openly expressed a political project that remained, for the most part, implicit; he formulated 'the geopolitical dream that motivates the funders of the SDA in 1990: the wish to bring back Bosnia-Herzegovina into the "house of Islam" (dar-al-islam) from which it had been torn away in 1878'. For Bosnian non-Muslims, this would mean a return to the *dhimmi* status that they enjoyed during Ottoman rule: 'protected' in the sense that they could practise their religion with certain limitations, but politically and legally subjugated to Muslims. Consequently, Izetbegović 'felt it was logical for Bosnia to become a state for the Muslims, as Croats and Serbs each already had a state of their own', as noted in the *Srebrenica Report* (328). On the same page, this *Report* also concludes:

Translators as Ambassadors and Gatekeepers

When Izetbegović, also as president, spoke of 'our people', he meant the Muslims and not the Croats and Serbs. On state occasions, the SDA flag often flew alongside the Bosnian one. At party meetings, those present expressed their support for the Iraqi dictator Saddam Hussein and saw Arab clothing. The many green flags flying on such occasions, some with half-moons, were a clear reference to Islam, not to any multi-cultural Bosnian identity.

The *Srebrenica Report* also records the claim by Rusmir Mahmutćehajić, one of Izetbegović's closest associates, from December 1990, that Serbs and Croats had to adapt all aspects of their development to those of the Bosnian Muslims (328). In the years preceding the war in Yugoslavia, Mahmutćehajić 'was the key strategist of Bosnian independence' and also 'instrumental in establishing the Patriotic League', the SDA's paramilitary wing, which would later grow into the Muslim-dominated Army of Bosnia and Herzegovina (Banac, 2000, x).[2] From 1991 to 1994 Mahmutćehajić was the vice president in SDA's government. Banac (2000, x) notes that 'all forces [...] that promoted the negotiated settlement of the Bosnian war' had a prominent adversary in Mahmutćehajić, and that the diplomats of important powers blamed him for obtaining military help for Bosnian Muslim forces from the 'wrong countries', namely, Iran. The founder of paramilitary forces, the opponent of negotiated settlement to end the war, and the link between SDA's government and the foreign Islamist forces began, as of 1995, to reinvent himself as a promoter of the image of Bosnia as 'unity in diversity', and of dialogue and tolerance. However, Mahmutćehajić's engagement on the side of unity, dialogue and tolerance is only 'at least official' as well.

Mahmutćehajić is an opponent of rationalism and secularism, liberalism and modernity, an anti-modernist of the René Guénon variety: from the time of the Enlightenment, the West fell into barbarity (Mahmutćehajić, 2000,

---

[2] Although the army 'at least officially' claimed to be all-Bosnian, in reality it was a Bosnian Muslim force only. Filandra recounts commander general Rasim Delić's visit to the First Battalion of the Seventh Muslim Brigade on 9 September 1993: for this occasion, the Battalion had three flags, one with the state coat of arms, one green 'national' flag, and one black flag of jihad with an inscription in Arabic, representing Islam. To greet the commander, the unit shouted 'sebiluna al-jihad' (our path is jihad), and sang a modified version of a song sung in the Second World War by fascist Ustaša units. 'This aspect made this unit a prestigious and elite one in the whole Army', concludes Filandra (2012, 326). More on the army's activities during the 1992–95 war in Schindler, 2007.

34); modern Western civilization is materialistic and intellectually barren because, sunk in positivism and agnosticism, it does not rely on transcendent principles (Mahmutćehajić, 2000, 56).[3] Salvation lies in returning to tradition, which in Guénon's manner stands for religion, or more specifically, the Tradition, i.e. the Koran. The 'being of Bosnia', which is 'the treasury of Tradition', cannot be understood without understanding the difference between the Tradition and the 'paganism of modernity' (Mahmutćehajić, 1997, 8), but the English translation substitutes the 'paganism of modernity' with 'the shallow vulgarity of our new-age outlook' (Mahmutćehajić, 2000, 6).

Christianity in his view is responsible for much of Europe's moral degradation: the genocide of Jews and Muslims in Europe, which has been going on for centuries, cannot be explained without taking into consideration Christianity as Europe's core feature (Mahmutćehajić, 1997, 204); crimes committed against Bosnia are always discussed only as simple, individual crimes, instead of analysing them from the perspective of the holy tradition of the perpetrators, which is Christianity (1997, 212). The English translation, however, modifies this sentence so that Christianity as such does not appear as the basis from which the crimes arise, and substitutes this with 'the use of Christianity by the anti-Bosnian elites' (Mahmutćehajić, 2000, 217). In spite of what he perceives as Christianity's dismal historical record, Mahmutćehajić (1997, 126) advocates *unity in diversity* as the 'Bosnian model', which stands for 'the trust in the possibility of a peaceful dialogue between the three Abrahamic traditions', 'a constant aspiration to establish permanent dialogue between different ways and laws, and between individuals exercising their right to seek perfection through following different paths' (Mahmutćehajić, 2000, 215).

This obviously does not mean that, historically, Bosnia has been the site of a constant and peaceful theological debate about the nature of God and inter-confessional tolerance: up until the twentieth century, different confessional communities barely communicated with each other (Sundhausen, 2014, 85–87). Mahmutćehajić does not dispute this, but boldly postulates the embodiment of unity in diversity in Bosniaks/Bosnian Muslims, 'the most numerous people of Bosnia' (Mahmutćehajić, 2000, 115): unity in

---

[3] I am quoting here from Marina Bowder's, Francis R. Jones's, Merima Osmankadić's and Oto Lukačević's translation *Bosnia the Good* (Mahmutćehajić, 2000). I will, however, also quote from the original (1997) to highlight the ways in which the translators modified the source text to soften its extreme edges. As the modifications are too numerous, only a representative sample will be included.

diversity is 'in the very essence of Bosniaks' being' (Mahmutćehajić, 1997, 211), as Bosniak identity stands for 'the essential unity of all sacred traditions' (Mahmutćehajić, 2000, 31). Thus, although absent from Bosnian history, unity in diversity still remains potentially anchored in the country through Bosniaks, while Serbs and Croats in all of Mahmutćehajić's publications appear only as Bosnia's relentless fascist destroyers. However, since 'religion is the nucleus of Bosniaks' culture' (Mahmutćehajić, 1997, 55), since Islam is their 'unifying and defining essence' (Mahmutćehajić, 1997, 130), it logically follows that 'Islam shoulders the unity in diversity' (Mahmutćehajić, 1997, 132). Modern culture, claims Mahmutćehajić (2000, 57), resembles a tree without a root: the social order of the contemporary world is not based on a 'transcendental principle' – meaning, it is secular, with sovereignty derived from people instead of from God and his holy book. 'But for a Muslim, law in its totality is a part of religion', claims Mahmutćehajić (1997, 55).

The English translation modifies this sentence by introducing a general religious perspective instead of the Muslim one: 'From the religious perspective religion and law are inseparable' (Mahmutćehajić, 2000, 57), which is neither a correct translation, nor a verifiable fact, as all other religions do not mind separating law and faith. This is, in a nutshell, the definition of Islamic political imagination: only God legislates, 'neither the people nor the parliament nor the sovereign can be sources of law' (Roy, 1994, 61). Mahmutćehajić rejects democracy quite explicitly: he lists Plato's main forms of political order, positioned on the scale from the best, which is aristocratic rule, via timocracy, oligarchy and democracy, to tyranny, as the worst. For him, 'aristocracy corresponds today to theocracy' (Mahmutćehajić, 2000, 35). 'Theocracy is the rule of the higher order', claims Mahmutćehajić (1997, 43), but the English translation omits this sentence (2000, 35). 'Democracy is, by its nature, the predecessor of dictatorship and demagogy', continues the author (1997, 43): it is in the *nature of democracy* to degenerate into dictatorship or demagogy. The translation kindly softens the edges again: 'Democracy is, however, always vulnerable to displacement or demagogy' (Mahmutćehajić, 2000, 35). In the future, Bosnians should be 'directed towards the "general good" which is realized by following transcendent principles' (Mahmutćehajić, 2000, 36); Bosnians should be steered away from the secular, popular sovereignty-based democracy, towards the theocratic system. 'This will require a fundamental and decisive reconsidering and denying of lower forms of freedom, and re-establishment of order' (Mahmutćehajić, 1997, 44). Naturally, in a theocracy, some forms of freedom will have to go, just as in the English translation the verb 'denying' had to go. What will this theocratic system be based on? The followers of Muhammad have

> a task of building a model community, guided by their obligation to establish a place where people will be brought into God's moral structure (*madina*). Wherever Muslims are living, they should order their community and their society on the basis of the Message and Example of God's Messenger. They should desire that the whole world be transformed into a *madina*, a community of believers. (Mahmutćehajić, 2000, 23–24)

Those who are not Muhammad's followers, such as Christians, 'are ruled by their own sacred laws'; however, '[t]heir independence ceases only at the point where it limits or endangers the priority of Islam as God's final and complete message' (Mahmutćehajić, 1997, 27–28). This is Mahmutćehajić's political vision: a theocratic state, based on Islamic law, in which non-Muslims can enjoy freedom as long as it does not contravene the primacy of Islam. They cannot be equal to Muslims; they are only tolerated so long as they submit to Islamic law. Even tolerance has its limits: tolerating what contravenes Islam is impossible, for otherwise '[t]olerance becomes the name for surrendering the fundamental principles without which religion is not possible' (Mahmutćehajić, 1997, 56). This view of the value of tolerance is, however, omitted in the English translation (Mahmutćehajić, 2000, 57). This vision is not limited to Bosnia and Herzegovina, it is global. Mahmutćehajić explains this in the following paragraph, which is also omitted in the English translation of *Bosnia the Good*: 'The world community of Muslims is the categorical and integral political ideal. This community is determined not by human, but by God's laws. No sovereign or authority can change these laws. This is the multiplicity of laws based on God's commands' (Mahmutćehajić, 1997, 31). This is, *pace* Mahmutćehajić, how Islam facilitates unity in diversity. This unity appears to be very clearly structured: Islam preserves its primacy, and from that position 'tolerates' those who submit to it, provided they respect Islam's priority. If unity in diversity is the dialogue between the sacred traditions, it is certainly not a dialogue of cultures, comments Nicolosi, as it is based on the recognition of Islam's supremacy (Nicolosi, 2010, 723). This is a crypto-nationalist thesis disguised as multiculturalism (Nicolosi, 2010, 725–26). In *Bosnia the Good*, one reads the following lyrical paragraph:

> The blood of *shaheeds, those who testified with their lives that there is no god but God and that Muhammad is His slave and His Messenger,*

cleanses this world, and enables the scent of the rose, its testimony to the love of God, and Paradise to open to the those who refuse to be enslaved to anything but God. (Mahmutćehajić, 1997, 134, my italics)

Shaheeds, Islamic martyrs who died to testify that Muhammad is God's Messenger, in the English translation surprisingly become martyrs for Bosnia's multi-confessional and multi-ethnic future: 'The blood of *those who died in the belief that Bosnia stands for all faiths and all peoples* cleanses the world' (2000, 143, my italics). This is not an example of an ethical, responsible and professional translation, but merely of an engaged, partial and committed one. There is nothing ethical in this modification of the source text: it radically changes the text's meaning and the political position of its author.

Mahmutćehajić's ethnonationalism is most obvious in his reinterpretation of Bosniak history. In almost all his publications, from *Živa Bosna* (1994) to the latest, *Andrićizam* (2015), he repeats the cornerstones of contemporary Bosniak mytho-history: in addition to the myth of the perfect tolerance of non-Muslims in the Ottoman state, there is also the representation of Muslims as the victims of a centuries-long genocide in Europe, the myth of the uninterrupted Bosnian statehood from the Middle Ages to the present and the famous *Bogomil* myth. Their main purpose is, as Džaja (2003, 58) noted, 'to marginalize the Serbian and Croatian presence in Bosnia' and 'to create the idea of Bosniaks as the corner-stone people' within it (Džaja, 2003, 53). The *Bogomil* myth was created at the end of the nineteenth and the beginning of the twentieth century by several Romantic historians and Austro-Hungarian officials, who strove to create a Bosnian nation to suppress already formed Serbian and Croatian identities in occupied Bosnia and Herzegovina. It crumbled when twentieth-century historians re-examined it. The myth maintained that the members of the mediaeval Bosnian Church collectively accepted Islam after the Ottoman conquest in the mid-fifteenth century, which would make them the ancestors of the present-day Bosniaks, who are thus their only true heirs. According to the *Bogomil* myth, the followers of the Bosnian Church were theologically similar to dualist, neo-Manichean Cathars, and were perceived as heretics by Roman Catholic and Serbian Orthodox churches, which instigated a genocidal campaign against them. As victims of their neighbours, the *Bogomil* saw salvation in Islam, and converted *en masse*. Twentieth-century historians, however, demonstrated that its ritual was similar to Catholic and Orthodox practice, that it was not persecuted, as the churches co-existed cordially and peacefully, that it was never a state church, and that there is no evidence that the majority of the population ever belonged to it, that by the time of Ottoman conquest only a handful of its members remained, and that *en masse* conversion to Islam never occurred.[4] Rather, it was a slow process, which accelerated only when the Bosnian Church was long gone.

The new Bosniak historiography, however, revived the *Bogomil* myth and transformed it into the founding Bosniak national myth. Mahmutćehajić not only frequently retells it in his books, but (2000, 117–39) extends it further into the past, constructing an 'uninterrupted' continuity composed of quite disparate and disconnected elements: from Alexandrian bishop Arius, exiled to Illyricum after the First Council of Nicaea (325 AD) and his Balkan followers, via some Muslim presence confirmed in parts of present-day Serbia and Croatia, to the first-known Bosnian *ban*, Borić (twelfth century), who bequeathed his estate to a Templar monastery, the Knights Templars being, in Mahmutćehajić's view (2000, 117–39), 'under the influence of Islam'. From the Templars to the Bosnian Church, formed in the mid-thirteenth century, is but a short step, and the Church naturally metamorphoses into Islam and present-day Bosniaks. What connects Arius's followers, the Knight Templars, the Bosnian Church and Bosnian Muslims is their religious difference, the status of heretics, and 'a historical experience of persecution and genocide' (Mahmutćehajić, 2000, 139). Mahmutćehajić (1997, 105) rejects any questioning of this construction, claiming that an 'exclusively rationalist and dogmatic-secular approach', which demands evidence and logical coherence, is not the right path to understanding 'the essence of Bosniaks' being'. This fable resembles early nationalist chronicles more than modern historiography; its expected effect on the reader should be to justify Bosniaks' claim on Bosnia, to prove that 'since the mediaeval foundations [they have an] active and historical right to Bosnia' (Mahmutćehajić, 1997, 39) at the expense of Serbs and Croats, who in the fable stand for persecutors coming from outside to eradicate different paths to God. In the English translation their 'historical right to Bosnia' becomes their 'historical rights within Bosnia and Herzegovina' (Mahmutćehajić, 2000, 33), a significantly different meaning, for the original implies that Bosnia belongs to Bosniaks only, while the translation allows for others having similar rights as well. Dubravko Lovrenović (2009, 276), a Bosnian mediaevalist who devoted a book to debunking nationalist myths of all three ethnicities in recent Bosnian historiography, maintains that this arbitrary construction of Mahmutćehajić is 'based on reviving stereotypes,

---

[4] On the Bosnian Church see Fine 2007; and a summary in Fine (2002, 3–6).

on conceptual and factual confusion, [and] unsustainable simplifications', and that he demonstrates 'intellectual arrogance [...] which laconically eliminates several generations of historians'.

This myth responds to the claim that 'Bosnia does not have its myth or its mythology', which Muhamed Filipović (2006, 10) put forward in 1967 in 'Bosnian Spirit in Literature – What Is It?', a manifesto from the earliest phase of modern Bosniak nationalism. This essay was apparently about literature, but its allegorical meaning was obvious to all: Bosnian literature is the embodiment of the Bosnian spirit, which emanates from the Bosnian nation. Filipović explicitly rejects the literature written in Bosnia before the 1960s as merely Serbian and Croatian literature, the literature that 'divided Bosnia more than many an army marching through' it (Filipović, 2006, 5). The new Bosnian literature will unite Bosnia by emitting the authentic Bosnian spirit, and is being written by Bosniaks alone. Thus – like Mahmutćehajić's various images of Bosnia – the Bosniak identity is superimposed on Bosnia, as supposedly the only authentic 'Bosnian' one. As an example of this literature, Filipović cited Dizdar's collection, *Kameni spavač* (*Stone Sleeper*, 1966). Dizdar gathered inscriptions from *stećci*, mediaeval tombstones in Bosnia, which ranged from trivial notes merely mentioning the names of the deceased, to more elaborate efforts to capture their lives in lapidary sentences that sometimes achieve unexpected poetic qualities. He developed some of them further, thus creating exemplary modern poetry based on mediaeval images of simple lives focused on basic existential situations: the reader hears the voices of those long gone who talk to him about love, death, fear, joy, hope, children, honour, etc. There is little specifically Bosnian in these elliptic verses: one poem mentions Bosnia, one 'good Bosnians', one lists several Bosnian rivers, and one several Bosnian rulers. Dizdar was not a Bosniak nationalist – he considered himself a Croat – and there is no evidence that he was attracted to mediaeval tombstones by the notorious nationalistic attachment to all things mediaeval. On the contrary, he once said: 'For me, the *stećak* is but an inspiration to address in poetic terms the existential [NB: not national – ZM] questions pertinent to all historical epochs. Hence a misconception that my poetry is only a representation of mediaeval times, or any other for that matter' (Buturović, 2002, 79). This is how Dizdar was read until the 1990s; since then, however, a host of critics have instilled in *Stone Sleeper* the whole repertoire of nationalist myths and transformed Dizdar into a poet of Bosniak nationalism.

An example of such a reading is the book *Stone Speaker* by Amila Buturović, to which Jones contributed his translations of Dizdar's poems.

Buturović (2002, 83) notes that in Dizdar's pre-1990s reception there were no traces of 'political and national concerns', but boldly postulates that Dizdar provides the 'sense of national history', and transforms 'the mediaeval burial ground into the cradle of national culture' (ibid., 84, 127). Throughout the book, Buturović manages to introduce many elements of current Bosniak mytho-history: the notion of Ottoman multiculturalism, *Bogomilism* as the 'precursor to Bosnian Islam' (ibid., 155), 'unity of Bosnian culture' (ibid., 115), 'unified Bosnian nationhood' (ibid., 2002, 33), even Bosnian 'continuity in territorial terms' (ibid., 127). Even though Buturović is aware of the mythical character of the *Bogomil* theory (ibid., 60–63), she nevertheless proceeds with an analysis based on the assumption that mediaeval *stećak* graveyards were *Bogomil* and that Dizdar 'accepted this proposition, turning it into the very basis of his poetry' (ibid., 71).[5] In Buturović's reading, Dizdar's *Stone Sleeper* becomes a 'national epic' about Bosnian unity and territorial integrity. This may well be a legitimate and valuable political programme, but it has no connection with Dizdar's collection; all these political and national concerns disappear as soon as Buturović begins to analyse individual poems, since a close reading of them cannot support them. Buturović's interpretation of Dizdar's poems is merely an example of political misreading: interpreting poetry is here used only as an opportunity to repeat, elaborate and fortify a national ideology. It is ironic that, although Jones (2009, 7) is well aware that 'the manipulation of literature often plays a crucial role in the process of ethnonational identity formation by generating "pseudo-histories" that create or reinforce national mythologies', he keeps repeating with reference to Dizdar's poetry this pseudo-history, which reinforces Bosniak national mythology (Jones, 2000, 2001, 2009, 2011).

From Gatekeeper to Ambassador

Jones frequently discusses what prompted him to translate and promote certain authors, and to use his gatekeeping capacity to exclude others. He deserves respect for being consistently open about his partisanship and partiality in all his publications, and turns the justification of his bias into a scholarly theme. Yet Jones (2009, 16) also maintains that it is 'crucial to have an awareness of the ethical and ideological implications of one's acts', and this

---

[5] Dizdar claimed, however, that under these mediaeval tombstones there could be members of other religions as well (Dizdar, 1971, 30).

is where our respectful spectatorship ought to give way to a more scholarly approach. As David Norris shows in Chapter One, the politics underlying theoretical anti-national(ist) approaches to the organization of world literature adopted by Western intellectuals are laid bare in the South Slav setting. Jones presents himself as a cosmopolitan opposed to every ethnonationalism, who put his professional skills to the service of the cosmopolitan forces in Bosnia and Herzegovina. Jones gave his support to the government led by Izetbegović's Party of Democratic Action, translated Latić and Mahmutćehajić, and, after translating Dizdar's *Stone Sleeper*, promoted an ideologically inspired interpretation of it. Yet we have seen that Izetbegović's government was hardly cosmopolitan in Jones's sense; it was ethnonationalist and Islamist, a fact recognized by all relevant literature on the Bosnian war. Jones's knowledge of the conflict is based on the media and personal accounts (Jones, 2011, 25), and if he refers to any literature on the war, it is to journalistic accounts like Silber and Little (1997), Malcolm (1996) and Judah (2000). The relevant, standard scholarly accounts of the war, written by professional historians and social scientists with appropriate language skills and a long-standing academic interest in the former Yugoslavia, in which Izetbegović's ideological platform is adequately presented, never appear as his sources: Burg and Shoup (1999) and Bougarel (1996) for the history of the Bosnian war, or Jović (2009), Hayden (1999) and Perica (2002) for the political, legal and religious aspects of Yugoslav dissolution, respectively. The standard history of Yugoslavia's dissolution, Woodward (1995), widely accepted as a non-partisan, non-biased, non-partial account of the events – such accounts are still possible, and not as exceptionally as some may believe – appears only once in all of Jones's writing (2009, 8), and then he imputes something to her that she did not claim: namely that Dobrica Ćosić was a prime mover behind the 1986 draft memorandum of the Serbian Academy of Sciences and Arts (Woodward, 1995, 71, 78). In his promotion of Dizdar's poetry, Jones contributed to furthering ethnonationalist myths, and thus actually might have harmed Dizdar's reception in English. *Stone Sleeper* was published by Anvil Press only in 2008, and had no reception to speak of: if you introduce someone as a poet who constructs 'a Bosnian identity through the country's medieval past' (Jones, 2009, 9), the reading public may be less inclined to read the author than if you introduce him as a great poet of existential situations that concern us all.

Presenting Latić and Mahmutćehajić as cosmopolitan writers is also incorrect, to say the least; both authors are ethnonationalists and Islamists from the extreme end of the political spectrum. The modifications we identified in Mahmutćehajić's translated prose amount to misrepresentation of the author's political and ideological position. A translator who is conscious of the ethical aspects of translating should abstain from mistranslating the source text or, where another translator is responsible for it, note that these 'improvements' drastically change the author's political and ideological position. Such a translator may even want to voice his concern regarding the morality and professionality of these changes – especially if analysing translators' decisions to alter or remove semantic features is one of his scholarly topics, as it is one of Jones's topics (Jones, 2016). Instead, Jones repeatedly presents as a cosmopolitan, anti-nationalist and tolerant advocate of multi-ethnicity an author who actually rejects tolerance, secularism and democracy, and promotes ethnonationalist myths, the primacy of Islam as political ideology, theocracy and Bosniaks' hegemony in Bosnia and Herzegovina. As a translator-as-ambassador, Jones accomplishes exactly what he explicitly opposes as a 'translator as gatekeeper': enabling the presence of ethnonationalist views in the lingua franca. 'Trustworthiness' is, as Pym notes (2012, 70), what translators exchange: it is the principal ethical value without which all talk about ethics, engagement and commitment, changing the world, but also about professionalism, makes little sense.

Conclusion

This case study points in two directions. The first concerns the limits of translators' ethics and the metaphor of ambassadors. In the complex web in which a translator must orient herself – the source text, its author and his background, the source culture, the translator's own politics and values, the world's ideological and military struggles, the ideal of a peaceful planet and of multicultural understanding, etc. – her primary loyalty must be to the source text that she renders into another language, and the accuracy of information that she supplies about it. A translator may find himself torn between his professional ethics, with its imperative of trustworthiness derived from accuracy and faithfulness, and his politics, with its vision of a better world. It is not enough to shrug and say 'the dirtier the situation, the dirtier our hands' (Jones, 2009, 20), for if we do, our hands are likely to be very dirty indeed. A part of this better world must be the idea of accurate translations and their *bona fide* knowledgeable and faithful promotion, and every politics that promises a better future without them, or at the expense of them, is not worth the trouble. It is plainly untrue that we must remain forever imprisoned in the prior intelligibility through which we understand something in advance, in a specific perspective or specific vocabulary: all these – constituting our partiality and bias – are subject to revision and modification through the process of interpretation. A translator should, like her relatives the historian, the social scientist or the literary critic, be judged by her success in overcoming her bias, not by the sincerity with which she confesses it. The metaphor of ambassadorship is inadequate here. Ambassadors are civil servants paid by governments to pass their views abroad; their independent thinking can only be exercised within the limits of policies set by their governments; it is to the government that they owe their loyalty; they need to achieve a political aim, and not necessarily be attached to truth. Translators should not pass on what governments want to be taken as their views – as occurred quite literally in the present case study – and should be independent, attached to truth and loyal to their source texts.

The second direction concerns the notion of intercultural dialogue and the gatekeeper metaphor. A gatekeeper does not facilitate a dialogue: he merely prevents some from entering and speaking. A translator as gatekeeper is engaged in the opposite of the translator's task: in non-translating. That a translator can follow his bias and be wrong, by mistaking the Guelphs for the Ghibellines or the other way around, by now needs no further evidence. Or, perhaps, could they all be Guelphs? Or all Ghibellines? Instead of *deciding for us* who is who, the translator should use his linguistic skills to *reproduce for us* the dialogue of Guelphs and Ghibellines as faithfully and accurately as possible, without fearing that she might 'legitimize' the bad ones in the process. Agreeing to translate a text with which one disagrees does not imply complicity, as Baker (2006, 105) believes; translators are not responsible for the content of their translations, as long as they are accurate. Even if the content is detestable, their professional task is to present detestable contents to a wider audience accurately. The fear of legitimizing such texts is unfounded: their abhorrent Guelphness or Ghibellinesness – depending on your particular bias in this quarrel – will shine through even in translation. Here, the modesty of 'humble language workers' (Pym, 2012, 17) mirrors the interpretative humility of historians and social scientists; the latter do not hesitate to present all positions they discuss as accurately as they can, confident that their adult audience will be able to tell its Guelphs from its Ghibellines. If we claim that this confidence has become unfounded, and that no one can rely on an audience mature enough to tell one from another, then everything we do as historians, social scientists and translators begins to lose its sense. If, however, we claim to be able to tell one from another, we should generously recognize that our readers might still have the same ability. Translators from major languages may not have this task; there are many readers who can inspect this dialogue themselves, or there may be other translators who translate exclusively Guelphs, while we stick to Ghibellines. Translators from small languages, however, because there are so few, must take on this task. Only thus will they be able to facilitate a dialogue in which, it is to be feared, the reader will see that there are Guelphs and Ghibellines on all sides. This may upset our ideological certainties, but will at least be the first step towards the intercultural dialogue for which, we all agree, translators are working.

Jones rightly claims that by translating or refusing to translate, a translator from a small language has the power to decide which writers and ideas can be heard in the target culture: publishers can easily make their own choices regarding which translations to commission from widely known languages, as they often read these languages themselves. With small languages, with as many translators as the fingers on one hand, publishers rely exclusively on translators to tell them what is out there, what should be let in and when the gates should be closed. In this way, translators from small languages have the power to create pictures of source cultures which become so hegemonic that trying to challenge them becomes a very risky and unpopular enterprise. This case study presents an extreme and perhaps exceptional example of misrepresentation, but its extremity and exceptionality point to an important aspect of the problem that this collection deals with: when it comes to small languages, the translator's power and consequently her responsibility, are incomparably greater than in the case of widely spoken ones.

Bibliography

Ali, Rabia and Lawrence Lifschultz (eds). 1993. *Why Bosnia? Writings on the Balkan War* (Stony Creek, CT: The Pamphleteer's Press).
Arnautović, Marija. 2009. 'Djeca iz "mješovitih" brakova: nevidljive žrtve rata', Radio Free Europe, 15 October 2009. Available from: www.slobodnaevropa.org/content/article/1852764.html [accessed 25 May 2016].
Baker, Mona. 2006. *Translation and Conflict: A Narrative Account* (London and New York: Routledge).
Baker, Mona. 2007. Reframing Conflict in Translation. *Social Semiotics*, 17 (2), 151–69.
Baker, Mona. 2013. Translation as an Alternative Space for Political Action. *Social Movement Studies*, 12 (1), 23–47.
Banac, Ivo. 2000. Foreword. In Mahmutćehajić, Rusmir, *Bosnia the Good: Tolerance and Tradition* (Budapest: CEU Press).

Beganović, Davor. 2011. Postapokalipsa u zemlji "dobrih Bošnjana". *Kulturkritik kao izvor kulturalnog rasizma. Sarajevske sveske*, 32–33, 417–42.
Bougarel, Xavier. 1996. *Bosnie: Anatomie d'un conflit* (Paris: La Découverte).
Bougarel, Xavier. 1999. Bosnian Islam since 1990: Cultural Identity of Political Ideology? Paper presented at the annual convention of the Association for the Study of Nationalities, Columbia University, New York, April 1999. Available from: https://www.researchgate.net/publication/32230183_Bosnian_Islam_since_1990_Cultural_Identity_or_Political_Ideology (accessed 17 June 2016).
Bougarel, Xavier. 2007. Bosnian Islam as "European Islam": Limits and Shifts of a Concept. In Al-Azmeh, Aziz and Effie Fokas (eds). *Islam in Europe: Diversity, Identity and Influence* (Cambridge: Cambridge University Press).
Bougarel, Xavier. 2017. *Islam and Nationhood in Bosnia-Herzegovina: Surviving Empires* (London: Bloomsbury, Kindle edition).
Burg, Steven L. and Paul S. Shoup. 1999. *The War in Bosnia-Herzegovina* (Armonk, New York and London: M.E. Sharpe).
Buturović, Amila. 2002. *Stone Speaker: Medieval Tombs, Landscape, and Bosnian Identity in the Poetry of Mak Dizdar* (New York: Palgrave).
Dizdar, Mak. 1966. *Kameni spavač* (Sarajevo: Veselin Masleša).
Dizdar, Mak. 1969. *Stari bosanski tekstovi* (Sarajevo: Svjetlost).
Džaja, Srećko M. 2003. Bosanska povijesna stvarnost i njeni mitološki odrazi. In Kamberović, Husnija (ed.). *Historijski mitovi na Balkanu* (Sarajevo: Institut za istoriju u Sarajevu).
Filandra, Šaćir. 2012. *Bošnjaci nakon socijalizma: O bošnjačkom identitetu u postjugoslovenskom dobu* (Sarajevo/Zagreb: Preporod/Synopsis).
Filipović, Muhamed. 2006. Bosnian Spirit in Literature – What Is It? *Spirit of Bosnia*, 1 (1).
Fine, John V.A. 2002. The Various Faiths in the History of Bosnia: Middle Ages to the Present. In Shatzmiller, Maya (ed.). *Islam and Bosnia: Conflict Resolution and Foreign Policy in Multi-Ethnic States* (Montreal and Kingston, London, Ithaca: McGill Queen's University Press).
Fine, John V.A. 2007. *The Bosnian Church: Its Place in State and Society from the Thirteenth to the Fifteenth Century: A New Interpretation* (London: Saqi).
Hayden, Robert M. 1999. *Blueprints for a House Divided* (Ann Arbor, MI: University of Michigan Press).
Izetbegović, Alija. 1990. *Islamska deklaracija* (Sarajevo: Mala muslimanska bibioteka). English translation at http://www.angelfire.com/dc/mbooks/Alija-Izetbegovic-Islamic-Declaration-1990-Azam-dot-com.pdf (accessed 25 September 2019).
Jones, Francis R. 2000. The Poet and the Ambassador: Communicating Mak Dizdar's *Stone Sleeper: Translation and Literature*, 9 (1), 65–87.
Jones, Francis R. 2001. Bringing Mak Dizdar into the Mainstream: Textual and Cultural Issues in Translating Dizdar's *Kameni spavač*. *Forum Bosnae*, 11, 261–85.

Jones, Francis R. 2009. Ethics, Aesthetics and *Décision*: Literary Translating in the Wars of the Yugoslav Succession. In Baker, Mona (ed.). *Translation Studies: Critical Concepts in Linguistics*, Vol III (London and New York: Routledge). Also in *Meta*, 49 (4) (2004), 711–28.

Jones, Francis R. 2010. Poetry Translation, Nationalism and the Wars of the Yugoslav Transition. *The Translator*, 16 (2), 223–53.

Jones, Francis R. 2011. *Poetry Translating as Expert Action: Processes, Priorities and Networks* (Amsterdam and Philadelphia: John Benjamins).

Jones, Francis R. 2014. Book review of *Interpreting the Peace: Peace Operations, Conflict and Language in Bosnia-Herzegovina*. *Translation Studies*, 7 (3), 360–63.

Jones, Francis R. 2016. Partisanship or Loyalty? Seeking Textual Traces of Poetry Translator's Ideologies. *Translation and Literature*, 25, 58–83.

Jones, Frances R. and Damir Arsenijević. 2005. (Re)constructing Bosnia. Ideologies and Agents in Poetry Translation. In House, Juliane, M. Rosario Martín Ruano and Nicole Baubgarten (eds). *Translation and the Construction of Identity: IATIS Yearbook 2005* (Seoul: IATIS).

Jović, Dejan. 2009. *Yugoslavia: A State that Withered Away* (West Lafayette, IN: Purdue University Press).

Judah, Tim. 2000. *The Serbs: History, Myth and the Destruction of Yugoslavia* (New Haven, Conn, London: Yale University Press).

Lovrenović, Dubravko. 2009. *Povijest est magistra vitae: O vladavini prostora nad vremenom* (Sarajevo: Rabic).

Mahmutćehajić, Rusmir. 1997. *Dobra Bosna* (Zagreb: Durieux).

Mahmutćehajić, Rusmir. 2000. *Bosnia the Good: Tolerance and Tradition* (Budapest: CEU Press).

Malcolm, Noel. 1996. *Bosnia. A Short History* (London: Macmillan).

Netherlands Institute for War, Holocaust and Genocide Studies. 2002. Srebrenica Report, Available from: http://publications.niod.knaw.nl/publications/srebrenicareportniod_en.pdf (accessed 7 June 2016).

Nicolosi, Riccardo. 2010. Dijaloška tolerancija. Konstrukcija bosanskog kulturnog identiteta i uloga islama (devedesete godine). *Sarajevske sveske* 27–28, 709–31 [in English: 'Dialogic Tolerance', available at academia.edu/RiccardoNicolosi].

Perica, Vjekoslav. 2002. *Balkan Idols: Religion and Nationalism in Yugoslav States* (Oxford: Oxford University Press).

Popa, Vasko. 1972. *Uspravna zemlja* (Belgrade: Vuk Karadžić).

Pym, Anthony. 2012. *On Translator Ethics: Principle for Mediation between Cultures* (Amsterdam/Philadelphia: John Benjamins).

Roy, Olivier. 1994. *The Failure of Political Islam* (London: I.B. Tauris).

Schindler, John R. 2007. *Unholy Terror. Bosnia, Al-Qa'ida, and the Rise of Global Jihad* (St. Paul, MN: Zenith Press).

Silber, Laura and Alan Little. 1997. T*he Death of Yugoslavia* (London: Penguin).

Sundhausen, Holm. 2014. *Sarajevo: Die Geschichte einer Stadt* (Wien-Köln-Weimar: Böhlau).
Tymoczko, Maria. 2000. Translation and Political Engagement. *The Translator*, 6 (1), 23–47.
Woodward, Susan L. 1995. *Balkan Tragedy: Chaos and Dissolution after the Cold War* (Washington, DC: Brookings Institution).

CHAPTER THREE

Supply-driven Translation: Compensating for Lack of Demand

Ondřej Vimr (Institute of Czech Literature, Czech Academy of Sciences)

The most widespread translation practice is non-translation; it is normal that most texts and utterances are never translated. If everything had to be translated, the resource implications alone would leave humanity in serious trouble. It nevertheless makes sense to study the phenomenon of non-translation in two contexts: first, when it is artificially induced (through censorship or ideological embargo) (see Duarte, 2000; Špirk, 2014) and second, when, as discussed in this chapter, individuals or institutions struggle against non-translation, as in the case of less widely translated European literatures. To understand the logic of these interventions in international literary flows, I will approach translation from the perspective of supply and demand.

Understanding Demand-driven Translation

Because of the time and effort required, it is much easier to find a reason for not translating a text or utterance. Demand is widely considered a key motivation for literary translation; someone (a particular person or an undefined set of individuals) in the target culture sees a book or a series of books (a repertoire, genre) in another culture, observes that it is missing in the target culture and that it may be useful in some way, and makes the decision to get it translated. As Gideon Toury (2012, 21–22) puts it:

Work on this chapter was supported by funding from the European Union's Horizon 2020 Research and Innovation Programme under the Marie Skłodowska-Curie Grant Agreement No.749871.

cultures resort to translating precisely as a way of filling in gaps, whenever or wherever such gaps may manifest themselves: either in themselves, or (more often) in view of a corresponding non-gap in another culture that the target culture in question has reasons to look up to and try to exploit for its own needs.

For example, consider the German interest in Scandinavian literature in general and Henrik Ibsen (1828–1906) in particular in the nineteenth century. Although the German openness towards Scandinavian literature was to some extent rooted in pan-Germanic cultural affinities, Ibsen and other Scandinavian authors of the late nineteenth-century boom were translated thanks to genuine interest in the new, radical voices of the source cultures. The demand-driven nature of these translations does not conflict with the fact that these translations were read in ways that somewhat contradicted their original reception and interpretation in their source cultures (see, for instance, Bruns, 1977; Gentikow, 1978; Baumgartner, 1979; Zernack, 1997).

This straightforward account of what might be called demand-driven translation becomes problematic, however, when applied to contemporary book industry practice. In Toury's view, three important aspects are involved: the existence of a gap in the target culture vis-à-vis a non-gap in the source culture, the prestige of the source culture and the 'needs' of the target culture. The following anonymized letter, however, sent by a large supranational literary agency to a mid-sized publishing house in a semi-peripheral country, offering publishing rights for a three-book series, gives a rather different idea of why a book might be translated:

> We have just signed an extraordinary debut author.
>
> [*The debut author*] is the first [*semi-periphery nation*] crime author that we have taken on since 2005, which was when we signed [*a world-famous crime author*]. Incidentally, [*the debut author*] has the same [*national*] publishing house, publisher and editor as [*the famous author*].
>
> [*The debut author*]'s [*book title*] is the most ambitious, well-written and suspenseful [*national*] crime debut of the past decade. The first book of a planned trilogy, [*the book title*] was published in [*the source country*] some weeks ago to rave reviews, and the book was reprinted after only three days.
>
> Attached please find the following material:
>
> English sample translation
>
> English detailed synopsis

Ondřej Vimr

> English translation of a review from [*a newspaper*] ([*source country*]'s biggest newspaper)
> English review quotes
> [*The*] original manuscript
>
> We are looking for closing [*sic*] a three-book deal.[1]

This letter exemplifies how part of the contemporary book industry works. It opens with a favourable comparison with a world-famous author, highlighting the similarities on multiple levels, including the genre, nationality, publishing house and editor. It then notes the quality and success of the first book using positive domestic reviews and sales. Lastly, it emphasizes that the whole package of three books must be taken, when only the first has been written and published. The language of the accompanying documents reveals that the acquisition editor at the target publishing house is not expected to know the source language, but the original manuscript is attached too, should there be any doubts and an expert (perhaps a translator) at hand. In the light of Toury's account, the letter prompts the question: where in the target culture is there a gap for books not written yet or books that are almost the same as a previous one? Moreover, the prestige of the source culture envisaged by Toury has apparently been replaced by the prestige of the previous author on the world market. Likewise, the exploitation of the non-gap in the source culture (the original book) for its own needs seems to apply to the target publisher, literary agency, original author and many others, but definitely not the target culture.

Toury's descriptive model, explaining the process of translation as filling in gaps of the target culture vis-à-vis non-gaps in the source culture, seems to work best retrospectively for the purposes of comparative literature, literary history or theory of translation, as in the example of Ibsen. While it also seems to explain the overall tendency of literary flows for high-brow literature, where the status of particular literary works in both source and target literary systems is scrutinized by literary experts, other rules may apply to strata of literary production like popular fiction, as we will see with the examples of Emily Flygare-Carlén (1807–92) and Marie Sophie Schwartz (1819–94).

---

[1] Email from a large supranational literary agency to a mid-sized publishing house in a semi-peripheral country, March, 2015. The three-book series was sold to 20 countries as of February 2016, with the second and third book still unpublished.

Supply-driven Translation

The practice exemplified by the quoted letter suggests a model where the international circulation of literature is not shaped exclusively by demand on the target side, but is heavily influenced by the source or supply side. In cases of supply-driven translation, the key impulse for a translation does not come from within the target literary system, based on the reflection on what source systems have to offer and what the target culture may need. Rather, it comes from an entity positioned outside the target literary system with limited interest in and knowledge of the target literary system, including its 'gaps'. With supply-driven translations, economic and other non-aesthetic factors come into consideration on the supply side and may become the driving force behind the international circulation of literature.

Toury rightly acknowledges that 'sometimes – e.g. in so-called 'colonial' situations – an alleged gap may be pointed out for that culture by a patron of sorts, who also purports to know better how the gap may best be filled' (2012, 22). While Toury does not develop this idea, it seems obvious that the author of the letter – a literary agency – can hardly be considered a 'patron of sorts', nor the practice labelled a 'colonial' situation. Similarly, André Lefevere introduced the notion of patronage to describe 'the powers (persons, institutions) that can further or hinder reading, writing, and rewriting of literature' (1987, 20; 2016, 12). Lefevere's patrons operate primarily outside the literary system, they are not writers, publishers or translators, yet they inform the actions of these professionals of literature and therefore control the system in terms of literary poetics, interpretation and more. Importantly, these patrons operate in the target system and therefore help to structure the demand side of the international translation process from within. In supply-driven translation, the supplier comes from outside the target system in its entirety and does not necessarily need to point to a gap in it or in culture as a whole. Indeed, the supplier may well emphasize the sameness of the supplied work of literature, revealing the systemic redundancy of the work for the target culture. Such a work may nevertheless prove a gap-creator as well as gap-filler for the target book market, if appropriate marketing measures are put into practice.

For both demand- and supply-driven translations, the actual function of a translated literary work in the target cultural and literary system is a matter of multiple factors and cannot reliably be foreseen. Demand-driven translation, however, envisages a function from the outset, an idea of where the translation would be positioned in the dynamic target cultural and literary system once it is published, while supply-driven translation does not. The presupposed function of a supply-driven translation is derived from factors that apply to its function in the source and global markets for this and similar works.

Although borrowed from economics, the terms of supply and demand applied to literary flows do not reduce literary circulation to a matter of buying and selling. The terms also have political and sociocultural dimensions. The dynamics of supply and demand in literary flows, inherent in literary circulation, expose the importance of translations for both source and target countries, cultures, institutions and individuals. Some translations are more important for the target side, others for the source side, while yet others are mutually important, but with different emphases. For each translation, there needs to be supply (at least the original text) and demand (someone willing to execute the translation), with possible extra stimuli and motivations on both sides of the spectrum. The range of stimuli on the supply side is variegated and includes, for example, letters sent by authors to foreign editors promoting their own work, public agencies subsidizing translation and author visits, literary agents stimulating competition on the target book market with auctions, state-funded publishers who publish translations in the source country and export them, etc. The scope of motivations on the supply side is also differentiated and includes economic and prestige benefits for the author, publisher, literary agent, culture and country. From this perspective, rather than the facts of the target culture in Toury's understanding, it seems more accurate to understand translations as cross-national transfers that imply the existence of a field of international relations of exchange (see Heilbron and Sapiro, 2007). It is in the field of relations and exchange that translation projects are negotiated and executed by both individuals and depersonalized institutions with their unstable position in the field and their own interests and needs. Translations are facts of the international field of relations of exchange and should be studied as such.

Supply-driven Translations in the Late Nineteenth Century: Individual Actors

The supply-driven model needs to be distinguished from a strategy designed in the target system, either by a publisher or any other actor operating within the target system. In 1875, the Czech publisher of the Swedish popular novelist Emily Flygare-Carlén had a promotional article printed in a Czech newspaper (Anon., 1875) that stated:

Supply-driven Translation

> The Swedish are actually very much like us in terms of their efforts, especially when it comes to the family literature. The writings of Flygare-Carlén, in particular, appear to stem from the Czech spirit and are equally popular in Czech translation as the work of the best Czech male and female authors.

The major quality of the translated work, as presented in the article, is the alleged spiritual similarity between the translated author and Czech authors, including their popularity among readers. The aspects of otherness, originality and novelty are disregarded altogether. However, unlike the more recent letter cited above, which also promotes a work of literature on the basis of similarity to other successful authors (rather than as a 'gap-filler'), this promotional article has been produced by the target publisher to increase the sales of a translated work chosen and published by the same publisher; it operates within the target system and is not a case of supply-driven translation. The letter, by contrast, works across national literary systems and is supposed to stimulate actors in the target system's literary field to translate and publish a work preferred and suggested by the supply side.

A glance into the recent history of translation reveals that, broadly understood, supply-driven translations are not an innovation of the globalized and market-driven book industry. Rather, as we see in the chapters that follow by Chitnis, Wolters, Hermansson and Leffler and others, supplying translations is a practice that has been consistently explored and used by various actors, especially from smaller source cultures, to fight non-translation and stimulate a lower-than-expected demand in potential target cultures for over a century. The following examples from the Scandinavian and Czech history of translation give us a sense of the phenomenon, its diverse facets and its historical dimension. It also underscores the importance and complexity of agency in the international circulation of literature.

Supply-side interventions in international literary flows can take many forms and can be easily traced to the latter half of the nineteenth century. While the institution of literary agents was in its infancy (Thompson, 2012, 59–61), the authors themselves helped pave the way for their international success in the late 1800s. For many authors from smaller European nations with limited national language readership, translation (into German and French in particular) was the only means of gaining international fame and prestige as well as making their living. Some authors did not need to promote their work at all and were still widely translated, some took minor steps, while others promoted their work vigorously. August Strindberg (1849–1912) made

53

every effort to get published in French, which he considered prestigious and important for the dissemination of his work. He employed three strategies while living outside Sweden: he wrote in French, self-translated his works into French and commissioned translations of his works into French: 'Everything that was published in French between 1884 and 1894 is either written directly in French, or translated by the author or by others at his instigation' (Balzamo, 2013, 172).[2] Strindberg's work was, however, translated extensively into German during the same years without any intervention on his part. While translations of his work into German were demand driven, translations into French were supply driven. Flygare-Carlén, like other cases discussed by Hermansson and Leffler in Chapter Eight, had no need to promote herself, but her comparably famous compatriot, Marie Sophie Schwartz, wrote incessantly to German publishers to promote her own work and solicit translation rights fees (Leffler, 2019, 15–16).[3] While the translations of Flygare-Carlén were demand driven, the translations of Schwartz into German were partially driven by supply. The availability and relative popularity of Schwartz in German, however, had a spillover effect and induced demand-driven translations into other languages such as Czech (Vimr, 2019).

The Interwar Period: The Rise of Institutional Interventions[4]

Supply-driven translations are not merely a matter of individual actors such as authors eager to earn international prestige and recognition (like Strindberg), as well as revenues (like Schwartz). This became apparent in the wake of the First World War when a number of new countries emerged in Europe, fighting for their international status. As Chitnis demonstrates in the next chapter through the example of Czechoslovakia, it was in this period that the first coherent attempts were made at using literary translation in cultural diplomacy, thus moving the supply-driven stimuli from an individual to an institutional level.[5] These institutionalized activities took place in

---

[2] For other recent studies on Strindberg in translation see Gedin et al., 2013.

[3] My thanks to Yvonne Leffler for bringing the case of Marie Sophie Schwartz to my attention. For an in-depth analysis of agency in the translation, publishing a reception of popular Swedish women writers into Czech in the nineteenth century see Vimr, 2019.

[4] For a more detailed discussion see Vimr, 2018.

[5] The concepts and terms of cultural diplomacy and soft power as known today

Supply-driven Translation

three distinct areas of diplomatic communication: unilateral, bilateral and multilateral (Vimr, 2018). Unilateral actions were linked to the work of cultural and press attachés promoting source literature in the target country and usually took the form of one-off *ad hoc* projects. Bilateral and multilateral programmes depended, respectively, on the long-term diplomatic relations between countries and the establishment of the multinational League of Nations; these were the first attempts at systematic institutionalized supply-driven translation activity.

Proactive bilateral support for fiction and non-fiction translation was gradually incorporated into bilateral cultural agreements, a new and popular tool of cultural diplomacy.[6] Until the outbreak of the Second World War, the four most active countries to enter into such agreements were France (with 13 signed bilateral agreements), Poland (10), Czechoslovakia (9) and Belgium (8) (Haigh, 1974, 47). The immediate statistical impact of these agreements on translation production is difficult to assess. The agreements did not include any procedure for the production and promotion of translations; rather, they were an open, mutual acknowledgement of the significance of translation for both the source and target countries and provided a diplomatic and political frame of reference. It was the duty of diplomats and officials to identify ways of accomplishing the practical side of supplying translations and supporting translation activity. These would range from forwarding original books (or translations into generally known languages, such as English or French) to the cultural gatekeepers in the intended target countries to publishing translations in the source country and exporting them.

The importance of translation for (cultural) diplomacy and for the construction of the international image of a country grew in the interwar period, and it was most natural for diplomats and politicians from minor countries to provide supply-side support for translation, with the printed word as the only major source of knowledge about the unknown and unseen. Countries with unfavourable asymmetrical representation in the target countries therefore warmly welcomed bilateral agreements. Negotiating a

---

were not in use at the time. Technically, the agenda was often shared between the department of foreign affairs and the department of education, usually referred to as propaganda (with neutral connotations) or simply promotion. (This information is based on my research in the archives of Czechoslovakia, Denmark, Norway and Sweden.) See also the discussion by Chitnis in the following chapter.

[6] The topic of bilateral cultural agreements and the institutional support for literary translation in the interwar era is further developed in Vimr, 2018.

cultural agreement between Czechoslovakia and Sweden, the Czechoslovak diplomats internally assessed its potential benefit quite frankly:

> We [the Czechoslovak Republic] will, moreover, be the main beneficiaries of the agreement, especially since not only the exchange of translations (300 books have been translated into the Czechoslovak language, compared to 15 translations in the opposite direction), but also other promotion work has always been completed swiftly on the Czechoslovak side, while fundamentally struggling in Sweden.[7]

The content of these agreements was rather similar across the European continent; they were short (about one page) and were built on the principle of reciprocity and openness. Cultural agreements were also of importance to Nazi Germany, which began concluding them with its allies soon after Joseph Goebbels became Minister of Propaganda (Hungary 1936, Japan 1938, Italy 1938, Spain 1939). These agreements, however, were much longer and featured detailed paragraphs on the censorship of texts unfavourable to the source country regime. Nazi Germany's use and meticulous design of such agreements only emphasizes the perceived importance of cultural diplomacy and translation for the source country at the time.

Between the wars, the first attempts were also made to establish support for fiction and non-fiction translation multinationally. Czechoslovakia, Romania and Yugoslavia, for instance, triangulated a more detailed version of the bilateral agreement for the Little Entente, the political and cultural entity, and planned to co-publish bilingual editions of their most prestigious authors and works, supporting financially the translations and publishing as well as supplying the published books to public libraries across the three countries (Vimr, 2014, 112–17).

The League of Nations and its International Committee on Intellectual Cooperation (the predecessor of UNESCO, established 1922) took the first practical steps in supporting translation on a supranational level by launching the Index Translationum (1932), a coordinated record of published translations. More importantly, it also introduced programmes designed to provide active support for translation in the latter half of the 1930s. The initiative did not arise from the West European centre of the

---

[7] 'Zpráva periodická č. 4 za 4. čtvrtletí 1935' [Periodical report no. 4 for the 4th quarter 1935], 7 February 1936, AMZV (Archive of the Czechoslovak Ministry of Foreign Affairs), Politické zprávy 1918–39, Švédsko, Stockholm 1929–39, Stockholm 1936, č. 90dův/1936; all translations into English are mine, OV.

Supply-driven Translation

Committee but from non-European and small European countries, which also financed the programmes. Two collections of translation – Japanese and Ibero-American – appeared, with the clear aim of supplying the most important works of the respective non-European national literatures in a world language (French). In Europe, the Romanian delegation proposed in 1936 that the Committee should 'publish a collection of translations into one or more big universal languages of representative and classical works taken from various European literatures in regional languages' (*Rapport* [...] 1936, 8). Both large and small nations were supposed to benefit from the translations from smaller European languages into more widely used languages. The benefit for the latter (except for the source country) would, however, be indirect, since they were supposed to 'have easier access to the literature and consequently be more able to acquaint themselves with the spirit of their neighbours, which may help reciprocal understanding' (ibid., 64). This initiative came too close to the outbreak of the Second World War for any volumes to be published.

Despite their limited practical impact, both bilateral and multilateral interwar attempts at a supply-driven translation practice, including their justification, are crucial to understanding the European modes of literary translation support developed during the second half of the twentieth century. In the interwar period, three important aspects came to the fore at the institutional level. First, literature is a tool of diplomacy: literature in translation is important for the source culture and country since it helps establish and develop its international image and position in the field of international relations and is of benefit for both parties as a path to mutual understanding and conflict prevention. Second, if the source country is in an asymmetrically weaker position in the international field of (cultural, political, economic) relations, interventions from the source side are needed and justifiable, supplying information and/or translations to the target countries to overcome the asymmetries. Third, the common issue arising from more detailed discussions and plans was how to choose works for promotion, translation and supply. The most widespread cultural agreements did not feature any suggestions at all; Nazi-German agreements only featured suggestions of the types of works to censor. The Little Entente and League of Nations projects suggested a focus on the national canon as determined by the source country, paying practically no attention to the tastes and expectations of the target readership or the 'needs' of the target system.

Ondřej Vimr

Post-Second World War: Experiments on the Path Towards Current Practice

After the Second World War, various projects emerged to support the translation of smaller European literatures, the earliest of which all shared one thing in common: failure. At the same time, the examples presented demonstrate a growing awareness of a lack of demand for translations from smaller literatures and a readiness to compensate for it at both private and public institutional levels. While the interwar period saw most institutional projects remain on the drawing table, supply-driven translation gradually became a widely acknowledged practice when there was more time to explore the options.

Perhaps the most ambitious was the Bridge project proposed and organized by the Prague publisher Bohumil Janda (Sfinx and ELK imprints) and the renowned editor and literary agent Max Tau, a German Jewish émigré to Oslo.[8] It was supposed to involve selected publishers from all small European countries in a publishing and marketing network scheme. The key idea was to choose the 'best books' from the participating countries on an annual basis, have them translated into all other participating languages and publish them simultaneously, with a multiplying marketing effect. From the perspective of supply-driven practice, one of the important goals was to have 'passive members' in large countries (Germany, France, UK and USA) who would publish a selection of the yearly Bridge production. Janda and Tau initiated the project in 1947. In March 1948, publishers from seven countries (Belgium, Bulgaria, Czechoslovakia, Denmark, Netherlands, Norway and Sweden) were supposed to attend the initial convention in Prague, with contact also established with publishers from seven other countries (Hungary, Romania, Finland, Iceland, Poland, Switzerland and Yugoslavia). The communist takeover in Czechoslovakia and the rise of the Iron Curtain put an end to the project.

The Bridge project is unique in supply-driven translation first because it reveals that publishers across countries were used to networking and were quick to realize the potential of a complex networking scheme in terms of information exchange (tips about promising authors and works) and coordinated promotion. The scheme was proposed and promoted within a group of individuals that had known each other personally and the literary

---

[8] For a more detailed account and analysis of the Bridge project see Vimr, 2011, 138–44.

agent (Max Tau) seems to have functioned as an advisor and negotiator rather than a promoter of particular authors' or publishers' interests. Second, already in the 1940s, publishers were open to imitate the publishing catalogues of similarly positioned publishers across countries to reduce the risk of making the wrong choice (cf. Franssen, 2015), since Janda and Tau deliberately chose publishers they knew had similar literary tastes and status in their national literary fields. Third, in contrast to most other supply-oriented schemes, it was a private project with the proponents fully aware of the commercial dimension of publishing.

There is not much information on the process of selecting the 'best books', but the few names that appeared in the discussions suggest a focus on well-established contemporary authors (Sigrid Undset, A. den Doolaard), while the plan was to have Max Tau as the final arbiter of the quality and suitability of the works proposed by the individual participating publishers. When trying to supply books from small countries to large countries, Janda and Tau did not want to rely on the fame and success of a particular work or author in the source country. Rather, they intended to build international fame within the group of smaller countries, supplying an internationally visible pre-selection of books from small countries for publishers from larger countries to choose from.

The 1950s saw the establishment of presumably the first state-subsidized organization charged with promoting a small national literature abroad, and its agenda was almost identical to that of similar institutions today. In 1954, a publicly funded foundation was created in the Netherlands for the promotion of Dutch literature that 'subsidized translations, established contacts with foreign publishers, commissioned trial translations, and diffused information about authors and their work' (Heilbron, 2008, 193). Far from being the only way of supporting literary export to the target countries, similar publicly funded agencies are probably the most visible means of supply-driven translation today. The Dutch scheme, however, faced fierce criticism as early as the 1980s: the number of translations remained low, the quality of translation was mediocre, the foreign publishers were obscure and only interested in the subsidies, and literary fame did not ensue (ibid.). Wolters' discussion of the Biblioteca Neerlandica in Chapter Five gives multiple answers to why a supply-driven translation project may fail, including book design and the choice of works that may well represent the source country's canon, but do not appeal to the target audience.

Despite criticism of the early Dutch foundation, comparable agencies for the promotion of literature that supply information, subsidize translations and perform other supporting activities have been on the rise in recent decades, with many new agencies established after the fall of the Iron Curtain.[9] Recent research shows the modest, yet positive impact of some agencies in semi-peripheral and peripheral countries and literatures like the Netherlands (HaCohen, 2014), Turkey (Akbatur, 2016), and Flemish (McMartin, 2016a, 2016b) and Catalan literature (Roig Sanz, 2016). Especially revealing is Ran HaCohen's study of the mutual exchange between two peripheral literatures, Dutch and Hebrew, from 1991 to 2010, which shows asymmetrically higher numbers of translation into Hebrew than in the other direction and links the fact to the labour conditions and state subsidies in the respective countries. Although supplying translations through national public-funded agencies for the promotion of literature abroad is widely practised today, more extensive research on the topic is needed, especially in the area of inter-peripheral relations.

Multinationally, the UNESCO Catalogue of Representative Works was established in 1948 and discontinued in 2005 due to lack of funds:

> The project's purpose was to translate masterpieces of world literature, primarily from a lesser known language into a more international language such as English and/or French. There were 1060 works in the catalogue representing over sixty-five different literatures and representing around fifty Oriental languages, twenty European languages as well as a number of African and Oceanian literatures and languages. (UNESCO, n.d.)

The end of the project may indicate the limited impact of such a broad initiative in respect to the funds and other resources needed. Likewise, through the Creative Europe action programme, the European Union supports literary translation (cf. Creative Europe, n.d.). The data or scholarly research on these programmes is currently scarce.

---

[9] While the Dutch Foundation for Literature has its roots in the 1950s, the Finnish FILI and Norwegian NORLA (established in 1977 and 1978 respectively) are perhaps the oldest institutions of the kind that have not undergone a major transformation. Most current agencies in Europe were established or transformed in the last 30 years (cf. *Survey of Key National Organizations Supporting Literary Exchange and Translation in Europe*, Budapest: Literature across Frontiers, December 2012).

Typology, Paradigm Shift and Agency in Translation

More complex research is needed to provide a comprehensive evaluation of supply-driven translation and its impact. This brief account nevertheless highlights the intricate nature of agency in translation as it has developed over the twentieth century, and also reveals the following. First, it facilitates the creation of a typology of interventions in supply-driven translation, illuminating the complexity of the phenomenon (see Table 1).

There are two basic types of agents on the source side involved in supply-driven translation: individuals (such as authors or individual literary agents) and institutions (publishing houses, public or private foundations, state departments, etc.). As a matter of course, individuals and diverse institutions may cooperate on a common goal of supply-driven translation to compensate for lack of demand while maintaining their respective agendas. In the 1930s and 1940s, Italian publishers were criticized for publishing too many translations. To avoid possible Fascist-regime restrictions, Mondadori, a leading Italian publisher, helped maintain translation balance by assisting in the translation of several dozen books, chosen in cooperation with the Italian Ministry of Culture, from Italian into French (Rundle, 2010, 55–59, 152–57). It was a supply-driven translation project shared by the actors of publishing and political fields with different agendas: commercial and political.

Table 1   Supply-driven translations: a typology

Type of agent	*Individual*	*Institutional*
Source of funding	Private	Public
Anchoring	Multinational	National
Focus	Periphery–periphery	Periphery–centre

While potentially profitable either in terms of economic or symbolic capital, supply-driven translation is a risky business and needs initial funding. This funding may come from private and public sources and a diachronic analysis of financial flows in supply-driven translation may provide a further stepping stone in understanding the logic and dynamics of international literary flows.

In terms of networking, cooperation and coordination, the national or multinational anchoring of supply-driven projects reveals different approaches to the management and control of the project. On the one hand, it seems that projects linked to the promotion of a particular (national) literature are ever more prevalent in comparison with multinational projects, as they may be easier to manage or fund, for instance. On the other hand, little research is available on multinational projects and their impact. At the same time, national publicly subsidized agencies supporting the export of books cooperate on a multinational level nowadays, as evidenced by the Traduki project, connecting southeast European and German-speaking literary systems, or the European Network for Literary Translation (ENLIT) established in 2016 and connecting 22 organizations across 19 countries and regions (Süßmann, 2016). Institutionalized supply-driven translation is a fully established practice nowadays, and multilateral cooperation is yet a further attempt to rebalance the globalized book market and draw attention to less central languages and literatures while respecting the market logic of contemporary publishing (see Heilbron and Sapiro, 2018).

In fact, supply-driven translation from non-central source contexts tends to target both more or less peripheral systems and the central and hyper-central language areas, if we apply Heilbron's distinction (1999). This double focus is clearly visible in both the Bridge project and ENLIT network. As the Bridge project illustrates, the justification and aims differ, depending on whether the focus is on peripheral or central contexts. Supply-driven translation aimed at dissemination in peripheral countries seems to be connected with symbolic value and seeks to accumulate symbolic capital. This symbolic capital can be an asset in supplying translations to the more central countries. A focus on central countries and languages, on the other hand, has two purposes, since these countries and languages act as both targets and mediators. A successful translation into a central (German, French) or hyper-central (English) language brings both financial and symbolic capital. The latter is of particular importance, since it may also help to provoke demand in other countries by gaining access to the peripheral countries either directly (via new translations into the peripheral countries prompted by success) or indirectly (benefiting from the fact that a more central language has a number of non-native speakers).

The second important aspect elucidated by this brief history of supply-driven translations is its dynamics and development over time. Assuming that demand-driven translation was a standard paradigm in the nineteenth century, with only individual authors gradually trying to influence literary circulation, we can see a clear paradigm shift towards a more multi-faceted model for literary exchange, with varied and ever more complex attempts at supply-driven translation during the twentieth century. This shift accompanied the rise of many important actors in the field of international literary exchange with the aims, roles and strategies of these actors being defined and redefined continuously. The supply–demand distinction makes it easier to account for these new and varied actors that have emerged in the past century to operate in the translation and publishing fields, such as literary agents – one of the most obvious, active actors in supply-driven translation nowadays, judging from their capability in selling the unwritten – or the agents of cultural politics and diplomacy.

The international diplomatic and political use of literature has, above all, undergone profound development. In the interwar period, methods of cultural diplomacy were gradually being established, with book translation merely a fraction of the agenda. It was only in the wake of the Second World War that cultural diplomacy gained a central status also for a hyper-central language country: 'When the United States assumed the mantle of global leadership after World War II, cultural diplomacy was considered a central part of its strategy' (Finn, 2003, 16). The US institutions supported cultural export, publishing and supply-driven translation on a global scale: in Latin America (Milton, 2008), Central and Eastern Europe (Saunders, 1999), or the Arab countries (Laugesen, 2017) where it gradually competed with supply-driven translation projects by other major countries such as the USSR since the 1960s, and France since the 1980s (Jacquemond, 2009, 21–24).

In many European countries, the decades following the 1970s gave rise to the national agencies supporting literary export. These have become the main engines of supply-driven translation in non-genre fiction. More recently, one of the most ambitious and expensive goals of a country (represented by its institution for the international promotion of literature) has been to become Guest of Honour at the Frankfurt Book Fair, which promises substantial impact in terms of media visibility in Germany (Matis, 1997; Körkkö, 2017) as well as an increase in the number of translations into German (McMartin, 2016b). However, the extent of the spillover effect, in terms of more frequent translations into other languages, seems rather unclear (Linn, 2006). This objective makes the link between the literary, political and diplomatic dimensions ever more visible, and was made explicit in a speech given by the Norwegian State Secretary, Tone Skogen, on the occasion of the signing ceremony confirming Norway's guest status for 2019: 'The government's decision to support Norwegian literature's big dream – Frankfurt 2019 – was based in part on the idea that culture is a part of politics, and that culture is also diplomacy' (Skogen, 2016).

Ondřej Vimr

A third aspect highlighted by this chapter is that it would be a mistake to understand supply- and demand-driven translation models as opposites. Rather than two polarities, they are intertwined approaches to the practical management of the international literary circulation system, reflecting the complexity of day-to-day decision processes in the translation and publishing business and the long-term impact these decisions have on the creation and reinforcement of literary and cultural representations of source countries. At the same time, the prominence of economic aspects of both the original and the translated product only underscores the interdependence of the supply and demand side, the source system, the target system and the intermediaries.

While it may seem that translators suffer most from this convoluted practical side of the global literary circulation, this need not necessarily be so. The most decisive moment for a translation is the acquisition of translation rights that allow a publisher to publish a particular book. These decisions are taken by acquisition editors positioned at the virtual centre of a gatekeeping network that provides them with masses of information about books (Franssen and Kuipers, 2013). Such a network may include literary agents, national promotion agencies, peer publishing houses and translators. Every part of the network furnishes the final decision-maker with a unique set of information that adds to the personal credit of the informant. While literary agents and national agencies, with their profit and prestige agendas, clearly position themselves on the supply side, and target publishers represent the (potential) demand side, translators as well as peer publishers in other countries may act as more independent opinion-givers in finding the right balance between supply and demand. A peer publishing house may give important information about the success of a particular title in another country. A translator, however, holds a unique position – especially in the context of minor languages – as the expert on both the source and target cultures and their literary systems, and is supposedly qualified to arbitrate on whether a particular text may succeed in the particular target culture and whether there would be real demand from readers for the supply-driven translation. The distinction between supply- and demand-driven models in translation, as well as the historical occurrences and dynamics thereof, may therefore empower translators since it makes the practical processes of global literary circulation more transparent and helps each party to become aware of their particular position and power in the system. The transparency that the distinction has the potential to deliver may also make it easier to see the limits of the struggle against non-translation. That struggle, from the 1920s to the present, forms the subject of the next four chapters.

Bibliography

Archives
AMZV: Archive of the Czechoslovak Ministry of Foreign Affairs, Prague, Czech Republic.

Works Cited
Akbatur, Arzu, 2016. Can We Go beyond '3%'? The Changing Perception of Turkish Literature through Translations into English. Paper delivered at the conference 'Small is Great: Cultural Transfer through Translating the Literature of Smaller European Nations', Budapest, 10–12 March 2016.
Anon. 1875. Emilie Flygaré-Karlénová a její spisy. *Posel z Prahy*, 251, 1.
Balzamo, Elena. 2013. Utländska öden och äventyr. Strindberg i översättning. In Gedin, David, Per Stam, Anna Cavallin and Elena Balzamo (eds). *Strindbergiana: Tjugoåttonde samlingen* (Stockholm: Atlantis), 171–82.
Baumgartner, Walter. 1979. *Triumf des Irrealismus: Rezeption skandinavischer Literatur im ästhetischen Kontext: Deutschland 1860 bis 1910* (Neumünster: Wachholtz).
Bruns, Alken. 1977. *Übersetzung als Rezeption: Deutsche Übersetzer skandinavischer Literatur von 1860 bis 1900* (Neumünster: Wachholtz).
Creative Europe. n.d. Literary Translation. Available at: https://eacea.ec.europa.eu/creative-europe/actions/culture/literary-translation_en [accessed 9 May 2016].
Duarte, João Ferreira. 2000. The Politics of Non-Translation: A Case Study in Anglo–Portuguese Relations. *Traduction, Terminologie et Redaction*, 13 (1), 95–112.
Finn, Helena K. 2003. The Case for Cultural Diplomacy-Engaging Foreign Audiences. *Foreign Affairs*, 82 (6), 15–20.
Franssen, Thomas. 2015. Diversity in the Large-scale Pole of Literary Production: An Analysis of Publishers' Lists and the Dutch Literary Space, 2000–2009. *Cultural Sociology*, 9 (3), 382–400.
Franssen, Thomas and Giselinde Kuipers. 2013. Coping with Uncertainty, Abundance and Strife: Decision-making Processes of Dutch Acquisition Editors in the Global Market for Translations. *Poetics*, 41 (1), 48–74.
Gedin, David, Per Stam, Anna Cavallin and Elena Balzamo (eds). 2013. *Strindbergiana: Tjugoåttonde samlingen* (Stockholm: Atlantis).
Gentikow, Barbara. 1978. *Skandinavien als präkapitalistische Idylle: Rezeption gesellschaftskritischer Literatur in deutschen Zeitschriften 1870 bis 1914* (Neumünster: Wachholtz).
HaCohen, Ran. 2014. Literary Transfer between Peripheral Languages: A Production of Culture Perspective. *Meta: Journal des traducteurs/Meta: Translators' Journal*, 59 (2), 297–309.
Haigh, Anthony. 1974. *Cultural Diplomacy in Europe* (Strasbourg: Council of Europe).

Heilbron, Johan. 2008. Responding to Globalization. In Pym, Anthony, Miriam Shlesinger and Daniel Simeoni (eds). *Beyond Descriptive Translation Studies* (Amsterdam and Philadephia, PA: John Benjamins), 187–97.

Heilbron, Johan. 1999. Towards a Sociology of Translation: Book Translations as a Cultural World-System. *European Journal of Social Theory*, 2 (4), 429–44.

Heilbron, Johan and Gisèle Sapiro. 2007. Outline for a Sociology of Translation: Current Issues and Future Prospects. In Wolf, Michaela and Alexandra Fukari (eds). *Constructing a Sociology of Translation* (Amsterdam and Philadephia, PA: John Benjamins), 93–108.

Heilbron, Johan and Gisèle Sapiro. 2018. Politics of Translation: How States Shape Cultural Transfers. In Roig Sanz, Diana and Reine Meylaerts (eds). *Literary Translation and Cultural Mediators in 'Peripheral' Cultures: Customs Officers or Smugglers?* (London and New York: Palgrave Macmillan), 183–208.

Jacquemond, Richard. 2009. Translation Policies in the Arab World: Representations, Discourses and Realities. *The Translator*, 15 (1), 15–35.

Körkkö, Helmi-Nelli. 2017. *FINNLAND.COOL – Zwischen Literaturexport und Imagepflege: Eine Untersuchung von Finnlands Ehrengastauftritt auf der Frankfurter Buchmesse, 2014* (Vaasa: Vaasan yliopisto).

Laugesen, Amanda. 2017. *Taking Books to the World: American Publishers and the Cultural Cold War* (Amherst, MA: University of Massachusetts Press).

Lefevere, André. 1987. 'Beyond Interpretation' or the Business of (Re) Writing. *Comparative Literature Studies*, 24 (1), 17–39.

Lefevere, André. 2016. *Translation, Rewriting, and the Manipulation of Literary Fame* (New York: Routledge). First edition published 1992.

Leffler, Yvonne. 2019. Transcultural Transmission: Emilie Flygare-Carlén and Marie Sophie Schwartz in Central and Eastern Europe. In Leffler, Yvonne (ed.). *The Triumph of the Swedish Nineteenth-Century Novel in Central and Eastern Europe* (Göteborg: Göteborgs Universitet: LIR-skrifter), 7–31.

Linn, Stella. 2006. Trends in the Translation of a Minority Language. The Case of Dutch. In Pym, Anthony, Miriam Shlesinger and Zuzana Jettmarová (eds). *Sociocultural Aspects of Translating and Interpreting* (Amsterdam and Philadephia, PA: John Benjamins), 27–40.

Matis, Herbert. 1997. *Medienresonanz auf den Österreich Schwerpunkt zur Frankfurter Buchmesse, 1995* (Wien: Verl. d. Österreich. Akad. d. Wiss.).

McMartin, Jack. 2016a. Public Grant Agencies as a Bridge from Periphery to Centre? The Impact of the Flemish Literature Fund on Literary Translation Flows from Dutch into English, 2000–2015. Paper delivered at the conference 'Small is Great: Cultural Transfer through Translating the Literature of Smaller European Nations', Budapest, 10–12 March 2016.

McMartin, Jack. 2016b. Transnational Pole Coherence and Dutch-to-German Literary Transfer: A Study of Book Translations Published in the Lead-Up to the Guest of Honourship at the 2016 Frankfurt Book Fair. *Journal of Dutch Literature*, 7 (2), 50–72.

Milton, John. 2008. The Importance of Economic Factors in Translation Publication: An Example from Brazil. In Pym, Anthony, Miriam Shlesinger and Daniel Simeoni (eds). *Beyond Descriptive Translation Studies* (Amsterdam and Philadephia, PA: John Benjamins), 163–73.

Rapport de la commission sur les travaux de sa dix-huitième session plénière. 1936. (Genève: Société des nations. Commission internationale de coopération intelectuelle).

Roig Sanz, Diana. 2016. Catalan Translated Literature: Between the Nation, the Market and the World. Paper delivered at the conference 'Small is Great: Cultural Transfer through Translating the Literature of Smaller European Nations', Budapest, 10–12 March 2016.

Rundle, Christopher. 2010. *Publishing Translations in Fascist Italy* (Bern: Peter Lang).

Saunders, Frances Stonor. 1999. *Who Paid the Piper? The CIA and the Cultural Cold War* (London: Granta).

Skogen, Tone. 2016. Tale ved signering av bokavtale. *Regjeringen.no*. Available at: https://www.regjeringen.no/no/aktuelt/signering_bokavtale/id2500657/ [accessed 15 May 2016].

Špirk, Jaroslav. 2014. *Censorship, Indirect Translations and Non-translation: The (Fateful) Adventures of Czech Literature in 20th-century Portugal* (Newcastle upon Tyne: Cambridge Scholars Publishing).

Survey of Key National Organizations Supporting Literary Exchange and Translation in Europe, December 2012 (Budapest: Literature across Frontiers).

Süßmann, Ingrid. 2016. ENLIT: European Network for Literary Translation Launched in Frankfurt. In *Publishing Perspectives*. 1 November. Available from: https://publishingperspectives.com/2016/11/enlit-european-network-literary-translation-launched-frankfurt [accessed 20 November 2016].

Thompson, John B. 2012. *Merchants of Culture: The Publishing Business in the Twenty-First Century* (Hoboken, NJ: Wiley).

Toury, Gideon. 2012. *Descriptive Translation Studies and Beyond* (revised edition) (Amsterdam and Philadelphia, PA: John Benjamins). First edition published 1995.

UNESCO. n.d. UNESCO Archives AtoM Catalogue: Series – Representative Works. Available from: http://atom.archives.unesco.org/representative-works [accessed 9 May 2016].

Vimr, Ondřej. 2011. Prescriptive Polysystems, Struggle-free Fields, and Burdensome Habitus: Translation Paradigm Shift in the Wake of the February 1948 Communist Overthrow in Czechoslovakia. In *Acta Universitatis Carolinae–Translatologica Pragensia* (Prague: Karolinum), 135–47.

Vimr, Ondřej. 2014. *Historie překladatele* (Příbram: Pistorius & Olšanská).
Vimr, Ondřej. 2018. Early Institutionalised Promotion of Translation and the Socio-biography of Emil Walter, Translator, Press Attaché and Diplomat. In Roig Sanz, Diana and R. Meylaerts (eds). *Literary Translation and Cultural Mediators in 'Peripheral' Cultures: Customs Officers or Smugglers?* (London and New York: Palgrave Macmillan), 41–68.
Vimr, Ondřej. 2019. Despised and Popular: Swedish Women Writers in Nineteenth-Century Czech National and Gender Emancipation. In Leffler, Yvonne (ed.). *The Triumph of the Swedish Nineteenth-Century Novel in Central and Eastern Europe* (Göteborg: Göteborgs Universitet: LIR-skrifter), 87–124.
Zernack, Julia. 1997. Svärmeriet för Norden och det germanska i det tyske kejsarriket. In Henningsen, B., J. Klein, H. Mussener and S. Söderlind (eds). *Skandinavien och Tyskland, 1800–1914: Möten och vänskapsband* (Berlin, Stockholm and Oslo: Deutsches Historisches Museum, Nationalmuseum, Norsk Folkemuseum), 71–80.

Chapter Four

Literature as Cultural Diplomacy: Czech Literature in Great Britain, 1918–38

Rajendra Chitnis (University of Oxford)

State support for the translation and international promotion of smaller European literatures forms a refrain of this volume. This generally modest support constitutes part of cultural diplomacy, in its vaguest definition as 'any undertaking to promote the culture of a country by people who identify themselves with that country' (Gienow-Hecht and Donfried, 2010, 10). Studies of cultural diplomacy tend to focus on the post-1945 period, particularly the Cold War, and major powers like the United States, the USSR and China, but as Ondřej Vimr notes in the preceding chapter, the origins of this formal state involvement in literary circulation can be traced back to the post-1918 period, when it was arguably the less familiar, militarily and economically weaker European states, created or restored after 1918, that pioneered modern cultural-diplomatic practices as they competed to secure the favour of France, the UK and the USA. Noting the shift to state-led cultural diplomacy after 1918, Jessica Gienow-Hecht and Mark Donfried (2010, 18) write:

> Prior to World War I, cultural diplomacy remained an informal effort. [...] Most politicians agreed that the presentation of culture abroad should remain confined to individual interest groups and entrepreneurs, and most administrators in the foreign offices in Paris, London, and Berlin were convinced that the active dissemination of culture was important, but none of their business. Their job consisted in monitoring and funding whatever musical production, exhibition, or show they felt might improve their nation's image in the world.

In the post-1918 successor states, however, this distinction between the vaguer, disinterested promotion of one's nation through its culture and the politicized promotion of a specific idea of the nation became obscured because the 'individual interest groups and entrepreneurs' – patriotic nobility and intellectuals – who had been informally promoting the national culture abroad before the emergence of the new states were often prominent in the new leadership or civil and diplomatic services. When cultural diplomacy becomes more narrowly understood as 'a policy designed to encourage public opinion to influence a foreign government and its attitudes towards the sender country' (Gienow-Hecht, Donfried, 2010, 14), the state may discriminate or be accused of discriminating against writers who do not share its politics or its conception of the country that it wishes to propagate.

This tension in definitions of cultural diplomacy may be quintessentially observed in the context of First Republic Czechoslovakia (October 1918– September 1938), which, of the post-1918 successor states, took greatest pride in what it called its 'propaganda' efforts. In her study of the cultural diplomacy practised by the first Czechoslovak president, Tomáš Masaryk and his foreign minister and presidential successor, Edvard Beneš, Andrea Orzoff (2009, 15) writes:

> In the eyes of the [Prague] Castle leaders and many observers, propaganda had materially contributed to Austria's downfall and had brought about the Czech national 'revolution'. Rather than seeing propaganda as a danger to independent civic thought, Masaryk and Beneš viewed it as a useful form of civic education and an essential tool of statecraft. They boasted of their wartime propaganda skill in their memoirs, carefully planned the new state's propaganda organizations, and kept them under their personal control, trusting only their closest intimates. Masaryk and Beneš understood propaganda to be a crucial means of communicating with the masses and besting their political foes; cultural diplomacy was a parallel effort to reach elites abroad.

These propaganda efforts were hardly exceptional to Czechoslovakia, which both domestically and internationally had to counter hostile German, Hungarian and Polish propaganda about the new state's treatment of its national minorities. Orzoff's study, however, contradicts traditionally reverential accounts of the First Republic's cultural diplomacy, which emphasize its energetic diplomatic activity and engagement with the ideals and ambitions of the League of Nations and its internal efforts to build a modern civil society from a nationally divided population. She argues instead that Masaryk and Beneš used manipulative, oligarchical practices to promote a national myth about the 'innately democratic, peace-loving,

Literature as Cultural Diplomacy

tolerant Czechs', who were historically oppressed by the Habsburgs, and thus to 'claim the moral high ground and legitimate their own power' (Orzoff 2009, 14, 11).

The Place of Literature in First Republic Czechoslovak Cultural Diplomacy

My archival study of Czechoslovak state involvement in the translation and promotion of literature, however, reveals the more prosaic reality of state officials, who sense the international potential of literary culture but are uncertain how to harness it and lack the finance, expertise and capacity to do so. In the Foreign Ministry's national and literary archives in Prague, I found no strategy document dating from between 1918 and 1938 that elaborated the goals of Czechoslovak government support for the translation or promotion of literature. There is no evidence of any sustained attempt to translate or promote literature from Czechoslovakia in languages other than Czech, perhaps reflecting Peter Bugge's assertion that 'the Czechs have tended to regard this [myth of] democracy as their national property, and themselves as its fathers, its only real guardians' (Bugge, 2006–07, 4). More pragmatically, the marginalization of Czechoslovak German writers appears motivated by a fear that foreign readers might not look beyond their perspective (see Orzoff, 2009, 163), while the neglect of Slovak and Ruthenian reflects the dominance of a Prague-centred perspective, hardly limited to adherents of Masaryk, who viewed these literatures with a condescension comparable to that once adopted by German critics towards Czech literature, even when endeavouring to be supportive (see, for example, Čapek, 1935). In practice, however, First Republic Czechoslovakia epitomizes Gienow-Hecht's description of the difficulties of state-led cultural diplomacy:

> the state cannot do much without the support of nongovernmental actors such as artists, curators, teachers, lecturers, and students. The moment these actors enter, the desires, the lines of policy, the targets, and the very definition of state interests become blurred and multiply. What is more, these actors frequently assume a responsibility and an agenda of their own, regardless of the program or organization to which they are assigned. (Gienow-Hecht and Donfried, 2010, 10)

As Orzoff (2009, 12) acknowledges, the narrative of a democratic nation freed from bondage proved sufficiently widely accepted and flexible to be emphasized and interpreted variously by different people, and its promotion was 'haphazard and creative'.

The developing role of literary translation in state efforts after 1918 to deepen international dialogue and understanding is documented by Vimr in his study of the translation of Scandinavian literatures into Czech. He notes that in the 1920s the League of Nations International Committee for Intellectual Cooperation marginalized the translation and international promotion of literature because it considered it more a vehicle of nationalism than an agent of better mutual understanding (Vimr 2014, 108–09). In 1928, however, Czechoslovakia sought to embed an ambitious programme of multilateral literary translation into the Little Entente with Romania and Yugoslavia:

> A further way of bringing the Little Entente nations systematically closer would be, on a higher level of propaganda, i.e. a purely literary level, to have libraries of systematic translations [...] In this library, *belles-lettres* would alternate occasionally with reference works [...] They would be published by a private publisher, but the costs of rights and translator's fee would be met by the relevant state, which might also purchase a substantial number of volumes for public libraries. (Cited in Vimr, 2014, 109)

Like a later Romanian proposal (in 1936) that the Commission '"publish a collection of representative and classic works from different European literatures written in regional languages translated into one or more of the big universal languages [so that] humanity is not deprived of [...] the spiritual contribution" of these unjustly rarely translated literatures' (Vimr, 2014, 110), these plans never left the drawing-board. Overtaken by events to which the slow-burning effects of literary circulation had no answer, these examples indicate the daunting levels of coordination required to realize such projects, and the uncertainty of either diplomatic or literary success.

The Case of Czech Literature in Great Britain

The practical difficulties of literary cultural diplomacy and the gap between ambition and outcome are examined here in the context of Czechoslovak engagement with Great Britain, at a time when the English-speaking world had not yet become the dominant arbiter of literary taste. The UK had been a target of nascent Czechoslovak cultural diplomacy since at least late 1914,

Literature as Cultural Diplomacy

when Masaryk discussed his plans for an independent Czechoslovak state with the historian, Robert Seton-Watson (1879–1951), and the *Times* journalist, Henry Wickham Steed (1871–1956). Many Czechoslovak intellectuals felt great affinity with what they imagined to be the British character and approach to life, and advocated the British example for Czechs as a more natural counterweight to German civic and cultural models and influences than the French. In a 1923 *Times Literary Supplement* review, the translator Paul Selver (1888–1970) quotes Masaryk in an attempt to win British readers' sympathy for him and, by association, for Czechoslovakia: 'If I were to say which culture I regard as the highest, I should say that of England. From my stay in England during the war and as a result of critical observations I am convinced that on the whole the English have approached nearest to humanitarian ideals' (Selver, 1923, 698). Jindřich Dejmek (1992, 236) notes, however, that in the 1920s Czechoslovakia, with some disappointment, gradually realized Britain's limited interest in post-1918 Central Europe and 'despite the practically conflict-free nature of British–Czechoslovak bilateral relations, after 1925 the "English factor" slipped palpably into the background of Prague's foreign policy'. In September 1938, it was the British prime minister, Neville Chamberlain, who most painfully emphasized the failure of Czechoslovakia's propaganda efforts when, in September 1938, he justified the approach that led to the Munich Accord, which required Czechoslovakia to cede its majority German-speaking border territory to Hitler's Germany by saying: 'How horrible, fantastic, incredible it is, that we should be digging trenches and trying on gas-masks here, because of a quarrel in a faraway country between people of whom we know nothing...' (Chamberlain, 1939, 174).

In 1918, unlike Czech music, Czech literature had no international reputation. In 1912, *The Scotsman*'s reviewer of Selver's *Anthology of Modern Bohemian Poetry* felt obliged to explain that the word 'Bohemian' was being used in a geographical sense (Anon., 1912, 2). James Naughton (1977, 165) blames 'a conventional Czech intellectual nationalistic establishment, clearly perceptible by the 1850s, narrowly historicist and cultivating an expurgated folklore and rhetorically didactic aesthetic', which 'was unable to make any real mark outside its own circumscribed bounds of ethnic loyalty. [That establishment] more or less had the monopoly of Anglo-Czech literary propaganda and the results were commensurate with its standards – quite mediocre.' Though the Symbolist Otokar Březina (1868–1929) was admired in Germany, the first genuine Czech entries into world literature came in the 1920s, with the playwright, novelist and journalist, Karel Čapek (1890–1938) and the novel originally translated into English in abridged form by Selver as *The Good Soldier Schweik* (*Osudy dobrého vojáka Švejka za světové války*, 1921; English 1930) by Jaroslav Hašek (1886–1921). Only one other writer, Jaroslav Durych (1886–1962), had a novel published in English by a British commercial publisher between the wars, *The Descent of the Idol* (*Bloudění*, 1929; English 1935).[1]

Karel Čapek's Promotion of Czechoslovakia

None of these examples owed anything to state support. Čapek achieved his international breakthrough through his dystopian 'robot' play *R.U.R.* (1921, English 1923), the Prague success of which was noted in the *Observer* in 1921 (Anon., 1921, 15). London rights were secured in April 1922 (Vočadlo, 1975, 57) and, as Jana Šlancarová (2015, 58–62) documents, its première at St Martin's Theatre in April 1923 was eagerly anticipated and then much discussed in the British press, ensuring the speedy entry into English of the Czech neologism 'robot'. The producer, Nigel Playfair (1874–1934), arranged with Oxford University Press for his adaptation of Selver's translation to be available to coincide with performance, ensuring good sales. Čapek was in demand, appearing in the 1920s and 1930s with publishers including Faber & Faber, Geoffrey Bles, Macmillan and especially Allen & Unwin.[2] Čapek burnished his reputation by visiting Britain in 1924, when he met, among others, G.K. Chesterton (1874–1936), John Galsworthy (1867–1933), George Bernard Shaw (1856–1950) and H.G. Wells (1866–1946), wrote a

---

[1] According to Kovtun, 1988, the only other book-length publications by single authors were the prison memoir *The Jail* (*Kriminál*, 1918; English 1921) by Josef Svatopluk Machar (1864–1942); and plays *The Land of Many Names* (*Země mnoha jmen*, 1923; English 1926) by Josef Čapek (1887–1945) and *The Wizard of Menlo* (*Čaroděj z Menlo aneb Pokolení prvních věcí*, 1934; English 1935) by Edmond Konrád (1889–1957).

[2] The papers of Prague PEN, whose existence evidently facilitated international publisher communication, include letters from Faber & Faber, expressing disappointment that, after their publication of *Tales from Two Pockets* and *Letters from Holland*, *Dashenka* has appeared with another publisher (Allen & Unwin, in 1933), and hoping to be able to publish another of his books, and from Michael Joseph, wondering if Čapek was planning an autobiography (LA PNP, fond PEN klub, korespondence přijatá: letter from Faber & Faber, 11 December 1933, letter from Michael Joseph, 24 October 1935).

hugely popular account of his travels around Britain, *Letters from England* (*Anglické listy*, 1924; English 1925), originally serialized in English in the *Manchester Guardian*, and became so enamoured of the London club that he agreed to take on the work of establishing a Prague branch of the PEN Club, his main direct cultural-diplomatic contribution to Czech literature.

Čapek used his access to the First Republic leadership to secure government funding for the Prague branch on the cultural-diplomatic grounds that 'the club constituted a unique opportunity to inform the world continuously about relations in the new state from the Czech perspective and to disrupt the one-sided flow of information from German circles' (Krátká, 2003, 132). Prague PEN brought international writers to Prague and enabled their Czechoslovak counterparts to feel part of a world literary community, but, as Krátká notes, the vast majority of foreign contacts made through PEN were very superficial. Krátká (2003, 25) highlights the original London centre's interest in promoting literary translation and its proposal that each branch produce a list of the 30 most translatable books published each year, but Prague PEN lacked the means, infrastructure or ambition to support any translation or promotion of literature.

Given Čapek's personal and ideological closeness to the political establishment of the First Republic, opponents of Masaryk's Czechoslovakia, including prominent poets of the left-wing avant-garde, and some Czechoslovak German, nationalist and Roman Catholic writers who disliked Prague PEN's bourgeois, Anglophile structure, viewed it as the government's literary wing and declined invitations to join. Their suspicions were fuelled when those joining included not only writers, journalists and academics (including Masaryk and Beneš as honorary members), but also government ministers, diplomats, Masaryk's personal secretary and doctor, and the mayor of Prague (see Krátká, 2003, 42). Krátká (2003, 39–40), however, shows that its membership nevertheless included writers from across the political spectrum from the Marxist left to the nationalist right, and eventually pro-Czechoslovak Germans, notably those who worked for government-funded German-language periodicals (Krátká, 2003, 42). In February 1925, Čapek (1993a, 82) wrote to the literary historian, Otokar Fischer: 'of course, politics is none of our business. But if one does not object to state subsidy, then one must also swallow the consequence that we are thus bound within the limits of literary evaluation to take account of the policy of the state, though not of course the policy of parties.' I found no evidence, however, that the state favoured writers close to the First Republic establishment. For example, the little-read, loss-making foreign-language periodicals funded by the Foreign Ministry like the *Central European Observer* or *L'Europe Centrale* featured short articles and translated extracts about writers from across the aesthetic and political spectrum.

Čapek made a greater contribution as an unofficial diplomat in his writing, but here too he faced criticism from ideological and aesthetic opponents, for whom his work encapsulated the broader mediocrity of contemporary Czech literature. In 1935, the once anarchist, now communist poet and critic, Stanislav Kostka Neumann (1875–1947) focused his attack on Čapek. Viktor Kudělka (1987, 68) summarizes:

> The fact that Čapek's work was widely translated into other languages was not for Neumann evidence that Čapek was a world-class writer like, for example, Balzac, Dickens or Tolstoy. According to Neumann, Čapek focused all his efforts on export, not on world-class art. Čapek, moreover, lacked precisely those qualities that almost all critics of Czech literature most miss: emotional and intellectual greatness, uncompromising character, a manly attitude to a reality that the world wants not only to know, but also to change, a passionate relationship to the vital questions of the time, etc.

Neumann's criticism reflects a broader perception that Čapek's work, far from representing Czech literature, sought primarily to imitate foreign models for commercial gain (for a rejection of this view, see Kudělka, 1988). In this period, Czech critics frequently lamented the enduring lack of Czech literary success abroad, which for them meant high literary recognition, not sales. In 1931, over several issues, *Literární noviny* surveyed prominent critics and writers about suggestions that Czech literature was failing internationally because it was 'petty-bourgeois' and lacked Dostoevskian 'demonic elements' (Redakce, 1931, 2–3). While the patriotic literary historian, Arne Novák, suggests that the dominance of petty-bourgeois and peasant literature is unsurprising, given the nation's pre-war social make-up, a translator of Czech literature into German, Anna Auředníčková (1931, 4) points out that petty-bourgeois writing sells. In her experience, the problem is that German publishers will not risk Czech works because Czech literature is not well known, and moreover 'today's reader prefers to buy jolly books, so-called "light reading" [...] Our best, most valuable novels are, however, mostly serious, heavy reading.'

From a cultural-diplomatic perspective, Čapek's work ironically appealed less to influential elites than to those whom Masaryk and his contemporaries, in their critique of Austrian education, labelled the 'semi-educated',

Literature as Cultural Diplomacy

and to the extent that he encapsulated the British literary image of his country, he also established a certain expectation of Czechoslovak writing. His bestselling books in Britain were his *Letters from England* – a foreign traveller's quaint, generally positive, sometimes idealizing view of the British character and countryside – and *The Gardener's Year* (*Zahradníkův rok*, 1929, English 1930) – a collection of light-hearted pieces about Čapek's suburban experience of a quintessential British hobby – titles bound to appeal to a petty-bourgeois audience, whose success reveals that readership's essential self-centredness and lack of curiosity about matters potentially relevant to Czechoslovak cultural diplomacy. Ashley Dukes's early faint praise for *R.U.R.* as 'the excellent work of a journalist' (Dukes, 1924, 116) foreshadowed the recurring verdicts of the committee of the Nobel Prize, for which Čapek was nominated every year between 1932 and 1938, when the winners included Galsworthy, Ivan Bunin (1870–1953), Luigi Pirandello (1867–1936), Eugene O'Neill (1888–1953) and Pearl Buck (1892–1973). As Olga Klauberová (2008) has documented, while acknowledging sufficient qualities to encourage his renomination each year, these reports refer, sometimes repeatedly, to his 'journalistic superficiality' and 'affected style', 'insufficient clarity of ideas' and uncertainty about whether he means what he says.

Perhaps most important, the correspondence in the Allen & Unwin archive between the two gatekeepers to Czech literature in the UK in the 1930s – the publisher, Stanley Unwin, and the translator, Marie Weatherall (née Isakovics, 1896–1972) – reveals the extent to which Čapek limits, rather than increases, opportunities for other Czech authors. Unwin was a product of early Czechoslovak cultural diplomacy, who had known Masaryk when he lived in London during the First World War, and was 'immediately impressed by his personality. No one could fail to be – he was so transparently good and so obviously wise; one instinctively felt it a delight to converse with him' (Unwin, 1960, 147). Unwin (1960, 147) also admired Čapek, 'a charming man': 'There are few writers, living or dead, from whose works I have derived more enjoyment than I have from those of Karel Čapek.' In October 1937, as the German threat to Czechoslovakia increased, Unwin received the country's highest honour, the Order of the White Lion, on the recommendation of the ambassador to Britain, Jan Masaryk (1886–1948), the first president's son. Marie Weatherall was born in Bohemia, but by 1927 had married the Eton master, Robert Weatherall (1899–1973), who would become her translation partner, and emigrated to England. Her private letters at this time to a friend in Prague reveal her unhappiness in England, amid the latent racism and disrespect for the middle and lower classes at Eton, and her main motive

Rajendra Chitnis

in taking up literary translation appears to have been her desire to 'have something that is entirely my own'.[3] Her attachment to First Republic ideals is evident from her letters, notably in a letter from December 1937 expressing her grief at Tomáš Masaryk's death.[4]

Weatherall remained in close touch with the Prague literary scene until the German occupation, and was thus able to advise Unwin of forthcoming publications by Čapek; one letter from 1935 alerts him to *War with the Newts* (*Válka s Mloky*, Czech 1936; English 1937) with the minor mistranslation of 'Mlok' (salamander) that was never subsequently corrected.[5] Weatherall, however, also provides Unwin with reports on other contemporary Czech novels, but these are rarely unequivocally enthusiastic, and none is translated before 1938. She considers both works that have become Czech classics, by Josef Čapek, Ivan Olbracht (1882–1952) and Vladislav Vančura (1891–1942), for example, and more popular commercial writers like Eduard Bass (1888–1946) and Vladimír Neff (1909–83).[6] In her letter-reports to Unwin, Weatherall tries to second-guess her British publisher and his audience. Her criteria include both the penetrability of the work for the British reader and the attractions and challenges of translating it, with Čapek manifestly the implicit yardstick. The work of writers like Bass and Neff is superficially more similar to Čapek's work, but inferior, while the work of the other authors is too exotic and – with the exception of Olbracht, whom she justifiably feels has potential – possibly also too difficult to translate.[7] It was thus not political discrimination, but a particular perception of Czech literature, established by translated Čapek, that hindered the publication of other authors.

[3] LA PNP, fond Weatherallové, Marie, letter to Božena Kuklová, 12 April 1928.
[4] LA PNP, fond Weatherallové, Marie, letter to Božena Kuklová, 24 December 1937.
[5] AUC 47/6, letter to Unwin, 19 September 1935.
[6] These include: Josef Čapek's philosophical essay *Kulhavý poutník* (The Limping Pilgrim, 1936, still untranslated); Olbracht's first novel, about a man blinded, *Žalář nejtemnější* (The Darkest Prison, 1916) and his Ruthenia-based works *Nikola Šuhaj loupežník* (1935; *Nikola the Outlaw*, 2001) and *Golet v údolí* (Exile in the Valley, 1937), from which the main story, 'The Sorrowful Eyes of Hannah Karajich', was published in English in 1999; Vančura's stylized mediaeval epic, *Marketa Lazarová* (1931, still untranslated), and *Konec starých časů* (1934; *The End of the Old Times*, 1965); Bass's novel about an amateur soccer team, *Klapzubova jedenáctka* (1922; *The Chattertooth Eleven*, 2008) and Neff's family novel, *Dva u stolu* (1937).
[7] See AUC 47/6, letters to Unwin (1935), AUC 52/34, letters to Unwin (1937).

The Problem of Švejk

Hašek's picaro, Švejk, established an alternative international stereotype for Czech literature, centred on the 'little man' and pub culture, which was arguably even more influential on world culture than *R.U.R.*, but, unlike Čapek, he presented a problem rather than an opportunity for cultural diplomacy. In a 1921 German-language review of a theatre production of the novel, the Prague German Jewish writer and critic, Max Brod (1884–1968) (1923, 213) described Hašek's central character as 'a figure emerging from the hidden depths of the national spirit, recognized almost immediately by the people as authentic'. Though Brod also emphasized the universality of Švejk, from the perspective of internal and external propaganda, it was Švejk as an image of Czechness that concerned establishment, nationalist and non-avant-garde communist critics, particularly after the successful 1926 German translation paved the novel's way into the world. As Radko Pytlík documents, beyond the vulgarity and ostensibly primitive form, many intellectuals were horrified that this image of Czech soldiery during the First World War superseded that of the lionized Czechoslovak legionaries who fought against the Germans and Austrians and then the Bolsheviks in the Russian civil war (Pytlík, 1983, 276–79). As with Neumann's and Durych's criticism of Čapek, it is the perception of unmanly passivity that concerned them. In a 1933 survey of Czech literature for German readers, Novák describes Švejk as a 'pitiful clown, coward, idiot, parasite and foul-mouth, who quite stubbornly and successfully gainsays not only the war, but also the state, manly honour, heroism and patriotism' (cited in Pytlík, 1983, 266). Selver's English translation was published first in New York, with a tag-line on the front – 'The book that laughed Austria to Peace' – ostensibly designed to deflect attention from Czechoslovakia towards the Habsburg Empire and the war. In March 1930, in advance of its British publication, the London Legation wrote to the Czechoslovak General Consulate in New York: 'Hašek's *Švejk* is coming out very soon in England and the Legation urgently needs the opinions of American newspapers about this book to use as it prepares the ground for Hašek's work in the English press.'[8] New York obliged with cuttings of generally positive reviews that often reflect the regurgitation of publisher publicity and received critical wisdom noted by Hermansson and Leffler in Chapter Eight. They obediently interpret the novel as an anti-war

---

[8] AMZV, ZÚ Londýn, Propagace vlastní: Anglie, 1925–32, Box 711: Letter, 17 March 1930.

satire targeting Austria, compare it with Cervantes and Rabelais, and focus on Hašek as a colourful individual rather than as a representative of his nation, again revealing the discrepancy between Czechoslovak preoccupations and those of international readers. Hašek's novel exemplifies how international reception can force the critical mainstream of especially smaller nations to revise its views; in 2014, Czech president Miloš Zeman proudly presented an edition of Cecil Parrott's 1973 complete English translation to visiting former British Prime Minister Tony Blair.

Agents of Czech Literary Translation

Ironically, only Durych, a major writer associated with Roman Catholic conservatism and an outspoken opponent of Masaryk's Czechoslovakia, really benefited from any propaganda agenda. *The Descent of the Idol* was subtitled 'A Story of the Thirty Years War', and marketed and reviewed as a rich and exciting historical novel, obscuring its contemporary cultural-diplomatic relevance.[9] This period was hardly distant in the context of Czechoslovak national mythology, in which the 1620 Protestant defeat at White Mountain and the 1621 executions of Bohemian gentry on Prague's Old Town Square – with which Durych's novel begins – signify the crushing of Czech nationhood and the absorption of the Bohemian kingdom into Roman Catholic Habsburg domination. The Czechoslovak government explicitly presented the 1920 redistribution of land as redress for White Mountain (see Glassheim, 2005, 88). Durych's novel, however, follows the historian, Josef Pekař (1870–1937), and writers like Jiří Karásek z Lvovic (1871–1952) and Miloš Marten (1883–1917), in offering a different portrayal of the period to that advocated by Masaryk and the First Republic establishment, which seeks to reconcile Czech patriotism with Roman Catholicism.

In his study of how Durych's German translator, Paul Eisner (1889–1958), secured the German translation of the novel, published as *Friedland: Ein Wallenstein-Roman* in Munich in 1933, Tilman Kasten (2014, 753) describes how Eisner became excited about the possibilities of the novel in German translation while it was still being written. Eisner hoped not only for commercial

---

[9] The *Aberdeen Press and Journal* wrote: 'In an amazing tale of plot and intrigue and misery which beset the Holy Empire, the author, with extraordinary minuteness, has collected an enormous mass of information, vivid with sanguinary incident and idyllic romance' (Anon., 1935, 2).

Literature as Cultural Diplomacy

success, but also to counter the condescending portrayal of Bohemia in the Thirty-Years-war novel *Wallenstein* (1920) by Alfred Döblin (1878–1957) and to give international readers an alternative example of Czech war literature to *Švejk*. Eisner, born in Prague to a bilingual Czech- and German-speaking Jewish family, was the editor of *Prager Presse*, a daily newspaper overseen by the Czechoslovak Foreign Ministry that sought to promote a positive idea of Czechoslovakia among German speakers at home and abroad. Although with the rise of Nazism, Eisner increasingly identified himself with the Czech perspective, Kasten (2014, 751) argues that his conception of national identity in Czechoslovakia did not arise from the prevailing Czech, anti-German historical narrative, but reflected the search, typical of Prague Jewish intellectuals of his generation, 'for an answer to growing Czech and German nationalism in the idea of a cultural symbiosis of the Czech and German', nurtured by centuries of coexistence in the Bohemian crown lands.

The novel's publication in English was not explicitly linked to this agenda, which was of little interest to British audiences. In November 1929, when only extracts of the imminent novel had appeared in the Czech press, Weatherall, in possibly her earliest bid for a project, wrote to Durych to ask about the translation rights, because she believed 'it would be good to translate it and possible to find a publisher for it'.[10] Durych, however, surprisingly replied that Eisner was already negotiating with a New York- and London-based publisher.[11] According to a letter from Durych's Czech publisher, Melantrich, in April 1934, serious interest – from the London literary agency, Alexander –came only after publication in German. Melantrich report that Eisner offered a choice between translating from his German translation or the shortened Czech version he created for that translation, and, despite his financial situation, forewent payment to ensure the book was published. The decision appears to be taken by telephone, and the novel eventually appeared with Hutchinson in 1935, translated by Lynton A. Hudson, and originally advertised using the German title, *Friedland* (Durych, 1935, appended brochure, 32).[12]

---

[10] LA PNP, fond Jaroslava Durycha, korespondence přijatá: letter from Marie Weatherall, 24 November 1929.

[11] LA PNP, fond Weatherallové, Marie, 2: 139/73, letter from Durych, 13 December 1929.

[12] See LA PNP, fond Jaroslava Durycha, korespondence přijatá: letter from Melantrich, 9 April 1934. Contrary to the statement on the title page of the English edition, Hudson, otherwise unknown as a translator of Czech literature, may therefore have translated from Eisner's German translation. This supposition

Rajendra Chitnis

I have also pieced together from the archives two examples where the Czechoslovak Foreign Ministry did lead an attempt to translate Czech imaginative literature in Britain. Both involved the two dominant agents of Czech literary translation into English in the 1920s – Selver and Otakar Vočadlo (1895–1974) – who exemplify Gienow-Hecht's account of cultural-diplomatic actors for whom the state agenda existed alongside their own priorities. Both worked for the Czechoslovak Legation in London in its early years and both sustained in their writing the prevailing Czech national narrative, but the Czechoslovak state lacked the financial and structural capacity to direct or control their activity. In 1921, Vočadlo, while 'lending a hand here and there' (Vočadlo, 1975, 27) at the Legation as a postgraduate student of English literature at University College London, agreed to respond to a request from Čapek, then a literary advisor at a Prague theatre, for recommendations of recent English-language plays, thus beginning a period as the Legation's expert for literary-related queries, and a lasting friendship with Čapek. From 1922 to 1928 Vočadlo lectured on Czech language and literature at the School of Slavonic Studies (co-founded by Masaryk at King's College in 1915). London PEN approached him in 1922 about founding a Prague branch, and through PEN he organized Čapek's 1924 visit to Britain. His correspondence shows a reluctance to be distracted from academic research by cultural diplomacy, from which he eventually withdrew. However, in his much discussed 1924 essay *V zajetí babylonském* (In Babylonian captivity), he argues that German-language culture before 1918 had not provided a conduit for Czech literature into the world, but on the contrary imprisoned it. Through his essentially voluntary activities promoting the translation of Czech literature, he put into action his contention that it was time for Czech writers 'to free themselves from the German environment and Viennese agencies [...] and join international circulation directly' through English and French translation (Vočadlo, 1975, 35).

Selver's motives are less clear, not least because of the almost complete absence of his voice from the archives, but they appear to combine a

---

would gain weight if Hudson's published translations from Hungarian and Italian could be shown to have been made from German versions. I am very grateful, however, to the Hungarian literature scholar and translator Peter Sherwood, who identified that at least one of Hudson's Hungarian translations – *Hungarian Melody* (*Magyar rapszódia*, 1936) by Zsolt Harsányi (1887–1943) – came out in the same year as the Hungarian original and seven years before the German edition.

sympathy for the Czechs with an ambition for scholarly recognition without conforming to conventional academic routes, and the need to make a living. His autobiography, *First Movement* (1937, written under the pseudonym Mark Grossek), ends as he begins university in London, a self-conscious Jewish working-class man, scornful of academia and his privileged peers, and the second volume was rejected by Unwin in 1942.[13] Selver had positioned himself as the dominant advocate of Czech literature in Britain since his 1912 anthology, and he offered his own emotive paraphrase of the national myth in his opening essay to a 1920 anthology:

> It is the poetry of a nation that has been labouring under a heavy yoke, but whose bonds have at length been shattered. And in its verse is heard the exultant cry of freedom, the vigorous utterance of young and lusty spirits. The poetry of the Czechs has won for itself a place among the poetry of more favoured nations, whose languages are widely spoken and who are able to look back upon a glorious literary past. (Selver, 1920, 20)

Selver was employed by the Legation after 1918 as an office translator; in 1940, Jan Masaryk, by now Foreign Minister in the Czechoslovak government-in-exile in London, wrote:

> Paul Selver was a very sympathetic spectator at the birth of the Czechoslovak Republic, and since then he and I worked together in London for many years in the cause of that country. It might be said that the result of our labours was very disastrous, and that neither he nor I should show ourselves in public after March, 1939 [the German occupation of Bohemia and Moravia]. But we have not reacted in that shy way – on the contrary, we are still actively labouring for the return of everything that Czechoslovakia stood for. (Selver, 1940, 13)

Selver nevertheless suffers from a negative reputation, shaped entirely by Vočadlo. According to Vočadlo (175, 43), Selver was simply lucky to be working at the Legation in 1921 when Čapek's friend, then a secretary at the Legation and inexperienced in literary matters, was looking for a translator for *R.U.R.* Through its success, Selver established himself as Čapek's lead translator in the 1920s. In his memoir of the period, Vočadlo fiercely criticizes Selver's practices with Čapek's work; he sold the rights to translations and permitted the free adaptations of plays for performance without contacting

---

[13] AUC 150/12, letter from Unwin to Selver, 4 November 1942.

Rajendra Chitnis

Čapek or his agent, and generally prioritized his own financial gain over the author (see 1975, 45–49, 60). Vočadlo (1975, 44) also mocks the howlers in Selver's translations, which prompted him to try – with limited success – to cultivate other British Czech literary translators from among his students.[14] Selver was only supplanted by Vočadlo's discovery of the Weatheralls, whom Unwin found much easier collaborators.

Selver's actions may well reflect, however, the weak position of translators in the period, who are poorly paid, and, as Vočadlo suggests, expected to do their work selflessly for the greater good. In 1946, Unwin published a book on literary translation, highlighting its importance to post-war rebuilding of international relations and setting out his experience of good and bad practice, including the need to pay translators 'adequately' (Unwin, 1946, 2). In a letter from 1970, however, Marie Weatherall remarks that '[Unwin] published Čapek and paid us shamefully little for the translations (8 pounds for *Dashenka*); he published Čapek because it was a political matter, and maybe the government at the time paid him to do so'.[15] This claim reveals Weatherall's awareness of the Czechoslovak government's close interest in literary translation and Unwin's personal connections with them, but is unsubstantiated by the archives, where there is no evidence of a willingness to subsidize imaginative literature, which would have been especially unlikely for such a commercial text.

The threat presented by personal conflicts to a small state's cultural-diplomatic ambitions is reflected in a letter from late 1926, in which Čapek has to tell Vočadlo: '[Jan Masaryk] would be glad if you could somehow make friends with Selver, since it would be much easier then to do all sorts of propaganda' (Čapek, 1993b, 360). Their bad relations were not, however, the reason that the Legation's forays into literary translation failed. The first foray involved Orbis, the semi-private, state-subsidized publisher launched

---

[14] Čapek records in a letter how Vočadlo's student, Lawrence Hyde, approached him in Prague to apologize for his poor translation of the 1924 novel *Krakatit*, published in English in 1925. The volume of Čapek stories, *Money and Other Stories*, published by Hutchinson in 1929, featured translations by three of Vočadlo's students, of whom one, Dora Round, who also later translated from Dutch and Spanish, published translations of two Čapek works with Allen & Unwin before 1938, and continued during and after the war.

[15] LA PNP: fond Marie Weatherallové, handwritten note, 11 June 1970. The Allen & Unwin archive shows that Unwin quarrelled about fees with Selver and with Dora Round, who points out that, unlike Weatherall, she needs to make a living from translation.

in 1923 and overseen by the Czechoslovak Foreign Ministry. The minutes of Orbis meetings suggest that it rarely engaged with imaginative literature, focusing its organizational capacity and finances instead on the translation, production and promotion of informative books about Czechoslovakia, certain academic texts (particularly in the social sciences), and memoirs and political texts by Masaryk and Beneš that were expected to appeal to a perceived influential elite of politicians, diplomats, academics and journalists. In April 1924, Oskar Butter (1886–1943), a senior civil servant at the Foreign Ministry, sent the Legation in London the manuscript of an English translation of a canonical cycle of dark, supernatural narrative poems, *Kytice z pověstí národních* (A Posy of Folk Tales, 1853) by Karel Jaromír Erben (1811–70).[16] The venture seems speculative, rather than carefully planned, though a well-translated and presented version might have succeeded commercially, given the British fondness in the period for Central European folk tales, and the fact that Erben's tales had inspired a cantata and symphonic poems by Antonín Dvořák (1841–1904). The translation was by Josef Štýbr (1864–1938), a Czech physician living in Pittsburgh, whose translation of another canonical verse cycle, the pastoral *Večerní písně* (Evening Songs, 1859) by Vítězslav Hálek (1835–74), had been published in Boston in 1920. In his introduction, Štybr does not hesitate to locate Erben within the national myth:

> the young man found himself at school at a time when to openly acknowledge his Czech birth and to proclaim adhesion to the Czech cause amid forced German surroundings was looked upon as a sort of heroism by his compatriots and was not devoid of danger of facing a certain displeasure and even reprisal from the Austrian ever suspecting officialdom.[17]

The archives show that Geoffrey Bles, which in 1925 published Čapek's *Letters from England*, agreed to publish the translation, on condition that it underwent correction by a British English native speaker to remove Americanisms and other infelicities evident from the above quotation, and

---

[16] AMZV, ZÚ Londýn, Propagace vlastní: Anglie, Osvěta a školství 262: Vědecký a literární styk, různé: 1923–26, letter from Butter to Legation, 22 April 1924.
[17] AMZV, ZÚ Londýn, Propagace vlastní: Anglie, Osvěta a školství 262: Vědecký a literární styk, různé: 1923–26, Introduction by Dr Josef Štybr, page 1 of 9.

that Orbis agreed to buy two to three hundred copies and supply illustrations. Orbis made these commitments, spending 1,000 crowns on engravings by Jan Konůpek (1885–1950), which may explain their persistence with the project. However, though Vočadlo supplied a brief scholarly comparison of Erben's tales and Scots and English ballads, the director of the School of Slavonic Studies, Bernard Pares, confirmed his misgivings about the translation, noting that 'to make the translation you sent me fully satisfactory would, I think, be almost as much labour as to translate it'.[18] Selver was not willing to improve another's translation, and the matter ended in 1927 with the Foreign Ministry agreeing to give Selver time to produce his own translation, and sending more recent editions of the original for this purpose. It was not until 2012 and 2013 that two English translations of the full cycle came along almost at once, from Marcela Malek Sulak for Twisted Spoon in Prague and Susan Reynolds for Jantar in London.

The second effort to publish Czech literature in English was much more ambitious and short-lived. In January 1926, Josef Hanč, who had just been transferred to the London Legation as press secretary from the Foreign Ministry, where he had been editing Orbis's English-language periodical, the *Central European Observer*, reported to Prague that Bles was willing to publish, without financial support, a series of suitable Czech novels.[19] Hanč approached Čapek for suggestions (see Čapek, 1993b, 355), and he proposed seven, almost all drawn from the last decades of Austrian rule. It is hard to argue that they were chosen for their political content or their authors' politics; indeed, his inclusion of a short novel by Durych looks generous given Durych's increasing hostility towards him in both the press and private letters. The list also includes women writers who, despite their prominence in any canon of modern Czech prose writing, were entirely neglected by translators in the period. The works are all, however, Realist, sometimes idyllic texts, as though Čapek is trying to predict the tastes of a petty-bourgeois audience, with no examples of the Decadent or Avant-garde Modernism that constituted the best Czech writing of the time. In any event, by August, the Legation effectively abandoned the project, telling the Ministry that it would take years, not months, because

---

[18] AMZV, ZÚ Londýn, Propagace vlastní: Anglie, Osvěta a školství 262: Vědecký a literární styk, různé: 1923–26, letter from Bernard Pares, 22 December 1926.

[19] AMZV, ZÚ Londýn, Propagace vlastní: Anglie, Osvěta a školství 219: Literatura – vydávání českých autorů ve V.Británii 1924–28, letter to Foreign Ministry, 28 January 1926.

of the publisher's demands for particular lengths of text and individual synopses.[20] By contrast, in Paris, through a collaboration between Grasset and the Prague publisher Aventinum, a comparable venture succeeded, but lasted only three volumes (Zanello-Kounovsky, 1998, 25), earning a caustic article in 1929 on the embarrassing vulgarity of Czechoslovak 'cultural propaganda' from the most influential Czech Modernist critic, F.X. Šalda (1929, 161), who foreshadows the theory of target culture gap-filling discussed by Vimr in the previous chapter:

> A proud free nation never trades its loves, never forces its loves on other nations [...] A foreign nation comes for them itself when it needs them for its further development and poetic, artistic, philosophical growth; and only this kind of poetic, artistic, philosophical coming-together, and no other – especially not a coming-together sold for external prestige – has a price and value [...] Recently, in his book *Genève ou Moscou* [1928], the French Modernist [Pierre] Drieu La Rochelle [1893–1945] said with impertinent irony about us and similar 'small nations' – small because we are small-minded and of little faith – [...] how ridiculously we had missed the point if all we can do is [...] artificially cultivate a tradition – which is like cultivating anaemia from incest – and doing cultural propaganda abroad that is nothing more than tickling petty-bourgeois vanity and throwing money out of open windows.

Conclusion

Šalda provides us with one assessment of Czechoslovakia's use of literature in cultural diplomacy during the First Republic, to which he objects not because it is driven by a narrow ideology or personal power interests, as Orzoff argues, but because literature is treated as an asset to be traded, a reflection of the First Republic's petty-bourgeois mores. Šalda, moreover, argues that the amateurish, wheedling manner of these efforts, as a mirror of general diplomatic efforts, cements Czechoslovakia's marginal international status. We have seen how other critics feared that an image of Czechoslovakia as weak, subservient and imitative was encouraged by the works that succeeded internationally. We might equally argue, however, that this chapter captures

---

[20] AMZV, ZÚ Londýn, Propagace vlastní: Anglie, Osvěta a školství 219: Literatura – vydávání českých autorů ve V.Británii 1924–28, letter to Foreign Ministry, 20 September 1926.

a state in transition from nineteenth-century nationalism to twentieth-century civil society building. What Gienow-Hecht presents as the problem of non-governmental actors serving as cultural ambassadors and gatekeepers might instead represent, in embryo, the type of cooperation that still appears to serve international literary circulation best. In this model, we see civil servants acting in the background as facilitators, passing on opportunities to translators, publishers and academics better placed to realize them, and attempting with limited resources to drive projects that seem promising, or in which they have invested without any reference to their narrow propaganda value.

While the heaviest burden of judgement and labour falls on translators, who alone are expected to work self-sacrificingly and are criticized when they complain, the ultimate obstacles to these efforts are the priorities of British readers, and therefore publishers. The eventually fateful gap between Czechoslovak and British perceptions of the depth of their affinity is captured in two ways by a letter written by Čapek (1993a, 391) to his 'unknown readers in Great Britain' in the aftermath of Munich, shortly before his death in late 1938. In the letter, Čapek asks uncomprehendingly why Britain and France would want to 'cripple' Czechoslovakia. His sudden uncertainty about how to talk to these readers is, however, also reflected in his multiple drafts and the fact that he never actually sent it. Ironically, it was not official Czechoslovak cultural diplomacy, but residual guilt among Western intellectuals over Munich, compounded by the post-1945 abandonment of Czechoslovakia to Stalin and Western helplessness in the face of the August 1968 Soviet-led military intervention to stop reform in communist Czechoslovakia, which prompted the next phase of international interest in Czech literature in the late 1960s. Then, however, the most successful writers, like Václav Havel (1936–2011), Bohumil Hrabal (1914–97), Ivan Klíma (b.1931), Milan Kundera (b.1929) and Josef Škvorecký (1924–2012), were those whose works could sustain a Western Cold War narrative about life in the Eastern Bloc, and perpetuate the twin images of the Czechs as plucky survivors and natural liberal democrats that were first fostered by Hašek's Švejk and Čapek. Given the discrepancy in power relations between the formal and informal cultural diplomats of small nations and their target audience, perhaps the biggest problem for those promoting Czech literature in Britain between the wars was that they were operating according to a myth concerning not only the Czechs, but also those they were trying to reach.

Bibliography

Archives
AMZV: Archive of the Ministry of Foreign Affairs of the Czech Republic, Prague.
AUC: University of Reading: Records of George Allen & Unwin Ltd, 1884–1983: Correspondence.
LA PNP: Literary Archive of the Museum of National Literature, Prague.
NA: National Archive, Prague.

Works Cited
Anon. 1912. An Anthology of Modern Bohemian Poetry. *The Scotsman*, 18 July, 2.
Anon. 1921. Man and Machine: Strange Frankenstein Play at Prague. *The Observer*, 23 October, 15.
Anon. 1935. Let's Look at the World in the Latest Novels. *Aberdeen Press and Journal*, 28 May, 2.
Auředníčková, Anna. 1931. Překladatelka o českém románu. *Literární noviny*, V (3), 4.
Brod, Max. 1923. Der gute Soldat Švejk. In his *Der Sternenhimmel* (Prague: Orbis), 212–15.
Bugge, Peter. 2006–07. Czech Democracy 1918–38 – Paragon or Parody? *Bohemia*, 47 (1), 3–28.
Čapek, Karel. 1935. O slovenské literatuře. *Přítomnost*, 12 (1), 4–6.
Čapek, Karel. 1993a. *Spisy XXII: Korespondence I* (Prague: Český spisovatel).
Čapek, Karel. 1993b. *Spisy XIII: Korespondence II* (Prague: Český spisovatel).
Chamberlain, Neville. 1939. *In Search of Peace* (London: Hutchinson).
Dejmek, Jindřich. 1992. *Československo, jeho sousedé a velmoci ve XX. století (1918–1992)* (Prague: Centrum pro ekonomiku a politiku).
Dukes, Ashley. 1924. *The Youngest Drama: Studies of Fifty Dramatists* (London: Benn).
Durych, Jaroslav. 1935. *The Descent of the Idol* (London: Hutchinson).
Gienow-Hecht, Jessica C.E. and Mark C. Donfried (eds). 2010. *Searching for a Cultural Diplomacy* (Oxford and New York: Berghahn).
Glassheim, Eagle. 2005. *Noble Nationalists: The Transformation of the Bohemian Aristocracy* (Cambridge, MA: Harvard University Press).
Kasten, Tilman. 2014. Pavel Eisner a *Bloudění* Jaroslava Durycha: literární transfer, tvorba kánonu a identita. *Česká literatura*, 62 (6), 745–83.
Klauberová, Olga. 2008. Karel Čapek a Nobelova cena. Available from: www.postreh.com/phprs/view.php?cisloclanku=2008102901 [accessed 10 January 2018].
Kovtun, George. 1988. *Czech and Slovak Literature in English* (Washington, DC: Library of Congress). Available from: http://lcweb2.loc.gov/service/gdc/scd0001/2007/20070628001cz/20070628001cz.pdf [accessed 10 January 2018].

Krátká, Petra. 2003. *Český PEN-klub v letech 1925–1938* (Prague: Libri).
Kudělka, Viktor. 1987. *Boje o Karla Čapka* (Prague: Academia).
Kudělka, Viktor. 1988. Čapkovo místo ve světové literatuře. In Vlašín, Štěpán et al. (eds). *Kniha o Čapkovi* (Prague: Československý spisovatel), 387–406.
Naughton, James. 1977. The Reception in Nineteenth-Century England of Czech Literature and of the Czech Literary Revival. Thesis. PhD. Available from: http://babel.mml.ox.ac.uk/naughton/jdn-cz-thesis.pdf [accessed 10 January 2018].
Orzoff, Andrea. 2009. *Battle for the Castle* (Oxford: Oxford University Press).
Pytlík, Radko. 1983. *Kniha o Švejkovi* (Prague: Československý spisovatel).
Redakce. 1931. Naše anketa o románu. *Literární noviny*, V (2), 2–3.
Šalda, František X. 1929. Kapitola velmi trapná, čili něco o národní hrdosti. In his *Šaldův zápisník: Ročník první* (Prague: Girgal), 153–65.
Selver, Paul. 1920. *Modern Czech Poetry* (London and New York: Keegan Paul, Trench, Trubner).
Selver, Paul. 1923. President Masaryk. *Times Literary Supplement*, 25 October, 698.
Selver, Paul. 1940. *Masaryk* (London: Michael Joseph).
Šlancarová, Jana. 2016. Čapkův anglický nakladatel. *Bohemica litteraria*, 19 (1), 107–23.
Unwin, Stanley. 1946. *On Translations* (London: George Allen & Unwin).
Unwin, Stanley. 1960. *The Truth about a Publisher: An Autobiographical Record* (Woking and London: Unwin Brothers).
Vimr, Ondřej. 2014. *Historie překladatele: Cesty skandinávských literatur do češtiny (1890–1950)* (Příbram: Pistorius & Olšanská).
Vočadlo, Otakar. 1975. *Anglické listy Karla Čapka* (Prague: Academia).
Zanello-Kounovsky, Nathalie. 1998. La Littérature tchèque en France, traduction et reception. *Štěpánská 35*, 4 (1–3), 20–30.

CHAPTER FIVE

Exporting the Canon: The Mixed Experience of the Dutch *Bibliotheca Neerlandica*

Irvin Wolters (UCL)

The Foundation for the Promotion of the Translation of Dutch Literary Works (De Stichting tot Bevordering van de Vertaling van Nederlands Letterkundig Werk), hereafter called The Foundation, was a state-funded, quasi-governmental organization established to oversee the translation of over 700 Dutch literary works into a variety of languages until 1989. It constituted the first steps in professionalizing and institutionalizing a Dutch literary foreign policy. The Foundation was established in 1954 under the initiative of Hendrik Jan Reinink, Secretary-General of the Ministry of Education, Arts and Sciences, in cooperation with four agencies: Maatschappij der Nederlandse Letterkunde (The Dutch Literature Society), Vereniging van Letterkundigen (The Literature Association), Nederlandsche Uitgeversbond (the Dutch Publishing Association) and PEN Club Netherlands.

The Foundation's principal aims, as stated in the charter, were to promote Dutch literature abroad by establishing contacts with Dutch and foreign publishing companies and academics, raising awareness of Dutch literature abroad and creating a portfolio of sample translations. In a statement of their raison d'être in *Stichting Ter Bevordering Van De Vertaling Van Nederlands Letterkundig Werk*, they attempt to account for the obscurity of Dutch literature outside the Netherlands. They acknowledge that the language barrier is a factor, but note that Dutch science has succeeded in crossing linguistic frontiers and that literatures of other small countries enjoy greater fame than Dutch letters. They contend that many works would interest readers outside the Netherlands because they shed light on a relatively little-known side of European life. They conclude by stating:

> There is no point in speculating about the reasons for this obscurity. It is better to examine whether and how this situation may be changed.

> This is precisely the aim which the Foundation is setting itself. It wants to do everything in its power to enable the foreign reader (and thus first and foremost the publisher) to acquaint himself with Dutch literature. (*Stichting Ter Bevordering Van De Vertaling Van Nederlands Letterkundig Werk*, n.d.)

One of The Foundation's first key projects was the development of a series of Dutch imaginative works translated into English, eventually called *Bibliotheca Neerlandica*, that would implicitly redress the imbalance in the international reception of Dutch literature and its fine-art counterpart in the Dutch Golden Age of painting. Initially planned to comprise of 17 volumes, ten were published between 1963 and 1967 before the series was abruptly abandoned. The micro-history of this venture therefore reads primarily as a cautionary tale for smaller literatures, in which inexperience, incoherent planning and organization, inconsistent production values and circumstances beyond The Foundation's control combined to undermine its ambitions. It particularly reveals the tensions between the interests of source and target cultures and between different parties in the process, including the state, academics, translators and publishers.

Dutch Literature and Post-war Cultural Diplomacy

In scholarship, Dutch often epitomizes those literatures written in less widely spoken languages from less well-known traditions that – it is argued – must be translated into dominating languages to enter 'world literature'. Pascale Casanova (2004, 256) states: 'Dutch is a language of ancient culture and tradition having few speakers, native or polyglot, and although it has a relatively important history and sizeable stock of literary credit, is unrecognized outside its national boundaries.' Elsewhere, she argues:

> If writers from dominated national literary fields such as The Netherlands wish to enter the world literary competition, they must work on importing capital by nationalizing their great universal texts through translation since if a work is translated into one of the great literary languages it becomes legitimate immediately [...] In the world literary universe, translation is one of the main weapons in the struggle for literary legitimacy. For a writer, struggling for access to translation is in fact a matter of struggling for his or her existence as a legitimate member of the world republic of letters. In the dominated regions of the literary

Exporting the Canon

field, translation is the only means of being perceived, becoming visible, of existing [...] Translation then functions like a kind of right to international existence. It allows a writer not only to be recognized as a literary figure outside their borders, but even more importantly it brings into existence an international position, an autonomous position inside the national universe. (Casanova, 2010, 5–11)

Jane Fenoulhet (2013, 5) supports this view, noting that after the Second World War few outsiders had access to Dutch culture because the language was not widely learned by fellow Europeans. For more on the international dissemination of Dutch literature, see Brems et al. (eds), 2017.

The ostensibly apolitical ambitions underlying translation into a dominant language are noted by Gisèle Sapiro (2014, 87), who suggests that, in the contemporary period 'in The Netherlands, support for translation is bestowed on literary works with no specific ideological objective except to the promotion of the national culture abroad'. While this assertion may apply now, it appears naïve in the context of my historical example. The creation of The Foundation in the 1950s constituted a cultural-diplomatic venture linked directly to a post-war Dutch colonial episode. Following the Japanese surrender in 1945, Indonesia declared independence from the Dutch, which resulted in a four-and-a-half-year struggle as they tried to re-establish their colony. In 1949, the Netherlands relented and formally recognized Indonesian sovereignty, but their aggressive methods had damaged their reputation in Europe. The creation of The Foundation formed part of a soft-power strategy by the Dutch government to change public opinion, using attractive examples of the national literature to repair this reputation. The Foundation received an initial yearly budget of 25,000 guilders (equivalent to £43,500 today) from the government to export Dutch culture through cultural diplomacy by developing contacts between Dutch and foreign publishers and acquiring translators. The priority of justifying its existence internally – to the state – is reflected in its publication in Dutch of a brochure marking its first ten years, summarizing its activities to date. The brochure notes that international contacts have markedly increased (*Tien Jaar Stichting Voor Vertalingen*, 1964, 4), but otherwise its parochial perspective and omission of data betrays the absence of a clear theoretical and practical strategy for achieving its key aims.

Irvin Wolters

Bibliotheca Neerlandica: From Committee to Dictatorship?

The roots of *Bibliotheca Neerlandica*'s difficulties may be traced to the organization of its commissioning body. In his analysis of organizational culture, Edgar Schein (1991, 14) argues that the goal in a committee is for everyone to work together with a single founder, each sharing their common vision. This approach is reflected in the minutes of the first meeting of the commissioning body for *Bibliotheca Neerlandica*, in Leiden in January 1955, where the members appear agreed that works will be selected based on both source and target considerations: how they had been received in the Netherlands and whether the work would be considered interesting abroad. The commissioning body was chaired by the prose writer, Ernest Lefèbvre, and was comprised of the poets and critics Emmy van Lokhorst (1891–1970) and Victor van Vriesland (1892–1974), and the literary historian and poet Piet Minderaa (1893–1968). The dynamics changed, however, when the charismatic Minderaa replaced Lefèbvre in 1956 and became the dominant voice in the process; subsequent minutes show, for example, that there was little collective deliberation about many volumes, notably the mediaeval anthologies discussed below.

The model that Minderaa favoured for *Bibliotheca Neerlandica* was the earlier *Bibliotheca Flandrica*, originally named the *Bibliotheca Belgica*, which was funded by the National Fonds voor Letterkunde (National Fund for Literature) and published by Diederich Verlag, Düsseldorf, between 1950 and 1954. Anne Marie Musschoot describes how each volume of *Bibliotheca Flandrica* was to be translated into English, French and German, but the three series would not be identical. As with *Bibliotheca Neerlandica*, a volume on the history of Dutch literature was planned for each language, though each would again be marginally different since 'the perception of what actually constitutes Dutch literature differs abroad from that in the Netherlands and Flanders' (Musschoot, 2004, 7). *Bibliotheca Flandrica* was not, however, a wise choice on which to base *Bibliotheca Neerlandica*. The venture collapsed in 1954 following the publication of the sixth translated Dutch work into German, a collection of anthologies called *Rauschendes Lied* (The Rustling of Song) (1954).[1] French publishers only wanted to publish

---

[1] The other five volumes in the *Bibliotheca Flandrica* series published in German by Eugen Diederichs Verlag Düsseldorf were: Gerard Walschap (1898–1989) *Houtekiet* (1939); Karel van de Woestijne (1878–1929) *Einsame Brände* (Flames in Solitude, 1952); Willem Elsschot (1882–1960) (*Käse*, 1933); Joseph Otto Plassmann

selected works from the series. English-language publishers wanted to inspect the texts before committing, and before they were translated, even though they may not have been able to read the Dutch originals. The minutes of the *Bibliotheca Neerlandica* commissioning body meeting of 28 November 1958 note that not even the Vlaamse Academie (Flemish Academy) rated the *Bibliotheca Flandrica* series, and Van Ardenne-Diephuis (2011, 71) adds that the six volumes published were poorly received, mainly due to the quality of the translations.

The Dutch Foundation, by contrast, prioritized English as the language of translation, mainly because of the difficulty in finding translators in other languages. The tenth-anniversary brochure, *Tien Jaar Stichting Voor Vertalingen* (1964, 6–7), states:

> It has become evident that finding good translators is a really difficult problem. In Italian, for example, many books have been translated via an intermediary language because there are insufficient people with the literary expertise to translate directly into Italian from Dutch. This has been the case even for French.

Like *Bibliotheca Flandrica*, however, the commissioning body for *Bibliotheca Neerlandica* under Minderaa was unknowingly canon-building. In the 1950s and 1960s, there was no 'official' Dutch literary canon, only a general list of over 1,000 literary works, and Dutch canon-building was conducted almost exclusively by a board of elite white men, a bias highlighted by Fenoulhet in her discussion of eight works on Dutch literary history published between 1925 and 1990, '[all] written by men, making them literally "master narratives"' (2007, 59). This situation effectively continued under Minderaa.

Els van Ardenne-Diephuis argues that Minderaa conceived *Bibliotheca Neerlandica* as a classical series biased towards Flemish literature (2011, 71). His doctorate in 1947 concerned the Flemish poet Karel van de Woestijne (1878–1929), and although born in Amsterdam, he favoured Flemish

---

(ed.), '*Altflämische Frauenmystik*': *Vom Göttlichen Reichtum der Seele* ('Old Flemish Female Mysticism': From the Divine Wealth of the Soul), an anthology containing: 'Brieven' ('Letters', c. 1240) and 'Visioenen' ('Book of Visions', c. 1240) by Hadewijch (c. 1210–60) and 'Seven Manieren Van Minne' ('Seven Manners of Loving', c. 1235) by Beatrijs van Nazareth (1200–68), and Wolfgang Cordon (ed.) *Altflämische Spiele* (Old Flemish Plays), an anthology containing *Lancelot und Sanderein* (Lancelot and Sanderein, c. 1400) and *Mariken von Nieumeghen* (Mary of Nijmegen, c. 1485), both by unknown authors.

literature, having written before the Second World War for the Flemish literary magazine *Het Kouter* and later in *De Spiegel der Letteren* as a member of the editorial staff. Van Ardenne-Diephuis suggests that, as chair, Minderaa coerced the members of the commissioning body into accepting his personal choices for works in the series: 'it was Minderaa who stamped his mark on the selection [...] The Dutch commissioning body members voiced little objection against his suggestions' (2011, 75). The ten volumes published included works by three Flemish authors, Elsschot, Walschap and Herman Teirlinck (1879–1967). Van Ardenne-Diephuis also notes Minderaa's preference for pre-1900 literature, for example *Sara Burgerhart* (1782) by Betje Wolff (1738–1804) and Aagje Deken (1741–1804) for the eighteenth century, and *Camera Obscura* (1839) by Nicolaas Beets (1814–1903), who wrote under the pseudonym Hildebrand, for the nineteenth century. Van Ardenne-Diephuis notes that 'his preference for these literary periods took precedence over the tastes of the English public' (2011, 74). Eleven of these works, selected on the basis of committee members' personal predilections, without consideration for their potential relevance to a wider readership, would later be included in the official Dutch canon, a list of 125 Dutch and Flemish classical masterpieces by 108 authors compiled in 2002 by Maatschappij der Nederlandsche Letterkunde te Leiden (Leiden Society of Dutch Literature) for the Dutch Ministry of Education.[2]

Between 1955 and 1961, the committee distilled from a huge number of suggestions the planned series of 17 volumes and when Minderaa stepped down as chair in 1961, the selection had already been approved. A major omission was more popular and contemporary literature, which might have prospered abroad. Van Ardenne-Diephuis (2011, 74) highlights Minderaa's dislike of successful contemporary literature by Gerard Kornelis van het Reve (1923–2006), Willem Frederik Hermans (1921–95) and Harry Mulisch (1927–2010), who were not considered for the series because 'they had evidently not proved themselves to Minderaa'. The committee similarly rejected Reinder Meijer's (1926–93) *Literature of the Low Countries*, which

---

[2] These were: *Max Havelaar* (1860), *Van den Vos Reynaerde* (c. 1225), *Beatrijs* (c. 1374), *Karel ende Elegast* (c. 1250), *Mariken van Nieumeghen* (c. 1485), *Van Oude Menschen de Dingen die Voorbijgaan* (1906), *Lijmen* (1924), *Het Been* (1938), Walewein (c. 1250), *Het Dwaalicht* (1946) and *De Koperen Tuin* (1950). For the complete 2002 canon, see https://www.goodreads.com/list/show/17883. Dutch_Literary_Canon [accessed 30 July 2019]. For more on the process of its formation, see D'Haen, 2011.

was eventually published in 1971 by Van Gorcum and became a standard work for scholars of Dutch literature until Theo Hermans' *A Literary History of the Low Countries* was published in 2009. Politics sometimes informed the commissioning body's choices, notably with *Max Havelaar* (1860) by Multatuli (1820–87), which acknowledges Dutch oppression of the Javanese during its occupation of Indonesia.

Selection Policy and Production Problems

In line with Vimr's account of supply-driven translation in Chapter Three, The Foundation ultimately prioritized source culture considerations, and failed to heed advice from their English publishing partner, Heinemann, and other publishers about the impression they were creating. 'Dutch literature looks like a provincial cousin, who rarely goes anywhere, except on coach tours to international conferences', wrote Peereboom (1963, 1045) in the *Times Literary Supplement*. In a letter from The Foundation's archive dated 18 June 1959, Heinemann wrote to the director, J.J. Oversteegen, about the translation *Droom Is Het Leven* (Dream Is Life, 1953) by Willem G. van Maanen (1920–2012): 'This book is not entirely suitable for an English readership. The novel is of course very short by our standards.' Further letters from this archive highlight the issue: the London publisher Eyre & Spottiswoode wrote to Oversteegen on 23 July 1958 about *Het Leven Op Aarde* (Life On Earth, 1934) by Jan Slauerhoff (1898–1936): '*Life on Earth* looks an interesting novel but I think its style would tell against it nowadays and that the risk of translating it would be commercially too great.' Hutchinson's editor-in-chief, Raleigh Trevelyan, wrote to Oversteegen on 14 July 1959 concerning *De Avonden* (The Evenings, 1947) by Gerard van het Reve: 'Quite honestly, having now been able to consider the entire book we do not feel that it would go down well in this country. Somehow the formula adopted is a little outmoded in our country.' Chatto & Windus wrote to Oversteegen on 8 September 1958 concerning Mulisch: 'Clearly he is a talented writer; both these pieces show much originality and skill. But they contain much that is not attractive, not to say – in the case of the novel – obscene.' Hutchinson wrote to Oversteegen on 4 July 1957 concerning the novels of Simon Vestdijk (1898–1971): 'However excellent in Dutch they may be, they will not transpose satisfactorily into English [...] His work could not reach a well-disposed market in this country.' Despite all these warnings concerning the length, style and formulaic nature of Dutch novels, the commissioning body pressed ahead. In her retrospective attempt to characterize the series, Rosalie Colie found only the three novels by Elsschot amusing, lamenting otherwise that 'there was an enormous preoccupation with physical needs and moral hypocrisies in middle class life' (1967, 110–18). This narrow-minded stuffiness and the inability to escape from the irresponsibility of small societies, hardly unique to *Bibliotheca Neerlandica* or Dutch literature, felt claustrophobic to Colie.

The shortcomings of the selection process were followed by inconsistent practice in the production of the volumes. *Max Havelaar* was one of four works chosen that already existed in English translation: this was a missed opportunity to introduce new works. Since *Max Havelaar*'s previous translators – Alphonse Nahuijs (1868) and Willem Siebenhaar (1927) – were both Anglophile Dutchmen, in this case a new version was commissioned from a native English speaker, Roy Edwards. By contrast, the volume that launched the series, *Van Oude Menschen, de Dingen die Voorbijgaan* (Old People and the Things that Pass, 1906) by Louis Marie-Anne Couperus (1863–1923), reprinted a 1906 translation by Alexander Teixeira de Mattos because of its success at the time. Colie (1967, 117) found the original translation, 'natural and often graceful'. A later critic, Ria Vanderauwera (1985, 53), was surprised that no editing had been done to the aged translation and questioned whether 'such infelicities as "een beste jongen"/"a capital fellow" and "kerel"/"old chap" really served the basic aim of making Dutch authors known to a present-day audience'. Her conclusion – 'one would expect extra care to be paid to metaliterature by translators, editors, publishers, and sponsors, especially with respect to the *Bibliotheca Neerlandica*, but this is not always so' – highlights an ominous lack of attention to detail from a notionally prestigious series launching its debut volume. Sales were nevertheless impressive.

Only half of *Bibliotheca Neerlandica*'s ten volumes contain a single work. It is perhaps understandable that Walschap's *Trouwen* (1933) and *Celibaat* (1934) appeared in one volume as *Marriage/Ordeal* (1963), since they thematically complement each other. Similarly, Elsschot's three novels *Lijmen* (1924), *Het Been* (1938) and *Het Dwaalicht* (1946), which appear in one volume as *Soft Soap, The Leg* and *Will o' the Wisp* (1965), are linked by their central character, Laarmans. By contrast, no explanation is either given or presents itself for the coupling in one volume of *Onpersoonlijke Herinneringen* (1936) by Frans Coenen (1866–1936) and *Willem Mertens Levensspiegel* (1914) by Jacobus Feylbrief (1876–1951), writing under the pseudonym J. Van Oudshoorn, as *The House on the Canal* and *Alienation* (1965). Advertisements in earlier volumes referring to *Willem Mertens*

Levensspiegel as *The Life of Willem Mertens* suggest disorganization and could later cause confusion.

The failings in production practice and rigour are epitomized by the two mediaeval volumes, each an anthology containing an eclectic selection of five works, of which some are extracts: 'Brieven' by the thirteenth-century poet Hadewijch of Brabant contains only 20 of the original 31 letters, while 'Walewein' (Gawein, c. 1250) by the thirteenth-century poets Penninc (his stage name) and Pieter Vostaert comprises just five pages of the original and is therefore difficult to put into context. Edmund Colledge had already translated the five works in the volume entitled *Mediaeval Netherlands Religious Literature* (1965) and was to translate the five works in the second, entitled *Reynard the Fox and Other Mediaeval Netherlands Secular Literature* (1967). After translating the four shorter pieces in the volume, however, he decided to enter a monastery, leaving *Van den Vos Reynaerde* (The History of Reynard the Fox, c. 1225) by Willem die Madoc maecte (n.d.) without a translator. Oversteegen eventually had to enlist a Dutch native speaker, Adriaan Barnouw, to translate it. Barnouw chose not to update the only English translation by William Caxton, favouring instead a new translation based on the work of J.W. Muller (1914).[3] Some pieces – 'Beatrijs' ('Beatrice', c. 1374), 'Karel ende Elgast' ('Charlemagne and Elbegast', c. 1250), 'Lanseloet van Denemerken' ('Lancelot of Denmark', c. 1400), 'Mariken van Nieumeghen' ('Mary of Nijmegen', 1485), and 'Nu Noch' ('Say that Again', c. 1400), all of which have an unknown author – were transposed from verse into prose, perhaps to make it easier to translate or for an English-speaking target audience to understand. Others – 'Brieven', 'Walewein', 'Seven Manieren Van Minne' by the thirteenth-century Flemish nun, Beatrijs van Nazareth, and 'Van den Blinckenden Steen' ('The Book of the Sparkling Stone', c. 1340) by the thirteenth-century Flemish mystic, John of Ruysbroek (1293–1381) – were all translated from prose to prose. 'Beatrijs' (c. 1374)

---

[3] Caxton printed his translation of the prose version of 'Reynard's Story' in 1481 and again in 1489. Editions followed by William J. Thoms for the Percy Society (London, 1844), by Edward Arber in *The English Scholar's Library of Old and Modern Works* (London, 1878), and by Edmund Goldsmid in the *Bibliotheca Curiosa* (Edinburgh, 1884). In *Van den Vos Reinaerde: Naar de thans bekende handschriften en bewerkingen critisch uitgegeven met eene inleiding door J.W. Muller*, Muller tried to reconstruct the original text from a collection of manuscripts: the Latin text of Balduinus's *Reinardus Vulpes*, the Cambridge fragments of the printed edition of 1487, the prose version of Reynard II, the chapbook of 1564 and the Low German version of 1498.

is regrettably the only work presented bilingually, with the Middle Dutch original on the opposite page.

The difficulties Oversteegen had in finding translators reflects the particular problem facing 'dominated languages', which are seldom taught abroad to more than an interested few, with a consequent shortage of able translators. The brochure *Tien Jaar Stichting Voor Vertalingen* (1964, 6–7) highlights the fact that the commissioning body found difficulty in finding translators of adequate competence: 'Candidates with a literary background were examined to test their translation skills, but no more than ten per cent of applicants were suited to this specialized, difficult task.'

Reinink saw the need for the development of a thoroughgoing translation policy because of the poor quality of translations, at a time when translation studies was in its infancy, and the number of translations published abroad was low. Johan Heilbron (1995, 230) points out that the number of translated Dutch novels rose from 127 in 12 languages between 1900 and 1909 to 701 in 28 languages between 1950 and 1957, but agrees that foreign publishers showed little zest for Dutch fiction and emphasizes that, thanks to the increased international trade in the twentieth century, the position of translators changed from a low-status hobby or means of supplementing income to a recognized profession (Heilbron 1995, 218–29). After the Second World War, translators in many European nations began forming organizations that were to be the driving force for the development of translation studies in the 1960s. In the Netherlands, het Instituut voor Vertaalkunde (the Institute for Translation Studies) was established in 1964 from the previously formed 1956 Nederlands Genootschap van Vertalers (Dutch Society of Translators).

Oversteegen understood better the need for a target-based approach to translated literature and assembled four native English-speaking translators, James Brockway, Neline Clegg, Roy Edwards and Alex Brotherton to look after the translations of the modern works. Although the translators were accomplished, with Brockway, Edwards and Brotherton later earning the prestigious Martinus Nijhoff Prize, awarded annually since 1955 to one or two translators for translation into or from Dutch, much of their work had to be edited at substantial additional cost to the publisher, Heinemann. A meeting of the commissioning body on 21 November 1963 had rejected as too expensive the idea of approaching academics to proof-read the works, but they might have considered the cheaper option of employing target readers. Heinemann's editor Roland Gant wrote to Oversteegen on 18 August 1965 complaining that 'all the extra work, reading, proof reading and copy editing,

Exporting the Canon

had not only cost much time but moreover a high amount of unexpected costs'. These costs were to prove a major factor in Heinemann prematurely abandoning the project.

Colie (1967, 117) perhaps unfairly blames the translators for causing this extra work:

> There are many typographical errors (because the typesetters are Dutch, and proof-readers are everywhere scarce, I suppose), which can be cleaned up in further printings. Translation is no easy task, as we know; but perhaps these books were done too fast, or were done by too-professional translators quick at giving the sense of a text but not its literary shadings.

Brotherton's partner, Betty Verheus, informed me during a personal conversation in Amsterdam that he often felt isolated, with no published academic resources to draw on, and had to make up the rules as he went along. These translators, some of whom were academics, were poorly paid. Oversteegen (1999, 153) writes that he realized soon after his appointment that The Foundation could not compete with the higher translation salaries paid in industry. In an 'Activity Report of the Foundation since 1 July 1953', Oversteegen (n.d.) notes that 'a translated biscuit-factory advertisement earned up to three times more than a translated long essay by Simon Vestdijk (1898–1971)'. An English version of a 'Memorandum of Agreement' from the Sijthoff archive at Leiden University, issued by the Dutch publisher Sijthoff and signed by Gilbert de Flines (1961, 1) shows that the translators earned only 1,000 guilders for each translated title (equivalent to £1,466 today). Later the commissioning body would adjust this according to the size and difficulty of the work in question.

Publishers and Sales

'Literary prestige', according to Casanova (2004, 15) depends on the existence of a more or less extensive professional 'milieu', including sought-after publishers, and three were to form part of the *Bibliotheca Neerlandica* operation. Sijthoff agreed to publish the *Bibliotheca Neerlandica* in conjunction with Heinemann in the UK. Later a small American company called London House and Maxwell would also come on board. The Foundation would have perhaps fared better if they had followed a publishing company like Penguin, whose series of classics had begun in 1946 with the translation of

Homer's *Odyssey* by Emile Victor Rieu, the first editor of a series that involved translations of well-known classics from over 25 languages. Indeed Meijer, a Dutch academic, writer and later professor of Dutch at London University, who wrote the rejected *Literature of the Low Countries* for the series, highlighted Penguin when he wrote to Oversteegen on 29 March 1965 in reply to their dissatisfaction of his handling of cultural history in the volume:

> I find it a pity that you have to focus on cultural history and I have an idea that you are overestimating the value of a cultural history situation. I am not against this but in a small work which concerns itself primarily with literary history, I would not want to place too much emphasis on this. You ought to look again at the Pelican histories of French and Italian literature where no mention is made of cultural history despite them being very usable. (Archief: Stichting ter Bevordering van de Vertaling van Nederlands Letterkundig Werk [Archive of the Foundation for the Promotion of Dutch Literary Works], Letterkundig Museum [Museum of Literature], The Hague)

Thomas Joy (1974, 15) notes that from the 1950s to the 1960s, the declining number of good stock-holding bookshops in the UK caused publishers great concern. Joy (1974, 1) attributes their closure to a failure to move with the times, particularly regarding business methods and improved window and interior displays. According to Allan Hill (1988, 153–54), however, UK book sales in fact doubled in this period. Rival companies Hodder, Collins and Macmillan were all prospering, but by 1957 Heinemann was heading for bankruptcy, with their main business of hardcover fiction having virtually stalled. Hill (1988, 155) suggests that they had failed to adjust to the paperback revolution, while Clive Bingley (1972, 27) points to ill-advised loss-making acquisitions like Peter Davies and Hart-Davis.

Heinemann blamed production costs and sales for their premature withdrawal from the project. In a letter from The Foundation's archive, their representative, Alwyn Birch, wrote to Gilbert de Flines at Sijthoff on 17 October 1966, indicating his desire to terminate the contract:

> Soon we will be publishing *Max Havelaar* by Multatuli and *Mediaeval Netherlands Secular Literature*. After this we are left with the unwritten *History of Dutch Literature* and several volumes of essays and poetry. As you will see the sales for the more recent volumes have declined. If we deduct the copies sold to the Dutch and Belgian governments then they have been small throughout [...] our editorial costs have been rising

Exporting the Canon

constantly. It was originally agreed that the Stichting [Foundation] would commission the translations and forward the final version to us complete [...] Many of the translations have been in poor English and have required a great deal of rewriting [...] They have turned a marginally profitable series into an unprofitable venture.

Table 2, which was attached to the letter from Birch to de Flines, suggests that the *Bibliotheca Neerlandica* sales from 1964 to June 1966 were acceptable, with all volumes selling a high proportion of their print run.

Table 2 *Bibliotheca Neerlandica* Sales: 1964 to 1966

Title	Print run	Sales 1964	Sales 1965	Sales 1966	Sales total
Old People	3,000	2,319	103	43	2,465
The Waterman	3,000	2,390	89	43	2,522
Marriage/Ordeal	3,750	2,771	68	11	2,850
The Man in the Mirror	3,750	2,743	90	23	2,856
The Garden	4,000	1,969	553	231	2,753
Mediaeval Literature	3,500	1,892	370	21	2,283
The House on the Canal	3,500	–	1,948	466	2,414
Three Novels	3,500	–	1,978	488	2,466
Max Havelaar	3,000	–	–	–	–
Mediaeval Secular Literature	3,000	–	–	–	–

One thousand copies of each print run were, however, bought by the Dutch and Belgian governments and given to libraries and institutions around the world, with Heinemann, the English publisher, selling its remaining stock to The Foundation at a considerable reduction. In a letter obtained from the Foundation's archive, Heinemann's representative, John Beer, wrote on 26 November 1969, to Johan Somerwil at the Foundation: 'I am authorized to say that we shall be glad to sell you the remaining stock of [*Bibliotheca Neerlandica*] at published price <u>less 80%</u>. It is understood that this transaction is confidential.' Oversteegen acknowledges in his 1963–64 report that he is seeing a turn in book production and that the market for classical works appears saturated, but Birch's explanation does not bear out Van Ardenne-Diephuis's view (2011, 82) that this context played a role in falling sales. Minderaa had already reported in the commissioning body's minutes of 16 December 1960 that Heinemann faced financial problems because their financiers in Birmingham had withdrawn. In 1962, Heinemann reported a loss of £65,544 (St. John, 1990, 525), and these broader financial difficulties seem the dominant reason for Heinemann's withdrawal.

For Vanderauwera (1985, 122–24), *Bibliotheca Neerlandica* was always likely to struggle in its target culture, where

> [c]ommercial success is rare, critical success, both qualitatively and quantitatively (the sheer number of reviews) is moderate, and some sort of idea about Dutch literature is in most cases non-existent or conveniently stereotyped. Literary works which have been primarily selected because of their classical status in the source-language such as is the case with *Bibliotheca Neerlandica* will be at best interesting but 'epigonal' curiosities to a target-pole which is notoriously indifferent to foreign work.

John Lehman from the *London Magazine* agrees and states: 'The English are not interested in their own literature, let alone that of other nations' (Oversteegen, 1999, 188). The Foundation could influence the promotion and translation of Dutch literary works, if not its distribution and reception, but Vanderauwera (1985, 127) argues that 'it may well be that its financial support sometimes had a reverse effect on the publisher's promotional endeavours: there is no great incentive to activate potential reviewers and buyers if the money problem is discretely solved'. In 1975, John M. Coetzee translated *Een Nagelaten Bekentenis* (A Posthumous Confession, 1894) by Marcellus Emants (1848–1923) for a joint venture by The Foundation and Twayne Publishers, the *Library of Netherlandic Literature*, which was discontinued after 11 volumes. Vanderauwera (1985, 127), however, highlights that he complained about the lack of reviews and thought that 'as the translation was subsidized from The Netherlands, the publishers put out the translation with the minimum of publicity and promotion'. She continues (1985, 127) that the editor of the series, Egbert Krispyn, drew a different conclusion:

To create a market one would absolutely need the cooperation of major journals and magazines. After some twelve years or more trying to get one of them to review the Twayne translations, without *any* success, I am convinced that they simply are not interested, don't want to be bothered, and will not review translations from the Netherlandic unless it is something particularly filthy. For some reason they will give space for third rate German books, but not even for second rate Netherlandic ones.

Conclusion

Should we, then, conclude that *Bibliotheca Neerlandica* was a total failure, brought down by its internal strategic and organizational shortcomings and an unfavourable external context? Fenoulhet (2013, 52) pertinently asks: 'What if a translated text fails to sell and therefore remains for the most part unread? Is it still part of the target community simply because it has been translated into the community's language?' She argues elsewhere that the debate about successful translated works is now shifting from simply being published to actually being read (Fenoulhet, 2013, 52). Sapiro (2014, 87) adds that although economic profit is not the only motivation of publishers, it underlies the very conditions of existence of trade publishing, with certain translations being undertaken only for the economic profit they are expected to provide.

The translation of literary works, however, is not always profitable, economically speaking, but seeks to acquire symbolic capital, as in the case of the Dutch government, seeking to redress its tarnished image after 1949. The series is now out of print, but it did enable some works to find a place in the English-speaking world market. Although the series ended prematurely, ten volumes, comprising 22 works, were published. *Of Reynaert the Fox/Van den Vos Reynaerde* was translated and published again in 2009 by André Bouwman and Bart Besmusca in an adult version, and by Simpson in 2015 in a children's edition; and Meijer's *Literature of the Low Countries* (1971) became a seminal volume at Dutch institutions. *Bibliotheca Neerlandica* translations have reappeared in other series, notably Vestdijk's *The Garden where the Brass Band Played* in New Amsterdam Books in 1989, Multatuli's *Max Havelaar* in Penguin Classics in 2005, and Couperus's *Old People and the Things that Pass* in 2008 with Dodo. Two other planned volumes appeared later with other publishers; The Foundation funded David H. Brumble III's 1982 translation of *De Spaanschen Brabander* (The Spanish Brabanter, 1617)

Irvin Wolters

by Gebrand Adriaenzoon Bredero (1585–1618), which was successfully put on in Texas, where a reviewer described it as 'a comic masterpiece and a feast for the senses' (Hulbert, 1982), while *Lucifer* (1654) by Joost van den Vondel (1587–1679) was retranslated by Noel Clark in 1990, following translations by Leanard Charles van Noppen (1898) and Jehangir Mody (1942). In 2019, a retranslation of Multatuli's *Max Havelaar* was published which was translated by Ina Rilka and David McKay. As Fenoulhet (2013, 41) argues: 'in a globalized world, the fact that Dutch writers have published in other languages is living proof, as it were, that Dutch literature has vitality and can bridge the gap between Dutch culture and other cultures, thanks to the work of intermediaries such as translators and publishers.'

Bibliography

Works Published in the Bibliotheca Neerlandica *Series*
Coenen, Frans, and Van Oudshoorn, J. 1965. *The House on the Canal/Alienation.* Trans. James Brockway and Neline. C. Clegg (Leiden: Sijthoff).
Colledge, Edmund (ed.). 1965. *Mediaeval Netherlands Religious Literature.* Trans. E. Colledge (Leiden: Sijthoff).
Colledge, Edmund and Barnouw, Adriaan (ed.). 1967. *Reynard the Fox and other Mediaeval Netherlands Secular Literature.* Trans. Adriaan J. Barnouw and Edmund Colledge (Leiden: Sijthoff).
Couperus, Louis. 1963. *Old People and the Things that Pass.* Trans. Alexander Teixeira de Mattos (Leiden: Sijthoff).
Die Madoc maecte, Willem. 1967. Van den Vos Reynaerde. Trans. Adriaan J. Barnouw. In Colledge, Edmund (ed.). *Reynard the Fox and other Mediaeval Netherlands Secular Literature* (Leiden: Sijthoff).
Elsschot, Willem. 1965. *Three Novels: Soft Soap/The Leg/Will o' the Wisp.* Trans. Alex Brotherton (Leiden: Sijthoff).
Multatuli. 1967. *Max Havelaar.* Trans. Roy Edwards (Leiden: Sijthoff).
Teirlinck, Herman. 1963. *The Man in the Mirror.* Trans. James Brockway (Leiden: Sijthoff).
Van Schendel, Arthur. 1963. *The Waterman.* Trans. Neline C. Clegg (Leiden: Sijthoff).
Vestdijk, Simon. 1965. *The Garden where the Brass Band Played.* Trans. Alex Brotherton (Leiden: Sijthoff).
Walschap, Gerard. 1963. *Marriage/Ordeal* Trans. Alex Brotherton (Leiden: Sijthoff).

Archive

Archief: Stichting ter Bevordering van de Vertaling van Nederlands Letterkundig Werk (Archive of the Foundation for the Promotion of Dutch Literary Works), Letterkundig Museum (Museum of Literature), The Hague.

Works Cited

Bingley, Clive. 1972. *The Business of Book Publishing* (Oxford: Pergamon).

Brems, Elke, Orsolya Réthelyi and Ton van Kalmthout (eds). 2017. *Doing Double Dutch: The International Circulation of Literature from the Low Countries* (Leuven: Leuven University Press).

Casanova, Pascale. 2004. *The World Republic of Letters* (Cambridge, MA: Harvard University Press).

Casanova, Pascale. 2010. Consecration and Accumulation of Literary Capital. Translation as Unequal Exchange. Trans. Siobhan Brownlie. In Baker, Mona (ed.). *Critical Readings in Translation Studies* (New York: Routledge), 285–303.

Colie, Rosalie. 1967. Review: Invitation to Experience. *The Kenyon Review*, 29 (1), 110–18.

D'Haen, Theo. 2011. How Many Canons Do We Need? World Literature, National Literature, European Literature. In Papadima, Liviu, David Damrosch and Theo D'Haen (eds). *The Canonical Debate Today* (Amsterdam: Rodopi), 19–38.

De Flines, Gilbert. 1961. *Memorandum of Agreement* (Leiden: Sijthoff).

Fenoulhet, Jane. 2007. Tijdgebonden. De onmisbaarheid van geschiedenis in het literatuurcurriculum. In Steyaert, Kris (ed.). *De historische dimensie in de Neerlandistiek* (Nijmegen: uitgeverij Vantilt).

Fenoulhet, Jane. 2013. *Nomadic Literature. Cees Nooteboom and his Writing* (Bern: Peter Lang).

Heilbron, Johan. 1995. *Waarin een klein land: Nederlands cultuur in international verband* (Amsterdam: Prometheus).

Hill, Alan. 1988. In *Pursuit Of Publishing* (London: John Murray).

Hulbert, Dan. 1982. Theater Review. *Dallas Times Herald*, 23 November.

Joy, Thomas. 1974. *The Bookselling Business* (London: Sir Isaac Pitman & Sons).

Musschoot, Anne Marie. 2004. Het Nationaal Fonds voor Letterkunde: Vijftig jaar ondersteunde werking in het literaire veld. In *Verslagen en mededelingen van de Koninklijke Academie voor Nederlandse taal-en letterkunde*. Available from: www.dbnl.org/tekst/_ver016200401_01/_ver016200401_01_0025.php [accessed 9 August 2016].

Oversteegen, J.J. n.d. *Activity Report of the Foundation since 1 July 1953* (Amsterdam: De Stichting tot Bevordering van de Vertaling van Nederlands Letterkundig Werk).

Oversteegen, J.J. 1999. *Etalage, uit het leven van een lezer* (Amsterdam: Meulenhoff).

Peereboom, J. Low Countries Literature. *Times Literary Supplement*. 19 December 1963, 1045.

Sapiro, Gisèle. 2014. The Sociology of Translation: A New Research Domain. In Bermann, Sandra and Catherine Porter (eds). *A Companion to Translation Studies* (Hoboken, NJ: Wiley), 82–94.

Schein, Edgar. 1991. The Role of the Founder in the Creation of Organizational Culture (1983). In Frost, Peter, Larry F. Moore and Meryl Reis Louis (eds). *Reframing Organizational Culture* (London: Sage), 14–25.

St. John, John. 1990. *William Heinemann: A Century of Publishing, 1890–1990* (London: Heinemann).

Stichting Ter Bervordering Van De Vertaling Van Nederlands Letterkundig Werk. n.d. Leaflet (Amsterdam: De Stichting tot Bevordering van de Vertaling van Nederlands Letterkundig Werk).

Tien Jaar Stichting Voor Vertalingen. 1964. Brochure (Amsterdam: De Stichting tot Bevordering van de Vertaling van Nederlands Letterkundig Werk).

Van Ardenne-Diephuis, Els. 2011. *De Stichting voor Vertalingen 1954–1999. De Bibliotheca Neerlandica: Nederlandse letteren op de internationale kaart 2011* (Groningen: University of Groningen).

Vanderauwera, Ria. 1985. *Dutch Novels Translated into English: The Transformation of a 'Minority Literature'* (Amsterdam: Rodopi).

Chapter Six

Creative Autonomy and Institutional Support in Contemporary Slovene Literature

Olivia Hellewell (University of Nottingham)

As with many other so-called small-nation contexts, research concerning literary translation from Slovene into the global language of English is virtually non-existent. Speakers of English with knowledge of Slovene, a language with two million native speakers, are few. Existing research into this pair of languages tends to originate from the source culture (SC) and therefore often focuses on the translation of literary works into Slovene, rather than examining how and why Slovene literature comes to exist in English translation. While a lack of research into this particular language pair can be easily explained, the lack of research into specific small-nation contexts within the field of translation studies more broadly results in an incomplete picture of the circulation of literary translation. As a result, our understanding of the wider sociocultural functions of translation cannot be considered comprehensive. This is because, as this chapter will show, studies from small-nation contexts like Slovenia complicate the picture that is commonly presented by theoretical translation models developed on the basis of more 'dominant' languages. Through an analysis of two case studies that detail two very different routes for translation into English, the research presented in this chapter seeks to construct a clearer understanding of the factors determining the existence and reach of literary translations in this particular small-nation context.

While this chapter examines the translation of Slovene literature into English, it does not claim that the institutional and non-institutional translation practices are exclusive to literary works destined for the anglophone market. Nor does it suggest that English is the most common language into which Slovene literature is translated. Indeed, data from the Index Translationum, though far from comprehensive, suggests that

Olivia Hellewell

German is the most frequent target language (TL) for literary translation from Slovene.[1] This is also corroborated by recent research from scholars at the University of Ljubljana, who note that German is a language into which Slovene literature is frequently translated, owing to a shared border between Slovenia and Austria, a sense of familiarity between the two SCs and a historical connection between Slovene, Austrian and German cultures (Moe et al., 2010, 47–48). In this chapter, the term 'Slovene cultural context' is thus used to describe the arena in which dealings concerning Slovene-to-English literary translations are conducted, which is not to suggest that the strategies described pertaain to the translation of Slovene literature into English alone.

In addition to examining the cultural institutions that are central to the selection, funding and promotion of literary translations from Slovene into English, this chapter will also explore the role played at institutional level of Slovene narratives of national identity, and will demonstrate how, given the presence of such narratives and their connection to language and literature, they must therefore be considered as influential factors in the field of literary production within this particular small-nation context.

How Small is Small?

Translation studies research has long drawn attention to unequal balances of power between languages, and consequently to the reach of national literatures on a global scale (Casanova, 2004; 2013; Cronin, 1995; 2003; Tymoczko, 1999; Venuti, 1995). The call by Pascale Casanova (2009, 285–303) for translation to be understood as 'unequal exchange' problematized discussions of translation as 'a "simple" operation of transfer, [which] presupposes the existence of national languages which are equal and juxtaposed'. Though translation and power dynamics have long been addressed as an object of study in their own right (notably Tymoczko and Gentzler, 2002), there nevertheless remains a lack of research into the specific structural conditions within what Bourdieu (1996) terms 'fields of cultural production' in small-nation contexts, which would further highlight the unequal nature of the exchange between national literatures

---

[1] Mona Baker (2010, 34) notes that 'existing sources for data [...] for example book statistics available in each country and databases such as the *Index Translationum*, are all flawed'.

through translation. Without sufficient case studies throughout small-nation contexts, the imbalance cannot hope to be redressed. An analysis of key Slovene cultural institutions would not in itself suffice to interpret the conditions in which Slovene literature is selected, funded and promoted for publication in English. As Ieva Zauberga (2005, 67) argues, the process of literary translation from a small-nation source language (SL) also constitutes a means of increasing 'recognizability of [their] culture in the eyes of the rest of the world'. And in Slovenia, a small nation whose national identity is narrated as being inherently linked to language and literature, the role of such narratives must be considered to understand the motivation for literary translation activity from a small-nation SC to a more linguistically dominant target culture (TC).

When the newly formed Slovene government declared independence from Yugoslavia on 25 June 1991, it marked the first time that Slovenia had ever existed as an independent nation state. Before the Socialist Federal Republic of Yugoslavia, Slovenia belonged to the Kingdom of Serbs, Croats and Slovenes, and before this the region had been governed for centuries by the Habsburgs. The earliest mention of a defined Slovene speech area exists in a preface to a 1557 translation of the New Testament by the Protestant priest Primož Trubar (1508–86). Speaking of his approach to the translation, he noted that he had tried, 'in terms of vocabulary and style, to make it so that every Slovene, whether he be from Kranj, Lower Styria, Carinthia, Kras, Istria, Lower Carniola or the Italian-Slovene borderlands, will understand' (Rupel, 1966, 60). As a result of Trubar's translation and subsequent definition of Slovene speech areas, his name is to this day synonymous with the symbolic function of language as a sign of national identity. Slovenia has not always had official flags or borders, but the language and its literatures are attributes that have been narrated as constant and have survived in the face of powerful linguistic and political forces. Narratives of Slovene national identity and its intrinsic connection to language and literature are thus pivotal to understanding the Slovene field of cultural production. The presence of such narratives, as an examination of the interview data will demonstrate, tells us much about the motivation for the production of literary translations from Slovene into English, which is why they must be analysed in addition to factors that are more typically seen as influential in small-nation contexts, as discussed by Michael Cronin (2003, 139–40), like the disparity between the number of translations read and produced, and the invisibility of minority cultures on a global stage and within translation studies itself. In this chapter, the term 'identity' encapsulates the notion of a socially constructed narrative that is influenced by specific historical, political and cultural conditions.[2]

Discussions of the role and function of identities in translation studies research have placed too much emphasis on the agency of a TC, and analyses have not been extended to include small-nation contexts where the fields of production differ greatly from those of the more dominant languages and literatures. In his 'Translation and the Formation of Cultural Identities', Venuti (1995, 10) writes that translation has the potential to 'produce far-reaching social effects [of which] by far the most consequential [...] is the formation of cultural identities'. Although Venuti claims that the 'process of identity formation [...] is double-edged', his discussion of this process does not extend to the role of the source culture (SC). The power to construct certain identities of a SC is placed solely with the TC, and assumes that the translation process is carried out within the TC, to serve the needs of the TC readership. The tendency to discuss the dynamics of translation and the creation or projection of identities in this way has obscured our understanding of the function of translated literature for smaller SCs, who must work harder than their linguistically dominant counterparts for their cultural voices to be heard. Venuti's later work shifts its focus from the way in which translation processes can form cultural identities to the role that translation has played in the construction of national identities. In *Translation Changes Everything*, Venuti (2013, 117) maintains that 'nations do indeed profit from translation', and furthermore that 'nationalist movements have frequently enlisted translation in the development of national languages and cultures, especially national literatures'. This, he argues, is the result of 'translation agendas' that exploit cultural differences within the ST 'to construct a national identity that is assumed to pre-exist the translation process'. As in his earlier writings on translation and cultural identities, Venuti sees the main consequence of these translation agendas occurring in terms of the TC. The examples that Venuti employs to demonstrate the process of identity formation all centre upon an idea of translation 'enriching national literatures'. If we look at the Slovene field of cultural production, there is evidence of literature

---

[2] This usage is informed by the social constructionist approach of Steph Lawler (2014, 24), who theorizes identity as being 'creatively produced through various raw materials available – notably, memories, understandings, experiences and interpretations'.

Contemporary Slovene Literature

translated into Slovene having enriched this 'national literature'.[3] There is, however, another sphere of activity carried out by Slovene cultural institutions that cannot be explained be a TC-oriented theory of identity formation. As Zauberga (2005, 67) has observed with her research into Latvian models of translation, 'translations of Latvian literature (and most probably other minor cultures) mostly start not with a need on the target pole but with a wish to become known generated on the source pole'. Much of the rhetoric analysed from Slovene cultural institutions both in printed form and in interview data suggests a similar trend.

Cultural Institutions and Their Roles

While, as Richard Mansell shows in the next chapter, a single cultural institution dominates the promotion of Catalan literature, there are five Slovene cultural institutions in Slovenia, in addition to the Ministry of Culture and individual publishing houses, for which a primary task, if not sole mission, is to promote Slovene literature through translation. These are Javna agencija za knjigo (the Slovenian Book Agency; JAK), Društvo slovenskih pisateljev (the Slovene Writers' Association; DSP), Center za slovensko književnost (the Centre for Slovenian Literature), Trubarjev sklad (the Trubar Foundation) and Slovenian PEN.[4] In this chapter I shall provide an overview of the first four institutions. Slovenian PEN has had an important role historically, and continues to be active in supporting literary translation today; however, as a regional branch of an international writers' association, its structural make-up requires a broader analysis that cannot be covered comprehensively here.

JAK is a government agency that works within the field of literature and publishing. It emerged in December 2008 as an institution connected to, but officially distinct from, the Ministry of Culture. Its sphere of activity is threefold: publishing, the promotion of reading in Slovenia and international cooperation, which is the strand that concerns this chapter's analysis. JAK's activities in the field of international cooperation include the distribution of

---

[3] A comprehensive study of literary translations into Slovene is Majda Stanovnik's *Slovenski literarni prevod, 1550–2000* (2005).

[4] The English translations of these associations are taken from official documents or the websites of the respective institutions, hence the variation between Slovene and Slovenian here.

state funds for translation projects, the organization of translation seminars that initiate contact between JAK and potential new translators of Slovene literature and the production of promotional materials to advertise Slovene literature in translation at international book fairs. JAK's translation seminar is a particularly good example of the effort and capital invested in the promotion of Slovene literature abroad, as the organization pays for translators to attend a week-long seminar, providing all-inclusive accommodation and daily translation seminars where translators can meet the authors of the selected texts, as well as Slovene translation scholars. In exchange for this investment, JAK is able to engage translators with texts of their choosing, and use the resulting translation samples to produce booklets that each showcase particular texts in a range of languages.

In terms of how JAK interacts with other cultural institutions working to promote Slovene literature in translation, it is useful to understand the agency as an umbrella organization. It overlaps with other institutions outlined here insofar as the others rely on JAK for the distribution of funding, since they must apply through public calls for tender to finance their activities. The agency's establishment was initially met with protest from writers who did not agree to two of the clauses in the law that the government had set out (MMC RTV SLO, 2007). These objections were related to the structure of the ruling body that would preside over JAK and to the allocation of funding (MMC RTV SLO, 2007). Despite these objections, the government's proposal went ahead and JAK has continued to operate since, albeit with a number of structural changes.

The second institution examined here is the DSP: a collective body of authors, poets and literary figures that can be traced back to Ljubljana in 1872 (Levec, 1885, 247). It was first formed following a newspaper article entitled 'Advice on How to Better Promote Literary Activity among Slovene Writers', dated 4 April 1968 (Lermavner, 1972, 1027). It was written by Davorin Trstenjak (1817–90), a writer, Roman Catholic priest and supporter of the Zedinjena Slovenija (United Slovenia) movement, which was established in 1848 to demand the establishment of a Slovene monarchy and equal language rights for Slovenes living within the Austro-Hungarian Empire (Štih et al., 2008, 269–70). This first incarnation did not endure, and the early political associations with United Slovenia are cited by literary historian Fran Levec (1885, 247) as one of the reasons behind this. It was however, just one of many formations of the DSP, which adapted according to the various governing powers in the years that followed. In 1885, the society re-emerged, with the aim of promoting Slovene literary activity and providing financial

Contemporary Slovene Literature

support to Slovene authors, though it was disbanded by Austro-Hungarian authorities again in 1915 (Društvo slovenskih pisateljev, 2019). After the fall of the Austro-Hungarian Empire in 1918, the DSP emerged again as 'Društvo slovenskih leposlovcev' (the Slovene Authors' Association) and from 1945 onwards, the DSP operated within Yugoslavia as a part of the Union of Yugoslav Writers and the Socialist Alliance of Working People of Yugoslavia (Društvo slovenskih pisateljev, 2019). In the 1980s the DSP was a significant mobilizing force against the central Yugoslav authorities and founded the Committee for the Protection of Freedom of Thought and Literary Expression (Štih et al., 2008, 503). In February 1990, Slovenia's request to leave the Yugoslav Writer's Association was formally accepted, and the organization has continued to operate as the DSP ever since. The current mission statement on the DSP's website outlines the organization's principal function: 'The Slovene Writers' Association is a voluntary, independent and non-profit organization that serves and furthers the professional, social and cultural interests of Slovene writers'.

It becomes clear that although the financial support of Slovene authors and the promotion of Slovene literary expression have been at the heart of the DSP's mission, it has nevertheless been a politically active association, acting in the interests of an independent Slovene state at several stages of its genesis. In addition to the DSP's union-type function in Slovenia today, it also describes a list of aims, functions and responsibilities, two of which are particularly relevant to understanding the role of the DSP in the field of literary translation: 'The association organizes literary performances, literary and cultural gatherings, symposia, meetings for writers and workers in the cultural sector, it cooperates with manifestations of this at home and abroad, [and] it takes care of the assertion of Slovene authors' works abroad.' The description of the DSP's activities strongly suggests similarities with the findings of Zauberga (2005) from her research on the Latvian cultural sphere: that the production of translations within small-nation contexts are often driven by an impetus to become known generated, as Ondřej Vimr argues in Chapter Three, at the source pole.

The Trubar Foundation is a joint enterprise of the Slovene Writers' Association, the Centre for Slovene Literature and Slovenian PEN, and exists to give financial support to the publication of Slovene literature in translation. Publishing houses outside Slovenia can apply to the Trubar Foundation if they are publishing the literary work of a Slovene author in translation, and they can receive up to 50 per cent of the printing costs. The Trubar Foundation applies for most of its funding from JAK – therefore state funds – but the Foundation does also cite 'other sources' of funding on its website. The Foundation and the work it has supported was the subject of an exhibition at the National University Library in Ljubljana, which stated in its promotional material (Narodna univerzitetna knjižnica, 2011):

> the Trubar Foundation financially supports and encourages foreign publishers with translations of Slovene authors into other languages. With the help of the Trubar Foundation's programme, every year a range of translations of Slovene authors are published by esteemed foreign publishers, therefore the programme is without doubt of exceptional importance for the wider international assertion of Slovene literature. The foundation's activity is led by the Slovene Writers' Association, while the foundation's direction is shaped by three partners: the Slovene Writer's Association, Slovenian PEN and the Centre for Slovene Literature.

The Trubar Foundation therefore seeks to promote itself as a significant actor in the network of cultural institutions that support the translation of Slovene literature into other languages. Its financial support, as the exhibition demonstrated, has resulted in the publication of numerous works of literature in translation. And the organization's title, named after the Protestant priest narrated as being 'the founding father of his language' (Gow and Carmichael, 2000, 63) provides a subtle reminder of the presence of narratives of national identity in the Slovene cultural context.

The Centre for Slovene Literature is another institution with an explicit aim of promoting Slovene literature abroad. The institution grew from foundations cast by a previous fund known as Sklad Vladimirja Bartola (the Vladimir Bartol Fund), named after the Slovene author Vladimir Bartol (1903–67), but evolved into and served its first year as the Centre for Slovene Literature in 1999. The Vladimir Bartol group was 'an informal group that was already working to promote Slovene literature', which as Brane Mozetič, the head of the Centre, explained in a personal interview in Ljubljana in June 2015, later evolved into the Centre when it was decided that the fund required an official account and workspace of its own. The promotional activities of the Centre for Slovene Literature can be divided into three main categories: the publication of works of Slovene literature into foreign languages, including anthologies and books about Slovene literature; the organization and promotion of events, the majority of which take place abroad; and the preparation of literary catalogues in multiple languages, containing abstracts from Slovene novels in translation that have been published domestically that year, which are used as promotional material at book fairs. Here we can see similarities between the Centre and JAK: the Centre for Slovene literature produces an annual publication entitled '10 Books from Slovenia', which provides summaries and sample translations that are chosen by literary critics, and JAK also produces booklets of sample translations, which are the product of its annual translation seminar. There are thus at least two sources separately publishing promotional material and sample translations to promote Slovene literature internationally.

The Centre for Slovene Literature differs structurally from its state-funded counterpart in international promotion, since it has no paid members of staff. It has a single office in a communal building in Ljubljana's Metelkova quarter, which is an artistic space shared by other creative enterprises. Mozetič, the current director, who is not employed by the Centre due to a lack of funds, describes the Centre to me as a 'one-man band', and sees himself as a 'freelancer'. The Centre for Slovene Literature relies on funding from JAK, and the remainder of funds must be secured from external sources. Despite these structural differences, there is visible overlap in the activities of the Centre and JAK, not only in the preparation of material to advertise to foreign publishers, but also in other areas such as the organization of literary exchanges. The number of institutions working in the same field and the subsequent overlap in activities could be read in one of two ways: that the plurality of institutions is evidence of a particularly powerful drive to increase the visibility of Slovene literature beyond the SC, or, by contrast, that the overlap in activities is the result of a crowded cultural sphere where institutions do not interact to coordinate their efforts. The latter view is supported by remarks made by Mozetič in interview, which suggest that the system is perceived as fragmented:

> Initially the Centre for Slovene Literature wanted to be the type of centre that would bring all the promotion together. So that it wouldn't be so fragmented – translators here, publishers there – but the Centre never received (and this was a political decision) that status because those in the Ministry of Culture didn't give it.

Mozetič's remarks recall the documented controversy surrounding the establishment of JAK, and hint at a struggle for control over the promotion of Slovene literature in translation and the reluctance of smaller organizations to relinquish roles that they have long held independently. Given this perceived fragmentation, it could be concluded that the relatively high number of cultural institutions working in the literary translation sphere is not necessarily indicative of a concerted effort to promote Slovene literature, but that it is instead due to a level of competition resulting from the emergence of new governmental organizations that has yet to be reconciled. Yet the four institutions outlined here continue to have active programmes and contribute to the production and promotion of Slovene literature in a variety of ways. The cultural machine, as it were, although fragmented, continues to function. Whether this perceived fragmentation can be proven to have a positive or negative effect upon the amount of Slovene literature in translation that reaches an anglophone audience is a question that requires further research.

Though more data are required before the overall efficacy of the Slovene cultural system can be discussed in any comparative sense, there is still much to be drawn from the testimonies of those who have navigated various routes within the system. Indeed, the function and motivation of the cultural institutions described above cannot be understood entirely without speaking to the individuals who have worked within them. As a response to the shortage of detail concerning the structures that select, fund and promote literary translations in small-nation contexts, the following section of this chapter examines two sets of interview data that provide specific examples of how literary translations from Slovene into English have been selected, funded and published.

An Institutional Route to Translation: Literary Festivals as a Platform for Visibility

The first example draws on data from a conversation with Slavko Pregl (b.1945), the Director of JAK from its inception in 2009 up until 2012, in Ljubljana in June 2015. Pregl is an author in is his own right, particularly known for his children's fiction; he served as President of the DSP from 2007 to 2009, and continues to be an active member today. My questions to Slavko Pregl sought to prompt discussion about his perceptions and expectations of his roles within these cultural institutions, as well as descriptions of how they functioned. He described one of the roles of the DSP as being a mobilizing force for Slovene authors and cited examples such as the organization of school visits, literary events and the international Vilenica literary festival. Pregl spoke about Vilenica with particular pride and described it as 'a big international literary festival [...] which is essentially a Central European literary festival where prizes are awarded, and where a number of distinguished authors from Europe have already received awards'.

His description stressed the size and international status of Vilenica, as well as the prestigious list of authors whom it has hosted. The status bestowed upon Vilenica by Pregl, and the language that is used to describe it in online promotional material, shows that he and the DSP consider the festival a successful platform for gaining international literary exposure.[5] His description of Vilenica as a 'Central European' festival also warrants further attention. This geographical delineation is typical of popular narratives of Slovene identity, which seek to emphasize that Slovenia is a Central European country, with a Central European cultural heritage. Such narratives typically define Slovenia's location in opposition to Eastern Europe, and particularly in opposition to the Balkans.[6] The naming of Vilenica as a specifically Central European literary festival could therefore be read as a subtle attempt to reinforce a narrative of Slovenia as a European nation state with a European cultural heritage.

Pregl then continued to talk about Vilenica specifically in relation to translated literature, and describes an example from a time where he was director at JAK:

> Vilenica is especially important for the translation of our things into foreign languages, and during the time when I was at the Slovene Book Agency we came to an agreement with Dalkey Archive Press from New York. Their editor comes to Vilenica, we prepare a sample of a wider selection of works, which he himself then gets for authors with translators, and he chooses one or two books a year, and they're translated and then published in America.

Dalkey Archive Press has published a series of Slovene novels in English entitled the Slovenian Literature Series, and it could be said that it is the most visible collection of Slovene literature published in translation.[7] The fact that this publishing contract was initiated at Vilenica shows that the DSP has been a particularly successful cultural actor in promoting Slovene literature on an international stage. This particular example also reinforces the hypothesis that, in small-nation contexts, the translation is initiated by the SC, and not

---

[5] Some of Vilenica's promotional material can be seen in English on the festival's website, www.vilenica.si.

[6] For further discussion of pro-European and anti-Balkan discourses in Slovenia, see Patrick Hyder Patterson (2003, 110–41).

[7] The full list of works in this series can be found online at: www.dalkeyarchive.com/product-tag/slovenian-literature-series/ [accessed 30 July 2019].

initially solicited by the TC. The literary festival provides the platform, and the DSP prepares a selection of texts, ready-made for the literary agent.

When asked about the selection process within the DSP and the amount of agency that individuals have when making decisions about works to be translated, Pregl was keen to stress that the DSP always prepares a širši zbor (wider selection) of literary texts: he used this phrase three times in his response. As in the previous example described with Dalkey, publishers or agents from the TC select works from a list curated by the DSP. According to Pregl, it is the editor who makes the final decision, and the selection is based on 'how much they like the text and how they get on with the translator'. It cannot be claimed from Pregl's responses that the DSP as an institution has an agenda as to what kind of literary works it seeks to promote, though Pregl did admit to having an idea about what kind of work typically succeeds on the anglophone market, despite not specifying what this was. This suggests that at present, any attempts to project a Slovene cultural identity occur predominantly in the creation of platforms for visibility, rather than through the content of literary texts.

A Non-institutional Route for Slovene Literature in Translation: One Author's Approach

In contrast with the interview with Pregl, which reveals what we might call an 'institutional' viewpoint, my second interviewee, also speaking in Ljubljana in June 2015, provides an individual author's perspective. Miha Mazzini (b.1961) is one of the most widely translated Slovene authors, with six novels published in English. When asked to describe how the first translation of one of his novels came about, he replied: 'I'm not a good example for your research [...] I funded my first translation myself, as that was my "second opinion"'. Mazzini used the metaphor of a medical 'second opinion' after being rejected by the cultural institutions that typically fund literary translations. Mazzini makes clear in the interview that he does not view the institutions that I have discussed as mechanisms of support, and his critique reveals much about alternative routes to literary translation in a small-nation context, as well as their consequences for his translation strategy.

Mazzini maintains that there are three ways for a novel to be funded for translation in Slovenia. Each of these scenarios, he said, has the same outcome: the readership will be zero. He claims that the way translations are funded promote indifference among publishers; for example, a TC publisher

Contemporary Slovene Literature

receives funding for five novels, paid for with government funding, and they, the publisher, can choose any novel that is presented to them and still receive the same fee. His responses suggested that this funding was in place to promote Slovene literature for the sake of Slovene literature being visible, with little regard for its content. This recalls the argument made by André Lefevere (1996, 146), which was reiterated by Ieva Zauberga (2005, 72), that 'such types of translation[s] of literature are obviously not aimed at influencing the masses, but rather at making the text of a foreign work of literature accessible to scholarly analysis'. This advance purchase of a set number of translations could indeed suggest that the reception of these particular novels in the TC is not a priority. Yet it could also point to an economic necessity and stands as an example of how a small-nation SC must adapt its translation practices to have its cultural voice heard on an international stage.

Mazzini realized that he did not want to follow what we might call the more institutional route for the funding of literary translations and publication of Slovene works in English. Escaping the institutional norms, however, did not mean that he escaped the difficulties that authors in small-nation contexts typically face. One statement made by Mazzini very clearly demonstrates how, as an author from a small nation, he is conscious of the obstacles in place, and shows how he adapts his working practices to counter these restrictions:

> And I noticed something really interesting, and I do this too, in agreement with the translator. When I send manuscripts – before it was written at the top 'novel by [...], translated by [...]' – and I immediately received rejections. Now the publisher doesn't write 'translated by', to ensure it gets read at all.

The words 'and I do this too, in agreement with the translator' reveal that when Mazzini sends his translated manuscripts to UK and US publishing houses, he actively disguises his work as a piece originally written in English. He assumes the role of a writer from the TC to avoid the bias that he has experienced as an author from a small-nation SC. He adheres to UK and US publishing norms to avoid the obstacles that the apparent stigma of translation creates.[8] He has thus achieved his personal goal of publication without having to satisfy the criteria of the Slovene funding institutions, of

---

[8] It could also be said that Miha Mazzini's name contributes to his ability to hide his Slovene origin. His surname is Italian, and the short form of his first name, 'Miha', is less recognizably Slavic in origin that the long form 'Mihail'.

which he is critical. In terms of translation strategy and what this means for the potential projection of Slovene narratives of national identity through his works, Mazzini's responses suggest that reaching an audience takes precedence over any concerns about retaining what we might to consider to be 'Slovene elements' in the text. This pragmatic use of self-translation contrasts with that described by Josianne Mamo using Maltese examples in Chapter Twelve. Ritva Leppihalme (2006, 789) states that 'from the point of view of a small language culture, the choice of translation strategies may be crucial as it is only in translation that its literature can reach the rest of the world'. From Mazzini's answers we can certainly agree that translation was crucial to his works reaching the wider world. Yet his story suggests that, if he wanted to get published at all, the choice of translation strategy was something that in reality did not exist. This necessity to adapt the translation norms of the anglophone TC in order to gain visibility also revealed consequences for the ST:

> If I know that when I finish a novel I'll pay for the translation, and that I'll then (because I'm able to edit in English) [...] I'll once again read the translation really carefully and then correct it [...] it's really great to hold back on publishing the Slovene original because I then correct the Slovene original too.

Mazzini thus takes responsibility for the final proofreading process and has the final decision as to whether the translated novel is sufficiently 'invisible'. He later went as far as to say that he even considers whether phrases within the Slovene source text could be adequately rendered into English, and adapts the source text if necessary. From this we could conclude two things: first, that there is little or no concern with promoting any 'Slovene-specific' elements of the text. If Mazzini, the author, is prepared to alter his ST and SL to facilitate the communication of his work in a TL, then he is prioritizing the TL choices over those of the SL. Second, we could therefore argue that in addition to the first point, Mazzini's priority is gaining readership. His decisions point towards a desire for his books first and foremost to be read, with his status as a 'Slovene author' not featuring in any of his responses. His rejection of the mechanisms that facilitate the majority of Slovene-to-English translations corroborates this: he has little desire to be associated with the cultural institutions that make it their explicit aim to promote Slovene literature and culture.

Conclusion

The interview data presented here raise many issues pertaining to the function of translated literature in small-nation contexts. On the one hand, they confirm many of the assertions made by translation studies scholars who have focused their research on the translation of literature within small nations, such as Zauberga's contention that translations are initiated by the SC, Ritva Leppihalme's view that translation strategy is crucial in order to obtain international visibility, and the assertion of Michael Cronin (2003, 140–41) in *Translation and Globalization*, that the same set of criteria cannot be used to judge translation processes in minority cultures as are used in dominant cultural contexts. As well as supporting observations made by translation studies scholars who have researched small-nation contexts, the data also reaffirm certain ideas expressed within translation studies more broadly. The interviews show, for example, how the route of Slovene literature into English translation can be considered an 'unequal exchange', to adopt Casanova's terminology. With both institutional and non-institutional routes to English translation, the process was initiated in the SC, with neither example documenting any particular effort on the part of the anglophone TC to obtain a work of Slovene literature in translation. Yet on the other hand, the data show how, in the small-nation context of Slovenia, there are additional layers of meaning that must be taken into consideration when understanding how and why Slovene literature comes to be in English translation. At an institutional level, narratives of Slovene national identity continue to be present, as Pregl and the mission statements of organizations like the Trubar Foundation demonstrate. Such narratives reinforce Slovenia's Central European rather than Eastern European or Balkan identity, and are products of Slovenia's specific historical and political circumstances. There are thus specific factors, unique to the Slovene cultural context, that have the potential to shape the production of literary translations, in addition to the structural challenges commonly faced in small-nation contexts. Despite being a small sample of the data that I have collected, these two case studies indicate that the Slovene cultural context can offer some particularly unique insights into the role of cultural institutions in the funding and promotion of translated literature, and furthermore how translations can function as a means of promoting a particular cultural narrative to a wider international audience.

Olivia Hellewell

Bibliography

Baker, Mona (ed.). 2010. *Critical Readings in Translation Studies* (Oxford: Routledge).
Bourdieu, Pierre. 1996. *The Rules of Art*. Trans. Susan Emanuel (Cambridge: Polity Press).
Casanova, Pascale. 2004. *The World Republic of Letters*. Trans. M.B. Debevoise (Cambridge, MA: Harvard University Press).
Casanova, Pascale. 2009. Consecration and Accumulation of Literary Capital: Translation as Unequal Exchange. In Baker, Mona (ed.). *Critical Readings in Translation Studies* (London and New York: Routledge), 285–303.
Casanova, Pascale. 2013. What Is a Dominant Language? Giacomo Leopardi: Theoretician of Linguistic Inequality. *New Literary History*, 44 (3), 379–99.
Center za slovensko književnost. Predstavitev. Available from: www.ljudmila.org/litcenter/ [accessed 16 October 2015].
Cronin, Michael. 1995. Translation and Minority Languages. *TTR: traduction, terminologie, redaction*, 8 (1), 85–103.
Cronin, Michael. 2003. *Translation and Globalization* (London: Routledge).
Društvo slovenskih pisateljev. Zgodovina. Available from: http://drustvo-dsp.si/zgodovina/ [accessed 2 October 2019].
Gow, James and Cathie Carmichael. 2000. *Slovenia and the Slovenes: A Small State and the New Europe* (London: Hurst).
Hyder Patterson, Patrick. 2003. On the Edge of Reason: The Boundaries of Balkanism in Slovenian, Austrian and Italian Discourse. *Slavic Review*, 62 (1), 110–41.
Lawler, Steph. 2014. *Identity: Sociological Perspectives* (Cambridge: Polity Press).
Lefevere, Andre. 1996. Translation and Cannon Formation: Nine Decades of Drama in the United States. In Alvarez, Román and Vidal Carmen Africa (eds). *Translation, Power, Subversion* (Clevedon and Philadelphia, PA: Multilingual Matters), 138–56.
Leppihalme, Ritva. 2006. 'Literary Gifts in Small Packages': A Case of Cultural Image-Making. In Utrera, Sonia Bravo and Rosario Garcia Lopez (eds). *Estudios de Traducción: Problemas y Perspectivas* (Las Palmas de Gran Canaria: Universidad de Canaria), 780–804.
Lermavner, Dušan. 1972. Prvo ali Trstenjakovo 'društvo slovenskih pisateljev'. *Sodobnost*, 20 (11), 1027–42.
Levec, Fran 1885. Društvo slovenskih pisateljev. *Ljubljanski zvon*, 5 (4), 247.
Moe, Marija Zlatnar, Tanja Žigon and Tamara Mikolič Južnič. 2010. *Center in periferija: Razmerja moči v svetu prevajanja* (Ljubljana: Znanstvena založba Filozofske fakultete Univerze v Ljubljani).
MMC RTV Slovenija. 2007. Slovenski pisatelji so se zbrali na protest. Available from: www.rtvslo.si/kultura/knjige/slovenski-pisatelji-so-se-zbrali-na-protestu/152720 October [accessed 26 April 2016].

Narodna univerzitetna knjižnica. 2011. Trubarjev sklad v NUK: slovenska literatura v prevodih. Poster.
Rupel, M. (ed.). 1966. *Slovenski protestantski pisci* (Ljubljana: Državna založba Slovenije).
Stanovnik, Majda. 2005. *Slovenski literarni prevod, 1550–2000* (Ljubljana: Založba ZRC, ZRC SAZU).
Štih, Peter, Vasko Simonitti and Peter Vodopivec, 2008. *Slovenska zgodovina: družba, politika, kultura* (Ljubljana: Inštutut za novejšo zgodovino).
Tymoczko, Maria. 1999. Post-colonial Writing and Literary Translation. In Bassnett, Susan and Harish Trivedi (eds). *Post-colonial Translation: Theory and Practice* (London: Routledge), 19–40.
Tymoczko, Maria and Edwin Gentzler (eds). 2002. *Translation and Power* (Amherst & Boston: University of Massachusetts Press).
Venuti, Lawrence. 1995. Translation and the Formation of Cultural Identities. In Schäffner, Christina and Helen Kelly-Holmes (eds). *Cultural Functions of Translation* (Clevedon: Multilingual Matters), 9–25.
Venuti, Lawrence. 2013. *Translation Changes Everything: Theory and Practice* (Oxford: Routledge).
Zauberga, Ieva. 2005. A Knock at the Door: On the Role of Translated Literature in Cultural Image Making. *Across Languages and Cultures*, 6 (1), 67–77.

Chapter Seven

Strategies for Success? Evaluating the Rise of Catalan Literature

Richard M. Mansell (University of Exeter)

Many literatures, not just those of smaller nations, aim to have works translated into languages of supposed prestige. Commenting on the Prix Formentor initiative from the 1960s, George Weidenfeld (the deceased Lord Weidenfeld) said that 'For an Italian book to become known internationally, it had to pass through the filter of English publishing' and 'Italian publishers were well aware of this fact' (de Glas, 2013, 172). The English-language market is renowned, however, for its resistance to translation, often expressed through the mythical claim that 3 per cent of books published in the UK and US are translations. Venuti (2008, 11) places this figure between 2 and 4 per cent, Nielsen at 3.5 per cent (Booker Prizes, 2016), and Literature across Frontiers' research says that the 3 per cent figure seems true for all books, but translated literature is consistently above 4 per cent (Büchler and Trentacosti, 2015, 5). There is also anecdotal evidence that UK and US publishers are simply not interested in foreign works: '"The English buy nothing except American products. As for Americans, they are only interested in themselves, that's all," says the female literary director of a large [French] house' (Bourdieu, 2008, 151). This, then, is a Catch-22 situation: English-language markets are key to wider international success, but are very difficult to enter. And if this is difficult for better-known foreign literatures, it proves even more so for smaller literatures. In this chapter, I shall analyse how a small European literature (Catalan) might reach an English-language audience, and how many books actually make it through. In this context, I shall discuss what 'small' means in the market for English-language translated literature, and why 'small' does not have to be a synonym for a lack of commercial success.

Strategies for Success? Evaluating the Rise of Catalan Literature

Catalan as a Literature of a Small European Nation

Catalan presents many of the difficulties encountered when trying to classify a language, literature or culture as 'small' or 'minority'.[1] Catalan is a language spoken by some 8.5 million people and understood by 12 million, mostly in the autonomous communities of Catalonia, Valencia and the Balearic Islands in Spain, the area of Southern France known to the Catalans as 'Northern Catalonia', and the city of Alghero in Sardinia.[2] It is also the sole official language of the Pyrenean state of Andorra, so it is technically not a stateless language. One of the languages of the mediaeval Crown of Aragon, Catalan lost out in official contexts to Castilian in the unification of the crowns of Castile and Aragon in the fifteenth century under Ferdinand and Isabella, and was banned from usage in the eighteenth century following the Bourbon victory in the War of Spanish Succession. In the nineteenth century, a Romantic revival of the language accompanied the industrial revolution taking place in Catalonia, and the growth of Catalan institutions and political autonomy continued in the twentieth century. This was interrupted first by the dictatorship of Primo de Rivera (1923–30/1931) and more brutally under the dictatorship of Francisco Franco (1936/1939–75). Some believe this still affects Catalan cultural identity today; in 2006, the Catalan historian Antoni Segura (2006, 16) declared:

> There is a void that can never be filled. And the message of the victors is imposed, even subtly on to the minds and political attitudes of the democrats who have survived the long night of the dictatorship. The process of nation building is smashed and what was normal, unquestionable and reasonable stops being so and beneath the long shadow of the Constitution – the representation of the collective rights of the Spanish, which denies the collective rights of the other Iberian peoples – we arrive at such irrational behaviour as denying the unity of the Catalan language and our common cultural heritage. Rights already won in the

---

[1] There are many who prefer the term 'minoritzada' (a sociolinguistic term that literally translates as 'minoritized'), pointing out that Catalan has more speakers than many European languages that are official in their states and so are official languages of the European Union (Torrents Vivó, 2012). See more on this below in terms of 'comparable' literatures.

[2] For more information, see the section 'Catalan in the 21st century' in Dols Salas and Mansell (2017, 7–10).

past are denied, and claims that were accepted in Republican times are now passed off as anachronistic.

Segura refers to the way historical disruption has led to claims that the Catalan language does not boast the numbers and range outlined above, but is rather smaller and disparate; for example, its official name in Valencia is *valencià*, and in the Balearic Islands there are constant attacks on the unity of the Catalan language.

It has therefore not always been possible for Catalan culture to present a united front outside its borders. In part this task now falls to the Institut Ramon Llull: 'a public body founded with the purpose of promoting Catalan-language studies at universities abroad, the translation of literature and thought written in Catalan, and Catalan cultural production in other areas like theatre, film, circus, dance, music, the visual arts, design and architecture' (Institut Ramon Llull, n.d.). It is currently funded by the Government of Catalonia and Barcelona City Council. The government of the Balearic Islands was part of the group from its creation in 2002 until 2012 (and left for 'economic and political reasons') (NacióDigital, 2015) and following a change of government in the islands in 2015, work began in July 2015 for them to rejoin, with a formal agreement signed in May 2016 (Institut Ramon Llull, 2016).

The role of translation in the development of Catalan literature and culture cannot be underestimated, especially given that in all its territories, it competes with a 'larger' language. On the one hand, translation was used extensively to provide models where these were missing owing to disrupted Catalan history between the sixteenth and nineteenth centuries (never mind the disruption of the twentieth). On the other, it was used to build a cultural identity for Catalan-speaking territories that was distinct from the rest of Spain, and even by regions of Catalan-speaking territories to reinforce differences between themselves and Catalonia, as is the case with Majorca at the beginning of the twentieth century. Translation into Catalan of great works thus came to be seen as a 'sacred duty' for Catalan intellectuals, and translation has always held a special prestige.[3] It also means that Catalan steadfastly refuses to be seen as a 'regional' language or culture; it sees itself as a distinct cultural entity from Spain, France and Italy. Matthew Tree (n.d.) argues that UK publishers have seen Catalan literature as regional, using (often poor) sales figures of Spanish translation

---

[3] For a full discussion of this history, see Mansell (2012).

when considering buying the rights to a book. He states, however, that now Catalan literature 'has never been in a better position to break out of the "regional" cocoon imposed on it by politics and prejudice, so finally giving foreign readers a chance to discover a major national literature which has been one of Europe's best kept secrets for far too long'. For Catalan, translation is a means of direct contact with other nations without having to pass through the filter of the Spanish state, which justifies the institutional measures they put in place.

The Institut Ramon Llull and the Promotion of Catalan Literature in Translation

The Institut Ramon Llull is the publicly funded body responsible for promoting Catalan language and culture abroad, and it strongly feels that translation into English is a key strategy in promoting the language and culture, but that the issue is not straightforward: 'One of the Institut Ramon Llull's missions is to broaden people's knowledge of the work of Catalan writers – from mediaeval classics to contemporary works – by supporting the translation of their works. [...] One of the main challenges faced by European literatures is translation into English' (Bargalló, 2007, 11). To help in achieving this aim, it has a series of grants available for publishers to promote the translation of Catalan works, and since 2012 there has been a particular focus on the English-speaking markets of the United Kingdom and North America. In terms of institutional support for translations, from 2002–14 the Institut Ramon Llull funded the translation of 962 works into 44 languages in 48 countries, through four separate initiatives. First and principally, there are grants to fund the translation of works themselves. These cover the translator's fees, and also the anthologist's fees in the case of poetry anthologies. Eligible applicants are publishers that have already acquired the rights for a work. There is a maximum total award per applicant of €200,000 over three years, and for 2015 €220,000 was earmarked for the awards. Second, there are awards available for the promotion of Catalan works, including events, festivals and promotional campaigns, monographs on Catalan culture, translation of excerpts and production of booklets for distribution abroad. Again, there is a limit of €200,000 over three years. There are grants to pay for residential visits of literary translators to Catalonia. Finally, there are travel grants of up to €2,000 for writers and translators to promote their works.

Richard M. Mansell

Thanks to these apparently generous grants, we might hypothesize a significant increase in the number of translations since 2002. To determine the number of translations published, there are two main databases available, each providing slightly different results. The deficiencies of UNESCO's Index Translationum[4] are well documented: there is a lack of consistency from country to country regarding what constitutes a book (Ginsburgh et al., 2011, 234) and there are no data on total book production (Franssen and Kuipers, 2013, 52). The Institut Ramon Llull also has its own TRAC database available for translations from Catalan,[5] as well as the accompanying TRALICAT database of literary translators from Catalan. The Index Translationum figures only give data for Spain, the US and the UK until and including 2008 (as of June 2016), and TRAC offers full figures up to 2014. The following results have been gained by searching for all translations between 1975 and 2015 on both databases: on the Index I searched for all translations from all versions of Catalan listed into all versions of English, and on TRAC I searched for all literary translations. See Figure 1 for the results if we aggregate the full and raw statistics offered, with Index Translationum represented by the dashed line and TRAC by the dotted line.

There is a significant difference between the two sets of figures in the middle of the last decade, with a huge spike in the Index figures in 2007 (38 entries). A comparison of the entries in both databases for these years show that the Index includes more children's books than TRAC (20 in 2007), and that the same book can appear multiple times, particularly if it is a multilingual version. Also of note is that in the TRAC figures between 1975 and 2007 more than ten books a year are translated and published in English only twice, and yet from 2008 to 2014 the figures dip below ten only once. The TRAC figures for children's literature are fairly easy to strip out, offering the following (with the Index figures included for comparison).

The figures change most significantly between 1996 and 2003. Following the dotted line, a picture emerges of a literature that was steadily growing in terms of English translations until the early 1990s, but then drops, only to begin to rise around 2006–07. Ironically, 2002 – the year when the Institut Ramon Llull was formed – marks the low point, with just a single literary translation published in English, an 899-page translation by David H. Rosenthal of the Civil War epic *Incerta glòria* (*Uncertain Glory*, 1956) by Joan Sales (1912–83).

[4] Available from www.unesco.org/xtrans/ [accessed 31 August 2016].
[5] Available from: https://www.llull.cat/catala/recursos/trac_traduccions.cfm [accessed 31 August 2016].

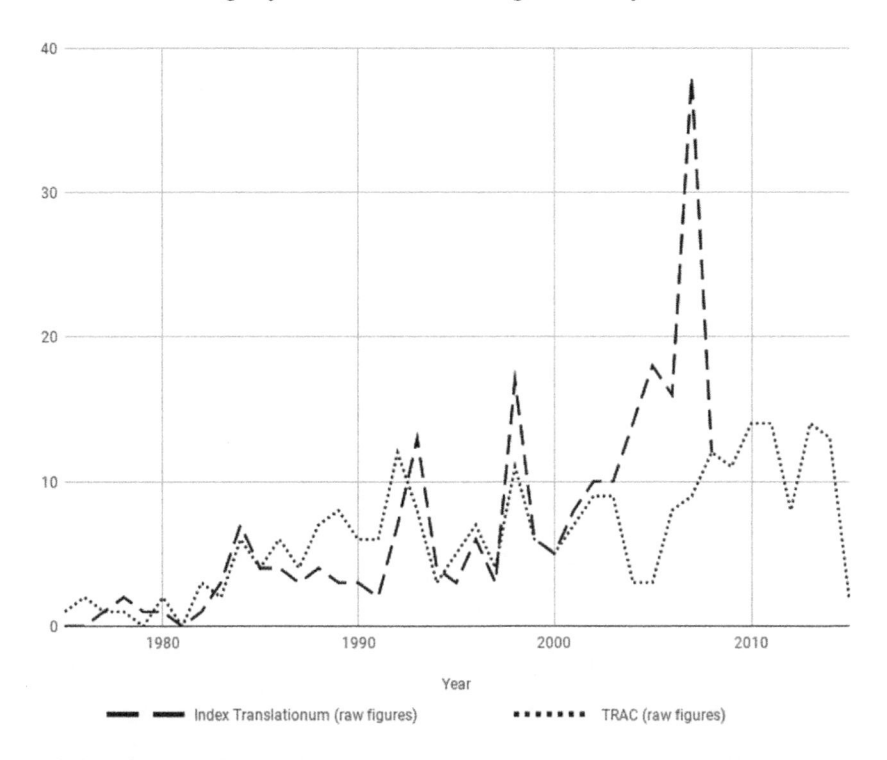

Strategies for Success? Evaluating the Rise of Catalan Literature

Figure 1. Index Translationum (raw figures) and TRAC (raw figures)

The statistics ostensibly indicate that the Institut Ramon Llull's initiatives have increased the number of literary translations from Catalan into English. It would, however, be naive to call this a raging success: the highest annual figure is 14 books (in 2011 and 2013), and it is vital to look at what is being translated (or retranslated), why, and where it is being published, both in terms of geographical location and publisher. Geographical location is important: of the 122 literary translations listed by TRAC between 1975 and 2000, the leading place of publication is in fact Barcelona with 31 texts, followed by New York with 21 and London with 18 (and fourth, Sheffield, thanks to the Anglo-Catalan Society).

These figures suggest that some translations could not find a publisher in English-speaking territories, or that 'agents', in the broadest sense, did not even try. The role of individuals becomes important in understanding the finer nuances of these figures. For example, D. Sam Abrams is the translator of ten volumes published in Barcelona at that time (and one in Terrassa) – all of them books of poetry – but none of his translations was published outside Catalonia. David H. Rosenthal is the translator of 19 different publications

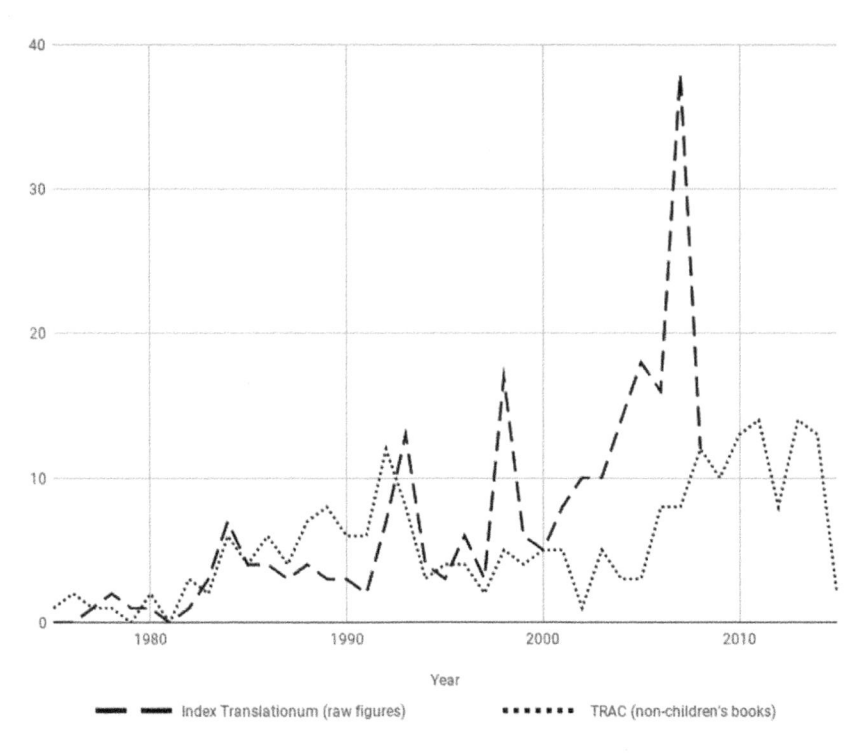

Figure 2. Index Translationum (raw figures) and TRAC (non-children's books)

(from 1980 to 1996), but three are the multiple editions of *The Time of the Doves* (*La plaça del Diamant*, 1962) by Mercè Rodoreda (1908–83), five are multiple editions of the mediaeval novel *Tirant lo Blanc* (1490) by Joanot Martorell (1413–68) and Martí Joan de Galba (?-1490), and four are multiple editions of *Natural History* (*Les històries naturals*, 1960) by Joan Perucho (1920–2003). Some of these are re-editions, some are concurrent editions published in both New York and London by associated presses. Indeed, if we look at the statistics for the translators themselves, we see that there are some translators with a great number of translations, and some with just one or two, but very few in between.

The Work of the Gatekeeper: The Case of Peter Bush

Moving to the figures for both numbers and people in the more recent period, since 2007, one translator, Peter Bush, has translated 16 works of fiction from Catalan into English that have been published in both the UK

Strategies for Success? Evaluating the Rise of Catalan Literature

and the US, dominating the field. An interesting case is his retranslation of *La plaça del Diamant*, a first-person narrative recounting the life of Natàlia, through the Spanish Second Republic, the Civil War and the subsequent dictatorship. Praised as not only one of the best Catalan, but also one of the best European novels of the twentieth century, it is not surprising that it is one of the most translated Catalan works of fiction and has been translated into 35 languages. Only *La pell freda* (*Cold Skin*, 2002) by Albert Sánchez Piñol (b.1965), a science-fiction-thriller-horror-comedy, has been translated into more (37). Bush's translation is in fact the third in English; the first was by an Irish translator, Eda O'Shiel, in 1967, and was translated as *The Pigeon Girl*. The second was called *The Time of the Doves*, and was translated by David H. Rosenthal and first published in 1980 (and again in 1986). There has been much academic criticism of these two previous versions, but Peter Bush – unusually in the context of retranslation – not only distances himself from this criticism, but also criticizes the critics, rather than the previous versions. Indeed, Bush suggests that readers will gain greater analytical insight into the source by reading all the translations than by reading the scholarship. For Bush (2013, 31), while literary translators are first and foremost concerned with finding a publisher, academics are concerned with outdoing each other in finding translation errors and mismatches between the source and target. His claims regarding translation as a valid form of analytical engagement and criticism are pertinent, and no surprise given the material he published in the last decade regarding the position of literary translation in research assessment exercises (with a lower case 'r', 'a' and 'e').[6]

Bush was in fact approached by the publisher Virago to translate *La plaça del Diamant*, and happily it was already on his list of works he wanted to translate. He states that of the works he translates, roughly 40 per cent come from pitching works to publishers, and the other 60 per cent from commissions (Bush, 2013, 37). These figures are important in highlighting the role of individual translators in introducing texts to publishers: with such small figures overall, as discussed below, the Catalan market is heavily

---

[6] The Research Assessment Exercise (RAE) was a method of evaluating the research produced in UK universities, and allocating public funding based on this. Results were published between 1986 and 2008, and after this the RAE was replaced with the Research Excellence Framework. For an excellent discussion of the frequent exclusion of translations from the definition of 'research' within these exercises, see 'Translation as Research: A Manifesto' (Diverse Signatories, 2015) and Nicholas Harrison's accompanying article (Harrison, 2015).

reliant on a few key 'agents'. We can see that Bush has a role as a gatekeeper between Catalan literature and the English market. On Bush's translation, Michael Eaude (2013) writes that he 'has taken enormous pains to capture its world. A translator like this is essential if books from a stateless culture like Catalan are to be ushered successfully on to the stage of world literature [...] The fierce beauty of Rodoreda's writing makes it one of the masterpieces of modern European literature.' As it stands, the authors translated by Bush are a mix of contemporary work and twentieth-century classics: as well as Rodoreda and Sales, we find Najat El Hachmi (b.1979), Kilian Jornet (b.1987), Empar Moliner (b.1966), Quim Monzó (b.1952), Josep Pla (1897–1981), Francesc Serés (b.1972) and Teresa Solana (b.1962). His work has received very positive reviews in the press; his 2014 retranslation of *Uncertain Glory*, for example, received excellent reviews in many papers including *The Guardian* and *The Independent* (with the standard statements that the translation is excellent because it reads well, of course), and was listed by *The Economist* as one of the top ten works of fiction for 2014 (*Economist*, 2014).

Franssen and Kuipers identify acquisition editors as 'the main gatekeepers in the acquisition process and the only ones involved in all stages of the decision-making' (Franssen and Kuipers, 2013, 56). Well-connected translators like Bush are, however, part of the 'gatekeeping networks' they identify, which provide 'provide crucial information and orientation [and are becoming increasingly] central to cultural production in this globalized age' (Franssen and Kuipers, 2013, 71). It is therefore instructive to understand his approach, as articulated to me in personal communication. The positive reviews can partly be attributed to Bush's view that a translation is first and foremost a work of literature in English, and so must work well as such. Bush, moreover, believes that reading is about enjoyment, and is therefore not only unprejudiced about the translation and publication of Catalan genre fiction alongside literary fiction, but in fact argues that the promotion of a range of genres is vital for any literature to succeed. As a gatekeeper in the truest sense, Bush has effectively established himself as one of the few figures with the power to create a canon of Catalan works in English, and returns repeatedly to his own list of works that he hopes to see published, like those he has already translated by Pla, Rodoreda and Sales.

Strategies for Success? Evaluating the Rise of Catalan Literature

Marketing Catalan Literature

One area where more work could be done to improve the low numbers of translations from Catalan is to examine what is done in Catalan-speaking areas to market books, such as literary prizes. Catalan has a 'wealth' of literary prizes; the Institució de les Lletres Catalanes database lists approximately 1,000 literary prizes for fiction and poetry, and many of these offer publication as the prize itself or part of it. It has, however, no prize comparable to the Booker, where a multi-stage process of announcing a longlist, then a shortlist and finally a winner engages the media over a period of time and creates a narrative. Likewise, there is concern that existing prizes are not transparent and are distanced from readers, since the current largest prize (the Sant Jordi prize) is given to an unpublished work:

> [P]ublishers can give all the prizes they like, of course, but we need one with the hallmark of a prestigious institution, like Òmnium, independent of strictly commercial interests, with completely incorruptible juries for works that have been through the filter of readers and critics. This elevates authors, Catalan literature, and publishers together. (Massot, 2016)

That said, similar models do not suggest that this type of prize would do anything to help translation. In her study of the German Book Prize, Sally-Ann Spencer (2013, 204–05) states that although the domestic sales of the winner of the prize are much higher than would be normally expected, it does not lead to a greater number of translations from German, nor does the fact that the book has won the German Book Prize increase sales of the translation. Indeed, in a personal communication, the critic Boyd Tonkin attributed the very high proportion of German longlisted and shortlisted entries in the 2015 Independent Foreign Fiction Prize to the willingness or desire of UK publishers to tie in with the twenty-fifth anniversary of the fall of the Berlin Wall. Catalan does have its own prize for literary translation, the Premi Internacional Ramon Llull, but this is for the best published literary translation from Catalan in the past year; it is publishers who put their books forward, and the prize does not necessarily lead to more translation. As for the perspective of publishers, Alex Gallenzi of Alma Books told me that source-culture prizes help more with identifying works to translate and publish than with marketing them to the target readership.

In comparing the picture for Catalan literature in translation with other literatures, we should look at the comparison first with Spanish, the majority language in Spain with which most Catalan-language publishers have to compete, and second with other European languages. Since 2011, the Spanish Economic and Commercial Office (ICEX) has published reports on books published in the UK from Spain in Basque, Catalan, Galician and Spanish, and Spanish books from the rest of the world. Spanish, which includes books from any country of origin, unsurprisingly has many more books translated into English and published in the UK, with 83 in 2011, 89 in 2012, 93 in 2013 and 84 in 2014. Nevertheless, Catalan, with five, one, eight and six titles in each year respectively, comfortably outperforms Galician and Basque, which total five titles between them in the four-year period (Gómez Muñoz, 2014a, 7; 2014b, 7). It is more enlightening to look at how Catalan compares with other European languages, and here Literature across Frontiers performs excellent research. The top ten European source languages in the UK market by numbers of titles published for the period 2000–12 is led by French (1,217 titles), then German (729), Spanish (481), Russian (432), Italian (383), Swedish (359), Norwegian (190), Dutch (185), Portuguese (121) and Danish (118) (Büchler and Trentacosti, 2015, 15). The remaining European languages go from Polish in eleventh place with 65 titles over the period, down to Sardinian in fortieth with just one (Büchler and Trentacosti, 2015, 16). Catalan is in eighteenth place with 23 titles, an ostensibly enviable position, but qualifications can be made. Danish, Dutch and Norwegian are all languages of similar sizes in terms of number of speakers, yet publish many more translations in the UK than Catalan. Norwegian may be an anomaly; according to Nielsen BookScan, in 2014 Norwegian books were worth £2.29 million in the UK market (second only behind Swedish at £2.95 million), which was entirely attributable to Jo Nesbo and Karl Ove Knausgaard: other books translated from Norwegian failed to make it into the figures, which means that they were either sold in UK bookshops not covered by BookScan, or sold no more than two copies.[7] For Catalan to match Norwegian in terms of revenue, it must find a literary phenomenon like Knausgaard or Nesbo.

The same conclusion can be drawn from Portuguese, a better example for comparison with Catalan, since its European base is on the Iberian Peninsula, the population of Portugal is roughly 10.5 million, and Portuguese is a Romance language. However, in terms of raw numbers of titles published, according to the LAF statistics, translations of books from Portugal outnumber their

---

[7] Nielsen's methodology is to analyse manually the top 100,000 books per year to create a corpus of translations, and then identify them by source language. By the hundred-thousandth position, books only sell two copies annually.

Strategies for Success? Evaluating the Rise of Catalan Literature

Catalan counterparts five to one. This is where some in favour of Catalan independence would claim that Portugal, being a state, can do things that the Catalan-speaking territories cannot. If we look at sales, though, virtually all the value of the Portuguese language market (over £0.5 million) comes from just two authors: the Nobel Prize winner, José Saramago (1922–2010), and the internationally acclaimed Paulo Coelho (b.1947), who, as a Brazilian, would not appear in the LAF figures. Josep Massot (2016) is therefore right when he says that 'For the first time there is a significant number of Catalan authors, both classic and contemporary, translated by commercial publishers in the English-speaking countries, although the works need to connect with readers there'. One route to commercial success for Catalan translations is not to translate more, but to identify one or two authors who can become huge successes, whether through international recognition like the Nobel Prize for Literature (in itself no guarantee of commercial success), or through prevailing trends in the industry and readership (like 'Scandi noir') or apparently fortuitous discoveries like Knausgaard, Elena Ferrante (b.1943), or Jonas Jonasson (b.1961), the author of 2013 and 2014's bestselling translations, *The Hundred Year Old Man who Climbed out of a Window and Disappeared* and *The Girl who Saved the King of Sweden*.[8]

These comparisons reveal a pattern in which a few translations sell in massive numbers, and many sell few copies. Prizes are no guarantee of commercial success: *The Iraqi Christ* by Hasan Blasim (b.1973) won the Independent Foreign Fiction Prize in 2014, but according to Nielsen still recorded fewer than 1,000 copies sold in that year. The only other books translated from Arabic to make the top 100,000 in 2014 are also by Blasim, but his 2009 book *The Madman of Freedom Square*, published by Comma, sold fewer than 100 copies, and his 2014 collection of stories *The Corpse Exhibition*, despite being published with Penguin, sold fewer than 50 copies. Further analysis of the top 100,000 makes disturbing reading for anybody hoping for regular sales of literary translations to rise above 1,000 with any frequency. The market for all literary translations in the UK in 2014 from the top 100,000 grossed nearly £13 million with almost 1.75 million copies sold of over 3,000 individual titles. Only 247 books sold more than 1,000 copies; only 340 more than 500; only 464 more than 250; only 678 sold 100 or more; 911 sold 50 or more; 1,279 sold 25 or more; 2,030 sold 10 or more. That means

---

[8] According to figures from Nielsen, *The Hundred Year Old Man* was the tenth bestselling fiction book of 2013 overall, and *The Girl who Saved the King of Sweden* was nineteenth in 2014.

that out of the top 100,000 fiction titles sold in the UK in 2014, there were 1,194 translations that sold fewer than ten copies. This does not include the approximately 150,000 other titles sold in the UK that year that sold two or fewer copies. The figures for gross value make even starker reading: 50 per cent of the market value for literary translation is taken by the top 27 titles, 75 per cent by the top 114, and 90 per cent by the top 272. A total of 2,952 titles – 91.56 per cent of titles – make up the remaining 10 per cent.[9] We can see that approximately 90 per cent of the market brings in just 10 per cent of the revenue. The space for bestsellers is small, and competition is fierce. Literary translations are fighting against non-translations for media coverage, for presence on the shelves of bookshops, and for readers' money. Finally, translations are fighting against each other, so how can Catalan and the literatures of other smaller European nations compete? Perhaps the answer lies in the phenomenon of the 'long tail'.

Literary Translation and the 'Long Tail' Business Model

The 'long tail' is a term coined by Chris Anderson in an article in *Wired* in 2004 to refer to the change in content creation, distribution and consumption taking place thanks to digital technologies. Over the twentieth century, entertainment was dominated by hits. 'Hits fill theaters, fly off shelves, and keep listeners and viewers from touching their dials and remotes' (Anderson, 2004). Not everybody's tastes are identical, however, and digital technologies allow for quick and easy storage and distribution of content: 'Hit-driven economics is a creation of an age without enough room to carry everything for everybody' (Anderson, 2004). The figures we have seen for literary translation indicate, however, that there are few hits, although there are many books that sell at least one copy.

Selling books in very small numbers is not a business model: rather, the long-tail business model comprises two parts: '[m]ake everything available' and '[h]elp me find it' (Anderson, 2009, 217). As Anderson (2009, 217) notes, '[t]he first is easier said than done'. He uses the example of the Sundance Film Festival, where '[f]ewer than a dozen of the 6,000 films [...] are picked up for distribution', and the vast majority of the rest cannot be shown outside

---

[9] It is a similar situation if we look at the entire top 100,000. The top 10,012 titles (10.01 per cent) bring in 90 per cent of revenue – a slightly larger proportion, but not vastly different.

of the festival because 'their music rights have not been cleared' (Anderson, 2009, 217). In literary translation, think of the cost of purchasing the rights to the translation, and how this hampers the publication of translations in the risk-averse environment of UK publishing where the overall cost of translations is stated as the greatest barrier to publishing works in translation (Dalkey Archive Press, 2011, 35). So, a top-to-bottom revision of translation rights may help the number of literary translations to grow in the UK, simply because if the initial cost of the work is lower, publishers may be more inclined to commission a translation (especially when many funding bodies pay the costs of translation, but not the costs of acquiring rights). This gives renewed support to Venuti's call (2008, 275–76) to open up rights solely for the purposes of translation:

> In the long run, it will be necessary to effect a more fundamental change, a revision of current copyright law that restricts the foreign author's control over the translation so as to acknowledge its relative autonomy from the foreign text. The foreign author's translation rights should be limited to a short period, after which the foreign text enters the public domain, although only for the purposes of translation.

Venuti approaches the problem of rights from the perspective of respecting the translator's position as author of the translation, yet this change could also benefit the overall literary translation industry, and increase its activity. This approach, however, challenges the basis of currently held concepts of authorship and ownership of works, and counteracts specific paragraphs of the Translator's Charter. It also requires either a rewriting of Article 8 of the Berne Convention for the Protection of Literary and Artistic Works (Paris 1971), which protects authors' rights to authorize translations of their work, or a redefinition of the minimum term of protection, which following article 7.1 is a minimum of the author's life plus 50 years, extended to the author's life plus 70 years under UK law (Copyright, Designs and Patents Act 1988, section 12).

There are, however, powerful arguments to persuade the source author and publisher to consider this approach, and the example can be found in music. In *The Long Tail*, Anderson (2009, 180) uses the example of house music as a long-tail phenomenon: DJs looked for records that had not made it as hits, or that had journeyed down the long tail. At the same time, producers rely on open-access strategies, allowing and encouraging work to be remixed, and Anderson (2009, 180) believes that this helps the value of the original product:

A house record that does well often attracts remixes from other producers; it becomes a kind of platform. Because these remixes are usually hyperspecialized for different microgenres, they're complements to the original track. As the number of complements increases, the value of the platform track snowballs. This snowball effect is another mechanism by which DJs-as-aggregators can efficiently navigate the Long Tail of music, quickly and easily discovering which tracks are snowballs within their respective niches.

What if we reconsider rights across the board, not just the translator's rights, but rights along the entire chain of production and distribution? Translations act as 'complements' to the source, creating their own value and adding value to the source, too. This approach ostensibly corresponds to Casanova's Bourdieusian concept of translation and literary circulation as the consecration of cultural capital, but using economic models and examples of where the Long Tail has succeeded in becoming financially viable.

The question of how Catalan literature can succeed in English is thus also the question of how other 'smaller' literatures – and translated literature itself – can succeed in English. English is often referred to as the dominant source language in global translation flows while having a very low proportion of published books as translations (Sapiro, 2016, 87), and in their study of the Dutch market, Franssen and Kuipers (2013, 67) even refer to translation from any other language than English as a 'niche market'. English is also the dominant language of communication in the global literary industry (Bourdieu, 2008, 150), all of which places English at the centre of global literary movement, with the consequence that from the point of view of English, all other literatures are peripheral, especially if we follow the sociological and Bourdieusian line of thought in which 'translation flows move from the core to the periphery' (Sapiro, 2008, 158). The problem of defining what 'small' means is therefore a problem for all translated literature in English.

The key here is the notion of niches. If we conceive of a single literary translation market, then we are falling into the same mindset where hits are the basis of a business model, and nothing else counts. As mentioned above, in that mindset, the main route to 'success' for Catalan literature and other smaller literatures is to find their Jonasson, Nesbo or Ferrante. However, as demonstrated by the figures above, such cases are a tiny minority in the number of works translated. There is no single reason why people read Catalan literature in translation, or literary translation in general. Out of those people who read a particular Catalan work in translation, some will go

Strategies for Success? Evaluating the Rise of Catalan Literature

on to read other Catalan works, some others will read literature from other smaller literatures, or politically similar areas, some will read works from similar genres, and some will go on to read works that are not translations at all. The greater the activity in each of these niches, however, and the greater the comment around it, the greater the chance that people will be directed down the long tail to get to it. Everyone has interests outside of hits (Anderson, 2009, 182), but they do not necessarily know where those interests can be met. Each niche needs to establish its own identity, and it can only do this through a following. A good example, discussed by Jakob Stougaard-Nielsen in Chapter Ten, is translated Scandinavian literature, Scandi noir (books and TV) and crime fiction, which all overlap, but are different niches for different but intertwining sets of people, depending on their tastes. This is the parallel culture that the long tail as a business model can exploit. To use an analogy, when Anderson (2009, 183) talked to friends and colleagues about internet memes that he thought were common knowledge, he in fact 'found that only about 10 percent of the audience had heard of any of them – and for each phrase it was a different 10 percent'.

If the right distribution channels can be matched to a strategy to direct people along the long tail, analogous situations suggest that the gross market for translated literature will grow. Referring to the times when Netflix lent physical DVDs and video rental shops existed, Anderson (2009, 218) states that Netflix customers on average rented three times more DVDs than 'bricks-and-mortar faithful'. The long tail is therefore a way not only of getting people to read more translated fiction, but, moreover, also to read more in general. In terms of marketing, this means that the traditional media are not the be-all-and-end-all. Indeed, personal communication with one marketing manager at a small independent press highlighted how publishers lament the ever-contracting space available in the traditional media for reviewing books, not just translation, and admit that translated literature is getting squeezed out. Instead, blogs and other social media come into play, which are essentially a form of massification of word-of-mouth. With this, though, is a loss of control over a marketing message; indeed, Anderson's rules six to nine of long tail marketing are entitled 'lose control' (Anderson, 2009, 221). This loss of control for publishers, however, would empower other figures across the chain of creation and distribution, from source authors right along to readers themselves. If we can engage with readers directly through blogs and social media a strong bond can be created, and such a reader will be 'a lasting evangelist' (Anderson, 2009, 231).

Richard M. Mansell

Conclusion

The Institut Ramon Llull is optimistic: there is the feeling that things are on the up, since English is the second highest target language by number of translations from Catalan (the first is Spanish), and that quality works are being translated by quality publishers. However, if this all forms part of a long tail selling only a few copies each year, then either the wrong books are being chosen for the UK market, or more needs to be done to direct people along the long tail so they buy and read these translations. Key for this is the translator; not only in creating high-quality translations, but also in taking part in the promotion of works to UK publishers, and promoting the translations once they are published. The figures above demonstrate that the work of single translators as champions for Catalan or indeed any other culture must not be underestimated. In the absence of the source author, a visible and respected translator can be the activist for a work, and be part of a long-tail marketing strategy, raising the profile of the work, of translation as a whole, and even, with the translation working as a complement to the source text, raise the profile of the source work at home too.

Bibliography

Anderson, Chris. 2004. The Long Tail. Available from: www.wired.com/2004/10/tail/ [accessed 31 August 2016].

Anderson, Chris. 2009. *The Longer Long Tail: How Endless Choice Is Creating Unlimited Demand* (London: Random House Business).

Bargalló, Josep. 2007. Participating in the Translation Debate. In Allen, Esther (ed.). *To Be Translated or Not To Be* (Barcelona: Institut Ramon Llull), 11.

Bourdieu, Pierre. 2008. A Conservative Revolution in Publishing. *Translation Studies*, 1 (2), 123–53.

Büchler, Alexandra and Giulia Trentacosti. 2015. Publishing Translated Literature in the United Kingdom and Ireland 1990–2012: Statistical Report. Available from: https://www.lit-across-frontiers.org/wp-content/uploads/2013/03/Translation-Statistics-Study_Update_May2015.pdf [accessed 18 January 2018].

Bush, Peter. 2013. Memory, War and Translation: Mercè Rodoreda's *In Diamond Square*. In Nelson, Brian and Brigid Maher (eds). *Perspectives on Literature and Translation: Creation, Circulation, Reception* (Abingdon and New York: Routledge), 31–46.

Dalkey Archive Press. 2011. Research into Barriers to Translation and Best Practices: A Study for the Global Translation Initiative. Available from: www.dalkeyarchive.com/wp-content/uploads/pdf/Global_Translation_ Initiative_Study.pdf> [accessed 31 August 2016].

De Glas, Frank. 2013. The Literary Prize as an Instrument in the Material and Symbolic Production of Literature: The Case of the 'Prix Formentor', 1961–1965. *Quaerendo,* 43 (2), 147–77.

Diverse Signatories. 2015. Translation as Research: A Manifesto. *Modern Languages Open,* 0 (0), 1–4.

Dols Salas, Nicolau, and Richard Mansell. 2017. *Catalan: An Essential Grammar* (Abingdon and New York: Routledge).

Eaude, Michael. 2013. The Monday Book. *The Independent,* 6 May, 46.

Economist, The. 2014. Page Turners. *The Economist.* Available from: www.economist.com/news/books-and-arts/21635446-best-books-2014-were-about-south-china-sea-fall-berlin-wall-kaiser> [accessed 31 August 2016].

Franssen, Thomas and Giselinde Kuipers. 2013. Coping with Uncertainty, Abundance and Strife: Decision-Making Processes of Dutch Acquisition Editors in the Global Market for Translations. *Poetics,* 41 (1), 48–74.

Ginsburgh, Victor, Shlomo Weber and Sheila Weyer. 2011. The Economics of Literary Translation: Some Theory and Evidence. *Poetics,* 39 (3), 228–46.

Gómez Muñoz, Beatriz. 2014a. *Informe Estadístico. Traducciones Literarias España-Reino Unido 2013* (London: Instituto Español de Comercio Exterior).

Gómez Muñoz, Beatriz. 2014b. *Informe Estadístico. Traducciones Literarias España-Reino Unido 2014* (London: Instituto Español de Comercio Exterior).

Harrison, Nicholas. 2015. 'Notes on Translation as Research', *Modern Languages Open,* 0 (0), 1–16. Available from: http://dx.doi.org/10.3828/mlo.v0i0.78 [accessed 9 May 2016].

Institut Ramon Llull. About Us. n.d. Available from: www.llull.cat/english/quisom/quisom.cfm [accessed 31 August 2016].

Institut Ramon Llull. 2016. President Puigdemont: 'Solemnitzem Amb Emoció La Reincorporació de Les Illes Balears a l'Institut Ramon Llull' – Notes Premsa. Available from: www.llull.cat/catala/actualitat/notes_premsa_detall.cfm?id=33402&url=president-puigdemont-solemnitzem-amb-emocio-reincorporacio-de-illes-balears-a-l_institut-ramon-llull.html [accessed 31 August 2016].

Mansell, Richard. 2012. Rebuilding a Culture, or Raising the Defences? Majorca and Translation in the Interwar Period. *Journal of Catalan Studies,* 15, 110–27.

Massot, Josep. 2016. El Sistema Editorial Catalán Se Mueve. *La Vanguardia.* Available from: www.lavanguardia.com/cultura/20160305/40205282199/sistema-editorial-catalan-se-mueve.html [accessed 10 March 2016].

NacióDigital. 2015. Les Illes Balears Tornen a l'Institut Ramon Llull Amb El Canvi de Govern. Available from: www.naciodigital.cat/noticia/90770/illes/balears/tornen/institut/ramon/llull/amb/canvi/govern [accessed 31 August 2016].

Sapiro, Gisèle. 2008. Translation and the Field of Publishing. *Translation Studies*, 1 (2), 154–66.

Sapiro, Gisèle. 2016. How Do Literary Works Cross Borders (or Not)? A Sociological Approach to World Literature. *Journal of World Literature*, 1 (1), 81–96.

Segura, Antoni. 2006. *Catalunya Year Zero*, trans. Richard Mansell (Birmingham: Anglo-Catalan Society).

Spencer, Sally-Ann. 2013. Prizing Translation: Book Awards and Literary Translation. In Nelson, Brian and Brigid Maher (eds). *Perspectives on Literature and Translation: Creation, Circulation, Reception* (Abingdon and New York: Routledge), 195–209.

Torrents Vivó, Eloi. 2012. El Català És Una Llengua Minoritària? *El Català Suma*. Available from: http://blogspersonals.ara.cat/elcatalasuma/2012/02/29/el-catala-es-una-llengua-minoritaria [accessed 31 August 2016].

Tree, Matthew. n.d. Waiting for the Breakthrough. *Transcript*, 3. Available from: www.transcript-review.org/en/issue/transcript-3-catalonia/contemporary-catalan-writing> [accessed 1 March 2016].

Venuti, Lawrence. 2008. *The Translator's Invisibility: A History of Translation*, 2nd edn (Abingdon, New York: Routledge).

Chapter Eight

Gender, Genre and Nation: Nineteenth-century Swedish Women Writers on Export

Gunilla Hermansson and Yvonne Leffler
(University of Gothenburg)

Today, as Jakob Stougaard-Nielsen discusses in Chapter Ten of this volume, Swedish literature is more widely translated and circulated than most literatures written in small languages. Swedish is only spoken by about ten million people and ranks as the ninetieth most spoken language worldwide. As an exporter of literature, however, Sweden has figured in the top 20 since the 1970s. Although literary imports exceed exports, Swedish is therefore currently more prominent as a literary language than might be expected (Svedjedal, 2012, 24–38). This chapter focuses on important, yet hitherto neglected parts of this story, which can and should be viewed in a much longer perspective. There are no reliable statistics before the mid-twentieth century, but research within the project *Swedish Women Writers on Export in the Nineteenth Century* has been able to show that Sweden had established its position as a literary European nation in the nineteenth century first and foremost through the international success of women novelists.[1]

In the early nineteenth century, Swedish literature, like many other small literatures, was 'discovered' for the first time by a wider, international audience. The present chapter examines this process by highlighting two contrasting cases of female authorship: the Romantic poet, Julia Nyberg (1785–1854) and the international bestselling novelist, Emilie Flygare-Carlén (1807–92). As their examples reveal, the opportunities for the translation and reception of smaller literatures changed in Europe and America during

---

[1] The chapter is based on a research project at the University of Gothenburg, on the transcultural transmission and reception of Swedish literature during the nineteenth century, financed by the Swedish Research Council: see Leffler et al., 2019.

the century. This was due not only to developments in book markets and readerships and fluctuations in the political climate, but also to shifting expectations and publication patterns relating to different combinations of genre, nationality and gender. The modest international reception of Nyberg's work was shaped by a complex exchange between domestic and international images of gender and nationality. It was fuelled by a desire for knowledge – even superficial knowledge – of other literatures and cultures, and functioned as part of different individual, regional and national identity projects. By contrast, Flygare-Carlén became a thoroughly international writer, whose novels in the mid-nineteenth century served as identification objects, entertainment and cultural commodities for large groups of readers. Ultimately, however, the strong gendering of the reception proved double-edged for both, creating opportunities as well as limitations.

The transnational translation and reception of works by women writers in Europe is a growing field of research, but so far most publications on nineteenth-century material have focused only on individual writers and mediators, bilateral examples, or on the impact of canonized writers from major literatures.[2] Until a broader and more refined picture has been established, comparisons and generalizations will be difficult to sustain. The Swedish example offers a combination of patterns shared by other small literatures during this period, and aspects that are specific to Swedish literature, particularly the attraction of exciting images of Europe's North. Contradicting assumptions on the patterns of cultural import and export made by Pascale Casanova and Franco Moretti, we will show how historical circumstances created different opportunities to disturb the balance between small and major – or dominated and dominating

---

[2] See publications by members of the COST action ISO910, *Women Writers in History: Toward a New Understanding of European Literary Culture*: see www.womenwriters.nl/index.php/Project_publications, the connected database project; *NEWW Women Writers*, see http://resources.huygens.knaw.nl/womenwriters [both accessed 31 July 2019]; and publications by the scholars in the series Studies on Cultural Transfer & Transmission (Petra Broomanns, ed. 2009 to date, Groningen. Barkhuis), which focus on cultural transmitters and mediators in Scandinavia and Netherlands. See also the series *The Reception of British and Irish Authors in Europe* (edited by Elinor Shaffer, 2002 to date), which at present includes Jane Austen (2007) and George Eliot (2016). Publications from the HERA project *Travelling TexTs 1790–1914: The Transnational Reception of Women's Writing at the Fringes of Europe* most certainly prove fruitful for more informed comparisons between different small literatures.

– literatures, and uncover the complex relationship between translation and other kinds of reception.

The Female Poet: National and International Assessments

In Sweden, Nyberg was considered *the* female poet, with a genuine talent, within the new Romantic school known as the Phosphorists. She published lyric poetry as well as verse dramas under the pseudonym Euphrosyne from 1816 towards the middle of the century, mostly in calendars but also as separate collections. Several of her poems were set to music and disseminated through songbooks. The reception in the Swedish press and literary circles was very appreciative, apart from the most conservative critics, who argued that women should not publish at all. No other contemporary female poet challenged her in terms of publication or domestic reception.

Like many of her counterparts in other European countries, Nyberg's male mentors were extremely important for her passage into the national public sphere. They helped and promoted her in several ways, but seldom valued her work unconditionally (Söderlund, 2000, 227–31). The longest review of Nyberg's first collection was actually written by P.D.A. Atterbom (1790–1855), the leader of the Phosphorist movement and Nyberg's first mentor. His assessment was an interesting mixture, simultaneously reproducing and undermining gender stereotypes (Borgström, 1991, 155–62; Holmquist, 2000, 82–85).[3]

The inconsistencies in Atterbom's review seem to reflect a sense of being at a crossroads both in terms of women's authorship and of the dynamics between cultural centres and the peripheries. Atterbom took the opportunity to develop some important aspects of his aesthetics and reflect on them in terms of gender. The world of Ossian, for example, was beyond a woman's grasp, including Nyberg's: how could a woman understand and master a godless universe? Atterbom (1870, 27) could think of only one possible exception to the rule: Madame Staël-Holstein (1766–1817). If any woman could succeed in translating Ossian, it would be her (1870, 27). When commenting on one of Nyberg's female predecessors, Anna Maria

---

[3] The ambivalences and discrepancies between theory and practice among Nyberg's male mentors/critics are similar to, albeit not quite as outspokenly paradoxical as what Helen Fronius has found in the German Goethe era (2007, 67–68). See also Behrendt, 2009, 23.

Gunilla Hermansson and Yvonne Leffler

Lenngren (1754–1817), Atterbom (1870, 3) reminded his readers that it would be almost ridiculous to compare the Swedish poetess with the French Sophie Cottin (1770–1807) and de Staël, or with the German Amalia von Helwig (1776–1831) and Dorothea Schlegel (1764–1839). He did not elaborate on these statements. Rather, this passage reveals an anxiety, a peripheral consciousness, which is projected onto female poets at the same time as it recognizes a growing female presence and importance on both the national and the international literary scene.

What, then, were Nyberg's chances of reaching a wider, international audience? Only one of her works was ever translated and published as a separate title, the dramatized legend *Christophorus*, which was included as recently as 1905 in a series of cheap editions (*Otavan Helppohintainen Kirjasto*) issued by a major Finnish publishing house. This is hardly surprising. Most translated European poetry during this period was published in anthologies and periodicals or scattered with original poems in collections by one poet-translator, not in full volumes dedicated to the translation of one author. At present, such contributions are much harder to map in a systematic way, compared to novels, but the importance of anthologies and periodicals should not be underestimated (see Essmann and Frank, 1991; Essmann, 1996, xii; France and Haynes, 2006, 138 and 143).

From existing bibliographies and searchable full-text databases, it has been possible to establish that at least six of Nyberg's poems were published in German, English and Icelandic translation before 1914. The translators were mostly male. Five of the poems appeared in different German anthologies of Swedish or Scandinavian poetry, including two stanzas of one song (later known as 'Vårvindar friska', 'Fresh Spring Breezes'), which was written to a traditional tune and translated anonymously as a 'Volkslied' in 1895 (Halbe et al., 1987–88). The same song (two and one stanza, respectively) was also translated and included in an Icelandic children's songbook, *Skólasöngvar* (Reykjavík, 1906–11) and in *Songs of Sweden: Eighty-Seven Swedish Folk- and Popular Songs* (New York, 1909). Two different poems were published in works that combined literary history and translations of Scandinavian literature in England (Howitt, 1852) and the Netherlands (Hansen, 1860). Some lines from another poem, which Flygare-Carlén used as mottos for two chapters in her novel *Gustav Lindorm* (1839), were translated with the novel and in this way thrived on the export successes of her younger colleague. The scale is not impressive, but it allows us to conclude that translation was typically motivated by a wider interest in Scandinavian or Swedish literature from 1840 onwards.

Nyberg's place in the Swedish canon was created in a dynamic between domestic assessments and expectations of Swedish poetry formed in the receiving countries. The Swedish Romantics oriented themselves towards German Romanticism, and Germany was also the natural starting point for promoting Swedish literature abroad. In 1821, publisher, writer and critic V.F. Palmblad approached F.A. Brockhaus by letter, presenting a range of ideas for introducing Swedish literature to German readers, including a periodical devoted entirely to Swedish and Danish literature. Brockhaus cunningly steered away from most of Palmblad's suggestions and instead used his new contact as an agent to export his own articles to the Swedish market (Berg, 1924).

Less than a decade later, however, Germany saw the first boom in Swedish literature. The prime motor for this development was *Frithiofs Saga* (1825) by Esaias Tegnér (1782–1846), an Icelandic saga transformed into a modern romance cycle. Tegnér elaborated on the notion of the strong, simple and brave Viking dedicated to masculine virtues, and combined it with Ossianic moods and Biedermeier values, including traditional gender norms. In contrast, Nyberg seldom chose historical subjects, and when she did, she often highlighted female agency. In Tegnér's own lifetime more than 20 editions of *Frithiofs Saga* were published in Germany, and by 1914 it had been translated to at least 14 languages. Across Europe and America it inspired other poems, novels, plays, operas, paintings and songs, as well as tourism in Norway, the land of the hero. The production of translations, retellings and adaptations continued throughout the century (Lundkvist, 1996; Wawn, 2000, 117–41).[4]

Unlike the novel, epic poetry was largely expected to be national, or rather to confirm certain images of the Swedish national character. In 1826 in France, Marianne von Ehrenström (1826, 96) saluted Tegnér as the Swedish Ossian, and proclaimed *Frithiofs Saga* to be 'à l'ordre du jour' (Mohnike,

---

[4] W.H. Saunders included poems by J.H. Kellgren, E.G. Geijer and Tegnér in *Poetical Translations from the Swedish Language* (Stockholm, 1828), and some poems by Tegnér appeared in J.E.D. Bethune's *Specimens of Swedish and German Poetry* (1848). Poems by these and Atterbom, E.J. Stagnelius, Bernhard von Beskow and Vitalis (Erik Sjöberg) had also been translated and commented upon in the *Foreign Review* and *Blackwood's Edinburgh Magazine* in the late 1820s. Data according to Swan, 1913; Afzelius, 1938; Bjork, 2005; and searches through library catalogues, WorldCat, Google Books, HathiTrust and the bibliographic database *Index C19*. See also Petersens, 1933.

2008, 174–75). Success in Germany reflected how readers projected onto Sweden a nostalgic longing for a vigorous and unspoiled culture (Rühling, 1996, 107–08). In 1852, Mary and William Howitt (1852, 1, 5; 1852, 2, 374) attributed the greatness of the British Empire to a healthy infusion of Viking blood, and they even found *Frithiofs Saga* somewhat tempered by Tegnér's mild spirit and sense of classicism. In effect, Tegnér succeeded in meeting many of the foreign expectations of Swedishness, where Nyberg – and quite a few of her male colleagues – failed.

Nyberg did not, however, go unacknowledged by readers. Indeed, Amalia von Helvig, known to be an important cultural mediator of Swedish romanticism in Germany, planned to translate Nyberg together with other Swedish poets in the early 1820s (letters to Lorenzo Hammarsköld, 3 January and 23 March 1824; Helvig, 1915, 133; 1950, 427). The project was, however, never finished, and von Helvig prioritized poets from what was known as the Swedish Gothic (Götiska) school, which boosted national identity by exploring the Norse heritage. Apart from her translation of *Frithiofs Saga*, she published translations of and introductions to Tegnér, Atterbom and K.A. Nicander (1799–1839) in *Morgenblatt für gebildete Stände* between 1822 and 1828. Nicander had also created new poems inspired by Norse traditions, which confirmed male stereotypes and notions of simple, honest, tough Viking life. A similar tendency is observable in one of the later German anthologies of Swedish poetry. According to an advertisement in 1860, poems by Euphrosyne were supposed to be included in one of the volumes of the *Hausschatz der Schwedischen Poesie* (1860). However, only Volume Three, with poems by Tegnér, Nicander and others was published, despite the fact that the prospectus presented the second, never finished, volume, containing Euphrosyne, E.J. Stagnelius (1793–1823) and the Phosphorists as the most interesting. It seems that poems from the Gothic school were easier – or safer – items to launch first.

Women Writers and Their Ghost-like Reception

Though virtually invisible internationally in terms of numbers of translations, Nyberg regularly features through short comments and references in surveys of Swedish literature, which appeared in magazine articles, travelogues, literary histories, records of famous women and encyclopaedias. Many of these reception genres – as we know – tend to be produced using translation, recycling and outright plagiarism (Collison, 1966, 175; Bödeker and Rohde-Gaur, 1996, 56). Nyberg's male mentors seem to have been no less influential when it comes to this 'superficial' or secondary dissemination of her work. They mentioned her with enthusiasm in letters to colleagues abroad and in introductions written for German periodicals and encyclopaedias. Whereas Brockhaus was reluctant to publish Swedish books in translation, he gratefully accepted another of Palmblad's ideas in the early 1820s. Until the late 1840s, Brockhaus commissioned Palmblad to write articles on Swedish authors and thinkers or to distribute the task to members of his network. The articles were published in the periodicals *Hermes* and *Blätter für literarische Unterhaltung*, as well as in the different editions of the *Conversations-Lexikon* (Berg 1924, 42–44). Translated and distributed all over Europe and in America, they repeatedly asserted that Nyberg had surpassed all her contemporary Swedish sisters in poetry (including Lenngren), and that her poems were full of intimate tenderness, which flowed from a pure and sensitive heart.

An article on Swedish literature in Brockhaus's *Neue Folge des Konversations-Lexicons* (1826) was especially influential and was recycled for decades, even after Nyberg's name was omitted again from the eighth edition of Brockhaus (1833–37). Other short and adapted versions also flourished in British periodicals and encyclopaedias, where she would be labelled 'The L.E.L. or the Mrs Hemans of the North'. After the publication of the Swedish biographical lexicon (*Biografiskt lexicon*, 1835–57), Nyberg even got her own brief entry in other German, French, Slovenian and British encyclopaedias.

These instances of superficial reception confirm the sketchy picture created by the few translations of Nyberg's poems. Where the intention was to cover the Romantic school as part of recent Swedish literary history, Nyberg would be included, if not highlighted, and then often with the double position as a Phosphorist and a female writer. Foreign assessments mirrored the domestic, and continued to be informed by them. The Howitts' characterization of Nyberg in 1852 explicitly relied on a history of Swedish literature by the critic O.P. Sturzenbecher from 1845, which was translated into German in 1850 and which confirmed her position as 'eine phosphoristische Notabilität' (Sturzenbecher 1850, 57).

We may reach a better understanding of this kind of canon formation and the purpose of such references by examining two puzzling articles in the American and British press from the 1840s. Unlikely as it would seem, Nyberg was mentioned *en passant* in 1842 in Edgar Allan Poe's review of Henry Wadsworth Longfellow's *Ballads and Other Poems*. He listed her as one representative of 'a bolder, more natural and ideal composition' among two French writers (Coëtlogon, Lamartine), three German (Herder, Körner, Uhland), two Danish (Brun, Baggesen), two Swedish (Bellman, Tegnér), four British (Keats, Shelley, Coleridge, Tennyson), and two American (Lowell, Longfellow) (Poe, 1842). A footnote explained that Nyberg was the author of 'Dikter *von* Euphrosyne' (our emphasis).

According to Adolph B. Benson (1952, 241), Poe probably did not read Swedish, and in 1842 (as it seems), only one of Nyberg's poems had been translated into German. Why should he mention her at all? Could it be that the attraction lay in the very combination of gender and nationality? In the list above, Poe covers the major literatures plus two small ones (Danish and Swedish), and along with 14 male poets includes two females (Nyberg and the German-Danish author Friederike Brun, 1765–1835). According to Leland S. Person (2001, 132–33), Poe often promoted and reviewed women writers in a manner that anticipated both the growing patriarchal views, marginalizing criticism, and much later the gynocentric views. In the case of Nyberg, the name-dropping must primarily be read as part of an attitude and a staging of himself as a well-informed and modern 'gentleman' critic, rather than a product of critical reading and appreciation.

In 1849, Nyberg was characterized more thoroughly in an article on 'Fredrika Bremer and her compeers' in *Chambers's Edinburgh Journal*, one of the most popular periodicals in Britain in the 1840s. It opened with this statement:

> Fredrika Bremer has had the good fortune not only to win popularity and esteem for herself, but also to create a general interest in behalf of the literature of her native country, so that translated copies of Swedish poets and historians now obtain a place on the shelves of our public as well as our private libraries and are inquired for with avidity by the ordinary class of intelligent readers. (Anon., 1849, 76)

If 'poets' includes novelists, then this is plausible enough; otherwise the overstatement is obvious. In 1849, volumes of Swedish poetry in English translation extended to a handful of separate translations of Tegnér's *Frithiofs Saga* and two of his romance *Axel* from 1822. Two collections of Swedish (and German) poetry from 1828 and 1848 included poems by J.H. Kellgren, E.G. Geijer and Tegnér.[5] In other words, if there were a copy of Swedish poetry in the libraries of the 'intelligent' readers in 1849, it would reflect the

---

[5] Translations data will be made available online in the project database SWED in 2019.

much earlier Tegnér craze. Perhaps, however, what was actually there is less important than the very idea of having Swedish poetry on the shelf. Was being a cultivated reader somehow linked to knowledge of peripheral or small literatures?

What *can* be established is that the article in *Chambers's* is not evidence of reading, at least not evidence of reading any of the female writers mentioned: Nyberg, Bremer, Sophie von Knorring (1797–1848) or Flygare-Carlén. This part of the article in fact consists of translated extracts from an 1845 introduction to Swedish literature by the German writer, traveller, and critic Eduard Boas (1845, 98–99). Boas, in turn, plagiarized the characterizations of Swedish female poets in the 1826 Brockhaus article.

As Chitnis shows in Chapter Four in his account of British reviews of Czech literature between the wars, superficiality forms part of all transcultural reception. In this case, it must be understood in the context of the boom for literary and miscellaneous journals, encyclopaedias and eventually literary histories in the period. There appears to have been a market for knowledge of other literatures – no matter how rudimentary – in which serious and influential works competed with exclusively profit-driven enterprises, and in which superficiality overlapped with the Goethean notion of world literature as an informed global, cultural intercourse and understanding. What is striking in Nyberg's case is that the ghost-like reception stands almost alone.

Gendered compartmentalization did not simply hamper the international reception of Nyberg and her status in Swedish literary history. In fact, a growing interest in Swedish women writers following the popularity of the great novelists would also spill over to their less well known 'sister'. A commemoration of Bremer in *The Monthly Religious Magazine* in 1866 includes a very imprecise list of other Swedish women writers, mentioning that 'Julia Nyberg publishes at Upsal tender lyrics', though Nyberg had by then died. When Selma Lagerlöf (1858–1940), like Bremer and Flygare-Carlén before her, was awarded a gold medal by the Swedish Academy in 1904, some drops of fame would also fall on Nyberg's name in a short anonymous news item in the Czech periodical *Národní listy* (Anon., 1905, 45, 3).[6] Her position in the women's section of Swedish literature furthered these kinds of remembering, however short or misinformed.

---

[6] Special thanks to Ursula Stohler for translating the text.

Gunilla Hermansson and Yvonne Leffler

A Literary Success Story About and By Emilie Flygare-Carlén

In contrast to Nyberg, Emilie Flygare-Carlén, an example of a small-nation success story, immediately became a major international bestselling writer with a substantial international reception. In some languages, her only rivals were Charles Dickens, Alexandre Dumas and Eugène Sue (Munch-Petersen, 1978, 982). After Flygare-Carlén's first novel was published in Swedish in 1838, she published about two or three novels a year over the following 13 years. Altogether, she published around 30 novels, just as many novellas, and a couple of biographical works. Unlike many other Swedish writers, she never travelled outside Sweden to promote her works and establish herself as a literary celebrity. Her novels travelled by themselves without much marketing by the writer or her Swedish publishers; there is no evidence that she or her publishers contacted translators, editors or publishers abroad to promote her novels. Instead, she was constantly approached by translators and publishers who wanted her to send them her latest manuscript for immediate translation, or who tried to persuade her to agree to some other favour, like a signed portrait or a preface to a new translated edition. Several contemporary writers were so inspired by Flygare-Carlén's novels that they published what would now be called 'fan fiction': continuations under their own and Flygare-Carlén's name. One example is the German writer Paula Herbst (1818–83), who published several novels based on Flygare-Carlén's works, such as *Der Erbe: Fortsetzung von 'Das Fideicommiss' von Emilie Flygare-Carlén* (1859).

Flygare-Carlén's debut in 1838 resulted immediately in translations into Danish and German. Some years after her debut, her novels were also translated into English and French. Translations into English instantly resulted in distribution in both Britain and the United States; one and the same novel was often translated the very same year into both British and American English and distributed by one publisher in London and another in New York. Translations into French were commissioned by both French and Belgian publishers, and therefore distributed in several French-speaking regions. Translations into French probably promoted translations into other Romance languages such as Italian and Spanish. At the end of the century, Flygare-Carlén's novels were translated into approximately 20 European languages.

The most widely circulated language in Europe at the time was certainly German because of the Austrian Empire and its cultural dominance in Europe. Literature in German was not only distributed in the regions of today's Germany, Austria and Switzerland, but also in those of today's Hungary, Czech Republic, Poland and Romania. This transcultural circulation in German created opportunities for translations into other languages, often via German. The first translations into small languages, like Dutch and Czech, were made from German translations. Most of the translations into other major languages, like French and English, were made from the original Swedish text, though some works, like *A Brilliant Marriage* (*Ett lyckligt parti*, 1851), published by Richard Bentley in London in 1852, were translated into English via German. In any event, these transcultural circulations owed much to Flygare-Carlén's German success.

Judging by the way Flygare-Carlén's novels were marketed in translation, her transcultural success was a result not of her exotic Scandinavian origin, or of her accounts of the unknown fringes of Europe, but of her instant recognition as an important European novelist. At home, she built her reputation by being the first writer to represent the Swedish west coast in literature, introducing a new geographical region and its colourful population (Leffler and Witt-Brattström, 1993). However, outside Sweden, her success was mainly due to her more regionally unspecified domestic novels, such as *One Year* (*Ett År*, 1846),[7] *Opposite Neighbours* (*Vindskuporna*, 1848), and *The Whimsical Woman* (*En nyckfull kvinna*, 1849). Nor is she presented in the prefaces to her translations primarily as a Swedish or Scandinavian writer. Instead, English and American translators and publishers often placed her in a Germanic tradition (Krause, 1852, v), and to the Italian audience she was introduced as a novelist in the English tradition (Mapelli, 1869, 3–10).

The Novel: By Women – For Women

Emilie Flygare-Carlén's European success can be attributed to the facts that her novels were instantly translated into a major language, German, and were circulating at a time when novels by women writers were in demand by a growing number of female readers. Her novels were distributed in the Austrian Empire as well as other parts of Europe dominated by German culture at a time when few other bestselling women novelists were published in German. Her bestselling predecessors were male novelists like Dumas, Dickens and Sue, who no longer answered the demands of the female readers for female protagonists and their everyday struggles. Educational stories of

---

[7] Another title in English is *Twelve Months of Matrimony*.

this kind were also encouraged by the national movements in Europe, where the modernization of society was linked to a well-run household and the mass-educated women in many rising European nations, such as Hungary, the Polish and Czech lands and Italy (Hawkesworth, 2001, 44–45; Romani, 2006, 3–11).

Flygare-Carlén's novels in translation were increasingly positioned in a gendered context addressing mainly female readers, both in German translation and in other languages, with the support of illustrations, titles, genre labels and forewords.[8] First, some translated novels were published with exquisitely illustrated and appealing covers, like the German edition of a collection of her novels, illustrated by Karl Ohnesorg and published in 'Ausgewälte Romane' by Franz Bondy in Vienna and Leipzig in 1895–99. The front cover shows a woman in a striking pose. She is displaying her fashionable outfit while a young male admirer sits behind her. In the background, a seaside resort is outlined. To a reader familiar with the novel, the picture does not refer to any recognizable episode of the plot of any of the novels. Instead, the cover resembles an advertisement in a women's fashion magazine. By having a woman in a conspicuous pose or engaged in a typically feminine activity, the front cover promotes the publication as an engaging story about an intriguing female protagonist, specifically of interest to women readers. At the same time, these elaborately illustrated books demonstrate that Flygare-Carlén's works were so commercially attractive that publishers were prepared to invest in costly new editions. Another similarly stunning cover was used for the Czech translation of Flygare-Carlén's *The Whimsical Woman* (*Rozmarná žena*), published in Prague by Šimáček in 1898: in light violet colours, it shows the lovely but whimsical heroine standing in a womanly setting, a fashionable parlour. The heroine is standing turned slightly towards the wall behind her so that she is facing a framed portrait of a woman, who appears to be the author, Emilie Flygare-Carlén. The cover thereby displays both the heroine of the novel and its female writer. By displaying these two women on the cover, the novel was certainly intended to attract female readers and customers.

---

[8] About these gendered publication strategies see also Yvonne Leffler, 2017. 'Gender and Bestsellers: The Swedish Novelist Emilie Flygare-Carlén outside Scandinavia', in Isis Herrero López, Celica Alvstad, Johanna Akujärvi and Synnøve Skarsbø Lindtner (eds) *Gender and Translation: Understanding Agents in Transnational Reception* (Vita Traductiva: Éditions québécoises de l'œuvre), 107–26.

Nineteenth-century Swedish Women Writers on Export

Second, the titles of Flygare-Carlén's novels were often changed in translation to emphasize the female dimension; in many cases the novel was named after its female protagonist (Moretti, 2013, 194–97). In Dutch, *The Heroine* (*Romanhjältinnan*, 1849) was launched as *Blenda van Kulen (de romaneske)* in 1851, while *The Home in the Valley* (*Familjen i dalen*, 1849) was marketed in Italian as *La signorina Nanny: Romanzo* in 1875. English and American publishers also frequently put the name of the female protagonist in the title. The novel *One Year* was launched by J. Miller in New York as *'Lavinia'; or, One Year: A Tale of Wedlock* in 1873, and *The Professor and His Favourites* (*Professorn och hans skyddslingar*, 1840) was circulated by the American newspaper *The National Era* as *Rosa and Her Suitors* in 1855–56. The same pattern is noticeable when the novel *Opposite Neighbours* was published in London and New York in 1858. The title is a forename: not the name of the male protagonist, the engineer William, but the first name of the proud and capricious young lady he is in love with, Marie Louise. Thus, the English title is *Marie Louise; or, the Opposite Neighbours*, thereby turning the female object of the protagonist's love and desire into the protagonist (Carlén, 1853, 1854).

The British distribution of Flygare-Carlén's first novel, *Waldemar Klein* (1838), is an even more striking example. The Swedish novel is titled after the male protagonist, Waldemar Klein, a young general practitioner in love with the delightful Maria. However, his dying father makes him swear to marry their neighbour's daughter, the vain and conceited Julia. Although Waldemar is soon released from his engagement, the title of one English edition is *Julia; or, Love and Duty* (1854) (Flygare-Carlén, 1854). The British title explicitly highlights a certain subplot of the novel, making the reader pay more attention to Julia's story. She is a young woman who makes the wrong decision and who is blinded by superficial glamour and vanity, and accordingly ends up in an unhappy marriage before she dies of tuberculosis. The title thus directs the reader's attention to the story about a woman who, because of her flaws, is severely penalized, punished with illness and death; the title stresses Julia's function in the novel as a cautionary example of a misled woman who has to pay for her mistakes. Thus, the title also labels the novel as a female *Bildungsroman*, or an educational novel of manners addressing female readers.

A third way to address the female audience was to launch Flygare-Carlén's novels as romances. Although her novels were never presented as romances in Sweden, they were often placed in a romance tradition outside Scandinavia. When her breakthrough novel, *The Rose of Thistle Isle* (*Rosen på Tistelön*,

1842), praised for its exceptional realism by Swedish critics, was translated into American English two years later, it was distributed as a romance. Her translators, Gustavus Clemens Hebbe and H.C. Deming, together with their publisher J. Winchester in New York, published it as *The Smugglers of the Swedish Coast, or, The Rose of Thistle Island: A Romance by Mrs Emilie Carlen*. Also, the novel *The Skjuts-boy* (*Skjutsgossen*, 1841), translated by Alex L. Krause, was advertised by her American publisher, Harper, as *Ivar; or, the Skjuts-boy: A Romance by Miss Carlén* in 1859 and then again in 1864. The subtitle 'Romance' was also added in some other languages, for instance, when *Six Weeks* (*Inom sex veckor*, 1853) was translated into Italian as *Sei settimani: romanzo* and published in Milan in 1876.

But it was not only covers, titles and subtitles that placed Flygare-Carlén's novels in a gendered context. Introductory forewords also highlighted the sex of the writer and the domestic setting of her novels. In general, Flygare-Carlén's femininity and qualities as a female writer and a woman were stressed more in Latin countries. The paratexts focused on her life as a married woman and housewife, although the biographical information was not absolutely correct. In a preface to a French edition of *The Rose of Thistle Isle* (*Les smogglers suédois*, Paris 1845), Flygare-Carlén is presented as the virtuous spouse of the poet Carlén (Coquille, 1845, 1). Another example is the Italian preface to *One Year*, written by her translator Clemente Mapelli, and published in Milan in 1869 as *Un anno di matrimonio*. In Italian, the rather vague Swedish title, *One Year*, is specified as 'one year of matrimony', and thereby also targeted at female readers. The introduction about the writer is also turned into a romance, or female Bildungsroman; here, Mapelli describes Flygare-Carlén's first marriage in detail as unhappy, noting that she was fortunate to be freed from it, and giving both her husbands more romantic professions than they actually had: an officer in the cavalry and a musician. When Mapelli stresses Flygare-Carlén's literary talents, he is eager to praise her capable female characters and the way she emphasizes the importance of good education for women as, according to Mapelli, it makes women good mothers (Mapelli, 1869, 13). This view that women should be educated to uphold and endorse family values corresponds to the ideal promoted by the national movement in Italy.

Another strategy to heighten Flygare-Carlén's female virtues and adapt her to domestic values is demonstrated by some American introductions. In the foreword to *One Year: A Tale of Wedlock*, published in New York in 1853, the translator Elbert Perce constructed Flygare-Carlén as an amiable heroine. He claimed that she started to write to provide for her parents. Her virtuous personality was further emphasized since, according to Perce (1853, iii), she was married to a clergyman, though in reality she was married to the lawyer and writer Carlén. For the American audience, however, she was a good Christian daughter and woman, who was rewarded by becoming a clergyman's wife. In another American foreword, written by her translator Krause to *Ivar; or, the Skjuts-boy* (1852), she is effectively turned into a good American citizen because of her ability to portray the lower classes. She is, he claims, 'the republican, *par excellence*' among female authors, meaning that she is at heart a true American (Hebbe and Deming, 1844, viii). She and her novels were thus incorporated and domesticated into an American context.

Gender and Nation: A Double-edged Sword

The striking similarities and differences in the transcultural transmission and reception of Nyberg and Flygare-Carlén demonstrate the importance of genre, nation and gender in the nineteenth-century circulation of literature. In Nyberg's transcultural reception, nationality, genre and gender were intertwined categories of selection. Without interest in Swedish or Scandinavian literature, there would have been no translation or mention at all. Her poems were recognized for certain feminine and romantic qualities, but failed to meet the foreign, preconceived ideas of the nation that were essential to the popularity of a poet in the early nineteenth century. Her international reputation might nevertheless be partly explained by the first boom in Swedish literature in German translation. Although her poems as such were not widely disseminated and read, she was often referred to in European and American surveys of Swedish literature. Reception based on non-reading and the recycling of superficial knowledge challenges standard traditional notions of world literature and of literature's afterlife. The power and scope of this kind of circulation should not be underestimated; the case of Nyberg demonstrates that superficial reception and canon-forming processes are very much connected.

Flygare-Carlén's novels met a demand in a different market. They were written when domestic novels by female writers were in demand by a rapidly growing audience of novel-craving European readers. In contrast to Nyberg's poetry, Flygare-Carlén's works were instantly translated and read on a large scale. Her triumph confirms the importance of choosing the right genre at the right time. With no serious competition from other female novelists at the time, her novels travelled by themselves. The widespread transnational circulation of Flygare-Carlén's novels demonstrates the preconditions for the rise of the bourgeois novel some decades later, in the mid-nineteenth century. The popularity of novels was endorsed not only by successful women writers – such as Flygare-Carlén – but also by a growing number of readers, especially female readers, and national movements in Europe that promoted women's reading as a means of mass education. Mapping the transcultural dissemination of Flygare-Carlén's novels in Europe confirms that, in the latter half of the nineteenth century, the European novel was increasingly launched by publishers and critics as a female-authored form to be read primarily by women. In addition, the success of Flygare-Carlén's novels proves that novels from small nations written in small languages could reach readers in almost any European language and most regions, especially if they were extensively launched by influential German publishing houses.

The actual circulation and reception of Nyberg's Romantic poetry and Flygare-Carlén's blockbusting novels may differ in extent and number, but the texts and the writers' fame travelled along the same route out of Sweden, into Europe and across the Atlantic Ocean. The two writers' international repute relied on their recognition by German publishers and critics; the literary hub in Europe was not Paris, as Moretti, Casanova and Mariano Siskind claim (Casanova, 2004, 23–34; Moretti, 2013, 22; Siskind, 2014, 8, 17), but Leipzig and Stuttgart, at least for Scandinavian literature. At the time, literary texts still travelled as physical objects by the same routes as people and goods, from Sweden via Denmark and then along the main land routes into the German-speaking regions in today's Germany, and then onwards, or alternatively by sea to England and across the Atlantic Ocean to the USA. It is therefore no coincidence that both Nyberg and Flygare-Carlén soon became well known both in Central Europe and in the United States.

They also share the fate of being women writers at a time when they were a minority, but rapidly growing in size and significance, provoking interest as well as a need to control among the male agents in the literary field. It seems that being able to name a few women writers in a survey often enhanced a nation's cultural status (Fronius, 2007, 78), and showing awareness of foreign female celebrities was equally important for the self-promotion of male critics, as was demonstrated in the cases of Atterbom and Poe. Over the nineteenth century, however, both Nyberg and Flygare-Carlén were progressively removed from the centre of literature into an increasingly gendered context, the ladies' room in the peripheral history of Swedish literature. Their possible recognition as European writers in the history of world literature therefore still lies ahead.

Bibliography

Archive
The Royal Library in Stockholm, KB1/Ep. H 2: Amalia von Helvig's letters to Lorenzo Hammarsköld.

Works Cited
Afzelius, Nils. 1938. *A Bibliographical List of Books in English on Sweden and Literary Works Translated into English from Swedish*, 2nd edn (Stockholm: Fritze's).
Anon. 1849. Fredrika Bremer and her Compeers. *Chambers's Edinburgh Journal*, 4 August.
Anon. [sign. Crito]. 1866. Fredrika Bremer. *The Montly Religious Magazine*, 35, 187–94.
Anon. [sign, Mr. Penn]. 1905. "Sizy spisy", *Národní listy*, 1905: 45, 3.
Atterbom, P.D.A. 1870. *Litterära karaktäristiker* (Örebro: Bohlin).
Behrendt, Stephen C. 2009. *British Women Poets and the Romantic Writing Community* (Baltimore, MD: Johns Hopkins University Press).
Benson, Adolph B. 1952. *American Scandinavian Studies, Selected and Edited with a Bibliography by Marshall W.S. Swan* (New York: American Scandinavian Foundation).
Berg, Ruben G:son. 1924. Palmblad och Brockhaus. Några anteckningar ur en brevväxling. *Samlaren*, 5, 1–58.
Bjork, Robert E. 2005. A Bibliography of Modern Scandinavian Literature (Excluding H.C. Andersen) in English Translation, 1533–1900, and Listed by Translator. *Scandinavian Studies*, 7, 105–42.
Boas, Eduard. 1845. *In Scandinavien: Nordlichter* (Leipzig: Friedrich Ludwig Herbig).
Booker Prizes. 2016. First Research on the Sales of Translated Fiction in the UK Shows Growth and Comparative Strength of International Fiction. Available from: https://thebookerprizes.com/resources/media/pressreleases/first-research-sales-translated-fiction-uk-shows-growth-and [accessed 20 July 2019].
Bödeker, Birgit and Sybille Rohde-Gaur. 1996. Zur Rezeption britischer Literatur in Deutschland (1800–1870). Grundlage und zwei Beispiele. In Essman, Helga and Udo Schöning (eds). *Weltliteratur in deutschen Versanthologien des 19. Jahrhunderts* (Berlin: Erich Schmidt), 51–76.
Borgström, Eva. 1991. *'Om jag får be om ölost': Kring kvinnliga författares kvinnobilder i svensk romantik* (Gothenburg: Anamma).
Carlén, Emilie. 1853. *Marie Louise; or, the Opposite Neighbours*, with numerous illustrations. Trans. Alex L. Krause (London: Ingram, Cook).
Carlén, Emilie. 1854. *Marie Louise; or, the Opposite Neighbours*, with numerous illustrations. Trans. Alex L. Krause (New York: Appleton).

Casanova, Pascale. 2004. *The World Republic of Letters* (1999). Trans.
M.B. DeBevoise (Cambridge, MA and London: Harvard University
Press).
Collison, Robert. 1966. *Encyclopaedias: Their History throughout the Ages*
(New York and London: Hafner).
Coquille, F. 1845. Avant-propos. In Flygare-Carlén, Emilie. *Les smogglers suédois*. Trans. F. Coquille (Paris: rue Grange-Bateliere No 1).
Ehrenström, Marianne. 1826. *Notices sur la littérature et les beaux-arts en Suède* (Stockholm: Eckstein).
Essmann, Helga. 1996. Einleitung. In Essman, Helga and Udo Schöning (eds), *Weltliteratur in deutschen Versanthologien des 19. Jahrhunderts* (Berlin: Erich Schmidt), pp. IX–XXI.
Essmann, Helga and Armin Paul Frank. 1991. Translation Anthologies: An Invitation to the Curious and a Case Study. *Target* 3(1), 65–90.
Flygare-Carlén, Emilie. 1854. *Julie, or, Love and Duty* (London: Richard Bentley).
France, Peter and Kenneth Haynes. 2006. The Publication of Literary Translation: An Overview. In France, Peter and Kenneth Haynes (eds). *The Oxford History of Literary Translations in English*, vol. 4: 1790–1900 (Oxford: Oxford University Press), 135–51.
Fronius, Hellen. 2007. *Women and Literature in the Goethe Era (1770–1820): Determined Dilettantes* (Oxford: Clarendon).
Halbe, Heinz-Georg, Fritz Paul and Regina Quandt (eds). 1987–88. *Schwedische Literatur in deutscher Übersetzung 1830–1980: eine Bibliographie* (Göttingen: Vandenhoeck & Ruprecht).
Hansen, C.J. 1860. *Noordsche Lettere (Talen, Letterkunden, Overzettingen) als vervolg op de Reisbrieven uit Dietschland en Denemark* (Gent: I.S. van Doosselaere).
Hawkesworth, Celia. 2001. Introduction. In Hawkesworth, Celia (ed.). *A History of Central European Women's Writing* (New York: Palgrave).
Hebbe G.C. and H.C. Deming. 1844. Translators' preface. In Carlén, Emilie, *The Rose of Thistle Isle*. Trans. G.C. Hebbe and H.C. Deming (London: Bruce and Wyld).
Helvig, Amalia von. 1915. *Amalia von Hevigs bref till Atterbom*. Edited by Hedvig Atterbom-Svenson (Stockholm: Bonniers).
Helvig, Amalia von. 1950. *Amalia von Helvigs brev till Erik Gustaf Geijer*. Trans. W. Gordon Stiernstedt (Stockholm: Bonniers).
Holmquist, Ingrid. 2000. *Salongens värld: om text och kön i romantikens salongskultur* (Eslöv: Symposion).
Howitt, Mary and William Howitt. 1852. *The Literature and Romance of Northern Europe*, vol. I–II (London: Colburn).
Krause, Alex L. 1852. Translator's Introduction. *Ivar; or, the Skjuts-boy; a Romance by Miss Carlén*. Trans. A.L. Krause (London: Illustrated London Library) [v]–viii.

Leffler, Yvonne and Ebba Witt-Brattström. 1993. Skräck och skärgård. Om Emilie Flygare-Carlén. In *Nordisk kvinnolitteraturhistoria II: Fadershuset 1800–1890* (Höganäs: Förlags AB Wiken), 261–68.

Leffler, Yvonne, Åsa Arping, Jenny Bergenmar, Gunilla Hermansson and Birgitta Johansson Lindh. 2019. *Swedish Women's Writing on Export: Tracing Transnational Reception in the Nineteenth Century* (Gothenburg: LIR skrifter). Available from: https://gupea.ub.gu.se/handle/2077/61809 [accessed 25 September 2019].

Lundqvist, Åke K.G. 1996. Frithiofs saga på väg. In Törnqvist, Ulla (ed.). *Möten med Tegnér* (Lund: Tegnérsamfundet), 33–73.

Mapelli, Clemente. 1869. Prefazione. In Carlén, Emilia. *Un anno di matrimonio*. Trans. Clemente Mapelli (Milan: E. Treves), 3–13.

Mohnike, Thomas. 2008. Att bilda Norden efter grekernas mått. In Hermansson, Gunilla and Mads Nygaard Folkmann (eds). *Svensk og dansk litterär romantik i ny dialog* (Göteborg: Makadam), 174–88.

Moretti, Franco. 2013. *Distant Reading*, London (New York: Verso).

Munch-Petersen, Erland. 1978. *Romanens århundrede: Studier i den masselæste oversatte roman i Danmark 1800–1870* (Copenhagen: Forum).

Perce, Elbert. 1853. Translator's Preface. In Flygare-Carlén, Emilie. *One Year, a Tale of Wedlock*. Trans. Alex L. Krause and Elbert Perce (New York: Charles Scribner), pp. [iii]–v.

Person, Leland S. 2001. Poe and Nineteenth-Century Gender Construction. In Kennedy, J. Gerald (ed.). *A Historical Guide to Edgar Allan Poe* (Oxford: Oxford University Press), 129–65.

Petersens, Hedvig af. 1933. Robert Pearse Gillies, Foreign Quarterly Review och den svenska litteraturen. *Samlaren*, 14, 55–106.

Poe, Edgar Allan. 1842. Review: Ballads and Other Poems by Henry Wadsworth Longfellow. *Graham's Lady's and Gentleman's Magazine*, XX (3).

Romani, Gabriella. 2006. Introduction: Scenes from Nineteenth-Century Italy: Delightful Stories on Those Long, Long Winter Evenings. In Arslan, Antonia and Gabriella Romani (eds). *Writing to Delight: Italian Short Stories by Nineteenth-Century Women Writers* (Toronto, Buffalo and London: University of Toronto Press).

Rühling, Lutz. 1996. Nordische Poeterey und gigantisch-barbarische Dichtart. In Essmann, Helga and Udo Schöning (eds). *Weltliteratur in deutschen Versanthologien des 19. Jahrhunderts* (Berlin: Erich Schmidt), 77–121.

Siskind, Mariano. 2014. *Cosmopolitan Desires: Global Modernity and World Literature in Latin America* (Evanston, IL: Northwestern University Press).

Söderlund, Petra. 2000. *Romantik och förnuft: V.F. Palmblads förlag 1810–1830* (Hedemora: Gidlund).

Sturzenbecher, O.P. 1850. *Die neuere Schwedische* Literatur (Leipzig: J.J. Weber).

Svedjedal, Johan. 2012. Svensk skönlitteratur i världen. Litteratursociologiska problem och perspektiv. In Svedjedal, Johan (ed.). *Svensk litteratur som världslitteratur: En antologi*. (Uppsala: Uppsala Universitet).

Swan, Gustaf N. 1913. The English Versions of Tegnér's 'Axel': A Bibliographical Sketch. *Publications of the Society for the Advancement of Scandinavian Study*, 1 (4), 179–84.

Wawn, Andrew. 2000. *The Vikings and the Victorians: Inventing the Old North in Nineteenth-Century Britain* (Cambridge: D.S. Brewer).

Chapter Nine

Translating as Re-telling: On the English Proliferation of C.P. Cavafy

Paschalis Nikolaou (Ionian University)

Poets from smaller European languages have always struggled to make their voices heard. Constantine P. Cavafy (1863–1933) presents us with a singular case of poetry translated into all major languages – indeed, retranslated at a rate unheard of for a modern poet – to the extent that we now speak less about a voice from Greece, primarily associated with a 'small' national literature. His publication history alone (listed at the end of this chapter) immediately shows how this body of work has long outstripped notions of minority; the fact that this poetry speaks for characters and settings that belong in the margins of antiquity, culture and sexuality makes this situation even more poignant. Though Cavafy's poetry nowadays exists in most languages, it is with English that a unique – even excessive – relationship has been forged. Alongside a wealth of imitations, in the early twenty-first century alone we can count at least ten extensive translation projects related to the accepted canon of 154 poems. There are rarely 'second chances' for a poet rendered into a major language, but in Cavafy's case, the consecutive acts of translation suggest not simply the reconfirmation of his value beyond his own culture, but the expression by translators and publishers of needs and *desires*, explored in this chapter.

For modern Greek writers, the enduring continuities with their ancient Greek counterparts – the diachrony of a language, where the gist of ancient texts can be somewhat understood without intralingual translation – are simultaneously a blessing and a curse. A key figure in the presentation of Greek literature to English-speaking audiences in recent decades, David Connolly (2003, 13, my emphases) laments in his foreword to a bilingual edition of a poetry collection by Yannis Kondos (1943–2015) how

> translators of modern Greek poets are perhaps further disadvantaged in their efforts to communicate their tradition in the English-speaking world. *The very fact of being obliged to refer to 'modern' Greek poets and not simply Greek poets is indicative of the problem.* Experience has taught me that any reference to 'Greek' alone is invariably identified in the mind of the audience or readership with Greek antiquity. *Many contemporary poets who have failed to make any impact in English translation have undoubtedly suffered from the legacy of Greece's ancient past and from a particular perception of Greece by Westerners.*

Introducing *The Greek Poets: Homer to the Present*, Robert Hass (2010, xxxi) echoes the experience of many readers when he acknowledges an absence

> between Callimachus, who died in about 240 bce, and the great flowering of modern Greek poetry that began with C.P. Cavafy, whose first poems appeared in the 1890s. It was a gap in my knowledge of about two thousand years that – it stuck me – was both typical and symptomatic. From the end of what we think of as the classical period to the beginning of the twentieth century, Greek poetry simply disappeared from the narrative of European poetry in the Western world.

Hass continues that it is 'in the footsteps of Cavafy' that Greek poetry returned with force, and that it is thanks to a poet who lived abroad – in Alexandria – that international attention came back to Greek poetry. A few decades later, Greece had two Nobel laureates in George Seferis (1900–71) and Odysseus Elytis (1911–96).

Why Cavafy?

While Cavafy's popularity owes something to his perceptive conversations with history and oblique encounters with the constancy of human passions, it is the dramatic new style he forged that has proved timeless, though it was vehemently resisted by Athenian critics and journal editors during the first two decades of the poet's career. In the early part of the twentieth century, Cavafy did not belong in the literary system, but came out of nowhere. Seferis (1966, 146, my emphasis) identifies a crucial antinomy:

> Very often in Cavafy's work, while the language itself is neutral and unemotional, the movement of the persons and the succession of the

events involved is so closely packed, so airtight, one might almost say, that one has the impression that his poems *attract emotion by means of a vacuum*. The vacuum created by Cavafy is the element which differentiates his phrases from the mere prosaicness which the critics have fancied that they saw in his work.

Cavafy perhaps consciously added to the allure of his work and shaped its reception throughout his life by personally distributing and editing his poems in sheets and small pamphlets, and thus purposely focusing readers' attention on the individual poem.[1] Moreover, for Nasos Vayenas (2010, 133):

> no other Greek poet has been such a good critical reader of his own work as Cavafy. The phrase 'Cavafy is a poet of the future', which he spread eloquently to the wider public through the small coterie of his admirers, was clearly less dictated by vanity and more by an awareness that a time would come when his poetry, even though out of step with the poetical norms of his day would one day be recognized as great, and not just within the narrow confines of modern Greek.

Central to the ease of Cavafy's transmission beyond his own language is the narrative perspective, the *poetic* use of tendencies usually found in prose. Cavafy's works are frequently experienced first through their storytelling, their articulation of the edges of events, motives and behaviour, communal as well as individual. Works that tell stories always fare better in translation and, indeed, W.H. Auden (1907–73) (Cavafy, 1961, especially xv–xvi) was among the first to note the translatability of the Greek originals, in his introduction to Rae Dalven's 1961 edition of Cavafy's *Complete Poems*, where he compares several existing English and French translations. The simplicity of Cavafy's construction is, however, rather illusory, given his intricate fusion of high demotic and purist strands of Greek and his painstaking exploitation of rhythm, metrical effects and punctuation. The relative absence or dissipation of these tensions and subtleties in the more uniform English of at least the early translations detracts much less from the tone and thrust of these works compared to other Greek poets, like Elytis, whose writing more ostentatiously foregrounds, often through neologisms, how language may also structure reality. Following Seferis, we might say that Cavafy's poems by means of a vacuum also attract *translation*.

---

[1] See Gregory Jusdanis's close study of this method in *The Poetics of Cavafy: Textuality, Eroticism, History* (1987, especially 58–63).

Paschalis Nikolaou

In examining the affinity between Cavafy and English, we should not neglect the dialogue between traditions that took place in his formative work. Cavafy spent his childhood years in Liverpool and London in the late nineteenth century, and his earliest poems were apparently written in English.[2] Between 1884 and 1895 there were also exercises in the form of translated fragments of works by Shakespeare, Keats, Shelley and Tennyson (collected in Cavafy, 2013a). Even once he began writing exclusively in Greek, Cavafy was known to self-translate and privately circulate poems in English, before this task was systematically assumed by his brother John, whose translations – often still in association with the poet – appeared in English journals until around 1920.[3] Importantly for their appeal to English readers, by addressing historical figures, these earliest renderings by John Cavafy and also George Valassopoulo, like 'Darius' or 'Alexandrian Kings' – preselected by E.M. Forster and Cavafy himself – match, at least thematically, certain norms also found in the target language.[4]

Interpersonal relationships also proved critical. Before his significant encounter with Forster, who would write the first introductory text on Cavafy in the journal *The Nation and Athenaeum* in 1919, and to whom we owe that poignant, oft-repeated description of an 'old man with a straw hat, at slight angle to the universe', Cavafy engaged with a circle of 'knowing readers' in Egypt, including Timos Malanos, who published the first study of Cavafy in 1933. Malanos's support certainly influenced Cavafy's gradual acceptance in Athens, and even though their relationship later became tumultuous, Malanos also wrote a few poems 'in the manner of' Cavafy, discussed below.

---

[2] '[More Happy Thou, Performing Member]' (1877), 'Leaving Therapia' and 'Darkness and Shadows' (both 1882). The authorship of the first and the third poem remains contentious (see Ekdawi, 1997, 223–30).

[3] John Cavafy's 63 completed translations were eventually published in 2003 and several can be accessed through the Cavafy Archive website at www.cavafy.com/poems/list.asp?cat=1 [accessed 31 July 2019].

[4] The Valassopoulo translations were completed at the instigation of E.M. Forster, largely for inclusion in *Pharos and Pharillon*, published in 1923. For the three-way discussion between Forster, Valassopoulo and Cavafy about this undertaking (culminating in the inclusion of 'Ithaka' in T.S. Eliot's *Criterion* in 1924, followed by 'For Ammones Who Died at the Age of 29 in 610' in 1928) see *The Forster–Cavafy Letters: Friends at a Slight Angle*, edited by Peter Jeffreys in 2009. The first letter to Valassopoulo is dated 8 October 1916, and the volume helpfully includes the complete texts of the resulting translations.

On the English Proliferation of C.P. Cavafy

Deeper individual motivations for what I label the 'polytranslation' of Cavafy (the growing number of translations also noted by other scholars, for example, Ekdawi, 2012) emerge from the paratextual comments of translators and editors that accompany publications in English from Dalven onwards. Beyond Auden's early assessment of Cavafy's translatability, Dalven's 'Acknowledgments' in the expanded edition (Cavafy, 1961, vi) also recognize the impulse given not only by the biographical criticism of Malanos (1933/1957), Peridis (1948) and Tsirkas (1958), but also the few previous translations: the English selection by John Mavrogordato and 'the translations in French of the same poems by George Papoutsakis and by Marguerite Yourcenar and Constantin Dimaras' (Dalven in Cavafy, 1961, vi). The most durable articulation of Cavafy's poetry in English before the 2000s, the *Collected Poems*, translated by Edmund Keeley and Philip Sherrard and first published in 1975, has also been the most frequently reframed. The 2009 bilingual edition, which superseded the revised 1992 edition, contains all paratextual material accumulated since 1975. The biographical note (Cavafy, 2009a, 453–58) uses information from Tsirkas's and Liddell's lives of Cavafy,[5] and the 'Translator's Note to the 1992 Revised Edition' emphasizes that, this time, Keeley and Sherrard 'have been especially sensitive to Cavafy's other formal concerns, for example his subtle use of enjambment and his mode of establishing rhythm and emphasis through repetition' (Cavafy, 2009a, xxiii–xiv). In his foreword, Robert Pinsky praises the significance of the Keeley/Sherrard translations for American poets, while appreciatively including other recent translations, and notes that anglophone readers should experience things differently now that they are equipped with a bilingual text:

> Readers who cannot read Cavafy – or any great poet – must be grateful for any translation, *as we triangulate and guess*. The warmth of the Rae Dalven translation, glints of difference or scholarship or idiom in the versions of Aliki Barnstone or Daniel Mendelsohn, contribute to the ongoing, imperfect perception of Cavafy. *And in this new edition, with the Greek page facing the English, matters like placement of rhymes and the length of lines are visible.* (Cavafy, 2009a, xx–xxi; my emphases)

The sense of triangulation increasingly extends to translators themselves as they seek to detail what differentiates their reformulations of Cavafy. At

---

[5] A year after the translations, in 1976, Keely published his *Cavafy's Alexandria: Study of a Myth in Progress*.

Paschalis Nikolaou

the onset of this recent spate of translations, Theoharis C. Theoharis strove for a completeness beyond that then known in English,[6] adding sections of unpublished, hidden, rejected and prose poems. This *'newly* translated' Cavafy is followed two years later, in 2003, on the seventieth anniversary of Cavafy's death and the eve of the Athens Olympic Games, by the edition of *154 Poems* that Evangelos Sachperoglou self-publishes in Greece, which reappears three years later in the Oxford World's Classics series billed as 'a new translation', retitled *The Collected Poems* (Cavafy, 2007b) and enriched by expert, lengthy introductory texts from Peter Mackridge and Anthony Hirst. Stratis Haviaras's return to *The Canon: The Original One Hundred and Fifty-Four Poems* was similarly first published in Greece in 2004 and reappeared in 2007 with Harvard University Press. Here, three initial paratexts (a foreword by Seamus Heaney, an introduction by Manuel Savidis and Haviaras's own translator's preface) assert how critical, poetic and translational faculties coalesce around another's voice. Seamus Heaney twice highlights the bonds of poet and translator in his foreword, arguing that '[Haviaras's] bilingual ear picks up the iambic pace of the Greek, measures it in two minds, and more or less keeps step with it in English. Haviaras is himself a poet, so he is at home in his medium and stays equidistant from metronome and monotone', before noting that the relationship is marked by a feeling 'not of appropriation, but of return and repossession' (Cavafy, 2007a, vi, vii). And Haviaras reflects on the genesis of the project thus:

> I had begun to 'translate' Cavafy in my mind thirty years earlier, not long after completing an undergraduate thesis on the poems, and shortly after the publication of the fourth collection of my poems (in Greek) in 1972. This was just one year before I began to write poetry in English. (Cavafy, 2007a, xii)

Another 'new translation' appears only two years later. Aliki Barnstone's introduction to *The Collected Poems of C.P. Cavafy* poignantly starts by remembering Auden's earlier comments on Cavafy, especially echoing those on national decline and patriotism as she finds herself

---

[6] In his foreword, Gore Vidal writes: 'I should note that my first visit to Athens took place in 1961, the year *The Complete Poems of C.P. Cavafy* was published by Hogarth Press, with an introduction by W.H. Auden. We were all reading Cavafy that season, in Rae Dalven's translation from the Greek. Now, forty years on, Theoharis Constantine Theoharis has given us what is, at last, all the poems that he could find' (Cavafy, 2001, xvi).

On the English Proliferation of C.P. Cavafy

especially aware of the history of conquest and defeat, of ruin and the desire to regain power, because I was lucky to translate most of the poems in this book on the island of Serifos in the Cyclades. Being in Greece allowed me to understand the poet's spirit of place, though the poetry seems at times willfully (though sorrowfully) to exile itself from location. (Cavafy, 2006, xxx)

Both the significance of place and the identity of the translator as another poet are again foregrounded in the introduction by Gerald Stern:

Barnstone is a poet, and she is able to construct, to create – or re-create – the poem. There is, in addition, the magical connection (between poet and translator) that there always is. I'll call it a sympathy, a fellow-feeling, she shares, or she has, with Cavafy. She herself writes in English, but her father, the scholar, translator, and poet Willis Barnstone is Jewish and her mother, the painter Elli Tzalopoulou-Barnstone is Greek, so she has lived in a double-diaspora, in Nevada now, of all places, which gives her even more kinship with Cavafy. (Cavafy, 2006, xviii)

While (auto)biographical identifications in the paratexts explain some translations, others, like Avi Sharon's selection for Penguin Classics (2008), reflect literary affinity. Sharon notes how Anglo-American readers recognized a 'universal poet and a proto-modernist' from the very first translations:

Suddenly Cavafy was seen to have written, along the lines of Eliot's thinking, with the tradition in his bones, leveraging themes and appropriating lines from Homer, Callimachus, Dante, Shakespeare and Browning [...] while Alexandria, Cavafy's 'unreal city', would be seen to rival in variety and richness Joyce's Dublin, Eliot's London or Pound's more extravagant commonwealth of *The Cantos*. (Cavafy, 2008, xvi)

More recent translations foreground this experimental aspect, seeking to intimate what may be foreign in the original. Daniel Mendelsohn's eagerly anticipated 2009 renderings, according to James Logenbach, signal a timely move away from overemphasizing a 'prosaic flatness' in English (Cavafy, 2009b). Through a conscious alternation of monosyllabic Germanic words chiming against Latinate ones, the translator at last attends to the artifice of Cavafy's language, in terms of the interplay between high and low diction. And in '[e]choing such effects, Mendelsohn makes me wonder if it wasn't the deliciously mongrel nature of English, which Cavafy spoke and wrote perfectly, that first provoked him to forge his own hybridized idiom' (Logenbach, 2009). Indeed, Logenbach further notes: 'the fact that the few poems Cavafy wrote in English contain phrases like "penetrating eye" and "transcendent star" (the Latinate word wedged against the Germanic) suggests that the poet's ear for English was at least as acute as the translator's'.

This continuous dialogue and 'fellow-feeling' with Cavafy, recognized by Stern, find ultimate expression in *Complete Plus* (Cavafy, 2013b), the most recent edition of an 'enriched' canon by George Economou. On the very last page, Economou gives us a 'Pantoum for C.P. Cavafy and a Translator', an articulation of emotional investment, in this traditional form, where we encounter stanzas like the following: 'To another was this task extended as a friend/who'd set it reaching for its fame and to/gain a breath of afterlife from that touch/as it passes the once and future poet's lips' (Cavafy, 2013b, 227). Economou indicates that the fluid relationship between translator and poet can itself be fully captured only through poetry, most clearly in the case of Cavafy's 'unfinished' poems, the drafts and fragments that he was still working on at the time of his death. Here, the modes of poet-translator and translator as scholar and editor operate in parallel as the original's half-realized intention meets the imagination of the later poet (or any member of Cavafy's audience) who must read between the lines. Karen Emmerich (2011 and 2017) has analysed the linking points of textual instability and inevitable interpretive acts in the more respectful, editorial translations by John Davis (1998) and Daniel Mendelsohn (2010), but in 'Finishing the Unfinished Poems', Economou (2015, 11–56) unfolds a structure far more ambitiously integrating poetry and translation:

> an approach of trans-composition, which combines the work of translator and poet in a collaborative process with Cavafy that I have previously described as *un métissage de l'écriture*. The balance between these two kinds of work within the approach to each poem necessarily differs according to the textual complexity of each of Cavafy's unfinished poems. The more drafts, variants and marginal comments and corrections in the condition of an original, the greater the possibilities the poet's work will play a major role in the refashioning of its elements into a finished poem in English.

This account is then followed by Economou's own 'Uncollected Poems and Translations'. In the poems (61–93), we re-encounter the 'Pantoum' that closed his 2013 translation of Cavafy, now acting as connective tissue between the two editions. The overtly autobiographical nature of several poems transfers,

On the English Proliferation of C.P. Cavafy

in this context, personal importance to the nine translations, ranging from Archilochos (680–645 bc) to Luis Cortest's 1983 poem 'Estación del metro', and including three early poems by Cavafy: 'Second Odyssey' (1894), 'The End of Antony' (1907), 'And I Leaned and Lay on Their Beds' (1915). The contents page thus suggests a narrative of poets' minds in dialogue. Translation processes are displayed within a larger mechanism of literary creativity, in a field where texts and structures comment on one another. It is the *unfinished* part of an oeuvre that may situate further completions of, as well as variations on, a voice. Economou's book is a literary experiment by way of Cavafy, a halfway-house between translation and imitation.

From Translation to Inspiration

Cavafy has attained his global status not only through translation, but also by inspiring and informing the poetry of others. Those poems that clearly channel Cavafy's style, or reference the circumstances of his life, often express a similar empathy to that propelling the relationship between translators and poets. Cavafy-inspired poetry is, indeed, so widespread that we may approach it through existing editions that attempt to catalogue a creative topos. Tellingly, the anthologies of foreign poems appear in Greek first; in asserting Cavafy's global reach, they inevitably feed back into the self-image of the national literature. *Synomilontas me ton Kavafi* (Conversing with Cavafy), a survey of more than 130 poems, was published in Greek translation in 2000, preceded a few months earlier by a much shorter, bilingual book, *Me ton Tropo tou Kavafi* (In the Manner of Cavafy), containing only 20 of those poems. Cavafy's particular hold on anglophone poets is obvious, with examples from Australia, Ireland, New Zealand and the USA, while verse from Albania, Holland, Romania, Sweden and Turkey reveals the extent of his journey.

Within this group, we find poems that are already part of literary history, of a critically observed dialogue between poets, like the sonnet-as-review by William Plomer (1903–73), 'To the Greek Poet C.P. Cavafy on his Ποιήματα (Poems) (1908–1914)' (in *The Fivefold Screen*, 1932) the first Cavafy-inspired poem in the language[7] and Auden's 'Rois Fainéants', written in 1968 (see in *Collected Poems*, 1991; it is a near-translation that transposes Cavafy's

---

[7] For an extensive survey of Plomer's relationship with Greece and Cavafy – with whom he corresponded briefly – see Georganta, 2012, 55–78.

Paschalis Nikolaou

'Alexandrian Kings' to a different cultural milieu). For Auden, as for others, these instances are emblematic of a longer relationship; Auden also has the Ithaca-echoing 'Atlantis' (1945), between homage and parody, and even earlier poems like 'Lullaby' (1937) owe a debt to a close reading of Cavafy. Indeed, Auden opens his introduction to the Dalven translations by stating:

> Ever since I was introduced to his poetry by the late Professor R.M. Dawkins, over thirty years ago, C.P. Cavafy has remained an influence on my own writing; that is to say, I can think of poems which, if Cavafy were unknown to me, I should have written quite differently or perhaps not written at all. Yet I do not know a word of Modern Greek, so that my only access to Cavafy's poetry has been through English and French translations. (Cavafy, 1961, xv)

Lawrence Durrell (1912–90) goes further, not only composing a sonnet addressed to Cavafy in 1946, but also fictionally representing the poet in his *Alexandria Quartet*, where several Cavafy poems also appear. In the first edition of *Justine*, we read: 'The words of the old poet came into his mind, pressed down like the pedal of a piano, to boil and reverberate around the frail hope which the thought had raised from its dark sleep' (Durrell, 1957, 160), followed by 11 lines from 'The City'. The entire poem appears at the end of the volume, alongside 'The God Abandons Antony', in Durrell's 'Workpoints' at the end of the volume, presaged thus:

> I copied and gave her the two translations from Cavafy which had pleased her though they were by no means literal. By now the Cavafy canon had been established by the fine thoughtful translations of Mavrogordato and in a sense the poet has been freed for other poets to experiment with; I have tried to transplant rather than translate – with what success I cannot say. (Durrell, 1957, 251–52)

Similarly, in three different passages of *Clea* (Durrell, 1960, 39, 40, 140) where 'the old poet of the city' is mentioned, asterisks lead the reader to the 'Notes' containing 'free translations' of 'The Afternoon Sun', 'Far Away' and 'Che Fece […] Il Gran Rifiuto'.[8]

---

[8] Thanks to Richard Pine, author of *Lawrence Durrell: The Mindscape* (1994/2005) and current Director of the Durrell Library of Corfu, for pointing me to some of these references in the original editions. For detailed discussions of the presence of Cavafy in Durrell's work see also Katope (1969) and J.L. Pinchin (1977).

On the English Proliferation of C.P. Cavafy

These early, better-known encounters, which blur the lines between appropriation, elective affinity and fictionalization, certainly contributed to Cavafy's myth, but are the first in a long and growing series. Three later examples from the 2000 Greek anthology epitomize the re-reading and recontextualization taking place *through* Cavafy. 'Poem Beginning with a Line by Cavafy' (1979) by Derek Mahon (b.1941) becomes a commentary on the 'Troubles' in Northern Ireland via 'Waiting for the Barbarians',[9] while 'Reading Cavafy in Translation' (1988/2007) by Mairi MacInnes (b.1925) dramatizes the distance between the poet and Cavafy's expression: 'He would never have liked me,/a woman who's ample and hopeful and hard-working' (2007: 34) starts the poem, and soon, from these more immediate impressions from the English, she moves to reach behind the translation:

> I understand too that the original contains
> A familiar sadness about the civilization
> Falling away behind us, and a dry contempt
> For our inept love of the present,
> That flares sometimes, like beacons before Armada.

James Merrill (1926–95), another poet whose work repeatedly converses with Cavafy, is represented by a poem that, like Mahon's, responds to 'Waiting for the Barbarians', but more like Auden's retreading of 'Ithaca'. The year is 1994 and in Merrill's 'After Cavafy' the Barbarians are poignantly replaced by Japanese: 'why do our senators, those industrious termites,/Gaze off into space instead of forming a new subcommittee?/Because the Japanese are coming today./Congress will soon be an item on their Diet' (Merrill, 1994, 13).

Anglophone appropriations only increase as we reach the present, notably in the book-length cycle *Imagining Alexandria* (2013) by Louis de Bernières (b.1954). Primarily a novelist, de Bernières (2013, 73–74, added emphases) reflects in his introduction that he is especially attached to the 'cameos of characters' and the way this poetry is 'stuffed with narrative'. He immediately proceeds to reveal that he 'can only speak Greek in song titles', therefore

> my 'Cavafy' poems herein come out *more like English translations than originals*, and in any case I have written under the influence of Cavafy,

---

[9] Cf. Joanna Kruczkowska's extensive study of the relationship between the two poets and Cavafy, in *Irish Poets and Modern Greece: Heaney, Mahon, Cavafy, Seferis* (2017). Mahon's long engagement is particularly reflected in the five versions ('The City', 'Voices', 'A Considered Pause', 'Old Men', 'The Life We Know') anthologized in his *Adaptations* (Mahon, 2006, 68–70).

> rather than in his manner. I do not follow his rhyme schemes, although I think that my metre is probably similar, and it is difficult to imitate his double game with katharevousa (a traditional, literary Greek) and demotic Greek, but there is something about his perspective and tone of voice that has, I think, *infected me. When I come across an intriguing anecdote in Suetonius or Plutarch, I like to think that my little bursts of inspiration might be similar to those he experienced.*

De Bernières thus not only highlights the points of contact between poetry and prose, but also, by describing his writing as 'under the influence rather than in [Cavafy's] manner', suggests how inner workings and impressions of – and distance from – the originals relate, agree and disagree with definitions and typology. De Bernières nevertheless still calls two poems ('Another House' and 'The Old Ones') 'direct plagiarisms' (de Bernières, 2013, 74).

The brief presence of Cavafy in England is more clearly contemplated in 'Cavafy in Liverpool' (2012) by Evan Jones (b.1973): 'in tweed and scarved, eyes closed/when the Mersey wind//calls his collar to his ear/on the strand near Albert Dock' before culminating in the lines: 'One less wave, he thinks, one less,/and then the Persians can get through' – the young poet intimating themes and lines to be composed years into the future.

'Cavafy's Things' (2013) by Josephine Balmer (b.1959) is narrated in the first-person plural of a family mourning the loss of a loved one. Under the title, she notes *'after* The Afternoon Sun and *i.m.* Darlene Balmer' (Balmer, 2013). Typical British town locales host fragments and phrases from 'The Afternoon Sun'. In the middle part, an old table that is part of the family history is rediscovered:

> Now here it was in the newly-opened cafe
> (had it been <u>an office for commercial affairs</u>?
> Or maybe <u>a solicitor's</u>? No, the baker's[...]),
> lined round in pine, tarnished, second-hand;
> a resting-place for dust-caked builders
> slumped over strong tea, the full English,
> as dark and heady as funeral incense.
>
> *They must always have been around somewhere,*
> *those worn-out old things* [...]

The italics indicate lines translated from the original, and the underlined words are also drawn from Cavafy's 1919 poem. Balmer consciously installs them in a structure that largely follows 'The Afternoon Sun'.

Intertextuality also occurs more subtly, for instance when translations are embedded in poetry collections, as in Heaney's *District and Circle*, where 'Cavafy: The rest I'll speak of to those below in Hades' (Heaney, 2006, 73) forms part of a complex dialogue between the living and the dead across the book (Heaney notably includes the poet's name in the title of this translation of one of the 'hidden poems'). And Don Paterson (b.1963) has a group of 'Three Poems after Cavafy' in 2003's *Landing Light* ('The Boat', 'One Night', 'The Bandaged Shoulder', 41–42), close enough to the originals to be designated translations, and followed by 'The Bowl-Maker' in his next collection, *Rain* (2009, 48). More recently, Christopher Reid also enlists Cavafy's voice in the list of 'Cs' that make up *The Curiosities* (2015). There, the poem shifts not only in title to reflect Reid's overall plan ('Before Time Could Change Them' now becomes 'The Circumstances'), but also typographically: each of the broken lines of the original unfolds in two lines in Reid's version which, while remaining close enough to be called a translation, nevertheless is double in length. Underlying these engagements, from recontextualization to poetic experiment, is a resolve to share a mind, which is realized in re-encodings that themselves engender further translations. In versions like 'The Circumstances' or poems like 'Cavafy in Liverpool', we recall more actively initial meanings, we sense that that familiar gaze is not only reaffirmed, but also extended.

Through Cavafy to his Greek Heirs

Just as Greek anthologies of Cavafy-inspired poetry inform Greece of its poet's influence, so we should inform the world of the creative reception of Cavafy's work in Greek literature. The 2015 chapbook I edited, entitled *12 Greek Poems After Cavafy*, somewhat mirrors a bilingual chapbook published in Greece in 2000 singling out six English poems that capture the initial and evolving reception of Cavafy's work in English literature.[10] While Plomer in 1932 marks the beginning of this process, Cavafy-inspired poetry in Greece begins

---

[10] Titled after a line by Cavafy, *Into a Foreign Tongue Goes Our Grief* […]: *Poems in English on, or after, Cavafy* included translations of W.H. Auden's 'Atlantis', Lawrence Durrell's 'Cavafy', Robert Graves's 'The Furious Voyage', Francis King's 'Cavafy', James Merrill's 'After Cavafy' and Russell Thornton's 'Epidaurus'; the poems by King and Thornton are taken from unpublished and undated collections.

over two decades earlier, and, significantly, the dominant mode for several years is not homage but parody (the 1960 poem 'Cavafy Writes to Malanos' by Angelos Parthenis (pseudonym of Petros Flambouris, 1935–2016), included in my selection, belongs to the later examples of this mode, hardly seen nowadays). My selections attempt to 'locate a kind of echo-chamber within Greek letters, which includes the attitudes forming within the SC, and the modulations in critical reception over the course of nearly a century of Greek poetry, between 1916 and 2015' (Nikolaou, 2015a, 3). Half the *12 Greek Poems After Cavafy* can be found in the two remarkable Greek anthologies (1997 and 2001) edited by Dimitris Daskalopoulos, which together hold 358 examples of Cavafy-inspired Greek poetry published between 1909 and 2001, with extensive notes. Four of the others were published later, and the last, '16 March 2015, 6 p.m.' by Dimitris Kosmopoulos (b.1964), was written especially for the chapbook; the publication of this poem in the original Greek is faced by its translation into English on the next page (Nikolaou, 2015a, 31–32).

The chapbook prioritizes the range of ways in which poetry can be Cavafy-inspired over the relative status of poets, and brings together new translations of poems by Seferis and Ritsos with works by six poets never before published in English. While the poems by Ritsos and Kapsalis come from narrative-inclined, book-length cycles, Ilias Margaris (1925–2017) constructs a collage, and the English translation, 'Compiling Verses from Cavafy' (Nikolaou, 2015a, 23) is itself a composite of existing translations. Yannis Voulis's 1963 poem 'From the Greek' (Nikolaou, 2015a, 17) finds translation, imitation and rewriting collapsing into one another: this near line-by-line repetition of Cavafy's poem 'Temethos, Antiochean, 400 AD' (1925) sees the poet in the original replaced by a translator who poignantly inserts the name of a lover in a translation of Callimachus:

> Anyhow it was not entirely for the love of poetry
> that this translation was made. One of Catlus's flames
> found his way into this elegant epigram.

These last three lines identify psychological spaces common to both poetry writing and translation. We witness simultaneously attachments shared by translators of, and poets after, Cavafy; they were also there and left a mark.

A project like *12 Greek Poems After Cavafy* can only happen when a poet's presence within world literature is pervasive enough for there to be an audience for the inner workings of another national literature. Cavafy thus provides an entry point into lesser known Greek poetry; the genealogy of influence permits the introduction of previous, unknown poetic voices in English. To make the selection representative enough, but manageable to another literary system and tradition, I imitated Ritsos's *12 Poiimata yia ton Kavafi* (12 Poems For Cavafy, 1963), a lasting model of poetic voices in dialogue. Here, Cavafy is observed in his surroundings, writing poems and conversing with members of his circle. This volume, *12 Greek Poems After Cavafy*, attempts a refraction of that existing shape; the variation in the title designed to reflect the proximity between poetries 'for' and 'after'.

Beyond examining the possibility of importing scenes from Greek literary history, the kind of 'philological translation' exemplified here also offered opportunities for a broader consideration of practices. 'A Note on Translating *12 Greek Poems After Cavafy*', which became available as a download-only pdf file at the publisher's website, included comment on the experience of collaborative translation (all but one of the translations were collaborations with Richard Berengarten) as well as on the status of, and reasons for, retranslation:

> Where translations already existed, as in the case of Ritsos and Seferis, the new version responds not just to the Greek original but also to a series of choices previously made; the palimpsest of sensibilities must also include translators working across the years. Retranslation becomes a gaze held; is not simply about, one hopes, improving on what has come before. (Nikolaou, 2015b)

The project became an active exploration of the thresholds and prospects for translated poetry originating from a small language, and more specifically, an enquiry into what may be accomplished in the confines of the 36-page chapbook. The concentration demanded by the limited space has much to recommend it, perhaps especially when it comes to considering paths from small into major languages/literatures. The four pages available for biographical notes combine communicating with English-speaking readers the extent and significance of the dialogue between Cavafy and each poet, alongside enough input to encourage further interest in their work, one hopes, in new English translations.

Conclusion

A sense of nearing saturation pervades recent translations of Cavafy. In his introduction to the Haviaras volume, Manuel Savidis argues that 'new, contemporary translation' is needed because we are not the same readers

Paschalis Nikolaou

we were decades ago: 'our sensibilities and our perception of language and poetry have been altered by the times' (Cavafy, 2007, xi). His argument would be more convincing if the volume had not been surrounded by several other translations around that year. In these editions, the introductions and notes repeat earlier scholarship while paradoxically arguing for greater innovation and precision. Even an elementary comparison of the translations suggests that they have long ceased originating from Cavafy's Greek alone; instead, most previous versions are set side by side, refer to each other and proceed as distant, unmarked collaborations, the new translator searching for small improvements, and the publisher for marketing angles.

Cavafy's international status and image is in fact defined by a synergy of actual translation and diverse forms of imitation. Over decades, this intense dialogue between literary systems has helped change Greek critical attitudes towards the poet. The mirror of an already English Cavafy faces the source culture. We can easily identify the dates when a consensus on his quality grows; they are also the points where Greek and foreign-language Cavafy-inspired poems begin to harmonize, follow similar ideas, and even agree on which poems to imitate most.

An extensive selection of the Cavafy-inspired work that exists in English might more fully and unequivocally show how a Greek poetic voice has continued in another language through a remarkable intertextual and paratextual operation, and how it materializes and is echoed through the cross-pollination of translational, critical and creative approaches. This has happened very rarely for other Greek poets; when it does, as with David Harsent's versioning of Yannis Ritsos (*In Secret*, 2012), the wider critical response reaffirms the need for varied approaches complementing one another, together serving to amplify a poet's reach. Regardless of quality, translation alone rarely proves enough, more so perhaps in the case of smaller languages. It is retellings of Cavafy's verse, those rich results of what has become code between poets, that both return energy to the originals and effect a visibility that engenders new translations.

Bibliography

Poetry By C.P. Cavafy
Cavafy, C.P. 1951. *The Poems of C.P. Cavafy*. Trans. John Mavrogordato. Introduction by Rex Warner (London: Hogarth Press).
Cavafy, C.P. 1961. *The Complete Poems of Cavafy*. Trans. Rae Dalven. Introduction by W.H. Auden (New York: Harcourt).

Cavafy, C.P. 1961. *Seven Unfinished Poems*. Trans. John C. Davis. *Conjunctions*, 31, 81–87.

Cavafy, C.P. 2001. *Before Time Could Change Them: The Complete Poems of Constantine P. Cavafy*. Trans. Theoharis Constantine Theoharis. Foreword by Gore Vidal (New York: Harcourt).

Cavafy, C.P. 2003. *Poems by C.P. Cavafy*. Trans. John C. Cavafy (Athens: Ikaros Books).

Cavafy, C.P. 2006. *The Collected Poems of C.P. Cavafy: A New Translation*. Trans. Aliki Barnstone. Foreword by Gerald Stern (New York: W.W. Norton).

Cavafy, C.P. 2007a. *The Canon: The Original One Hundred and Fifty-Four Poems by C.P. Cavafy*. Trans. Stratis Haviaras. Edited by Dana Bonstrom. Foreword by Seamus Heaney. Introduction by Manuel Savidis (Cambridge, MA, and London: Center for Hellenic Studies & Trustees for Harvard University; 1st edn, Athens: Hermes Publishing, 2004).

Cavafy, C.P. 2007b. *The Collected Poems*. Trans. Evangelos Sachperoglou. Edited by Anthony Hirst. Introduction by Peter Mackridge (Oxford: Oxford University Press; 1st edn, *154 Poems*, Athens: publisher unknown, 2003).

Cavafy, C.P. 2008. *Selected Poems*. Trans. Avi Sharon (London: Penguin).

Cavafy, C.P. 2009a. *Collected Poems*. Trans. Edmund Keeley and Philip Sherrard. Edited by George Savidis. Foreword by Robert Pinsky, revised edn (Princeton, NJ: Princeton University Press; 1st edn 1975).

Cavafy, C.P. 2009b. *Collected Poems*. Trans. Daniel Mendelsohn (New York: Alfred A. Knopf).

Cavafy, C.P. 2010. *The Unfinished Poems*. Trans. Daniel Mendelsohn (New York: Alfred A. Knopf).

Cavafy, C.P. 2011. *C.P. Cavafy: Poems – The Canon*. Trans. John Chioles. Edited by Demetrios Yatromanolakis. Harvard Early Modern and Modern Greek Library (Cambridge, MA: Harvard University Press).

Cavafy, C.P. 2013a. *Apokyrigmena: Poiimata ke Metafraseis (1886–1898)* (Athens: Ikaros Books).

Cavafy, C.P. 2013b. *Complete Plus: The Poems of C.P. Cavafy in English*. Trans. George Economou with Stavros Deligiorgis (Bristol: Shearsman Books).

Cavafy, C.P. 2014. *Selected Poems*. Trans. David Connolly (Athens: Aiora Press).

Economou, George. 2015. *Unfinished and Uncollected: Finishing the Unfinished Poems of C.P. Cavafy and Uncollected Poems & Translations* (Bristol: Shearsman Books).

Publications Featuring Cavafy-inspired Material

Auden, W.H. 1991. *Collected Poems*. Edited by Edward Mendelson (New York: Vintage International).

Balmer, Josephine. 2013. Cavafy's Things. *Agenda*, 47 (1–2), 90.

Daskalopoulos, Dimitris (ed.). 1999. *Parodies Kavafikon Poiimaton 1917–1997* (Athens: Patakis).

Paschalis Nikolaou

Daskalopoulos, Dimitris (ed.). 2003. *Ellinika Kavafoyeni Poiimata (1909–2001)* (Patras: Publications of University of Patras).
De Bernières, Louis. 2013. *Imagining Alexandria* (London: Harvill Secker).
Durrell, Lawrence. 1957. *Justine* (London: Faber & Faber).
Durrell, Lawrence. 1960. *Clea* (London: Faber & Faber).
Heaney, Seamus. 2006. *District and Circle* (London: Faber & Faber).
Jones, Evan. 2012. Cavafy in Liverpool. In his *Paralogues* (Manchester: Carcanet), 34.
MacInnes, Mairi. 1988/2007. Reading Cavafy in Translation. In her *The Girl I Left Behind Me: Poems of a Lifetime* (Nottingham: Shoestring Press), 34.
Mahon, Derek. 2006. *Adaptations* (Loughcrew: The Gallery Press).
Merrill, James. 1994. After Cavafy. *New York Review of Books*, 41, 14 July, 13.
Nikolaou, Paschalis (ed.). 2015a. *12 Greek Poems After Cavafy* (Bristol: Shearsman Books).
Paterson, Don. 2003. *Landing Light* (London: Faber & Faber).
Plomer, William. 1932. *The Fivefold Screen* (London: Hogarth Press).
Reid, Christopher. 2015. *The Curiosities* (London: Faber & Faber).
Ritsos, Yannis. 1963. *12 Poiimata yia ton Kavafi* (Athens: Kedros).
Serefas, Sakis (ed.). 2000. *Into a Foreign Tongue Goes Our Grief...: Poems in English on, or after, Cavafy* (Paeania: Bilieto).
Vayenas, Nasos (ed.). 1999. *Me ton Tropo tou Kavafi* (Thessaloniki: Kentro Ellinikis Glossas).
Vayenas, Nasos (ed.). 2000. *Synomilontas me ton Kavafi* (Thessaloniki: Kentro Ellinikis Glossas).

Works Cited
Connolly, David. 2003. Translator's Foreword. In Kondos, Yannis, *Absurd Athlete* (Todmorden: Arc Publications), 12–16.
Ekdawi, Sarah. 1997. Cavafy's English Poems. *Byzantine and Modern Greek Studies*, 21 (1), 223–30.
Ekdawi, Sarah. 2012. 'Definitive Voices of the Loved Dead': Cavafy in English. *Journal of Modern Greek Studies*, 30 (1), 129–36.
Emmerich, Karen. 2011. The Afterlives of C.P. Cavafy's Unfinished Poems. *Translation Studies*, 4 (2), 197–212.
Emmerich, Karen. 2017. The Unfinished Afterlives of C.P. Cavafy. In her *Literary Translation and the Making of Originals* (London and New York: Bloomsbury Academic), 131–59.
Forster, E.M. 1919. The Poetry of C.P. Cavafy. *The Nation and Athenaeum*, 25 April, 4643, 247–48.
Georganta, Konstantina. 2012. *Conversing Identities: Encounters Between British, Irish and Greek Poetry, 1922–1952* (Amsterdam and New York: Rodopi).
Harsent, David. 2012. *In Secret: Versions of Yannis Ritsos* (London: Enitharmon Press).

Hass, Robert. 2010. Introduction. In Constantine, David, Rachel Hadas, Edmund Keeley and Karen Van Dyck (eds). *The Greek Poets: Homer to the Present* (New York: W.W. Norton), ix–xxxiii.

Jeffreys, Peter (ed.). 2009. *The Forster–Cavafy Letters: Friends at a Slight Angle* (Cairo and New York: American University in Cairo Press).

Jusdanis, Gregory. 1987. *The Poetics of Cavafy: Textuality, Eroticism, History* (Princeton, NJ: Princeton University Press).

Katope, Christopher G. 1969. Cavafy and Durrell's *The Alexandria Quartet*. *Comparative Literature*, 21 (2), 125–37.

Keeley, Edmund. 1976. *Cavafy's Alexandria: Study of a Myth in Progress* (Cambridge, MA: Harvard University Press).

Kruczkowska, Joanna. 2017. *Irish Poets and Modern Greece: Heaney, Mahon, Cavafy, Seferis* (London: Palgrave Macmillan).

Liddell, Robert. 1974. *Cavafy: A Critical Biography* (London: Duckworth).

Logenbach, James. 2009. A Poet's Progress. *The New York Times*, 17 April. Available from: www.nytimes.com/2009/04/19/books/review/Longenbach-t.html?_r=0> [accessed 4 May 2016].

Malanos, Timos. 1933. *O Poiitis K.P. Kavafis –O Anthropos ke to Ergo tou* (Athens: Govostis; revised/expanded edn, Athens: Difros, 1957).

Nikolaou, Paschalis. 2015b. A Note on Translating *12 Greek Poems After Cavafy*. Available from: https://irp-cdn.multiscreensite.com/12e499a6/files/uploaded/A-Note-on-Translating-12-Greek-Poems-after-Cavafy.pdf [accessed 4 November 2018].

Peridis, Michalis. 1948. *O Vios ke to Ergo tou Konstantinou Kavafi* (Athens: Ikaros).

Pinchin, Jane Lagoudis. 1977. *Alexandria Still: Forster, Durrell, and Cavafy* (Princeton, NJ: Princeton University Press).

Pine, Richard. 1994. *Lawrence Durrell: The Mindscape* (London: Palgrave Macmillan; 2nd revised edn, Corfu: Durrell School of Corfu, 2005).

Seferis, George. 1966. *On the Greek Style*, trans. by Rex Warner and Th. D. Frangopoulos (New York: Little, Brown).

Tsirkas, Stratis. 1958. *O Kavafis ke i Epochi tou* (Athens: Kedros).

Vayenas, Nasos. 2010. Cavafy's Poetry of Irony. In Berengarten, Richard and Paschalis Nikolaou (eds). *The Perfect Order: Selected Poems 1974–2010* (London: Anvil Press Poetry), 133–36.

CHAPTER TEN

Criminal Peripheries: The Globalization of Scandinavian Crime Fiction and Its Agents

Jakob Stougaard-Nielsen (UCL)

Crime Fiction from the Global Peripheries

Crime fiction has always been an international genre, yet, until the late 1990s, the dominant locations of widely translated and canonized crime novels have coincided with the major and shifting centres of the publishing and media industry. Although their detectives are often displaced, travelling or negotiating the tensions between urban or geopolitical centres and geographical peripheries, Poe and Simenon's Paris, Conan Doyle and Christie's London, and Chandler's Los Angeles, to mention a few, replicate the dominance in translated fiction of a few major languages and locations. However, as Andrew Pepper and David Schmid (2016, 1) assert:

> It is only in the last twenty years or so that crime fiction has really mushroomed beyond the familiar scenes of its foundational texts [...] to become a truly global literary genre. Indigenous crime fiction cultures are now emerging from, and speaking to, their own sites of production and, aided by the globalization of the literary marketplace and a new emphasis on translation, traveling to all corners of the globe to the extent that we can now arguably describe crime fiction as a world literature par excellence.

From an Anglo-American central perspective, it undoubtedly appears that 'indigenous crime fiction' (like Kirino's Japanese, Camilleri's Sicilian or Arion's Romanian crime novels, Mendoza's Mexican narconovellas and Deon Meyer's South African thrillers) is only just now emerging from hitherto 'dark' countries and continents on the map of world literature, and that these must 'naturally' arise from 'foundational texts' familiar to critics and non-professional readers in the global centres of the West. This habitual framing of contemporary 'crime fiction as world literature' as peripheral, national fungi feeding on the cosmopolitan crime fiction capitals of the Western world, resembles a view of globalization described by Cairns Craig (2007, 29) as a world system wherein 'the cultural distinctions on which peripheries could draw to resist the processes of "globalization" are [...] erased: difference at an economical level turns into sameness at a cultural level'. In other words, the internationalization of crime fiction is a pertinent example of 'global literature', propelled by global market forces that capitalize on the exposure, management and exploitation of the exotically different local expressions of a global marketplace (Stougaard-Nielsen, 2016).

Crime fiction has proven remarkably marketable and mobile, and today the literary form or commodity perhaps best suited to take advantage of a globalized literary marketplace and a consequent new emphasis on translation. However, the marketization of these new, peripheral 'indigenous crime fiction cultures' also threatens to confirm their peripheral position in the literary system by condemning them to their own quirky foreignness, distinct only by their national or regional colour, or locate them at the 'commercial pole' of a homogenized bestseller culture alongside other rootless 'world fictions', crowding out 'the avant-garde' quality literature and small publishers, thereby confirming Pascale Casanova's prediction (2004, 172) that 'a genuine internationalism is no longer possible'.

Crime writers recently emerging from the global and European literary peripheries would be the first to acknowledge influence from seminal Anglo-American innovators in the many sub-genres of crime fiction, thereby exemplifying Franco Moretti's 'wave-theory' (2000) of the transnational spread of novelistic genres, emanating from literary and cultural centres and influencing the peripheries through translations, adaptations and mimicry. However, as Paulina Drewniak demonstrates in the next chapter, local traditions evidently have deeper, more eclectic and entangled roots sustained by literary and cultural traditions that also transcend the presumed narrow confines and static forms of Anglo-American genre fiction. Only very recently have critics begun to explore a more rhizomatic map of the world of genre fiction. For instance, the anthology *Crime Fiction as World Literature* (2017) challenges established centre–periphery conceptions of the dissemination of literature across national borders, upheld by Casanova and Moretti, and the rarely challenged Western history of crime fiction: 'It is notable that the first modern detective stories were written not in Europe or the United States but in China' (Nilsson et al., 2017, 2).

Jakob Stougaard-Nielsen

A significant factor in the more recent deterritorialization of the crime novel's origins and centres, according to the editors, is the wider 'globalization of the novel', driven by 'worldwide literary systems of distribution' involving 'complex, overlapping, disjunctive networks and sub-networks' (Nilsson et al., 2017, 3). The crime novel presents a particularly relevant case for considering the processes involved in the making of contemporary transnational literatures, since this genre, perhaps more than any other, is both the result of and itself propels such 'disjunctive networks', which characterize what Galin Tihanov (2014, 187) has called 'the regime of a complex (and constant) marginocentricity, in which centre and periphery become fluid, mobile, and provisional, prone to swapping their places and exchanging cultural valences'.

While the world of transnational publishing is undoubtedly dominated by multinational media conglomerates, Anglo-American centres and global English, there are clear signs of a more marginocentric regime on the rise especially, but not exclusively, in the market for bestsellers. 'Today', the editors of *Crime Fiction as World Literature* speculate, 'American crime writers are as likely to be inspired by Swedish authors as the reverse' (Nilsson et al., 2017, 3) – and, most likely, in translation. While this assertion is perhaps overstating the fact, it is certainly more probable today that readers across the world will pick up a crime novel originally written in a language other than English from independent, chain or online book stores, supermarkets or libraries. This new global regime, with its concomitant transnational 'democratization' of the traditional hierarchies of the book trade aided by new digital and social media such as 'BookCrossing, GoogleBooks, book blogs, pirated e-books, cooperative writing communities, and fan fiction' (Steiner, 2014, 320), is marked by its unpredictability:

> The rise to global prominence of Nordic detective fiction over the last twenty years, with writers like Peter Høeg [b.1957], Stieg Larsson [1954–2004], Henning Mankell [1948–2015], Matti Joensuu [1948–2011], Yrsa Sigurdsdottir [*sic*] [b.1963], Arnaldur Indridason [b.1961], Anne Holt [b.1958], and Jo Nesbø [b.1960], all of whom write in minority languages in countries with small populations and advanced welfare systems is another good example of the unpredictability of success. All these writers have acquired global access through translation. (Bassnett, 2017, 149)

The phenomenon of the global, bestselling crime novel may justly be considered significant – at least in terms of market share – but perhaps also an anomaly in the wider field of publishing today, where genre fiction and bestseller culture is still considered by some a closed system of purely commercial interests reaching a large group of 'common' readers, who read merely for entertainment and are characteristically reluctant to cross-over into other parts of the literary field (Venuti, 2008, 155; Rønning and Slaatta, 2012, 111). However, as it will be argued here, we should look to the recent 'unpredictable success' of Scandinavian crime fiction in the English-speaking world as an example of what it takes to traverse the borders between the contemporary publishing markets of small nations and those of global centres.

In the following, I shall explore aspects of this 'Scandinavian miracle', the 'unpredictable' international success of Scandinavian crime fiction, by considering various consecration processes (i.e. literary prizes and academic canonization) that have participated in stimulating the transnational flow of crime fiction, and the function of national and regional publishing and media environments in the promotion of literature in translation (including regional translation practices and the rise of literary agents), which, I shall suggest, have both helped shape and been shaped by the success of the genre. In such exchanges between Scandinavian and particularly anglophone markets, which predate the 'Scandinavian miracle' in the twenty-first century, I shall argue that we witness the emergence of a new regime of marginocentricity in transnational publishing in the particular case of small-nation literatures.

The Scandinavian Miracle?

Though Scandinavian literatures include a variety of recognizable crime fictions going back to nineteenth-century contemporaries of Poe,[1] and more sporadic examples of widely translated and internationally adapted crime novels in the late 1960s, notably by the Dane Anders Bodelsen (b.1937) and the Swedish writing team Maj Sjöwall (b.1935) and Per Wahlöö (1926–75),[2] the

---

[1] Kerstin Bergman (2014, 13) suggests that 'Sweden – as well as Denmark and Norway – all have stories similar to Poe's that predate the American author's'.
[2] Bodelsen's *Think of a Number* (1969 [1968]) was translated into several languages, including Czech, French, German, Italian, Japanese, Russian, Spanish and English. It was adapted for a Danish film in 1969 and an English-language remake in 1978 as *The Silent Partner* (Stougaard-Nielsen, 2017, 31). Sjöwall and Wahlöö's 'Novel of a Crime' series has been translated into most European languages, Turkish, Russian, Hebrew, Estonian, Chinese, Japanese and Korean,

'wave' of globally successful Scandinavian crime novels gathered momentum in the early 1990s with the international successes of Høeg's *Miss Smilla's Feeling for Snow* (1993 [1992]) and Mankell's 11-volume Wallander series (1991–2009). The wave broke in the first decades of the twenty-first century with the global publishing phenomenon of Larsson's *Millennium* trilogy (*The Girl with the Dragon Tattoo*, 2008 [2005], *The Girl Who Played with Fire*, 2009 [2006], and *The Girl Who Kicked the Hornets' Nest*, 2009 [2007]), the advent of Nordic Noir TV crime series including Denmark's *The Killing* (2007–12) and Scandinavian co-productions such as *The Bridge* (2011–18).[3]

According to David Geherin (2012, 4), Larsson's *The Girl Who Played with Fire* became 'the first translated novel in 25 years to top the coveted *New York Times* best seller list'. He uses the example of Larsson to suggest that, at least in crime fiction, the borders between nations and publishing markets are coming down. Indeed, several Scandinavian crime series have been translated into more than 30 languages, and authors like the Norwegian Nesbø, the Swedes Arne Dahl (b.1963), Camilla Läckberg (b.1974) and Liza Marklund (b.1962), and the Dane Jussi Adler-Olsen (b.1950) are selling millions of copies of their crime novels outside Scandinavia. In the twenty-first century, Scandinavian crime fiction has become a local as well as global obsession, often described as a sub-genre and forming a recognizable international brand with its stock of morose and often unhealthy detectives, cold, desolate landscapes and penchant for social and political criticism (Forshaw, 2012; Bergman, 2014, 173; Stougaard-Nielsen, 2017).

While locally produced crime fiction has dominated the national bestseller lists in Sweden and the rest of Scandinavia since the 1990s, the international success of translated crime novels, particularly their recent success in anglophone markets, has given birth to expressions such as 'Scandimania', 'the Nordic invasion' and 'the Swedish crime fiction miracle' (Svedjedal, 2012, 209), which suggest how rare it is for small-nation literatures

and *The Laughing Policeman* (1970 [1968]) was adapted for film in 1973 by 20th Century Fox.

[3] According to Pia Majbritt Jensen (2016): 'Danish audio-visual drama series are currently experiencing an unprecedented global boom in exports [...]. By the end of 2013, one or more of [*The Killing*'s] three seasons [...] had been exported to approximately 100 countries and territories in all continents, including Afghanistan and Argentina, Greece and Guatemala, Iran and Italy, Tadzhikistan and Taiwan, Mozambique and New Zealand [...] [T]he series has also been re-made into a US version (*The Killing*, AMC/Netflix, 2011–13) and a Turkish version (Cinayet, Kanal D, 2015).'

The Globalization of Scandinavian Crime Fiction and Its Agents

and cultures to make an impact on the UK and US markets. Monitoring the language spread of bestsellers on several European markets between 2008 and 2014, Miha Kovač and Rüdiger Wischenbart (2016, 25–27) found that

> the impact of Nordic authors remains striking, establishing a cohort very similar to English [...] The readers' rush for Nordic crime is the tip of a giant iceberg that has grown over several decades when as early as in the 1960s and 1970s, Henning Mankell [*sic*], Maj Sjöwall and Per Wahlöö had set out finding their readership in continental Europe. After Larsson's success, a new dynamics led to an explosion of translations.

Kovač and Wischenbart suggest that the 'unpredictable' recent publishing success is only the visible part of a much deeper and wider Nordic genre tradition, and one for which moreover the older generation, such as Mankell in the 1990s, paved the way because they had already 'set out' successfully to find their international readership. Nevertheless, how this breakthrough came about is an important story; its details will help us understand the internationalized publishing context in which the more recent successes of Scandinavian crime fiction in translation can be demystified. Kovač and Wischenbart's report also prompts the question: what characterizes the 'new dynamics' that 'led to an explosion of translations' following Larsson's success? The success of Scandinavian crime fiction in the UK, in the first decades of the twenty-first century, does indeed suggest that 'a new dynamic' has appeared, but one that was not created solely by 'the Larsson craze'. Instead, Larsson's success may be viewed as a fortunate result of consecration processes and publishing dynamics already in place in Scandinavia and in the UK.

The Consecration of Scandinavian Crime Fiction in Translation

A driver traditionally seen as belonging exclusively to the business end of the literary field is literary prizes. In Scandinavia, literary prizes for crime fiction, both within and between the nations, continue to play an important role in the popularization of the genre; in particular, the breakthrough of bestselling women crime writers in the late 1990s owed much to awards targeted precisely at broadening the authorship and readership for crime writing to women.[4]

---

[4] In the 1990s, the Swedish crime journal *Jury* instituted the Poloni Prize for

Jakob Stougaard-Nielsen

Consecration through literary awards is an epitextual phenomenon, a significant agent in the literary field, which must be examined if we want to understand the extent of the processes (and agencies) involved in the making of the 'Scandinavian miracle', perhaps better characterized as a fortuitous constellation of agents and phenomena both within Scandinavia and in receiving markets. Literary prizes are, as James F. English (2005, 3) reminds us, fundamentally about cultural prestige'. Literary prizes, according to Claire Squires (2009, 97), 'turn the attention of the media to books, and so support the consumption of literature generally'. In the literary field, the intervention of literary prizes has the dual function of both indicating and conferring value on authors and their books and, therefore, as agents they play an integral part in choosing and promoting works that may relate or conform to current tastes and values (Squires, 2009, 97–101).

The rise to prominence of international crime writing in the UK has been promoted by and reflected in the Crime Writers Association Daggers awards. Since 1955, according to the association (CWA Daggers), these literary awards 'have been synonymous with quality crime writing'; the CWA Gold Dagger, for instance, 'is awarded to the best crime novel of the year'. Curiously, 'up to 2005, books in translation were eligible for this prize', but 'in 2006, the CWA established a separate dagger for books in translation, recognizing the work of the translator as well as that of the original author'. Before the change to distinguish between English language and 'international' crime writing, the Gold Dagger was won by Mankell in 2001, by Spanish writer José Carlos Somoza (b.1959) the following year, and in 2005, four out of five nominated writers wrote in a language other than English. In the end, the award went to the Icelandic writer Arnaldur Indriðason. This 'accidental' internationalization of the CWA Gold Dagger prize, according to Geherin (2012, 4), 'illustrates a situation that was either encouraging or alarming, depending on one's view point'. When the CWA decided to preserve the Gold Dagger for crime fiction written in English, the committee was criticized for literary xenophobia, but the CWA's decision to expand its inclusion of crime fiction in translation to also award translators could be viewed as a natural recognition of 'a growing body of work by foreign writers that was rapidly becoming available in translation for English-speaking readers' (Geherin, 2012, 4).

promising female crime writers. Marklund won the first award in 1998. Three years later the prize was withdrawn thanks to the large number of female crime writers who had made the bestseller lists (Berglund, 2012, 38). A similar award was also established in Denmark in 2002.

The Globalization of Scandinavian Crime Fiction and Its Agents

While a few Scandinavian crime writers had benefited from the prestige of the Gold Dagger before 2006, with the International Dagger a larger number of 'new' writers, publishers and translators gained from the consecration and visibility of the award: Håkan Nesser (b.1950) was shortlisted in 2006 and the following year, a Dane (Christian Jungersen (b.1962)), two Swedes (Karin Alvtegen (b.1965) and Åsa Larsson (b.1966)) and a Norwegian (Nesbø) were shortlisted; Stieg Larsson was nominated in 2008, and in 2009 five Scandinavian writers and their translators were shortlisted (Nesbø, Johan Theorin (b.1963), Stieg Larsson, Indriðason and Alvtegen) – the French writer Fred Vargas (b.1957) won in 2006, 2007 and 2009. In 2010, the International Dagger went to the Swede Theorin, in a year where both Indriðason and Stieg Larsson were shortlisted again, followed in 2011 by the award going to the Swedish writing team Anders Roslund (b.1961) and Börge Hellström (1957–2017). Since then, Scandinavian crime writers and translators have regularly been among the nominated; yet, while their dominance in the category of the International Dagger has waned in recent years, a new prize, the Petrona Award for the Best Scandinavian Crime Novel of the Year, was first given out in 2013 at the international Crimefest convention in Bristol.[5]

A similar internationalization within the consecration of crime writing in translation in English-speaking countries can be seen in the academic reception, which plays a significant role in canonization processes. A growing number of studies are being published where the generic term 'crime fiction' is no longer assumed to mean crime fiction written in English. Despite the continuing dominance of British and American crime fiction, 'the field of crime studies not only seems to have expanded greatly, but also to have become increasingly international' (Kärrholm, 2014, 99). Whereas seminal studies by Priestman, Knight and Scaggs in the early 2000s dealt almost exclusively with crime fiction in English with the exception of a few French-language examples, Peter Messent's *The Crime Fiction Handbook* (2013) includes 14 case studies of key works in crime fiction of which two are Scandinavian (Sjöwall and Wahlöö and Larsson) and the rest British and American – and in Forshaw's anthology *Detective* in Intellect's *Crime Uncovered* series (2016), almost every other case study features a

---

[5] The Petrona Award was established to celebrate the work of Maxine Clarke, one of the first online crime fiction reviewers and bloggers, who died in December 2012. The award administrator, Karen Meek, is a former CWA judge for the International Dagger.

Scandinavian sleuth (Beck, Wallander, Hole, Lund/Noren, Van Veeteren). Kärrholm suggests that such examples demonstrate that 'there are still only a few Nordic authors thought important enough to be included in general handbooks on international crime fiction'. However, one could also conclude that the continuing absence of other crime fiction traditions in such general studies suggests that Scandinavian crime fiction has become consecrated both by literary prizes and academic canonization as *the* international crime fiction *per excellence* in the English-speaking world.

Consecration processes such as literary prizes and academic reception have played significant roles in the promotion of crime writing in translation in the UK beginning with the visibility provided by the CWA Dagger award to Mankell, well before the Larsson phenomenon, and a subsequent wider selection of Nordic crime writers and their translators with the inauguration of the CWA International Dagger award. We may assume that although academic interest in translated crime fiction has been slower to materialize, the popularity of (especially) Nordic crime writing, as evidenced by bestseller lists and literary awards, has resulted in a less Anglo-centric appreciation of the genre.

Regional Publishing in a Global Field

Consecration processes belonging predominantly to the commercial field (bestseller lists and literary prizes) have a significant, yet belated, impact on analogous processes related to the cultural prestige and literary value, or canonization, of 'peripheral' literatures in translation in the receiving cultural 'centres'. In the first decade of the twenty-first century, these (together with numerous other agents including literary festivals, cultural institutions, social media, publicists, publishers, agents and book clubs) have participated in promoting Scandinavian crime fiction as the source of a new popular world literature or the latest example of a global literature created by and for an increasingly commercialized and transnational publishing market.

Squires (2007, 408–09) describes the global publishing field as being under the hegemony of global English and dominated by a bestseller culture, which has resulted in a lack of diversity when it comes to reader access to a wider range of languages in translation. The global market for bestselling titles is dominated by transnational media and publishing conglomerates, where, according to Eva Hemmungs Wirtén (2007, 401), 'publishing is seen as

The Globalization of Scandinavian Crime Fiction and Its Agents

more of a commercial rather than a cultural activity', evidenced, for example, in media conglomerates' proclivity for trading in 'content' rather than books. This, according to Wirtén, is 'central to convergence as another of the main traits of late modern publishing'.

Global bestsellers are judged less culturally valuable because their success is mostly credited to well-funded promotion campaigns, the ability of conglomerates to benefit from promoting their 'content' through media convergence, and the wider marketization of publishing, where the lack of literary quality is no hindrance to success and, according to Venuti, where bland foreign literature is consumed in domesticated translations (Squires, 2007, 409; Venuti, 2008). This perception is exemplified by Stieg Larsson, who authored one of the most globally widespread books in 2009: 'the result of media conglomerates and hype', which 'may have little to do with what we understand as world literature' or a 'truly international literature' (Steiner, 2014, 316).

Concurring with Wirtén, Steiner (2014, 317) argues that transnational media conglomerates have influenced, 'and possibly dictated', the production and distribution of world literature as never before, through media and content development. These are 'agents [who] largely determine which literary works will travel across borders and become transnational'. However, Steiner (2014, 317) continues, 'book-market systems are not the same around the globe, and the publishing conglomerates do not control every part of the trade, which is, rather, a complex and often contradictory structure of domestic markets juxtaposed with international markets'. Though the principal agents in the global book trade are multinational conglomerates, 'publishing is regionally specific' (Steiner, 2014, 319), and a global bestseller is not always or exclusively the result of media conglomerates' interference. Larsson's posthumously published *Millennium* trilogy was, for instance, first published by Sweden's oldest independent publishing house, Norstedts, and, according to Kovač and Wischenbart, was

> sold for translation into several languages, but only the French translation at independent publisher Actes Sud triggered a frenzy that had been unanticipated. The third step in the saga of the trilogy going globally through the roof came with the launch of the UK edition by Quercus, another independent publisher. (2010, 31)

The example of Larsson's success, therefore, contradicts prevalent structures and tendencies in the global publishing market and demonstrates that, as Ondřej Vimr describes in Chapter Three, at least initially, a transnational publishing success can be driven by peripheral actors and small publishers in several markets by way of 'disjunctive networks'.

According to Helge Rønning and Tore Slaatta (2012, 102), 'a major finding in recent research is the prevalence of regional markets for publishing'. Publishing in the four large Nordic countries is dominated by a few national or Nordic conglomerates, such as Bonnier in Sweden, Aschehoug in Norway and Gyldendal in Denmark, followed by several medium-sized publishers and a number of smaller ones (Rønning and Slaatta, 114). So far, Nordic publishers have not been a major interest for multinational conglomerates, and therefore a less oligopolistic trend is still to be found in Nordic publishing, which may be attributed to relatively small national markets, and the way in which 'national languages, cultural policies and historically embedded cultural commitments still dominate in the Nordic publishing industry' (Rønning and Slaatta, 2012, 119).[6]

The general book market, according to Rønning and Slaatta (2012, 111), 'demands an ever greater number of bestsellers', and the fact that only a few writers like Larsson, writing in languages other than English, make one or two bestseller lists outside of their own language area demonstrates that 'bestseller thinking currently favours English-language writers and publishers' and 'the continuing and increasingly lopsided relationship between centre and periphery in international publishing.' While the Nordic countries demonstrate nation- and region-specific structures and conditions, they are also traditionally import cultures, still influenced by international consumers, publishers and literary trends. In her study of the impact of national and foreign literature in translation on Swedish bestseller lists, Ann Steiner finds that Swedish originals dominate; for instance, in 2010, 70 per cent of the most purchased titles were originally written in Swedish (2012, 24). Historically, translated literature in Sweden has constituted about half of the market, though in 2010, Steiner (2012, 25) concludes that this is no longer true, since only about 16 per cent of new published titles were actually translations, though the share of fiction titles is larger, with about 35 per cent translated titles. Translation from English is following a recently emergent pattern, in which English-language books play an unfamiliar, less dominant role internationally. In the last decades of the twentieth century, 80 per cent

---

[6] With the success of Scandinavian crime writing, we may be witnessing a change to this dominant system with, for instance, the appearance of HarperCollins Nordic, which publishes both international authors in Scandinavian translations and Scandinavian authors in their home markets.

The Globalization of Scandinavian Crime Fiction and Its Agents

of translated titles in Sweden were from English, a share that dropped to 70 per cent in 2010. Steiner (2012, 26) attributes this change to several smaller publishers venturing into the translated-fiction market.[7]

While UNESCO's *Index Translationum* indicates that over half of the translated fiction in Sweden, which comprises 50 per cent of published fiction, is from English, 'the bestseller lists show that English titles may not always sell as easily as they are translated', according to Steiner (2014, 321–22): 'In the case of Sweden, only two out of the top ten fiction titles were translations. No matter what some critics say about the global dominance of the English language, it is not visible in book-buying patterns.' Steiner's rather surprising conclusion that, in bestseller lists where global English should dominate, 'English-language literature does not dominate the globe', correlates with Kovač and Wischenbart's study of European bestseller lists in the period 2008–09 (Kovač and Wischenbart, 2010). Only 30 per cent of top 40 titles were originally written in English, while a small nation such as Sweden sported eight titles, mostly due to the success of crime fiction (2009). According to Steiner (2014, 322), 'the Swedish crime fiction author Stieg Larsson [...] is an illuminating example, showing that international success is more often linked to genre than to language'.

However, the fact that translation is itself an important consecration process in the international publishing market suggests that the regional Nordic publishing field has become a factor in the marketing and promotion of crime fiction within and beyond the region (Lindqvist, 2012, 203). The Nordic publishing field harbours not only a long-standing tradition for state-funded literary, publishing and translation endeavours, but also regional infrastructures based on historic, social, cultural and linguistic ties. These find expression in transnational and national support for translations of literature between the Nordic languages and the consecration of a Nordic literature in the annual Nordic Council Literature Prize awarded since 1962, whose purpose it is 'to promote interest in the literature and language of the neighbouring countries' and the Nordic community.[8] Such factors have helped promote a strong internal translation practice within the region, giving authors and

---

[7] A similar trend is noticeable in Denmark, where foreign fiction titles in translation led Danish titles by 30 per cent in 2009, but now the ratio is 50:50. There has been a rise in new Danish titles since 2009 and a little drop in translations from English (Books and Literature 2015, 2015, 13–14).

[8] See the description of the literature prize on the Nordic Council website (Nordic Cooperation, n.d.).

publishers a cross-national and regional exposure that has helped strengthen the visibility of Nordic literatures in translation more widely. According to Yvonne Lindqvist (2016, 174), the Nordic countries constitute 'a relatively autonomous' regional 'translation (sub)field in the global translation field', in which Nordic languages get translated into each other first. While English is still the dominant source language for translations in Sweden (in her data from 2010, it comprises a surprisingly low 16 per cent of the total publishing market, dropping from 30 per cent in 2002; the share of translations in Denmark and Norway is around 30 per cent), more proximate languages such as Danish and Norwegian come in second and third; and in Denmark and Norway, Swedish is second, far exceeding the third most frequent source language in Denmark: German (Lindquist, 2016, 177, 180). The data Lindqvist (2016, 181) has collected demonstrates the 'close interaction of the Scandinavian languages by means of translation and reveals the centrality of the Swedish language in the Scandinavian literary space'. Furthermore, Lindqvist (2016, 185) notes 'the odd fact' that despite their relatively restricted number of speakers, Scandinavian languages 'rank among the ten most important source languages in the global translation field today', and suggests that 'there is no direct relation between the number of speakers of a language in the world and the prestige of the language as source language on the global translation field'. The constitution of a Scandinavian translation (sub)field is, for Lindqvist (2016, 185), central to understanding the 'high prestige of the Scandinavian languages in the global translation field'. However, in the case of Swedish literature in translation, its marginocentric or semi-peripheral position on the export market was already noted by Johan Heilbron (2000) and an established fact by the 1980s, according to Agnes Broomé (2014, 38).

The relative success of translations from the Scandinavian languages generally and Swedish in particular is not an entirely new phenomenon – it certainly predates the 'Scandinavian crime fiction miracle' – but the significance of translations to the accrual of cultural prestige and, not least, the book business, has in recent decades been driven by the visibility of Nordic crime writing, as crime fiction has played a substantial role in the rise of income from translation rights, which has more than doubled in Sweden from the 1990s to 2012.[9]

---

[9] According to Broomé (2014, 39), 'the contribution to the Swedish publishing industry from sales of translation rights was about SEK60 million annually in the 1990s [...] By 2012, that number had more than doubled, to roughly SEK150 million, a considerable sum for companies in a relatively small market.'

Research into the Scandinavian translation (sub)field and the contemporary European market for translations points to the fact that, although English still dominates the markets, the source language, in Wischenbart's formulation (2016, 7), 'does not really matter', particularly in the 'bestselling' part of the business where 'authorial brands rule'. However, as Wischenbart also points out, an author's successful 'branding' is dependent on the choice of genre, which 'has become a factor that can override the marketing power of even the biggest corporations', as Stieg Larsson has demonstrated. As the Scandinavian example shows, branding through genre has proven a successful means of increasing the sale of international rights and thereby authors' consecration at home and abroad, especially if the chosen genre lends itself easily to media convergence. Wischenbart (2016, 7) argues, however, that in the contemporary market for fiction, an author may only overcome the perceived limitations of writing from within a small nation in a language other than English through the sale of translation (and adaptation) rights, 'provided that he or she can rely on the organizing muscle of a good agent'.

The Rise of the Nordic Agent

The publishing industry in Scandinavia witnessed a dramatic change in the last years of the twentieth century. In Sweden, as Berglund (2014) documents, the bestseller lists were taken over by domestic crime writers. Regionally, the same occurred in Denmark and Norway, and Scandinavia became relatively self-sufficient in the most popular of genres around 2000. Berglund's quantitative studies of the Swedish market for crime fiction over the past decades suggest that the crime fiction 'boom' was intricately linked to the rise of literary agents. Literary agents, according to Squires (2009, 35), reflect a 'cultural shift' in publishing towards a marketing-led publishing culture, and has been part of 'the growing professionalization and business-based practice of publishing'. Particularly in today's global, multimedia leisure and information industry, 'the literary agent's power has grown alongside the diversification of rights sales', with the agent 'effectively acting as the author's business manager' (Squires, 2009, 35). According to John B. Thompson (2010, 61, 73, 93), 'by the late 1990's [...] an agent was a necessity: a writer who wanted to publish with a major trade house now *needed* an agent' to orchestrate and exploit 'the sale of rights' associated with a work. In Scandinavia, where only a few literary agents had operated, in Sweden at the turn of the millennium, the 'need' for an agent was becoming apparent, as successful crime writers sought to sell not only translation rights but also rights to exploit their work in other media.[10]

The rise of agencies in Sweden has played a significant role in turning what was mostly an import country into an export country successfully selling titles beyond the traditional Nordic and Germanic markets. Similarly, in Denmark, the sale of international rights is a fast-growing business with a third more rights sold in 2015 compared to just four years previously.[11] Since 2000, according to Berglund (2014, 68), 'more than ten literary agencies have been founded in Sweden, and new ones are constantly being added'. The biggest, Salomonsson Agency, was founded in 2000 and focuses mostly on crime writers and other bestsellers. This boom in literary agencies coincided with 'the commercial success of Swedish crime fiction all over the world'. This structural transformation meant that Swedish publishing adjusted to the global book market both by growing the domestic field of popular fiction, with genres approximating forms well known in the global publishing centres and beyond, and developing media and market structures that allowed for a competitive advantage when potentially marketable books, like Larsson's, would eventually appear.

Mankell's Publishing Networks

Mankell constitutes a good example of the impact of a literary agent on the ability of an already nationally bestselling writer to make an impact on the international market. This case also demonstrates that the Scandinavian twenty-first-century publishing phenomenon is the tip of an iceberg of strategic coordinated practices between small-nation actors established in the early 1990s, which came to provide a 'marginocentric' model for successfully entering the international mainstream.

In Forshaw's assessment (2012, 21), 'if there's one modern writer who is the market leader for foreign crime in translation, it is Sweden's Henning

---

[10] Gunhild Agger has pointed out the centrality of adaptation to the success of Scandinavian crime fiction (Agger and Waade, 2010, 19–34). Broomé (2014, 152) also contends that the success of Swedish crime fiction is 'in no small part due to the synergy generated by their multi-modal form'.

[11] According to the Danish Agency for Culture, the number of rights sold for Danish books in 2015 was the highest for many years with 360 rights sold, 100 more rights than in 2011 (Secher, 2016).

Mankell'. According to Stephanie Craighill, 'Mankell's Swedish origins mean that he has become an emblem for the success of small-nation authors on an international scale' (2013, 202). The case of Mankell, therefore, could be viewed as pivotal in assessing the wider and subsequent success of Scandinavian crime fiction in translation. Mankell was a writer who had a perceptive approach to promoting his authorship in rapidly changing local and global markets for bestselling fiction. In 2001, he established his own publishing house, Leopard Förlag, together with his publisher, Dan Israel, which allowed Mankell not only to assert control over the rights to his own works, but also to use some of the revenue to publish less profitable translations, especially from African and Asian literatures. Having witnessed the impact of early film adaptations on the rising sales of his crime novels in Sweden in the 1990s, Mankell's decision to establish the production company Yellow Bird in 2003, together with the Danish producer Ole Søndberg, provides another example of Mankell taking control over the rights to exploit his own 'content', anticipating and helping to promote the growing importance of convergence in the market for bestselling fiction.[12]

Mankell's grasp of how to exploit his rights and establish and make use of publishing networks in the context of the national publishing business and the potential for remediations in the 2000s has a precedent in the way he and Dan Israel sought to achieve international success particularly in the UK and US markets in the early 1990s. Though Israel had managed to secure French and German publishing deals for Mankell's first Wallander novel *Faceless Killers* (1991) (with mediocre sales in the still primary German market), he adopted a different strategy for negotiating translation rights for the US market, which would seek to exploit the developing global success of Høeg's hybrid crime novel *Miss Smilla's Feeling for Snow* (Thomson and Stougaard-Nielsen, 2017, 241–42).

Høeg's novel had originally been picked up by the Danish editor Charlotte Dyssegaard at Farrar, Straus and Giroux, even before the book was published in Denmark (Wirtén, 2004, 41). Adopting a common 'central position' perspective on the potential of *Smilla*'s exotic Danish–Greenlandic settings

---

[12] Yellow Bird went on to produce several iconic Scandinavian crime films (e.g. the *Millenium* trilogy) and TV series including the popular TV series *Wallander*, featuring Krister Henriksson, and the international co-production (with Left Bank Pictures) of the English-language *Wallander* series featuring Kenneth Branagh as Kurt Wallander (BBC One, 2008–16). See interviews with Dan Israel and Bo Søndberg in Agger and Waade, 2010, 205–11.

and its equally exotic heroine, Smilla Qaaviqaaq Jaspersen, Dyssegaard had been waiting for a book by Høeg that would 'travel'; however, she might also have been persuaded by *Smilla*'s obvious echoes of still-fashionable Latin American magical realism, philosophical global thrillers and the growing success of feminist crime fiction in the US. *Smilla* would go on to reach number seven on the *New York Times* bestseller list, backed by major advertising campaigns that included 'Think Snow' baseball caps and snow pillows, special book-club editions and advertisements in major magazines and newspapers (Wirtén, 2004, 43).

According to Craighill (2013, 205), 'Israel was interested in how Peter Høeg's *Miss Smilla's Feeling for Snow* managed to achieve remarkable sales across the globe. He contacted Høeg's literary agent, at the Denmark based operation Leonhardt and Høier Literary Agency, Anneli Høier, and she started working with Mankell in [1992].'[13] Placing Mankell in the publishing network that had worked so well for Høeg was, according to Israel, integral to Mankell's global success, including in several European markets, where in many cases he would be published by the same publishers who published Høeg (like Christopher MacLehose in the UK, who also 'incidentally' published Larsson). While Craighill (2013, 210) still insists that 'international success begins with a good story, an engaging character, culturally non-specific content situated in a culturally specific context', its success in translation is dependent upon 'the work of an influential publishing network which brings that story to a global audience'.

Conclusion

The cases of Mankell, Larsson and the wider international success of Scandinavian crime fiction in translation in the twenty-first century are certainly not representative of the wider situation for small-nation literatures in the international mainstream. To reiterate Mete Hjort's formulation (2005, 31) from our introduction, 'What the concept of small nation acknowledges is that the game of culture [...] is more accessible to some groups than others, more hospitable to some aspirations than others and, in the long run a process involving winners and losers'. However, the Scandinavian case also

---

[13] Craighill suggests that they started their collaboration in 1991, but according to Anneli Høier the collaboration started in 1992, following the publication of the second Wallander novel in Sweden (see Høier, 2010, 189).

illustrates that certain genres, consecration processes, local and regional publishing networks and pioneering authors and agents in combination may produce a more 'fluid, mobile and provisional' 'marginocentric' publishing regime where centres and peripheries, as Tihanov suggested, are 'prone to swapping their places and exchange cultural valences'. The 'disjunctive networks' through which Scandinavian crime fiction became a transnational publishing success are as much part of the present 'deterritorializing properties of globalization' as the more static, yet still relevant, centre–periphery hegemony, which has dominated perspectives on the fate of literatures from 'small nations' in the field of transnational publishing (Tomlinson, 2011, 288).

Bibliography

Agger, Gunhild and Anne Marit Waade, (eds). 2010. *Den skandinaviske krimi: Bestseller og blockbuster* (Göteborg: Nordicom).
Bassnett, Susan. 2017. Detective Fiction in Translation: Shifting Patterns of Reception. In Nilsson, Louise, David Damrosch and Theo D'Haen (eds). *Crime Fiction as World Literature* (London: Bloomsbury), 143–56.
Berglund, Karl. 2012. *Deckarboomen under lupp: Statistiska perspektiv på svensk kriminallitteratur 1977–2010* (Uppsala: Avdelingen för litteratursociologi).
Berglund, Karl. 2014. A Turn to the Rights: The Advent and Impact of Swedish Literary Agents. In Helgason Jon, Sara Kärrholm and Ann Steiner (eds). *Hype: Bestsellers and Literary Culture* (Lund: Nordic Academic Press), 67–87.
Bergman, Kerstin. 2014. *Swedish Crime Fiction: The Making of Nordic Noir* (Milan: Mimesis International).
Books and Literature 2015. Annual Report of the Book and Literature Panel. Available from: www.kulturstyrelsen.dk/bogen-2015 [accessed 28 August 2017].
Broomé, Agnes. 2014. Swedish Literature on the British Market, 1998–2013: A Systemic Approach. PhD Thesis (London: UCL).
Casanova, Pascale. 2004. *The World Republic of Letters*. Trans. M.B. DeBevoise (Cambridge, MA: Harvard University Press).
Craig, Cairns. 2007. Centring on the Peripheries. In Thomsen, Bjarne Thorup (ed.). *Centring on the Peripheries: Studies in Scandinavian, Scottish, Gaelic and Greenlandic Literature* (Norwich: Norvik Press), 13–38.
Craighill, Stephanie. 2013. Henning Mankell: European Translation and Success Factors. *Publishing Research Quarterly*, 29 (3), 201–10.
CWA Daggers. Available from: http://cwadaggers.co.uk/ [accessed 28 August 2017].

English, James F. 2005. *The Economy of Prestige: Prizes, Awards, and the Circulation of Cultural Value* (Cambridge, MA: Harvard University Press).
Forshaw, Barry. 2012. *Death in a Cold Climate: A Guide to Scandinavian Crime Fiction* (Houndmills: Palgrave Macmillan).
Geherin, David. 2012. *The Dragon Tattoo and Its Long Tale: The New Wave of European Crime Fiction in America* (Jefferson, NC and London: McFarland). E-Book.
Heilbron, Johan. 2000. Translation as a Cultural World System. *Perspectives: Studies in Transatology*, 8 (1), 9–26.
Hjort, Mette. 2005. *Small Nation, Global Cinema: The New Danish Cinema* (Minneapolis, MN: University of Minnesota Press).
Høier, Anneli. 2010. Marked for skandinavisk krimilitteratur? Agger, Gunhil and Anne Marit Waade (eds). *Den skandinaviske krimi: Bestseller og blockbuster* (Göteborg: Nordicom), 189–94.
Jensen, Pia Majbritt. 2016. Global Impact of Danish Drama Series: a Peripheral, Non-commercial Creative Counter-flow. Kosmorama #263. Available from: www.kosmorama.org [accessed 28 August 2017].
Kärrholm, Sara. 2014. Bestseller Culture and its Effects on Research: The Case of Stieg Larsson's *Millennium* Trilogy. In Helgason, Jon, Sara Kärrholm and Ann Steiner (eds). *Hype: Bestsellers and Literary Culture* (Lund: Nordic Academic Press), 89–108.
Kovač, Miha and Rüdiger Wischenbart. 2010. *Diversity Report 2010: Literary Translation in Current European Book Markets: An analysis of authors, languages, and flows* (Vienna: Rüdiger Wischenbart Content and Consulting, 2010). Available from: www.wischenbart.com/upload/Diversity-Report_2010.pdf [accessed 28 August 2017].
Kovač, Miha and Rüdiger Wischenbart. 2016. *Diversity Report 2016: Trends and References in Literary Translations across Europe* (Vienna: Rüdiger Wischenbart Content and Consulting, 2016). Available from: http://wischenbart.com/download_diversity.php [accessed 9 November 2016].
Lindqvist, Yvonne. 2012. Det globale översättningsfältet och den svenska översätningsmarknaden: Förutsättningar för litterära periferiers mote. In Carlsson, Ulla and Jenni Johannison (eds). *Läsarnas marknad, marknadens läsare: En forskningsantologi utarbetad för litteraturutredningen* (Göteborg: Nordicom), 197–208.
Lindqvist, Yvonne. 2016. The Scandinavian Literary Translation Field from a Global Point of View: A Peripheral (Sub)field? In Helgesson, Stefan and Pieter Vermeulen (eds). *Institutions of World Literature: Writing, Translation, Markets* (New York and London, Routledge), 174–90.
Messent, Peter. 2013. *The Crime Fiction Handbook* (Oxford: Wiley-Blackwell).
Moretti, Franco. 2000. Conjectures on World Literature. *New Left Review*, 1, 54–68.

Nilsson, Louise, David Damrosch and Theo D'Haen (eds). 2017. *Crime Fiction as World Literature* (London: Bloomsbury).
Nordic Cooperation. n.d. About the Nordic Council Literature Prize. Available from: https://www.norden.org/en/nordic-council/nordic-council-prizes/nordisk-raads-litteraturpris/about-the-literature-prize/the-literature-prize [accessed 28 August 2017].
Pepper, Andrew and David Schmid. 2016. Introduction: Globalization and the State in Contemporary Crime Fiction. In their *Globalization and the State in Contemporary Crime Fiction* (London: Palgrave Macmillan), 1–20.
Rønning, Helge and Tore Slaata. 2012. Regional and National Structures in the Publishing Industry with Particular Reference to the Nordic Situation. *Journal of Media Business Studies*, 9 (1), 101–22.
Secher, Mikkel. 2016. Danske bøger hitter i udlandet – her er de vilde med os. *Tv2 Nyheder*, 12 March. Available from: http://nyheder.tv2.dk/business/2016-03-12-danske-boeger-hitter-i-udlandet-her-er-de-vilde-med-os [accessed 28 August 2017].
Squires, Claire. 2007. The Global Market 1970–2000: Consumers. In Eliot, Simon and Jonathan Rose (eds). *A Companion to the History of the Book* (Oxford: Wiley-Blackwell), 406–18.
Squires, Claire. 2009. *Marketing Literature: The Making of Contemporary Writing in Britain* (Houndmills: Palgrave).
Steiner, Ann. 2012. Läsarnas marknad, marknadens läsare: Reflektioner över litteraturens materiella villkor. In Carlsson, Ulla and Jenny Johannison (eds). *Läsarnas marknad, marknadens läsare: En forskningsantologi utarbetad för Litteraturutredningen* (Göteborg: Nordicom), 23–37.
Steiner, Ann. 2014. World Literature and the Book Market. In D'Haen, Theo, David Damrosch and Djelal Kadir (eds). *The Routledge Companion to World Literature* (London and New York: Routledge), 316–24.
Stougaard-Nielsen, Jakob. 2016. Nordic noir in the UK: the allure of accessible difference. *Journal of Aesthetics & Culture*, 8 (1). Available from: http://dx.doi.org/10.3402/jac.v8.32704 [accessed 9 November 2016].
Stougaard-Nielsen, Jakob. 2017. *Scandinavian Crime Fiction* (London: Bloomsbury).
Svedjedal, Johan. 2012. Svensk skönlitteratur i världsperspektiv. In Carlsson, Ulla and Jenny Johannisson (eds). *Läsarnas Marknad, marknadens läsare: En forskningsantologi utarbetad för Litteraturutredningen* (Göteborg: Nordicom), 209–20.
Thompson, John B. 2010. *Merchants of Culture: The Publishing Business in the Twenty-first Century* (Cambridge: Polity).
Thomson, C. Claire and Jakob Stougaard-Nielsen. 2017. 'A Faithful, Attentive, Tireless Following': Cultural Mobility, Crime Fiction and Television Drama. In Ringgaard, Dan and Mads Rosendahl Thomsen (eds). *Danish Literature as World Literature* (London: Bloomsbury), 237–68.

Tihanov, Galin. 2014. Do 'Minor Literatures' Still Exist? The Fortunes of a Concept in the Changing Frameworks of Literary History. In Biti, Vladimir (ed.). *Reexamining the National-Philological Legacy: Quest for a New Paradigm?* (Amsterdam: Rodopi), 169–90.

Tomlinson, John. 2011. Ubiquitous Locality. In Thomsen, Bodil Marie Stavning and Kristin Ørjasæter (eds). *Globalizing Art: Negotiating Place, Identity and Nation in Contemporary Nordic Art* (Århus: Aarhus University Press), 285–90.

Venuti, Lawrence. 2008. *The Translator's Invisibility: A History of Translation*, 2nd edn (London and New York: Routledge).

Wirtén, Eva Hemmungs. 2004. *No Trespassing: Authorship, Intellectual Property Rights, and the Boundaries of Globalization* (Toronto: University of Toronto Press).

Wirtén, Eva Hemmungs. 2007. The Global Market 1970–2000: Producers. In Eliot, Simon and Jonathan Rose (eds). *A Companion to the History of the Book* (Oxford: Wiley-Blackwell), 395–405.

Wischenbart, Rüdiger. 2016. *The Business of Books 2016: Between the first and the second phase of transformation: An overview of market trends in North America, Europe, Asia and Latin America, and a look beyond books*. White Paper, Frankfurt Book Fair, Summer 2016. Available from: www.buchmesse.de/pdf/white_paper_business_of_books_june_2016.pdf [accessed 28 August 2017].

CHAPTER ELEVEN

Literary Translation and Digital Culture: The Transmedial Breakthrough of Poland's *The Witcher*

Paulina Drewniak (University of Wrocław)

In June 2015, something unusual happened in the field of small European literatures. *The Last Wish* (2007), an English translation of a Polish collection of fantasy short stories, appeared among the *New York Times*' 15 bestselling mass-market paperbacks in the US.[1] It was the only translated book on the list, which otherwise included *Game of Thrones*, romance novels and the latest instalments of Clive Cussler (b.1931) and Lee Child (b.1954). Four years earlier, the then Prime Minister of Poland had presented the same book to President Obama during his state visit in Warsaw. If interested, the American president could have read on the cover that he had been given a 'European superstar, in English for the first time'.

Anyone familiar with contemporary popular culture will recognize the anomaly. Given the absolute dominance of English in this field, especially in the fantastic (Bhabha 1994, 21; Gouanvic, 1997), the 'aggressive monolingualism' of anglophone audiences (Venuti 2008, 13), and the normal direction of exchange between English and most other languages in the world, such cases are as rare as unicorns, and equally sensational. How did this book get translated and become a bestseller is such a translation-resistant market? How could something that ostensibly resembles a piece of genre fiction simultaneously hold so much significance for a Central European nation that it becomes its symbol? Can one be a fantasy superstar without speaking English? What does this all mean for smaller literatures?

The answer lies in modern digital cultures. *The Last Wish* is a part of what we now call a transmedia franchise, known as *The Witcher* (*Wiedźmin*

---

[1] See www.nytimes.com/best-sellers-books/2015-06-14/mass-market-paperback/list.html. The rankings 'reflect sales for the week ending May 30, 2015'.

Paulina Drewniak

in Polish). It consists of a body of short stories and novels published between 1986 and 1999 by the Polish author Andrzej Sapkowski (b.1948), a trilogy of videogames based on them by the Polish studio CD Projekt RED (2007–15) and numerous ancillary texts and products by various creators. The original books are a model of cultural hybridity, a Western fantasy formula saturated with Slav folklore and mythology, which helped them achieve cult status in Poland and fed into their initial popularity across Central and Eastern Europe. It was only after the commercial triumph of the Polish video game, however, that Sapkowski's books became available in English, initially only in fan translations as the traditional publishing industry failed to deliver. The emergence of transmedia entertainment facilitated translation of both a specific literary work and general cultural experiences, normally given little attention in anglophone cultural space. But once *The Witcher* became an international phenomenon, while retaining awareness of its foreign origin, it also became a platform for intercultural communication in an unprecedented manner.

This chapter uses the case of *The Witcher* to demonstrate the new possibilities for translated literature – and indeed for communication with and within the new, digitally literate generation of creators and audiences – created by the rise of digital cultures. *The Witcher*'s complex trajectory in English illustrates the multitude of forces that may potentially influence the circulation of peripheral literatures once modern media become involved.

'The Misery of Small Nations'

The Witcher's original context was Poland, reflecting stereotypical Polish national self-perceptions, preoccupations and attitudes to the wider world and the country's place within it. With 40 million speakers in the country alone, not to mention a vocal diaspora, Polish is not a 'small European nation'. In Heilbron's world system of translation (2010), it is listed as a 'semi-peripheral' language (middle-sized rather than small). Unlike the many stateless or minority languages of the world (Basque, Catalan, Occitan), it is not administratively disadvantaged; as the state language in Poland, and an official language of the European Union, it enjoys full legal protection, freedom of expression and substantial funding. It is not new either. Polish literature has a rich tradition, dating to the Middle Ages, and produces high quantities of books every year. Overall, Polish language and literature seem alive and well; indeed, one could say that the conditions for their development

Literary Translation and Digital Culture

and dissemination now are more favourable than any time in the past 200 years.

In European narratives, however, Poland is repeatedly conceptualized as small, both by dominant European countries and its own intellectuals. 'The cultural contempt of Europe for the "small eastern nations" makes us furious, bitter, and sad',[2] writes Maria Janion (2006) in her influential book *Niesamowita Słowiańszczyzna* [Sclavinia[3] the Uncanny]. The phrase comes from Istvan Bibo's essay 'Misère des petits états d'Est' (1986, in Janion, 2006) referring to the Poles, Hungarians and Czechs. The attribute 'small' reflects not only the unimportance of these nations to European history, at least as seen by the British or French. It also means, among other symbolic connotations, 'fearing for their existence', a fear of physical extermination arising from the region's troubled history that is alien to the West Europeans. The most recent examples of threats are Nazism and Stalinism, but Janion reaches far deeper. Drawing on Said's *Orientalism*, she argues that the Slav lands have always suffered from a disease of identity, which began with the brutal christening of these lands and the subsequent loss of the Slav religion, memory and myth. The Celts are lucky, she says, because they have kept their stories, and have even seen them brought to life in popular culture, in works such as *The Lord of the Rings*. We shall see how *The Witcher* plays on this apparently lost Polish mythology.

Why physical largeness and imagined smallness? Such paradoxes of definition are in fact common in translation studies. Albert Branchadell (2005, 1–19) runs into an analogous difficulty trying to find a common category for all the languages whose cultural output is similarly marginalized, but for vastly different reasons: some are persecuted, others spoken only by minorities, and others are historically peripheral. He concludes that in case of what he ultimately dubs 'less translated languages', the problem

---

[2] *Kulturowa pogarda Europy dla 'małych wschodnich narodów' budzi w nas wściekłość, gorycz i smutek.* Janion's discussion (2006, 20–38) on Poland's place in Europe is filled with a deep sense of marginalization.

[3] Note on the title: as of 2016, the book has not been translated into English. Marek Radziwon at Culture.pl translates the title as 'Uncanny Slavdom' (http://culture.pl/en/work/uncanny-slavdom-maria-janion). In this version I chose the Latin *Sclavinia*, from a tenth-century illustration depicting four women, personifications of mediaeval communities, bringing offerings to Holy Roman Emperor Otto – the other three being Germania, Gallia and Roma. This illustration is featured extensively in Polish historiography as early evidence of Slav peoples becoming 'equal citizens' of Europe.

often boils down to power differentials, which again invites postcolonial readings (cf. Janion).

Neil Lazarus (2012) criticizes some aspects of the appropriation of postcolonial discourse to Central and Eastern Europe, but his insightful paper offers one of the best characterizations of the conceptual 'situatedness' of the countries between Riga, Budapest, Minsk and Berlin. Lazarus traces the evolution of the concept of East and West in European history and scholarship: from the division of the Roman Empire towards the end of the fourth century AD, through the Great Schism of 1054, the Great Discoveries, the rise of imperial Russia, and eventually the Cold War. Out of those, he repeats after Sophie Bessis, 1492 marks the birth of both the division between East and West and of Reason-based European founding myths (Lazarus, 2012, 123). As a common European identity was forged in these defining moments, Poland repeatedly found itself on the wrong side of the emerging binaries, as each of those events marginalized Central Europe. Each also produced an ambivalence in the modern Polish identity. The division into Roman and Greek Christianity eventually placed the Slav nations into two opposite camps, with profound consequences (see Janion, 2006, on Slav liturgy). The Age of Discoveries saw the rise of seaward-looking colonial empires, and turned the Polish gaze towards the vast plains in the east, eventually creating an essentially imperial mindset, which took a sharp blow when the country itself was vassalized in the nineteenth century. Finally, after 1945 the countries of Western Europe, by building what became the EU, successfully defined 'core Europe' around themselves.

As a result, paradoxes emerge, starting with geography. What is known as Central Europe in Warsaw, Prague and Budapest is dismissed as 'Eastern' Europe in Berlin, Paris and London. This in turn produces a strong reaction, where the Central European countries affirm their supposed Westernness. Reflecting on the direction in which post-communist postcolonial scholarship often tends, David Chioni Moore writes that, in the post-Soviet contexts,

> postcolonial desire fixates not on the fallen master Russia but on the glittering Euramerican MTV-and-Coca-Cola beast that broke it. Central and Eastern Europeans type this desire as a return to Westernness that once was theirs. Any traveller to the region quickly learns that what for forty years was called the 'Eastern Bloc' is rather 'Central Europe'. One hears that Prague lies west of Vienna and that the Hungarians stopped the Turk, and one witnesses an increasingly odd competition to be at Europe's 'geographic centre'. The claimants for this mythic,

definition-dependent prize range from Skopje, Macedonia, to a stone plinth twenty miles east of Vilnius, in Lithuania. (Quoted in Lazarus, 2012, 126)

The Polish still aggressively assert both their Westernness and their undue marginalization. Roman Catholicism, the Latin alphabet and the long-standing tradition of democracy and civil rights (as opposed to Byzantine autocracies) become the markers of the country's cultural identity, firmly in the hegemonic white West.[4] The most significant consequence of this for translation is the immense cultural prestige and value Western content holds in these countries – especially in popular culture – and the parallel desire to produce something equal to imported models, exemplified by the phenomenon of Hungarian pseudo-translations of fantasy and science fiction described by Sohár (1999).

In terms of its relationship to the wider world, Poland may be seen as part of the privileged North, as understood by Jacquemond (1992) (note the Northern Kingdoms in the *Witcher* storyworld, the home of the protagonist and its ensemble cast of misfits). Poles do not identify with the non-white colonized peoples of the world. As Moore implies, despite the appropriation of postcolonial theory and the correct recognition of the aspects where they are dispossessed, the Polish are remarkably blind to instances where they are the privileged. This is largely because the only partner they aspire to convince is Western society at large, and not the other dispossessed. As a colonized nation, Poles are probably most likely to identify with the Irish, as English-speaking, white Europeans. A corollary to this is the homogeneity of contemporary Polish society, which results in peculiar conservatism, even racism, and a significant lack of awareness of racial tensions in the wider world, which comes to life in the reception of the *Witcher* franchise.

Polish is thus not small in terms of size or output, or the visions it harbours for itself. It is small on the 'invisible' plane, the conceptualization of the continent shared by its inhabitants. Modern nations are Benedict Anderson's 'imagined communities', in the sense that their constitutive principle is less in physical reality (e.g. territory, ethnicity, state borders) and more in the very specific awareness of other people 'like me', facilitated by technologies of mass communication, most importantly print. (We see

---

[4] Velickovic, 2012, observes how Central European immigrants in the UK after 2004 were perceived as 'less threatening' because of their white skin, and the deduced cultural proximity.

Paulina Drewniak

a parallel in new media; the emergence of digital technologies allows the emergence of vibrant online communities.) The construct of an imagined community includes its origin, since time immemorial (Anderson 2006, 11–12),[5] which links us in the imagined plane to the ancient peoples of Europe: Norse, Celts, Slavs, which modern nations perceive or construct as their ancestors. More importantly, the construct includes an opinion on a nation's place in the world. The self-perception of imagined European communities translates into an imagined literary geography of Europe, in which Poland is seen and sees itself as peripheral, even in areas where this is counterfactual. In the eighteenth century, Herder famously stated that Slavs 'occupy more space on the map than in recorded history' (in Janion, 2006). We may echo him and say that modern Poland occupies more space on the map than it does in the imagined space of Europe.

Transmedial Worlds

If Polish national identity in relation to 'the West' explains the zeal of Polish creators to become part of modern, Americanized popular culture, the other driving force behind the *Witcher* phenomenon are the mechanisms through which that culture itself operates, with the central notion of 'transmedia storytelling'. The term 'transmedia entertainment' was popularized by Henry Jenkins is his seminal book *Convergence Culture* (2006). His key thesis is that the development of modern media, and especially digital environments, leads to media convergence and gives rise to readership cultures that are qualitatively different in their behaviour from traditional audiences. He characterizes transmedia franchises as 'stories that unfold across multiple media platforms, with each medium making distinctive contributions to our understanding of the world, a more integrated approach to franchise development than models based on urtexts and ancillary products' (Jenkins, 2006, 293).

In other words, a franchise is more than an aggregate of texts. There is an intimate relationship between them on several levels: commercial (they are branded as part of a single universe), narrative (characters recur, plots

---

[5] If nation states are widely conceded to be 'new' and 'historical', the nations to which they give political expression always loom out of an immemorial past and, even more importantly, glide into a limitless future. It is the magic of nationalism to turn chance into destiny. With Debray we might say, 'Yes, it is quite accidental that I am born French; but after all, France is eternal' (Anderson, 2006, 12).

intertwine) and reception (they are seen as a single story-tree by the audiences, who then freely migrate between the various instalments). To Jenkins, the prototypical transmedia franchise is *The Matrix*. The world and story were introduced through film, expanded through games, comics and other content, and created a full, mysterious, addictively rewarding environment for the fans.

Other theorists develop and refine Jenkins's model. Klastrup and Tosca (2004) take the most important factor – world-building – to its logical conclusion, and introduce the notion of the transmedial world:

> Transmedial worlds are abstract content systems from which a repertoire of fictional stories and characters can be actualized or derived across a variety of media forms. What characterizes a transmedial world is that audience and designers share a mental image of the 'worldness' (a number of distinguishing features of its universe). The idea of a specific world's worldness mostly originates from the first version of the world presented, but can be elaborated and changed over time. Quite often the world has a cult (fan) following across media as well.

They emphasize the notion of a world's *worldness*, i.e. the defining features without which a fictional universe would lose its identity. For example, *Star Wars* would not be itself without the Jedi mythos. But the world's 'worldness' can be subtler, as it can rest in a particular mood or mode. The two authors also complicate Jenkins's view of authorship, stating that transmedia universes actually do tend to have 'originals', that is, canonical texts that establish the universe, which typically have one author, like Tolkien's *The Lord of the Rings*. Further research goes into narratology, examining the relationship between transmediality, transfictionality, intertextuality and other concepts tangential to our analysis, but narratology-oriented authors also emphasize the notion of a storyworld – storyworld before storyline – as the key defining element of a transmedia entity (Ryan, 2013; Maj, 2015).

Audiences in turn develop a set of special competences to navigate the complex web of content they receive, becoming 'informational hunters and gatherers' (Jenkins, 2006, 129). They employ collective intelligence and collaborative efforts to piece together scattered clues or develop alternative interpretations; they invest a lot and actively participate. They are also voracious and migratory in search of the kind of entertainment experiences they want (Jenkins, 2006, 282). This means, crucially, that avid gamers can easily become book fans, or that film-goers can play the game based on their favourite film. Any part of the franchise can serve as a point of entry, substantially broadening the potential audience. We will see how this played a significant role in the *Witcher* franchise, pushing the book to the bestseller status simply by being a tie-in with the game. It is no coincidence that the book, *The Last Wish*, appeared on the NYT list in the last week of May, 2015; the game, *The Witcher 3: The Wild Hunt*, premiered in the US on 19 May, that year.

In contemporary popular culture, especially in the fantastic, the patterns described by transmedia and convergence theorists are ubiquitous, and decisive. For better or worse, many big game franchises, blockbuster films and successful books are designed as transmedial, or at least designed to harness the participatory mindset of fans. This is especially visible in young adult content (*Harry Potter, Star Wars* etc.). Despite occasional resulting copyright hiccups (as in the 'Potter wars'), the entertainment industry seems to have fully adopted the convergence logic.

Transmedia storytelling typically involves world building, dispersed authorship (since different media instances can be authored by different creators), and unified branding. The last factor means that a transmedia franchise functions as a whole, which proves important for translation. It also typically inspires a cult following. Drawing on Eco's thoughts on *Casablanca*, Jenkins (2006, 97–101) identifies the key element: a cult film is made to be quoted. The work needs to provide a 'completely furnished world so that its fans can quote characters and episodes as if they were aspects of the private sectarian world'. It is an immersive environment, the experience of which can be easily shared by quoting creative one-liners, evoking characters or visual cues. In translation, this significantly expands the scope of communication by moving beyond the lexical paradigm and into the visual paradigm. If we operate in medium other than writing, intercultural communication can happen on additional levels: visuals, music, movement. We will see how this was utilized in the *Witcher* franchise in order to consciously showcase what creators believe to be Slav culture.

Across languages and cultures, convergence creates a peculiar dynamic, based on the east–west distinction:

> The flow of Asian goods into the Western market has been shaped by two competing forces: the corporate convergence promoted by media industries, and the grassroots convergence promoted by fan communities and immigrant populations. [...] [In corporate convergence] three distinctive kinds of economic interests are at play in promoting these new cultural exchanges: national or regional producers who see the global circulation of their products not simply as expanding their revenue

stream but also as a source of national pride; multinational conglomerates who no longer define their production or distribution decisions in national terms but seek to identify potentially valuable content and push it into as many markets as possible; and niche distributors who search for distinctive content as a means of attracting upscale consumers and differentiating themselves from stuff already on the market. (Jenkins, 2006, 109–10)

Despite Poland and Japan being very distant culturally, this description captures very well the factors that operated in case of *The Witcher*.

In summary, for our discussion, transmedia and convergence matter in three key areas: marketing, audience experience and audience participation. All these areas produce phenomena important for translation: the process, the product and the cultural impact. In the marketing dimension, the status of a potential translation can change from supply-driven to demand-driven. This is undoubtedly the most important thing that happened in case of *The Witcher*. Audience participation produces fan translations. Audience experience is a powerful tool to reframe certain cultural content, such as Slav mythology, to change its status, popularize it or elicit a reaction from the community.

The *Witcher* Franchise

Wiedźmin/The Witcher fully realizes the model of a transmedial world as defined by Klastrup and Tosca. It consists of several standalone works, each of which can serve as a point of entry. It presents a universe whose worldness is distinct and unmistakable. It is 'made to be quoted', with clever one-liners and some tongue-in-cheek political commentary. It did inspire a cult following, first in Poland, later in Central Europe and ultimately worldwide. The cooperation between the elements of the franchise has not always been smooth, mostly due to tensions between Sapkowski and authors of other instalments (the video game, the comics). Nevertheless, the relationship in the commercial layer as well as in the fan engagement layer exists, and in these areas, it works very well.

In fact, *The Witcher* became transmedial before the term had even been coined. The media consumption and production patterns described by Jenkins originate largely from American science fiction fandom. The *Fantastyka* magazine, where the first short story 'Wiedźmin' ('The Witcher',

Paulina Drewniak

'The Hexer' or 'Spellmaker', depending on the version) was published, was an outpost of the international fan movement in Poland. In the first years of its existence the magazine attracted a community fully acculturated to the same patterns that transmedia theorists later codified: participatory mindset, world building as a creation norm and immersion as a reception norm, and migratory behaviour. Sapkowski himself quickly adopted multiple roles; he began by promoting tabletop gaming. As a result, it was only a matter of time before the hugely successful *Witcher* world was be presented in other media. Between 1990 and 2000, the short stories were not only developed into a full-blown saga, but the story of the *Witcher*, Geralt, was also turned into a series of comics (co-authored by Sapkowski) and a tabletop RPG game system (i.e. a game manual) *Wiedźmin: Gra wyobraźni*, and filmed by Heritage Films and national TV (*Wiedźmin/The Hexer*, 2001). Although the production of the film was not coordinated with the fan movement (in fact, the casting choices were strongly contested), it nevertheless aimed to harness the emergent transmedia-friendly audiences.

It was the new generation of digital creators, however, that turned the story into a worldwide phenomenon by producing the video game *The Witcher* (2007). These were people born in the 1970s, who grew up consuming American-made entertainment, including games. Many of those involved in producing the first game were members of organized Polish fandom. The studio owners, two young businessmen who made their living selling localized Western games in the early 1990s, were avid fans of the saga themselves. The first copyright arrangements were made at a convention.

Wiedźmin's Hybridity

Beneath the transmedia framework lies a world whose *worldness* is distinctly Central European. Sapkowski's world-building strategy subverts many of the traditional fantasy tropes. If a default fantasy universe is Anglo-Saxon in its cultural layer, since it recombines the cultural items best known to anglophone audiences and reproduces their worldview (for instance using anglophone toponyms and anthroponyms, placing the protagonists in a typical British boarding school as in Rowling, or situating 'the barbarians' in the east, as in Tolkien (see Oziewicz, 2010)), the *Witcher* world employs Eastern European or Polish material instead. This is most visible in proper names. The geography uses names from throughout the continent: Polish, Slovene (Maribor), German, Serbian (Yaruga), Dutch, Italian, French. The same goes for the names of characters. Although the protagonists are called Geralt and Yennefer – arguably tweaked anglophone names – they are surrounded by Hungarian-sounding dwarves (Zoltan Chivay) and vampires (Emiel Regis Terzieff-Godefroy), Celtic earls (Crach an Craite), and rudely nicknamed Polish peasantry. Sapkowski's sensitivity to detail yields evocative descriptions of plants, animals and landscapes that are also unmistakably Polish. In fact, many readers, including Gollancz's commissioning editor Marcus Gibbs, point to the landscape as an important part of their experience of the books, distinguishing them from the canon. Sapkowski also effortlessly includes intertexts taken from fantasy classics, but also earlier legendary works in the fantastic (e.g. Romanticism, both Polish and European), Arthurian legends or classic Polish literature, and his selection of monsters matches almost exactly Janion's Romantic imaginarium, including the vampire and the devil, two creatures very prevalent in Slav folklore. All this creates a very linguistically rich world, which stands out in comparison to most anglophone-genre fantasy translated and published in Poland.

The mood and mode of the stories blur the distinction between good and evil, man and monster. According to translator and editor, Michael Kandel (2014),[6] this moral greyness is the distinctive feature of Polish fantastic worlds; for him, unlike Western monsters, Polish monsters 'come from within'. Similar observations come from other critics studying East European fantasies. Tkacz (2012) and Kaczor (2014) both comment on the gloominess and brutality of Polish fantasy worlds, which they attribute partly to Sapkowski's influence. That the phenomenon may be wider is evidenced in Sohár's discussion of speculative fiction in Hungary. Although her study covers only the period between 1989 and 1995, she observes that the Hungarian writers differ from translated counterparts in that their works rarely feature a typical adventure-story happy ending (1999, 252–53). If we take Julia Kristeva's notion of monsters as 'abjects' – personifications of what we repress and reject in ourselves – in *Witcher* stories they are often sentient, and more human than the people. The *Witcher* himself, a monster-killer by trade, rather than killing them, often empathizes with them. It is easy to see how a century of difficult choices where no evil was necessarily 'lesser' produced such an existentialist philosophy. This philosophy is strongly emphasized in the games; the quests are deliberately written to make it hard to tell who exactly the villain is and even the right outcome comes at a high

---

[6] Kandel translated and edited of a collection of Polish fantasy short stories (2010) in which 'Wiedźmin' (1986) was included.

cost. Dubbed 'choice and consequence' mechanics, this became one of the most highly praised aspects of the games.

Double Status

The early 1990s in Poland were a strange time. The Red Army had not yet left, and capitalism had already arrived. The country woke up to an identity void, and to the 'fixation on the Coca-Cola beast' that ended the Soviet stranglehold on the region. And *The Witcher* was perfectly and consciously timed for this moment, both by the author and the publisher. It combined the symbolic capital of a Western formula with the affirmatory value of placing familiar content within it. It gave Poles back their Slav mythology, or at least something like it. It did not matter that Sapkowski himself was ambivalent about the Slav material, nor that the material itself was sometimes fabricated. In a way, the books were also a socio-political commentary in the form of a genre fantasy novel (Majkowski, 2013) that nevertheless took itself seriously as a fantasy novel, i.e. mass entertainment. The plot included more or less veiled allusions, for example, to the Polish Round Table of 1989 and the behind-the-scenes way politics is often done, a hot topic in a country where many were becoming disillusioned with the transformation. The books even addressed some of the most troublesome of Polish narratives – the uprisings – arguably before anyone else did. The first full novel in the cycle *Blood of Elves* portrays the elves as a persecuted minority, cherishing the memory of a young female freedom fighter who led the elven youth into an uprising and ultimately to their deaths, but with a bitter commentary suggesting that this achieved nothing. In the 1990s, when the sense of the 1945 Warsaw Uprising was only beginning to be questioned, this sort of pragmatism could only be articulated within the neutralizing frame of popular culture. Paired with undeniable literary craftsmanship, it all made for an explosive combination. As a result, *Wiedźmin* became a staple of Polishness, and its author a literary celebrity, showered with praise and awards not only in the 'ghetto' of the fan community, but in mainstream literary circles.

Translation Process

Unusually, the *Witcher* books bypassed the normal route for translations of Polish literature, because they have a dual identity: as works of Polish literature and as pieces of world popular culture. As the former, they intimately engage important Polish narratives in a fresh framework. As the latter, they actively participate in global trends. The result is a peculiar mixture, where elements of Central European themes are showcased within digital media.

The translations came in several groups. First, 2005 – the year in which marketing for the forthcoming game started influencing the translation market – acts as a clear dividing line. The translations before that were driven by factors other than transmedia. The earliest, across Central and Eastern Europe (Czech, Lithuanian, Russian, Ukrainian; also German), were motivated first and foremost by Sapkowski's popularity in the respective national fandoms and the cultural proximity of the stories to the respective cultures, usually in that order. The stories' cultural identity made them familiar to the usually underprivileged audiences in these countries, and provoked a powerful response. Interestingly, much later Ukrainian and Russian authors took to writing tribute stories set in the *Witcher* universe. The translations after 2005 are clearly motivated by the games; indeed, many feature the game logo, a stylized wolf's head, on the cover. When we move to the English translation, the duality becomes particularly clear. *The Last Wish* in its British edition does feature the game logo. (The US edition displays a piece of game artwork instead.) At the same time, it declares that it was financed by the Poland Translation programme, run by the state-funded Polish Book Institute, as does the next publication, *Blood of Elves*. The British edition was, moreover, released practically alongside the first video game, in 2007 (for more details on the translation process, see Drewniak, 2015).

Sapkowski's cooperation with Gollancz, the publisher, did not go as planned. After the publication of the first two books in Danusia Stok's version (*The Last Wish*, 2007, *Blood of Elves*, 2008; US editions a year later) a legal battle began between the author, the publisher and the translator. As a result, for four years the translations were frozen. During this time, in 2011, the second instalment of the game *The Witcher 2: Assassins of Kings* was released, awakening voracious fan interest. Since the official publishing industry did not deliver, the fans took matters in their own hands. They wrote a petition (around a thousand votes online) to 'publishing firms', and when calls did not have any effect, they utilized the official Witcher game forum to crowdsource translations. These versions were often done by people who did not speak Polish, but used French, Russian or other languages as intermediaries. Since 2013, the translations have resumed with David French. These versions no longer credit the institutional patronage of

Paulina Drewniak

the Book Institute. They also opt for different cover art, though still advertise their relatedness to the games.

The details of why the translations were halted are not known. Sapkowski's statements at conventions suggest that he values translators who consult him with their choices, regardless of the language. Legend has it that he authored or suggested the first English rendering of *wiedźmin* as *hexer* (from the German word for witch, *die Hexe*, which works well with *hexes*, a type of spell popular in fantasy games), or that he backed the word choice with his personal authority. Both the film and the first official English translation (by Agnieszka Fulińska, in the volume *Chosen by Fate*, 2000) adopt this version.

The English Texts

Do the English translations of the cycle domesticate Slavic elements? Yes and no, and everything in between. Since each translation originated in a different time and circumstances, what we receive is a spectrum of attitudes, which in turn results in prismatic splitting of the storyworld. For example, in the earliest English translations before the iconic 'witcher' took root, the protagonist is called a *witchman, hexer, spellmaker, conjurer, sorceror* or even *medicine man*(!) Moreover, in the earliest as well as the fannish translations,[7] we witness a flattening of the storyworld's archaized language into the lingo of American action movies. In Fulińska's *Hexer* (2000), the mayor (*kasztelan*) of Wyzima at some point addresses Geralt as 'man' ('This is not the same, man …'). Similarly, Fieldmarshal's Coehoorn's 'skurwysyny' ['sons of bitches'], which David French eventually translates as 'whoresons', has been rendered as 'motherfuckers' in the fan translation of *The Lady of the Lake*. This is a wider trend; in general, the fan translations gravitate towards the generic language more than the official ones do. Eventually though, all versions domesticate to some degree, as popular culture prioritizes the story over philological faithfulness or the careful ethics of power difference that often informs the translation of high classics.

Nevertheless, the later translations by David French end up partially shielded from full domestication thanks to CD Projekt's adoption of

---

[7] A fannish translation here means a somewhat professionalized fan translation, that is, a translation which went through normal book publishing channels, but still originated and or/circulated in the organized fandom circles, or was authored by someone involved with those circles.

Slavicness as the differentiator in Western markets. While keeping the games internationally relatable, the studio's writers and translators consciously played upon the Slavic in the same way the books did, i.e. by liberally inserting Slavic toponyms and anthroponyms, recreating the Central European physical and social landscape in the structure of the game world (see Richards' review, 2015), or populating the game's otherworld with the ghosts of Polish Romanticism (like in the quest *Dziady/Forefathers Eve*, based on Mickiewicz; see Schreiber, 2017). This left many traces of linguistic and cultural difference, including the *striga* (the central monster featured in trailers). And those elements in the games in turn created some room for David French to experiment. French domesticates names that are either expressive (or inherits domesticated ones from Stok, like *Jaskier/Dandelion*) or meaningfully embedded in the story (the village *Zazdrość/Jealousy*). He also naturalizes elements of continental mediaevalism into Anglo-Saxon 'equivalents' (*wójt/alderman*). But he leaves many of the place names (*Chotla, Pereplut*), character names and realities intact, and goes out of his way to recreate Sapkowski's linguistic games. This stands in contrast to the earliest version (2007), in which Michael Kandel goes for what we might call 'violent domestication' of the vulnerable Polish text (with seemingly random changes of Sapkowski's proper names, such as *Velerad of Wyzima* thus becoming *Ethmond of Klothstur*). Predictably, part of the books' flavour is lost, if only by recontextualization, which severs the cultural links and renders references unrecognizable. Still, there is enough otherness left to make an English reader aware, and even curious. Most importantly, though, the game versions effectively codify the *Witcher* storyworld into a somewhat coherent whole, making it an attractive transmedia environment.

Official and Fannish

As for the attitude of the official translators to fan translators and vice versa, three possible scenarios can be distinguished. There is virtually no relationship between the 'national coryphées' (i.e. the state-funded institutions promoting Polish culture, funding translators and disseminating Polish classics, such as the Book Institute) and the vibrant online fan communities. The publishers have probably never heard of the fan translations and these two groups neither respect nor understand one another. To proponents of high culture, gamers are a faceless mob of orcs, hardly conducive of behaviours beneficial to national culture; to gamers and other digital natives, the inner workings and realities of the traditional publishing industry are incomprehensible. The 2011 fan petition was addressed vaguely to 'publishing firms', as if they were capricious gods withholding the publication of translations out of spite. As one frustrated fan declared in 2011, when the translation of the subsequent Witcher books was still frozen: 'Fuck Orbitbooks and fuck Danusia Stok, the fan versions are perfectly readable.'

A relationship does exist between the big speculative fiction publishers like Gollancz and the fans. These publishers know the value of fan engagement, and know how to leverage it. They also understand the logic of transmedia branding, hence the game logo on the cover of *The Last Wish*. Marcus Gibbs of Gollancz reports that more tie-in covers were considered. In this area, the professionals have usually heard of fan translations, but are indifferent to the phenomenon. This may reflect the fact that, counter-intuitively, there is actually no conflict of interests here. An avid fan, especially in the West, may devour the bootlegged versions but will always buy the official product in the end, even for an outrageous price. The translation activity is merely the extension of voracious interest and missionary zeal to promote the beloved franchise, and therefore, as a sign of fan investment and a free promotional machine, is either harmless or beneficial to the publisher. The fan translators gathered at the *Witcher* forum notably see their work as provisional, and remove their translations as the official ones are released. They are grassroots activists responding to the needs (demands) of their fellow enthusiasts, not business people trying to capitalize on the franchise's success.

The third scenario to examine is how translators relate to one another and how they are seen in the fandom community. In the case of speculative fiction, official translators are often translator-fans in the sense that aca-fans are academics; these are fans who have married their interests to their profession. Such translators participate actively in the fandom life and events, and are revered as specialists or even gurus. Moreover, they usually translate only the speculative genres (fantasy, science fiction, horror and related forms). If a 'traditional' (non-fandom) translator happens to translate a speculative work with a significant fanbase, he or she is quickly assimilated and acculturated into the community (Guttfeld, 2006). Many translator-fans are initially motivated by the same missionary zeal, as unpaid (or modestly paid) fan translators. Both Gouanvic and Chung describe how in France and Taiwan the advent of speculative fiction happened thanks to the efforts of dedicated translators. Many missionaries of speculative fiction start out this way; Sapkowski himself began as a translator.

Is the White Wolf 'White'?

The franchise's anglophone reception frequently features clashes between Polish self-perception and anglophone culture, exemplified by the online discussion following Polygon's review of the final instalment of the game (*The Witcher 3: The Wild Hunt*, 2015). An American reviewer named Arthur Gies, while generally enthusiastic, commented on what he perceived as the aggressive misogyny of the *Witcher* world,[8] and noticed a complete absence of characters of colour. A storm ensued, but this time it was Polish readers who were confused. Not only are many of them conservative compared to the current trends in gaming, but also, aside from open conservatives like Adrian Chmielarz,[9] who reject any idea of social justice or equal representation in fiction, many who see themselves as representatives of the privileged found this approach a new, almost incomprehensible experience. Polish public discourse simply did not have categories for it. As one blogger declared (an expat Pole living in Australia), Polish fans saw the presence of Sapkowski's prose and the games as *Poland's* one chance to be represented as a minority language and culture;[10] that someone might see Poles primarily through their Europeanness, or white skin colour, was inconceivable.

Unintentionally but powerfully, the issue of Slav mythology rose to the surface. Foreign readers found themselves examining Central European history in search, for example, of potential characters of colour, and Poles found themselves explaining their history and heritage to that audience, which forced them to express it in whole new terms. The value clash was evident. Aside from standard arguments raised in discussions about representation (such as the artistic freedom to create a world as one likes, or authorial integrity, since Sapkowski's world is indeed white), the dubious historical accuracy of Slav mythology became central. Though none of the commenters expressed it openly, the debate made it clear that the

---

[8] For instance, the third game features a dialogue option where the player can sympathize with an NPC (non-player character) who beat his pregnant wife to death. Michael Kandel (2014) states that a sort of 'chivalrous sexism' is a very pronounced feature of Polish culture.

[9] A Polish game developer and online personality. He was the first to solicit the rights to turn *The Witcher* into a game, in 1996.

[10] See Bleja 2015: www.volnaiskra.com/volblog/the-melting-pot-and-the-salad-bowl-why-the-witcher-3-is-a-step-forward-for-ethnic-diversity-in-games [accessed 6 August 2019].

real problem is not what really Slav *is*, but what people *believe* to be their heritage. In other words, history was proven secondary to the imagined layer where identity is built.

Conclusion

Several morals emerge from this story. First, it helps us identify some deficiencies in translation studies themselves. The route by which Sapkowski's prose entered English, and became so successful as to earn its author the World Fantasy Lifetime Achievement Award, is hard to explain using traditional concepts of literature-oriented translation studies. Like Ondřej Vimr in Chapter Three, we have to question Toury's assertion that translations happen to fill gaps in the TC (2012, 21–22), since English hardly suffers from a scarcity of paperback genre fantasy. In this case, Toury is proven right, but the gap does not come from literature. It was created by the systems of modern popular culture, which blur the boundary between the narrative content created across various media. This shows that, to understand the dynamics of intercultural communication today, one needs to look more broadly, especially where popular culture is concerned. It is time to start bridging the gaps created by the growth of the discipline and the resulting compartmentalization of research. Game localization, the translation of minor literatures and alterity are all extensively studied. But studies of alterity focus mostly on 'mainstream' high culture. Game localization studies in turn often focus on the technical aspects of the process, which create blind spots in translation theory itself. This situation is illustrated by the confused translational relationship between transmedia industries and the traditional literary cultures. These two do not understand one another, mostly because this distinction coincides with the distinction between high and popular culture. Since most academic translation studies are also biased towards high culture – even more so in the case of small languages – much is slipping under the radar. Few realize that popular culture is worthy of attention, though it is often the best seismograph for identifying wider trends.

In the case of the *Witcher* franchise, we are able to map a connection between two big areas: gaming and literature. We have identified a symbiotic relationship arising between the components of a transmedia franchise that influences translation processes. The success of one may, and typically does, create demand for additional material. This is how the *Witcher* books became NYT bestsellers; the presence of the games changed the status of translations of Polish fantasy from supply-driven to demand-driven. This is clearly visible when we look at the two collections in which 'Wiedźmin' (the original short story from 1986) appeared: *Zajdel Awards Winners* by SuperNOWA (2000) and *A Polish Book of Monsters* by PIASA (2010). Though the first was driven by traditional fan culture (fandom), and the second enjoyed patronage from a high-culture institution, neither was particularly successful. In fact, neither were any of the similar collections, such as Wiesiek Powaga's *Dedalus Book of Polish Fantasy* (1996). It is new media literacy that creates new types of audiences, and channels of intercultural communication that interact with traditional industries and can influence the dissemination of smaller literatures, especially when grassroots activity comes into play. New generations of bicultural creators merely harness the power of these relationships.

One would, however, be mistaken to believe that the new media completely supersede older cultural layers. 'Nation' is still the most powerful word in Polish culture. This is shown in the missionary attitude of both the creators of the *Witcher* franchise and the industrious fan translators. In both cases, the creation process was accompanied by a belief that Sapkowski's fiction constitutes an important contribution to world fantasy literature, if not in terms of literary novelty then in entertainment value. More broadly, contemporary audiences are bicultural also in the sense that they are both digital natives and members of their respective culture of origin. They take to new media to retell their story using the shared media literacy as a communication platform, just as the old Finnish shaman can retell the story of Odin's crows to a group of bikers by renaming them Harley and Davidson.[11] At the same time, the reception aspect shows that in the phrase 'small European nation', European may still be key; as postcolonial studies explains, even if you do not matter much in Europe you are perceived as part of it. Ultimately, the realities created by new media are not as completely new as some academic books would suggest. The hegemonies inherited from centuries of history still play a significant role, though sometimes in an unexpected way. In other words, it may be a three-dimensional chessboard, but the rules of the game are largely the same.

---

[11] The story told by Gunnar Roxen, a game developer and novelist, at the 2014 Eurocon in Dublin.

Paulina Drewniak

Bibliography

Primary Sources
Published English Translations of *Witcher* Stories
Sapkowski, Andrzej. 2007. *The Last Wish*. Trans. Danusia Stok (London: Gollancz).
Sapkowski, Andrzej. 2008. *Blood of Elves*. Trans. Danusia Stok (London: Gollancz).
Sapkowski, Andrzej. 2013. *Time of Contempt*. Trans. David French (London: Gollancz).
Sapkowski, Andrzej. 2014. *Baptism of Fire*. Trans. David French (London: Gollancz).
Sapkowski, Andrzej. 2015. *Sword of Destiny*. Trans. David French (London: Gollancz).
Sapkowski, Andrzej. 2016. *Tower of the Swallow*. Trans. David French (London: Gollancz).
Sapkowski, Andrzej. 2017. *Lady of the Lake*. Trans. David French (London: Gollancz).

Collections of Polish Fantasy Stories Containing *Witcher* Stories
Powaga, Wiesiek (ed.). 1996. *The Dedalus Book of Polish Fantasy* (Sawtry: Dedalus Books).
Sapkowski, Andrzej. 2000. The Hexer. Trans. Agnieszka Fulińska. In Gepfert, Elżbieta, Grzegorz Kozubski and Piotr W. Cholewa (eds). *Anthology: Chosen by Fate; Zajdel Award Winners* (Katowice, Warszawa: Śląski Klub Fantastyki, superNOWA).
Sapkowski, Andrzej. 2010. Spellmaker. Trans. Michael Kandel. In Kandel, Michael (ed.). *A Polish Book of Monsters; Five Dark Tales from Contemporary Poland* ed. by Michael Kandel (New York: PIASA Books).

Videogames
CD Projekt RED, *The Witcher*. 2007. PC and other platforms.
CD Projekt RED, *The Witcher 2: Assassins of Kings*. 2011. PC and other platforms.
CD Projekt RED, *The Witcher 3: Wild Hunt*. 2015. PC and other platforms.
For detailed information about the franchise, consult the Witcher Wiki, available from: http://Witcher.wikia.com/wiki/Witcher_Wiki [accessed 24 September 2016].

Works Cited
Anderson, Benedict. 2006. *Imagined Communities: Reflections on the Origin and Spread of Nationalism* (London and New York: Verso).
Bhabha, Homi. 1994. *The Location of Culture* (London and New York: Routledge).

Bleja, Dave. 2015. The Melting Pot and the Salad Bowl: Why the Witcher 3 is a Step Forward for Ethnic Diversity in Games. Available from: www.volnaiskra.com/volblog/the-melting-pot-and-the-salad-bowl-why-the-Witcher-3-is-a-step-forward-for-ethnic-diversity-in-games [accessed 20 September 2016].

Branchadell, Albert. 2005. Introduction. In Branchadell, Albert and Lovell Margaret West (eds). *Less Translated Languages* (Amsterdam/Philadephia: John Benjamins), 1–23.

Drewniak, Paulina. 2015. Are We There Yet? A Snapshot in the Haphazard History of *Wiedźmin's* English Translations. In Dudziński, Robert and Joanna Płoszaj (eds). *Wiedźmin – polski fenomen popkultury*. Available from: http://tricksterzy.pl/download/wiedzmin-polski-fenomen-popkultury/ [accessed 21 September 2016].

Gies, Arthur. 2015. The Witcher 3: Wild Hunt Review: Off the Path. www.polygon.com/2015/5/13/8533059/the-Witcher-3-review-wild-hunt-PC-PS4-Xbox-one [accessed 20 September 2016].

Gouanvic, Jean-Marc. 1997. Translation and the Shape of Things to Come. *The Translator*, 3 (2), 125–52.

Guttfeld, Dorota. 2006. *English–Polish Translations of Fantasy and Science-Fiction* (Toruń: Wydawnictwo Naukowe Uniwersytetu Mikołaja Kopernika).

Heilbron, Johan. 2010. Towards a Sociology of Translation: Book Translations as a Cultural World System. In Baker, Mona (ed.). *Critical Readings in Translation Studies* (London and New York: Routledge), 304–14.

Jacquemond, Richard. 1992. Translation and Cultural Hegemony: The Case of French-Arabic Translation. In Venuti, Lawrence (ed.) *Rethinking Translation: Discourse, Subjectivity, Ideology* (London and New York: Routledge), 139–58.

Janion, Maria. 2006. *Niesamowita Słowiańszczyzna: Fantazmaty literatury* (Kraków: Wydawnictwo Literackie).

Jenkins, Henry. 2006. *Convergence Culture: Where Old and New Media Collide* (New York and London: New York University Press).

Kaczor, Katarzyna. 2014. Bogactwo polskich światów fantasy. Od braku nadziei do *eukatastrophe*. In Konefał, Jakub Sebastien (ed.). *Anatomia wyobraźni* (Gdańsk: Gdański Klub Fantastyki), 181–98.

Kandel, Michael. 2010. Introduction. In Kandel, Michael (ed.). *A Polish Book of Monsters; Five Dark Tales from Contemporary Poland* (New York: PIASA Books), vii–xxi.

Kandel, Michael. 2014. Translation is Quixotic. A Conversation with Michael Kandel. Available from: www.restlessbooks.com/blog/2014/1/27/a-conversation-with-michael-kandel [accessed 13 March 2016].

Klastrup, Lisbeth and Susana Tosca. 2004. Transmedial Worlds – Rethinking Cyberworld Design. Available from www.itu.dk/people/klastrup/klastruptosca_transworlds.pdf [accessed 8 May 2016].

Lazarus, Neil. 2012. Spectres Haunting: Postcommunism and Postcolonialism. *Journal of Postcolonial Writing*, 48 (2), 117–29.

Maj, Krzysztof M. 2015. Transmedial World-building in Fictional Narratives. IMAGE Issue 22, Special Issue: *Media Convergence and Transmedial Worlds*, Part 3, 83–96.

Majkowski, Tomasz Z. 2013. *W cieniu Białego Drzewa: Powieść fantasy w XX wieku* (Kraków: Wydawnictwo Uniwersytetu Jagiellońskiego).

New York Times. 2015, New York Times Best Sellers. Available from: www.nytimes.com/best-sellers-books/2015-06-14/mass-market-paperback/list.html [accessed 20 September 2016].

Oziewicz, Marek. 2010. Representations of Eastern Europe in Philip Pullman's *His Dark Materials*, Jonathan Stroud's *The Bartimaeus Trilogy*, and J.K. Rowling's *Harry Potter* Series. *International Research in Children's Literature*, 3 (1), 1–14.

Radziwon, Marek. 2007. Uncanny Slavdom – Maria Janion. Available from: http://culture.pl/en/work/uncanny-slavdom-maria-janion [accessed 21 September 2016].

Richards, Laurie. 2015. Social Justice Witcher. Available from: http://theleveller.org/2015/08/social-justice-witcher/ [accessed 26 December 2017].

Ryan, Marie-Laure. 2013. Transmedial Storytelling and Transfictionality. *Poetics Today*, 34 (3), 361–88.

Schreiber, Paweł. 2017. How The Witcher Plays with Polish Romanticism. Available from: http://culture.pl/en/article/how-the-witcher-plays-with-polish-romanticism [accessed 27 September 2017].

Sohár, Anikó. 1999. *The Cultural Transfer of Science Fiction and Fantasy in Hungary, 1989–1995* (Frankfurt/M., Berlin, Bern, Bruxelles, New York and Wien: Peter Lang).

Tkacz, Małgorzata. 2012. *Baśnie zbyt prawdziwe: Trzydzieści lat fantasy w Polsce* (Gdańsk: Gdański Klub Fantastyki).

Toury, Gideon. 2012. *Descriptive Translation Studies – and Beyond* (Amsterdam/Philadephia: John Benjamins).

Velickovic, Vedrana. 2012. Belated Alliances? Tracing the Intersections between Postcolonialism and Postcommunism. *Journal of Postcolonial Writing*, 48 (2), 164–75.

Venuti, Lawrence. 2008. *The Translator's Invisibility* (London and New York: Routledge).

Chapter Twelve

Towards a Multilingual Poetics: Self-translation, Translingualism and Maltese Literature

Josianne Mamo (University of Glasgow)

> Two male crabs Dos jueyes machos no caben
> can't root in the same lair dentro de una misma cueva
>
> Rosario Ferré, *Language Duel/
> Duelo de Lenguaje*, 2002, 2–3

In her bilingual text *Language Duel/Duelo de Lenguaje* (2002), the Puerto Rican writer, Rosario Ferré (1938–2016), dramatizes the contest between English and Spanish in the Americas. This war is so fierce and loud, with cannonballs roaring above, that the advantages of taking a double perspective seem inaudible for these 'two male crabs' interlocked in an ever-lasting power struggle for linguistic dominance. We can observe this linguistic power struggle not only in the Americas, but globally, and with shifting and more complicated power dynamics when the struggle becomes one between minority and majority languages, as in Europe.[1] Cronin (2003, 139) shows how the postcolonial critique of Europe's role in history as colonizer often tends to 'reduce Europe to two languages, English and French, and to two countries, England and France'. He cites Niranjana's references to 'European descriptions' and 'European languages', which aptly expose the double pall of invisibility that minority cultures and languages experience (Cronin, 2003, 140). In telling Europe's story as one single story, postcolonial critics risk homogenizing languages, cultures and experiences, thus

---

[1] For more on the dynamics of representation, translation and imperialism see Baker (2014, 16) and on the invisibility of lesser used languages, including European ones, see Cronin (2003, 139).

reducing them to 'invisible minorities' (139). The single story, the one that does not study specificity, as Chimamanda Adichie (2009) warns, risks creating and perpetuating stereotypes (see also Tanoukhi, 2013). What is being perpetuated here is an essentialist narrative of Europe as a colonialist's narrative, which renders invisible the story of a post-colony within Europe. It also renders invisible Europe's multicultural experiences, not only beyond borders (e.g. the diaspora) but also within them, as exemplified by Malta, a small Mediterranean island-state that is generally absent from such debates.

The absence of smaller literatures from scholarly debates or in translation can render that literature invisible. Joseph Brincat (2011, 34) illustrates this well in his history of Maltese linguistics, in which he identifies contemporary translations of an ancient Arabic text, *Kitābar-Rawḍ al-Mitar* (*The Book of Fragrant Gardens*) that exclude the sections about Malta. For Brincat, these exclusions make it more difficult to trace the origins of the Maltese language, the only European language that is part-Semitic, part-Romance. This exclusion of the passage on Malta from both studies of Arabic sources and those concerning Italy not only created a gap in national knowledge, but also made it difficult to see how the Maltese language, with its multilingual influences, came to fit within the wider collective story of Semitic and European languages.

In his 'Incongruity and Scale', Callus (n.d.) offers two reasons for the absence of Maltese literature in centrally located discussions. First, the scale of Maltese literature is very small: 'The shock is that Maltese literature is minor in a scale and to a degree that makes it indiscernible to the other's critique. The other, it seems, will not be bothered.' Maltese literature is so small that it fails even to register on the radar of international literature. Here, small is used literally; the island is only 27 kilometres long and its language is spoken by half a million people. The small pool from which quality writing can arise, the small volume of content that the 'other' might be interested in reading, its tiny place in world markets and therefore its almost non-existent reception render a literature like Maltese imperceptible. But how can the 'other' be bothered with, and thus be inclusive of, something it cannot see? For Callus, it is an incongruous situation for which he recommends a practical (if ambitious) solution: establishing a literary magazine like *Wassifiri* and *Granta* to rectify the lack of 'appropriate' publication outlets in Malta for new creative writing.[2] Maltese literature thus finds itself in a 'double

---

[2] Callus takes as his starting point a 2009 criminal case brought against a writer who published an explicit story in a publication distributed at the

Self-translation, Translingualism and Maltese Literature

bind' (Callus, n.d.): unseen by the 'other' but lacking an autonomous literary infrastructure making it visible on a wider scale that would allow for its dissemination and analysis.

As for so many of the literatures discussed in this volume, writing literature in Maltese, best understood as an act of self-preservation, resistance, and insistence on speaking one's own language, predestines that literature to be always heard in translation. A constant process of mediation and negotiation occurs before the other can see or hear it. Ferré and Brincat's examples highlight the role translation plays in the circulation of ideas and knowledge across borders (and how a lack of translation can hinder that same circulation). Translation, however, is not the only way that ideas circulate across borders. People also cross borders, taking with them their culture, their literature and their languages, and this transfer is dramatized in the work of translingual writers. Like translators, translingual writers are engaged in producing transcultural meaning, except that when translingual writers produce a heterolingual text, the lived multilingual experience becomes visible on the page. It 'takes advantage of the double [I would say triple, or quadruple] perspective', and thereby shifts the 'parallel rails' to make languages meet and interact on the page (Ferré, 2).

While translingualism has attracted the attention of various writers and scholars in America, particularly Latin American literature, there is less focused discussion of it in Europe. This chapter aims to bridge this gap by examining how studies of the Latin American and African heterolingual text can be applied to a reading of the self-translated and heterolingual Maltese text. Despite the foregoing, I shall focus more on the poetics than the politics of multilingual writing, examining the creative strategies adopted by translingual writers using languages other than what others perceive as their first, and how such practices may be accounted for, valorized and read as part of literature and literature in translation, in the fields of translation and literary studies. I shall first explore the distinctions and convergences between self-translation (writers who translate their own work from one language to another) and two types of translingual writing (using multiple languages on the page, and writing an ostensibly monolingual text that

---

University of Malta's campus. This caused a major furore in the country and an ensuing national debate on censorship laws in print and television. However, while the criminal charges had the effect of censorship, Callus is more interested in the underlying cultural, religious and political conditions under which Maltese writers operate.

is a conveyor of another language) to determine how far a translational approach is used in the creation of a heterolingual text. This analysis will provide translation scholars and practitioners with a new vocabulary for understanding creative strategies used in the heterolingual text and serve as a springboard for future research into literary multilingualism. Second, I shall employ Francine Prose's approach to literary texts in *Reading like a Writer* (2006), which shifts the focus from what is being said to how it is being said. This will be then applied to the heterolingual text. By studying the techniques and creative strategies used by multilingual writers to achieve a particular effect on the reader, practising translators acquire tools that enable them to reproduce a similar effect (rather than just the message) in the target language(s) of their translations.

Revisiting the Definition of Self-translation

Self-translation and translingualism have captured the imagination of many scholars but few have made a connection between them, possibly because of the way we perceive them as two distinct and unrelated processes. For example, Anton Popović defined self-translation as 'the translation of an original work into another language by the author himself' (quoted in Grutman and Van Bolderen, 2014, 323). Inherent in this statement is the movement between languages and the coexistence of two final manuscripts in the source and target language. Grutman (2009, 257) later defined 'self-translation' as 'the *act* of translating one's own writings into another language and the *result* of such an undertaking' (my italics). This shifts the emphasis from Popović's 'original works', which suggests published texts, to Grutman's 'own writings', denoting anything from published texts to writers' notes. However, most examples Grutman gives are still of self-translators who 'repeat what they have already written in another language'. Grutman (2009, 257) illustrates this with a bilingual text from 1579 with two languages (French and Dutch) sitting 'side by side'. Contemporary equivalents would be Ferré's *Duelo de Lenguaje/Language* in the US and *A Bird is not a Stone* in the UK (Bell et al., 2014). Even if, in the latter case, the poet and translators are different (hence the text is not self-translated), it is an interesting example of a bilingual text published in Europe. While these texts make visible the two languages on the page, they still sit on 'two parallel rails'.

Linguistic separation remains integral to the final product, and entrenched in contemporary discussions of self-translation. For example, while Klimkiewicz (2013, 191–92) demonstrates successfully how a narrative whole can be broken into different linguistic segments in the process of writing, her discussion remains located in a language of separation. Her choice of words such as 'fragmentation', 'discontinuity' and 'divided consciousness' all point to fragmentation and a troubled psyche. In fact, while she suggests that translation and self-translation make 'the two parts of the self physically present, visible and audible tools', in her analysis they remain separated on different pages. Postcolonial writers and translation have, however, shown us that it is not always possible or desirable to separate languages on the page. Consider, for instance, the significance of including discussions of postcolonial writers (rather than translators) in *Postcolonial Translation* (Bassnett-McGuire and Trivedi, 1999). While Bassnett and Trivedi never use the term 'self-translation', the juxtaposition of postcolonial writing with Translation Studies suggests that there are various commonalities in the process of writing as both are involved in the cross-cultural transfer of meaning. Set side by side like this, the postcolonial writer can be seen as a self-translator as much as a translator can be seen as a writer. Of particular interest is Bassnett and Trivedi's reference (1999, 12) to Salman Rushdie, 'who writes in English in the first place and therefore does not need to be translated'. In his own words, however, Rushdie (1992, 9) is a 'translated' man, a British Indian writer who conquers both the English language and the novel form: 'The word "translation" comes, etymologically, from the Latin for "bearing across". Having been borne across the world, we are translated men. It is normally supposed that something always gets lost in translation; I cling, obstinately, to the notion that something can also be gained' (Rushdie, 1992, 17). This approach to self-translation contrasts with that of the Slovene Miha Mazzini, described by Olivia Hellewell in Chapter Six.

At first glance, what seems to be translated in Rushdie's case is the 'self' who adopts a new language as a result of his relocation, thus situating Rushdie's words in a discussion of identity politics. The relocation here does not, however, happen only at the metaphorical level but also at the textual level. What can be gained is a new 'English' reshaped to bring across transcultural meaning. We hear an echo of Rushdie's words – 'we can't simply use the language in the way the British used it' – because the language is needed to reflect a different social, cultural and political experience. It needs 'remaking for our own purposes' (Rushdie, 1992, 17). In this famous aside, then, the literal and the metaphorical converge, and in these gaps, language can be created anew.

Josianne Mamo

Even an etymological study of the word 'translate' allows for such a reading. In 'Interpreting the Meaning of Translation', Andrew Chesterman (2005, 6) moves away from 'translation universals', arguing that even the word on which Translation Studies is founded has plural etymologies. If even the literal meaning has multiple interpretations, imagine the creative possibilities of the metaphor 'to carry across'. This leads us to the translingual text– the text that is created in the liminal space, or 'the contact zone' (see also Pratt, 1991; Bhabha, 1994; and Zabus, 1991), where two cultures and their languages meet, a contact zone where poems like 'Bilingual Blues', by Gustav Pérez Firmat (b.1949) (1995, 28), are born:

> I have mixed feelings about everything.
> Soy un ajiaco de contradicciones.
> Vexed, hexed, complexed,
> hyphenated, oxygenated, illegally alienated,
> psycho soy, cantando voy:
> You say tomato,
> I say tu madre;
> You say potato,
> I say Pototo.
> Let's call the hole
> un hueco, the thing
> a cosa, and if the cosa goes into the hueco,
> consider yourself en casa,
> consider yourself part of the family.

This extract shows how the writer visibly manifests his bilingualism on the page. What is intriguing is the mental process behind this creation, the movement between ideation and implementation, and whether this can be called self-translation. The questions posed here deal more with the workings of the mind, hence questions that neurolinguists may be better equipped to answer (see Kager, 2015). Basing her argument on de Groot's theory that 'forgetting one language is directly related to second language acquisition', Kager suggests that writers may shift between languages when one word or a concept in a particular language does not have a corresponding translation. Writers switch languages when the creative possibilities end in one and begin in another. Studying a bilingual writer's notebooks can be illuminating here. For example, Knowlson illustrates how Beckett started writing 'La Fin' in English and, 29 pages into it, continued in French (quoted

Self-translation, Translingualism and Maltese Literature

in Kager, 2015, 70). Kager traces Beckett's words in a letter he wrote to Axel Kaun. In his letter, originally written in German, Beckett uses the metaphor of boring holes ('Loch') in languages: 'To bore one hole after another into [a language], until what lurks behind it – be it something or nothing – begins to seep through' (Kager, 2015, 71).

Kager shows how in languages, words do not always fall neatly onto each other, exposing existing gaps within them. In this liminal space, and unlike monolingual writers, translingual writers (and translators) are able to expose and bridge these gaps in and between languages. A similar concept is suggested in the extract from Pérez Firmat's poem with the words, 'Let's call the hole/un hueco, the thing/a cosa'. What is happening with this *hueco* is not only a literal translation but also a sexual pun on words as a result of the linguistic interplay between Spanish and English. 'Un hueco' can mean both a 'hole' and 'hollow' and 'if the cosa goes into the hueco' we all know what happens. The family is enlarged. Propagation happens: of people, of ideas, cultural identity and attachment. This interpretation seems supported by the next two lines, 'consider yourself en casa,/consider yourself part of the family'. This family (both the nuclear unit and America at large) is, however, complex and the words 'illegally alienated' and 'psycho soy, cantando voy' lend a sarcastic tone to it exposing the conflicting relationship between the two cultures. Words, concepts and two cultures are translated within the space of a stanza, sometimes a line. For Pérez Firmat, shifts in languages carry poetic signification (or function).[3]

Language shifts are not, however, always visible on the page, which means it takes a carefully attuned reader to pick up on these movements and interpret their poetic signification. It is thus important to distinguish between two types of translingual texts:

1. The text where the movement is visible on the page (as we have seen in Pérez Firmat's 'Bilingual Blues' and as we will see in the perhaps more complicated example by Antoine Cassar).

2. The text that shows visual evidence of only one language on the page, where that visible language carries across the sounds, rhythms, linguistic patterns and cultural references of another language.

---

[3] For more on poetic signification in heterolingual texts, see Marie Lauret's *Wanderwords: Language Migration in American Literature* (2014), in which the term 'migrant' is not used exclusively to refer to the movement of the people who write but also to the migratory aspect of language itself.

The latter may be described as a fusion of languages. Chinua Achebe's *Things Fall Apart* is one such example (for a textual analysis of the novel see Zabus (1991, 115)). Zabus (1991, 111) refers to the latter as the 'indigenization' of languages, where the lesser known language is 'grafted' onto or 'interbred' with the wider known language. Looked at it in this way, self-translation in translingual writing ceases to be a metaphor and becomes a translational technique in the writer's process. The fact that Zabus traces this creative strategy in African writers' work is not purely coincidental. In the spirit of true Calibans, rather than transforming their 'self', postcolonial writers transform the English language to 'curse' in it, 'contaminating' it with native sounds, rhythms and nuances. To go back to Rushdie's words, literary translingualism does not 'simply use the language the way the British did' (1992, 17) but makes that language the user's own. This suggests a conscious artistic decision to create a new language or third code (see also Bhabha, 1994; Simon, 1995; Zabus, 1991). Such decisions often arise in writing novels or poetry that are native-culture-based, like those analysed below.

Self-translation and Translingualism

It has already been established that the translator is a writer (Bassnett and Bush, 2006), but the extent to which the reverse analogy is true – that the translingual writer is a translator – is still an ongoing debate (Bandia, 2014). Drawing the distinctions and convergences between self-translation and translingual writing has deeper implications than meet the eye for both the field of Translation Studies and the actual practice of translation. First, despite the proliferation of creative writing courses (and unlike what happened in the 1990s with the cultural turn in Translation Studies: Bassnett-McGuire and Lefevere, 1998), Creative Writing and Translation Studies remain two distinct fields, which is a shame considering the tools with which creative writing courses equip a writer. Most importantly, they teach you how to close-read texts not only for what they say, but for how they say it. They study the effects of techniques (e.g. rhyme, repetition or silence) and how words, phrases and other strategies function within a text. In other words, considerations about content, function and effect are studied concomitantly with the reader's experience in mind, a paradigm familiar to literary (self-)translators. This is how heterolingual texts like 'C'est La Vie' by the Maltese poet, Antoine Cassar (b.1978) (2008) will be read here, with an eye and an ear for how multiple languages meet and interact on the page:

Self-translation, Translingualism and Maltese Literature

> Run, rabbit, run, run, run, from the womb to the tomb,
> de cuatro a dos a tres, del río a la mar,
> play the fool, suffer school, żunżana ddur iddur,
> engage-toi, perds ta foi, le regole imparar,
>
> kul u sum, aħra u bul, chase the moon, meet your doom,
> walk on ice, roll your dice, col destino danzar,
> métro, boulot, dodo, titla' x-xemx, terġa' tqum,
> decir siempre mañana y nunca mañanar,
>
> try to fly, touch the sky, hit the stone, break a bone,
> sell your soul for a loan to call those bricks your home,
> fall in love, rise above, fall apart, stitch your heart,
>
> che sarà? ça ira! plus rien de nous sera,
> minn sodda għal sodda niġru tiġrija kontra l-baħħ,
> sakemm tinbela' ruħna mill-ġuf mudlam ta' l-art.

Poems like 'C'est La Vie' show how literatures across the world can defy national borders and initiate cross-cultural conversations. Sliding in and out of English, Spanish, Maltese, French and Italian, 'C'est La Vie' is an example of how the heterolingual text is a by-product of different literary, cultural, and linguistic systems. Implicit in their very existence is that culture is neither fixed nor restrained within borders. Even the form the poet chooses (the Petrarchan sonnet with an octave and a sestet) epitomizes cross-cultural literary production, given that the sonnet has travelled from Italy, to France, to Britain and elsewhere (Kennedy, 2011), to be used here to frame a heterolingual text. The sonnet's structure and rhyme are developed into something new thanks to the differences between Italian and English, most notably in sound. For example, Samuel Johnson considered the Italian sonnet too 'foreign', 'not very suitable' to the English language and 'required the rhymes to be often changed' (quoted in White, 2011, 172). These structural and rhyming modifications demonstrate the challenges of translating the sound of one language into another. It can be argued that the translingual writer in the heterolingual text will have a larger pool of sounds to choose, so if sounds from one language do not fit, they can be taken from another. On the other hand, carrying across rhyme, rhythm and sound becomes more complicated when there is more than one language used within the constrictions of the poetic form. Given the phonological differences across languages, sounds may not exactly map. Cassar's word endings, however, exploit these differences quite successfully.

Translingual writers are therefore those who move beyond real and imagined borders, shifting between languages, cultures, and locations (e.g. Leila Aboulela (b.1964) writing about Khartoum in Scotland, Jhumpa Lahiri (b.1967), an American of Bengalese descent, writing about learning Italian in Italy), but not necessarily between texts. While the self-translator carries meaning from a source language to a target language, the language movement for translingual writers happens within one text. That single text becomes a visible manifestation of the multilingual writer's lived reality. In addition, the text's very existence acknowledges the existence of a multilingual reader. We may thus pinpoint a significant distinction between self-translation and translingualism. Whereas the practice of translating from a source to a target language assumes the readership is monolingual, translingualism presupposes a multilingual writer *and* audience. Such an assumption can pose a problem not only for monolingual readers (or readers unfamiliar with the language combination), for whom the heterolingual text (or parts of it) may become inaccessible, but also for the translingual writer, for whom the number of readers who can access their text will shrink. This scenario is further complicated if one introduces a majority/minority language power dynamic (e.g. English versus Maltese) into the picture. The translator of the heterolingual text into a monolingual text must then determine whether the function of the shift in languages is to draw in or alienate the (monolingual) reader.

Another point of convergence between self-translation and translingualism is the negotiation of meaning between cultures and the creative effect achieved in this negotiation. Cultural transposition is important for this discussion because translingual writers, just like translators, are concerned with how the message affects a reader's experience of the text. If the monolingual target audience's system of conceptualizing the world is different from the translingual writer's, then the writer needs to negotiate the meaning between (or within) these two worldviews (or five, in the case of Cassar's poem) (Mamo, 2014, 31). From this perspective, translingualism does take a translational approach in negotiating meaning across cultures, and this approach closely resembles the mapping of what Lefevere calls the 'textual and conceptual grids' in different cultures and languages. Translingualism, thus, functions similarly to translation in

> negotiating the passage of texts between [cultures], or rather, by deciding strategies through which texts from one culture can penetrate the textual and conceptual grids of another culture, and function in that other culture. (Bassnett-McGuire and Lefevere, 1998, 7)

Self-translation, Translingualism and Maltese Literature

Just like translators, translingual writers – in creating the heterolingual text and considering how to transfer meaning from one host culture to another – work within 'the domain of cultural capital to construct cultures' (Bassnett-McGuire and Lefevere, 1998, 7). The difference lies in that the cultures constructed by translingual writers are those in which multilingualism is not just a tool to translate from one language to another, but also a state-of-being where languages coexist and the negotiation of languages and cultures happens in only one space, whether the text or one's personal life. In keeping with François Grosjean's concept that the bilingual is not two monolinguals in one person (Grosjean, 1989, 3), this hybrid space denotes a space of existence rather than a transitory space en route from one language to another (Bhabha, 58). It is a space that the multilingual audience (the one familiar with Cassar's languages) shares with the writer and a space where a third code is born. This third code is where interlingual and cross-cultural interplay occurs. For this interplay to succeed, however, the translingual writer must negotiate effectively the passage of meaning not only between languages, but also in what results from their interbreeding. Consequently, while the self-translated text need only 'function' in the host culture, the heterolingual text may need to function within both monolingual and multilingual cultures. If so, then the translingual writer's creative strategies will need to reflect the different needs of her audiences.

In 'C'est la Vie', for example, five different textual and conceptual grids are being mapped (or overlaid) to make a coherent whole. Not knowing one of those languages (and its cultural references) is like missing a piece of the jigsaw puzzle. One can still get a general picture but a specific piece of the puzzle is lost, and with it, a certain nuance the author is trying to achieve. Questions regarding the transposition of cultural reference, faithfulness and equivalence (of meaning, content, idea, sound, function, effect achieved, and so on), and reader accessibility are as much a concern here as for the self-translator. However, while the latter solves this in parallel texts, the translingual writer has to adopt creative strategies that work within one heterolingual text. Such is the case with 'C'est la Vie', a poem about the cyclical nature of life, the futility of our efforts in the face of death. We are born, we strive to improve our station in life and we die. What is interesting about the poem, however, is the tone this fusion of languages creates, the dizzying, breakneck pace at which we live our lives. This pace is established through the repetition of 'run' in the first line '[r]un, rabbit, run, run, run, from the womb to the tomb' a line written in English, a language familiar to the majority of readers, which suggests that the poet wants to draw that

Josianne Mamo

majority in. The line, moreover, alludes to a children's song: 'run rabbit, run, run, run/here comes the farmer with his gun, gun, gun'. There is a sense of comfort in the form, but also an implicit fear of being chased.[4] The rabbit is reminiscent of the rabbit in *Alice in Wonderland*, running with a watch in his hand and Alice following him down the proverbial 'rabbit hole' to find herself in a dizzying, surreal world. The rabbit is also known for its reproduction rates, captured vividly in a common Maltese phrase, and the sexual puns will not be lost to readers familiar with the Maltese language.

The vertiginous quality of life and the interlingual strategy is captured using a Maltese phrase 'żunżana ddur iddur', a reference to 'a Maltese game' (Cassar, 2008). In this game, children sit in a circle facing each other, except for one child who plays the wasp. This child (the wasp) runs around the circle while the group sings the rhyme, 'Iż-żunżana ddur iddur'. By the end of the rhyme, the running child must tag (or place a ball behind) one of the sitting participants who becomes the hunter and must thus hunt the wasp. The aim of the game is for the wasp to take the hunter's place before the hunter tags him/her. If the hunter does not manage to tag the wasp, he/she will take the wasp's role, and the game continues until the participants are either too dizzy or too bored to continue. Cassar thus replicates the paradoxical effect of comfort in form and the anxiety (of the chase). Cassar provides a monolingual English translation of his poem on his website with the phrase 'żunżana ddur iddur', translated as 'the wasp goes round and round' as shown in the lines, 'play the fool, suffer school, the wasp goes round and round*, get involved, lose your faith, learn the rules' (Cassar's use of asterisk to explain reference to a Maltese game).[5] The choice of English draws in a much wider audience and could be further evidence that the interbreeding of languages in the heterolingual text is not meant as an alienation technique but rather an experiment in how different languages, with their respective textual and conceptual grids, can work together on the page. The word choice sounds literal rather than idiomatically equivalent to Duck, Duck, Goose – a game similar to ż-żunżana ddur iddur – as if the writer is either avoiding loading this particular phrase with the cultural inferences from outside the Maltese context or domesticating it for the English reader.

---

[4] The discussions I had over this poem with my editor were illuminating in extracting various transcultural meanings such as reference to this particular children's song. Collaborative translations (or readings) may open up new discussions on how a text relates to and within different cultures.

[5] The full English version of the poem can be found on Cassar's website (2008).

Consequently, the cultural transposition that was so effectively rendered in the heterolingual text and was accessible to the multilingual reader is not in-built in the monolingual translation. A footnote is required to explain the Maltese cultural reference. Perhaps it is there to remind the reader that even if an 'equivalent' idiom exists the cultural nuances will be stripped away. Its function becomes explanatory, factual and supplementary. A minority cultural reference is thus reduced to a footnote and becomes paratext rather than an interlingual and co-existing interplay. The footnote, in this case, becomes symbolic of the linguistic power struggle between majority and minority languages in a bid for a heterolingual text to become accessible to a wider audience, because even a footnote can have a significant function in a text (Maloney, 2005, 28). Consider how footnotes function in *The Brief Wondrous Life of Oscar Wao* by the Dominican American writer, Junot Díaz (b.1968). They carry the story of the (fictive) nation and are interwoven with the protagonist's story in the main text. In this case, the narrative in the footnote is intrinsically interwoven with the main plot, thus the footnote has a discursive and autographic function (it is the author speaking). In 'C'est la Vie', the footnote is more factual and allographic (a translator/editor's note), as if Cassar has swapped the writer's hat for a translator/editor's hat. Maloney seeks the origins of the footnote, whether the writer/fictive narrator or the editor/ translator's voice. In our case, this distinction becomes more blurred because Cassar is both writer and self-translator and takes different roles in the production of the text. Since, however, we have established that the translator is indeed a writer, this changing of hats may not be required if the function of 'żunżana ddur iddur' is carried over to the translated version.

Alfred Sant's *l-Għalqa ta' l-Iskarjota* / *The Iscariot Field*

I turn now to the self-translated text, *l-Għalqa ta' l-Iskarjota* / *The Iscariot Field* by Alfred Sant (b.1948), a novel that sits between comic horror and satire in its portrayal of Maltese media. This section analyses creative strategies discussed earlier in this chapter with an awareness of three types of readers for Sant's texts: the monolingual Maltese reader, the monolingual English reader, and the bilingual Maltese/English reader.

On the surface, the story is about a television production team (*Kwis Kwam*) frantically trying to pull off a last-minute show. The story is hardly 'inaccessible' (Pratt, quoted in Zabus, 1991, 183) to a non-Maltese audience, but its cultural references may be. Familiarity with the Maltese political scene,

Josianne Mamo

especially in the years closely preceding the novel's publication, gives the text a more complex edge and lends it allegorical meaning, as with *Animal Farm* and knowledge of communist ideology. The only difference (and biggest challenge) is that the references are to a lesser known culture. For a monolingual English reader who is unfamiliar with the cultural context in which the text was produced, the fictive *Kwis Kwam* is just a television programme rather than an allegory of island politics. While some may invoke Barthes' essay, 'The Death of the Author' (1977, 142) here, claiming that a text has a life of its own, an author-oriented analysis such as Klimkiewicz suggests will uncover the monolingual reader's loss: the third code that remains concealed without knowledge of the Maltese cultural milieu. It is in this spirit that the text will be analysed. While Cassar's heterolingual text allows for an open manifestation of language shifts on the page, Sant's shifts in this self-translated text may be less apparent or frequent. The limited use of visible multilingual manifestations, however, gives even more resonance to when they occur and validity to reading the text as an allegory of the Maltese cultural milieu.

The first clue lies in the name of the fictive television programme, *Kwis Kwam*. A reader familiar with the Maltese cultural milieu will know that Sant was the prime minister of Malta between 1996 and 1998. Diverging opinions on social matters within the party led to an early election in 1998, in which the media played an important role. Sant subsequently refused to appear on a television programme, *Xarabank*, which he likened to a Jerry Springer show (see Anon., 2005; Azzopardi, 2002; Sant, 2002) and which is also reminiscent of *Kwis Kwam*, the programme in the novel. The cultural context is no longer extraneous if the novel is to be read as a social and political satire. The risk here is that the third code created within the text may be lost without knowledge of the Maltese cultural milieu, and may lead to the stripping away of the text's allegorical and satirical meaning. However, *Kwis Kwam* is not a familiar phrase in Maltese, either. The English rendition makes more evident the interlingual play on Quis Quam, which comes from Latin and means 'Anybody'. The rendition of 'q' into 'k' in *Kwis Kwam* follows orthographic rules of early Maltese phonetic transcription (for more on orthography in the postcolonial text see Zabus, 1991, 47; and on Maltese orthography, Brincat, 2011, 108). In real life, the show *Xarabank* is produced by a team called 'Where's Everybody?'. Could the fictive 'Anybody' in Quis Quam be an interplay with the word 'Everybody' in the real production team's name? And could the use of early orthographic rules be a strategy to disguise this link, thus masking the text's engagement with real-life politics? While we cannot know the writer's intentions, what can be concluded at this point is that the orthographic change

Self-translation, Translingualism and Maltese Literature

conceals, somewhat, the word's origin from Latin. Sant brings 'strangeness' to the Maltese text.

Thus, these two words (*Quis Quam/Kwis Kwam*) demonstrate how the bilingual writer can access different systems of conceptualizing the world, but how does the writer deal with the cultural transposition of what Sherry Simon calls a 'local reality' (Simon, 1995, 10), shared by approximately half a million people, in the English version? Culture-bound allusions may not be common knowledge outside the culture in which they were produced, so the writer must choose between finding a corresponding idiomatic expression or allusion in the target language, and indigenizing the text. Sant's rendition of *Quis Quam* in Maltese suggests the writer creates rather than finds an equivalent (Simon, 10). It also suggests an element of defamiliarization, possibly for the Maltese reader.

Let us take another example of how Sant (2009, 328) deals with the local Maltese reality in idiomatic expression in order to assess whether the defamiliarization process occurs in the English version too:

'jilgħabha tal-ors'	⟶	Source text
'(he) pretends to be/plays/bear'	⟶	Literal meaning
'began to play games'	⟶	English text[6]

What the above suggests is that Sant favours finding a corresponding English idiom rather than 'indigeniz[ing]' the target text (Zabus, 1991, 4). This seems a typical translation where 'substitution is made not on the basis of the linguistic elements in the phrase, nor on the basis of a corresponding or similar image contained in the phrase but on the function of the idiom' (Bassnett-McGuire, 2002, 32). Postcolonial literature has shown us instances of writers 'using the European language as conveyor of [one's] culture' (Zabus, 1991, 4). One such case is Achebe, whose English becomes a 'New English', a hybrid between the native tongue and the English language. Language becomes a tool for appropriating representations that others have created of the self. Zabus (1991, 3) calls this the 'indigenization' of the text, where a third code is born. Some creative strategies include pidginization, multilingualism and relexification, a process that refers to the textual representation in a Europhone language of the native speech (Zabus, 111). Thus, in translating idioms, Achebe creates new linguistic signs in the target language, such as

---

[6] For more on the translation of proverbs into English, contextualized to the Igbo culture, see Zabus (1991, 155).

Josianne Mamo

the word 'leper', to transfer the Igbo culture-bound image of religion as the 'white-disease'. It raises questions as to whether there is evidence of indigenization in Sant. This analysis becomes more pertinent when considering the element of 'insistence' on speaking/writing the minor language evident in the country. The next example of how Sant deals with idioms and place names, however, does not show traces of indigenization:

> Hu u jsuq lejn <u>tal-Qroqq</u>, Bertrand fehem li l-professur Dillinger kien irnexxielu <u>jġib il-boċċa qrib il-likk</u>: din iż-żjara ta' Wali Aħmed bil-fors thasslet ilbieraħ waqt ir-riċeviment ... (Sant, 2009, 19)

> On his way to the <u>University</u>, Bertrand concluded that Professor Dillinger <u>had got what he wanted</u>. Wali Ahmed's visit was surely decided yesterday at the reception. (Sant, 2011, 15)

Readers grounded in Maltese 'local reality' know that the University is situated at 'tal-Qroqq', hence they can also infer that if Bertrand is heading there he is going to the University. Moreover, the word 'professor' reduces risks of misinterpretation as there is only one University in Malta with a concentration of 'professors' at 'tal-Qroqq'. In the English version, Sant states where he is going outright. But more interestingly, and perhaps disappointingly, is how Sant translates the idiom '*jġib il-boċċa qrib il-likk*':

'*jġib il-boċċa qrib il-likk*'	⟶	Source text
'(he) brings (to) the marble/bowls/boules near the target marble'	⟶	Literal meaning
'he got what he wanted'	⟶	English text

Again, a corresponding English idiom was substituted for the Maltese version. 'Boċċi' (also known as *bocce, boules,* or *petanque*) is a traditional game played in Malta and other Mediterranean countries where heavy balls ('boċċi') are thrown at a smaller target ('il-likk').[7] The Maltese version is charged with a very specific cultural allusion that is lost in the English translation. The 'strangeness of the text' (Gentzler in Bassnett-McGuire and Lefevere, xviii) is stripped in a bid to remain faithful to the target language and audience, thereby the text is somewhat domesticated.

There are moments of interbreeding between languages in Sant's work that occur mostly at the morphological level. For example, he describes a

---

[7] *Il-likk* is also known as *jack* (English), *pallino* or *boccino* (Italian).

member of the audience as 'it-Torta' (332). Translated literally to English, *it-Torta* could be either a pie or a tart. The Italian *torta* also means cake. In the Maltese version, Sant does not add an adjective but his solution in English is jam tart. Compared to a cake, a jam tart is flatter. Read in the context of a social satire, *torta* here acts as a pejorative term – what Pérez Firmat (2005, 92) calls an 'ill-tempered, nasty' interlingual pun – to poke fun at this member of the audience. Rather than favouring a translation based on corresponding meaning here, Sant focuses on translating the comic register instead, in a way that recalls Bakhtin's discussion of Latin parody. According to Bakhtin (1981, 75), although only Latin is visible on the page, 'this language is structured and perceived in the light of another language, and in some instances not only the accents but also the syntactical forms of the vulgar language are clearly sensed in the Latin parody'. Parody, of course, evokes the comic and the farcical, sometimes even ridicule. It uncovers the nature of the glottopolitics between the 'dominant' Latin (in our case, Latin and English) and the 'vulgar' (Maltese) conversational language. The multilingual resonance of the text and the parody thus lie in the allegorical use of the TV show's name: *Kwis Kwam/Quis Quam*. Because if an analysis of the text points towards a preference for domesticating cultural references, then that singular multilingual act becomes charged with significance.

Conclusion: Towards a Multilingual Poetics

There is a positive consequence of reading heterolingual text as a by-product of a lived multilingual reality that speaks to a multilingual audience. Awareness of a text's multilingual poetics can lead to the improved extraction and understanding of transcultural meaning, which any reader, but especially the monolingual reader, should not forget. To be attuned to the text's multilingual poetics is to let the text breathe and speak to us about a local reality with which the reader may not be familiar. This point applies even more so to a text that speaks of a lesser known culture, language and reality, because we cannot evaluate a text's aesthetics (and cultural value) and how it fits within a wider literary network if we are unfamiliar with the context in which it was produced and what it is speaking of/to. A text might have a life of its own in a reader's hands (be it a general reader, literary scholar or translator), but culturally attuned research makes for a more sensitive reading of culture-bound narratives. This becomes more complex for the heterolingual text

Josianne Mamo

as the cultures to which it is 'bound' (or connected to) are multiple and overlapping, like a Venn diagram, so a reader may need knowledge of all the textual and conceptual grids of these languages, unless the desired effect is to exclude the reader.

Further research in reading and writing multilingually will not only have an impact on Translation Studies by broadening its theoretical frameworks and vocabulary. It is also instructive for the practising translator who will be better equipped to translate the heterolingual text. But most of all, it can lead to a cultural transformation in how we read and talk about lesser known literatures. The Maltese examples discussed here expose not only the hybrid experience of millions in Europe, but also the ways we currently study literature produced in Europe. Moving towards research that is sensitive to specificity will in turn help us fill the gaps in the collective European narrative.

Bibliography

Aboulela, Leila. 1999. *The Translator* (Edinburgh: Polygon).

Adichie, Chimamanda. 2009. The Danger of a Single Story. TED Talks, October 2009. Available from: https://www.ted.com/talks/chimamanda_adichie_the_danger_of_a_single_story [accessed 28 April 2016].

Anon. 2005. Xarabank on Alfred Sant without Alfred Sant. *Malta Independent*, 11 May. Available from: www.independent.com.mt/articles/2005-05-11/news/xarabank-on-alfred-sant-without-alfred-sant-75269/ [accessed 18 January 2016].

Azzopardi, Peppi. 2002. Sant and Springer. *Times of Malta*, 17 November. Available from: https://www.timesofmalta.com/articles/view/20021117/opinion/sant-and-springer.162583 [accessed 18 January 2016].

Baker, Mona. 2014. *The Changing Landscape of Translation Studies* (Oxford: Wiley).

Bakhtin, Mikhail M. 1981. *The Dialogic Imagination*. Trans. Michael Holquist (Austin, TX: University of Texas Press).

Bandia, Paul F. 2014. Translocation: Translation, Migration, and the Relocation of Cultures. In Bermann, Sandra and Catherine Porter (eds). *A Companion to Translation Studies* (Hoboken, NJ: Wiley-Blackwell), 271–84.

Barthes, Roland, and Stephen Heath. 1977. *Image Music Text* (London: Fontana).

Bassnett-McGuire, Susan. 2002. *Translation Studies* (London and New York: Routledge).

Bassnett-McGuire, Susan, and Peter R. Bush (eds). 2006. *The Translator as Writer* (London: Continuum).

Bassnett-McGuire, Susan, and André Lefevere. 1998. *Constructing Cultures: Essays on Literary Translation* (Clevedon: Multilingual Matters).
Bassnett-McGuire, Susan, and Harish Trivedi. 1999. *Post-colonial Translation: Theory and Practice* (London: Routledge).
Bell, Henry, Irving, Sarah and Liz Lochhead (eds). 2014. *A Bird is not a Stone: An Anthology of Contemporary Palestinian Poetry* (Glasgow: Freight Books).
Bhabha, Homi K. 1994. *The Location of Culture* (London and New York: Routledge).
Brincat, Joseph M. 2011. *Maltese and Other Languages: A Linguistic History of Malta* (Sta Venera: Midsea Books).
Callus, Ivan. n.d. Incongruity and Scale: The Challenge of Discernment in Maltese Literature. In *Transcript 38: Malta*. Literature across Frontiers Publication. Available from: www.lit-across-frontiers.org/transcript/incongruity-and-scale-the-challenge-of-discernment-in-maltese-literature-by-ivan-callus/ [accessed 28 August 2016].
Cassar, Anton. 2008. C'est La Vie. Available from: https://antoinecassar.wordpress.com/muzajk/cest-la-vie/ [accessed 29 August 2016].
Chesterman, Andrew. 2005. Interpreting the Meaning of Translation. In Aejmelaeus, Anneli and Päivi Pahta (eds). *Translation – Interpretation – Meaning*. Studies across Disciplines in the Humanities and Social Sciences, 7. Helsinki Collegium for Advanced Studies. Available from www.helsinki.fi/collegium/journal/volumes/volume_7/index.htm [accessed 29 August 2016].
Cronin, Michael. 2003. *Translation and Globalization* (London: Routledge).
Ferré, Rosario. 2002. *Duelo de Lenguaje/Language Duel* (New York: Vintage).
Grosjean, François. 1989. Neurolinguists, Beware! The Bilingual is not Two Monolinguals in One Person. *Brain and Language*, 36, 3–15.
Grutman, Rainier. 2009. Self-Translation. In Baker, Mona and Gabriela Saldanha (eds). *Routledge Encyclopedia of Translation Studies* (London: Routledge), 257–60.
Grutman, Rainer, and Trish Van Bolderen. 2014. Self-Translation. In Bermann, Sandra and Catherine Porter (eds). *A Companion to Translation Studies* (Hoboken, NJ: Wiley-Blackwell), 323–32.
Kager, Maria. 2015. Comment Dire: A Neurolinguistic Approach to Beckett's Bilingual Writings. *L2 Journal*, 7.
Kennedy, William J. 2011. European Beginnings and Transmissions: Dante, Petrarch and the Sonnet Sequence. In Cousins, A.D. and Peter Howarth (eds). *The Cambridge Companion to the Sonnet* (Cambridge: Cambridge University Press).
Klimkiewicz, Aurelia. 2013. Towards an Understanding of the Self's Multilingual Dialogue. In Cordingley, Anthony (ed.). *Self-Translation: Brokering Originality in Hybrid Culture* (London and New York: Bloomsbury Academic).
Knowlson, James. 1996. *Damned to Fame: The Life of Samuel Beckett* (London: Bloomsbury).

Lahiri, Jhumpa. 2015. *In Altre Parole* (Milan: Ugo Guanda Editore).
Lauret, Maria. 2014. *Wanderwords: Language Migration in American Literature* (London and New York: Bloomsbury Academic).
Maloney, E J. 2005. Footnotes in Fiction: A Rhetorical Approach. PhD, Ohio State University. Available from: https://etd.ohiolink.edu/!etd.send_file?accession=osu1125378621 [accessed 29 August 2016].
Mamo, Josianne. 2014. Shifting Centres: Crafting a World through Language in Translingual Writing. *Oxford Research in English*, 1, 25–35. Available from: https://oxfordresearchenglish.files.wordpress.com/2016/12/orewin14marginsfull.pdf [accessed 29 August 2016].
Orwell, George. 2010. *Animal Farm: A Fairy Story* (London: Harvill Secker).
Pérez Firmat, Gustavo. 1995. *Bilingual Blues: Poems, 1981–1994* (Tempe, AZ: Bilingual Press/Editorial Bilingüe).
Pérez Firmat, Gustavo. 2005. 'On Bilingualism and its Discontents', *Daedalus*, 134, 89–92.
Pratt, Mary Louise. 1991. Arts of the Contact Zone. *Profession*, 33–40. Available from: https://serendip.brynmawr.edu/oneworld/system/files/PrattContactZone.pdf [accessed 29 August 2016].
Prose, Francine. 2006. *Reading like a Writer: A Guide for People Who Love Books and for Those Who Want to Write them* (New York: HarperCollins).
Rushdie, Salman. 1992. *Imaginary Homelands: Essays and Criticism, 1981–1991* (London: Granta).
Sant, Alfred. 2002. Partnership: Can, Should, Will Be. *Times of Malta*, 10 November. Available from: https://www.timesofmalta.com/articles/view/20021110/opinion/partnership-can-should-will-be.163073 [accessed 7 January 2016].
Sant, Alfred. 2009. *L-Għalqa tal-Iskarjota* (San Ġwann: Publishers Enterprises Group).
Sant, Alfred. 2011. *The Iscariot Field* (San Ġwann: Publishers Enterprises Group).
Simon, Sherry. 1995. *Culture in Transit: Translating the Literature of Quebec* (Montreal: Véhicule Press).
Tanoukhi, Nirvana. 2013. The Movement of Specificity. *PMLA*, 128 (3), 668–74.
White, R.S. 2011. *Survival and Change: The Sonnets from Milton to the Romantics* (Cambridge: Cambridge University Press).
Zabus, Chantal. 1991. *The African Palimpsest: Indigenization of Language in the West African Europhone Novel* (Amsterdam: Rodopi).

CHAPTER THIRTEEN

Does Size Matter? Questioning Methods for the Study of 'Small'

Rhian Atkin (CLEPUL, University of Lisbon)

> My sisters: But what can literature do?
> Or rather: what can words do?
> (*New Portuguese Letters*)
>
> Ok, one last time. These are small, but the ones out there are far away. Small... far away.
> (*Father Ted*)

Discourses that construct the world into binary opposites of centre and periphery, small and large, are so prevalent that, as Venuti (1998, 67–68) observes, they must be a major contributing factor to the fixation and reproduction of stereotypes about cultures, at least in the anglosphere. With their focus on 'size', theoretical discussions of the translation of the literatures of European nations deemed 'small' risk reproducing and reinforcing the very hegemonic systems that they seek to counter. There remains significant work to be done to examine thoroughly the decision-making patterns that lead to the promotion and perpetuation of certain views about given countries, and the exclusion of other voices that do not support those views. This chapter contributes to the detailed exploration of what is translated, by whom and how, extending the disciplinary boundaries of the discussion about the circulation of literatures in translation to incorporate approaches from social and gender studies. In so doing, I propose a reinvigorated qualitative

My warmest thanks are due to David Frier, Rachel Haworth, Tilmann Altenberg, Céire Broderick and Carol O'Sullivan for their willingness to read, comment on and debate at length the ideas contained in this article.

approach that might be a means of not only identifying the imbalances of power between the literatures and cultures of nations perceived as 'small' or 'large', but also exploring where and how those imbalances come about and thus finding ways to illuminate and even alter the hegemonic culture of the centre (Venuti, 1998, 4).

Any discussion of the processes, pathways and networks through which the literatures of 'small' European nations come to be translated is a discussion about power. The project from which this book arises tacitly acknowledges the cultural hegemony of certain countries or languages, and opens a dialogue with the fields of world literature (a field that is dominated by perspectives from Anglo-American and French academia) and book history, as well as translation studies. By viewing translation from the perspectives of 'small' European nations, this project counters and challenges some of the assumptions that are made about the literary marketplace, and even the links that are assumed to exist between language and nation state (Casanova, 2004, 17–18). Ideas about a country's 'literary capital' (Casanova, 2004, 21), and the theorizing and modelling of the ways in which books, literatures and cultures travel, tend, on the one hand, to treat literature as an object for capital exchange rather than as an epistemic object, and on the other, to accept (even where this acceptance involves challenging the grounds for defining specific regions as such) an established order in which some cultures and countries are perceived to be 'central', and others 'peripheral', or, in the terminology of this project, 'small'.

Reading Between the Lines: Approaches to Studying Networks

Feminist and postcolonial theoretical traditions urge caution about the claims to cultural or epistemic authority inherent in notions of centre/periphery, and about how generalizing theoretical models can easily become a means of homogenizing what is diverse and neglecting or making invisible the real stories and experiences of the people involved (see Scott, 1991, 775–76; Harding, 2002, 92–93). The focus on sales figures as a primary indicator of a book's success, and on the circulation of books purely as commodities excludes the multifarious, complex and often extraordinarily revealing stories of epistemic, intellectual and affective exchange across and within cultures that a close, qualitative engagement with the same topic might reveal. Furthermore, one of the end results of a focus on the book as commodity is to obscure the ways and means by which existing inequalities are perpetually reproduced, both within criticism and within what is translated and sold. Countries are made up of people, and literatures are produced and read by people and for people. The qualitative relationship between readers and texts is the reason why, for me, the epistemic rather than the capital function of a text is the primary concern.

My case studies, drawn from the literature of Portugal, challenge assumptions and contest the paradigmatic, generalizing and homogenizing models that are used to discuss how literatures in translation circulate. Such models not only fail to represent reality as it really is; they also serve to construct and maintain a patriarchal, capitalist and imperialist order. I propose as an alternative a renewed focus on the qualitative and a painstaking investigation of the ways in which texts and their readers interact, and the effects of such interactions on the ways in which literary works are selected, talked about and circulated in translation. In this approach, I emphasize the importance of that which is not empirically verifiable and I valorize anecdotal and experiential knowledge as a complement to conventional scholarly forms of evidence (see also Paulina Drewniak's valorization of fan translations in Chapter Eleven), because I believe that this approach is necessary to question the ways in which 'knowledge' is constructed and in order to acknowledge that, at times, we simply cannot indisputably 'know' everything.

While English uses the separate terms 'net' for a material object and 'network' for a less tangible set of connections, the Portuguese 'rede' means both network and net (such as a fishing net). In fishing, the holes of a net are designed to trap what is larger and will therefore be most financially productive, allowing in the process the small, undesirable and insignificant to slip through the gaps. The metaphor is useful for the study of the circulation of literature in translation. At our project conference, Stephen Watts asked: how do we account for and measure the circulation of books from lending libraries, for example? The ways in which we gather information about networks, and the networks themselves that we seek to map, have much in common with the fishing net, because they allow vast amounts of information to slip through the gaps as we focus primarily on what has the highest value and most obvious function as commodity in a system of capital exchange. From my personal, critical and political position, the apparent 'commodity turn' in the arts and humanities generally is worrying because it moves our understanding of literary value and success away from the unmeasurable epistemic and towards the privileging of more easily quantifiable data.

Rhian Atkin

Many of the efforts to map and model the pathways by which literary works come to exist in translation construct networks in which neat, straight lines of communication connect the human actors, such as literary agent, publisher and cultural promotion agency. In the theorization of 'world literature' and literary 'polysystems', intangible ideas and innovations are taken to be tangible objects of exchange, valorized as capital (Damrosch, 2004, 4; Even-Zohar, 1990, 47). In Robert Darnton's (1982) influential 'communication circuit', the reader is posited as the start and end point of what becomes a continual loop of reproduction, although Darnton does not expand in his article on the necessity of readership to the circulation of the book as a commodity. While Darnton (1982, 79) himself admits that reality may not correspond to his diagrammatic representation of how books circulate, and while he accepts that this type of model has clear limitations, he nevertheless proposes that this neat, orderly model be used to represent a much more complex reality. In other words, he suggests that we merely tweak the model to make it fit our case studies. But what would happen if we chose not to put the theoretical cart before the real horse? What is the picture if we commence from the case study, and not from the model?

Bruno Latour (2005, 21–25) observes how the sociological penchant for fixing connections in fact obscures them in many cases, and he questions why we, as academics, prioritize order to construct a narrative, rather than telling and engaging with the world as it is. As an alternative in which we might have more epistemic confidence, Latour proposes that we embrace the uncertainty that exists, that we tell what we can, and that we acknowledge that no story is ever the full story. This position is echoed by scholars such as Sandra Harding and Boaventura de Sousa Santos, who define what enters scientific 'knowledge' as part of the hegemonic order, and what is left out as corresponding to the marginalized (Harding, 2002, 96–97; Santos 2014a, 21; Said, 2003, 7). The story of how the novella *O Físico Prodigioso* (1966) by Jorge de Sena (1919–78) came to be published in a new translation is a useful illustration of how the widely used models of theorizing the circulation of literatures fail to account for the interactions that take place between academic scholars and various agents in the translation industry, even while they attempt to highlight the relevance of the humanities in a world that is focused on the circulation of commodities and money.

Does Size Matter? Questioning Methods for the Study of 'Small'

O Físico Prodigioso: A Case Study in Communication Reality

The first translation of Sena's novella into English, by Mary Fitton, was published by Dent in 1986. The edition contains no introduction and seems to have received little attention, critical or otherwise. Indeed, the information available within the book is so scarce that it would be impossible to apply any models such as the communication circuit to understanding how this translation came about, or how the book was circulated once it was available in English. The 2016 translation, by Margaret Jull Costa, does tell a story, however. First, the reverse side of the title page acknowledges the support of two cultural agencies in the production of the book, and so the intervention and interaction of external agents with the publisher in the production of the text in English is evident. Such interventions are precisely the types of processes that our project and its report have sought to map. It starts to become possible, from an initial reading of the book's paratexts, to identify a number of actors or agents in the publication of this text: the publisher is Dedalus Books; the cover design was produced by Marie Lane and the editor is her son, Timothy Lane. The book was funded, at least in part, by the Portuguese *Direcção-Geral do Livro e das Bibliotecas* and the Arts Council England. The translator was Margaret Jull Costa and I wrote the introduction.

The interventions of funding bodies might encourage us to speculate on whether the author was considered by the source and/or host culture as particularly worthy or important for translation, despite potentially low sales figures. Equally, the introduction by an academic might suggest that the publisher is seeking to add contextual support to this publication of a book by a writer whose name is barely known in the anglosphere. As the scholar who wrote that introduction, I am in the privileged position of knowing some of the combination of factors that led to the book being retranslated. It is necessary to stress that the content of the book and not the prestige of the author, the intervention of any cultural agency, or anticipated sales figures, was the principal impetus for this second translation. I had been working on the novella in Portuguese and felt unable to recommend the existing translation to non-lusophone colleagues and friends, for as Mike Harland (2006) observes, Sena's 'rich classical style, recreating both the prose and poetry of another age, is unfortunately lost in Fitton's translation, which ends up more as a paraphrase, in the style of a jolly and fanciful tale by T.H. White [1906–64]'. The novella is linguistically complex, mixing discourses and registers, poetry and prose, and deliberately creating ambiguity through language use. While such experimentation is one of the Portuguese text's

251

most compelling qualities, it requires great creativity and sensitivity to produce a translation that would successfully convey its playfulness and literary innovation. Based on my knowledge of her translations of the work of José Saramago (1922–2010), and in particular *Levantado do Chão* (1980, English 2012), I was sure that Jull Costa had the lyrical capacity to produce such a translation, and begged her to read the novella. I was delighted when she called me to declare her enthusiasm for the translation project.

As an academic, I had repeatedly tried to interest publishers in *O Físico Prodigioso*, but had no success because of some of the preconceptions about literature from Portugal: anecdotally, I heard that the author (a huge name in Portuguese letters but barely recognized in English) was not considered important enough to translate; nobody wanted to read literature from Portugal because they knew little about it already; publishers were unable to make their own qualitative judgement on the text because they did not have the linguistic capacity; and – importantly – prospective publishers did not think it would sell. As a prize-winning translator with an international reputation, Jull Costa was able to use her professional contacts to propose and secure publication with Dedalus Books and the publishers went on to seek support from the Arts Council and the Portuguese Ministry of Culture, while I wrote an introduction to accompany the translation. This story reveals that the impetus for translations and for the circuits of communication that are established around texts are much more complex and difficult to trace in many cases than the neat models suggest. Even this story does not immediately reveal that I know Jull Costa because – in the relatively small world of Portuguese literature in the UK – I had used her translations to support my own academic publications on Saramago. The chain of decision-making that led me to encounter this text by Sena can be traced back at least four steps further, through university courses and lecturer–student and author–lecturer relationships that eventually, over a period of decades, brought this book into my hands – and then Margaret's. Rather than the apparent simplicity of a Darntonesque communication circuit, the reality of the communication pathways along which this particular text travelled is revealed to be complex, messy, lengthy and rather serendipitous.

The 'circuit of communication', if such can be established at all, relies on the text not as a neutral object passed from one person to another in the production process, but as a 'mediating object'. In this view, the text's specificity must be accounted for, because although it looks like a simple object, its contents and the relationship that comes to exist between individuals who encounter that text, and one another, will lead in multiple directions, variously transforming and modifying the meaning that they are supposed to carry (Latour, 2005, 39). The mediating potential and function of the text is important because it implies agency. The 'actors' or nodes in a network like that explicated by Darnton may not be fully conscious of *why* they are acting in a particular way when the text is understood only as a commodity. Agency, by contrast, implies change, making a difference to something (and that difference may be positive or otherwise) (Latour, 2005, 52–53). By focusing on the text as mediating object, I am not refuting altogether the text's additional intermediary function as a commodity. However, by exploring the agency that emerges from the text as it circulates between readers, we might start to reveal and unpick the complex structures, discourses, processes and actions by means of which the notions of 'centre' and 'periphery' are constructed and maintained.

The attraction of a model like the communication circuit is that it constructs easy-to-account-for, straight lines between the nodes in the network. As Tim Ingold (2007, 167) has observed, such lines seem to offer reason and authority, yet that very reason has frequently and repeatedly been shown to be irrational and even to mask intolerance and oppression. Ingold's observations caution against the idea that it is possible conclusively to map networks. They underline the necessity that we be ready to hear the other stories and voices that may be masked by a neat, network model. Our project report cites the account of the publishing director at Penguin, Simon Winder, who explained how decisions to translate texts from Romanian were taken because a trusted office colleague, who is Romanian, recommended them (Chitnis et al., 2017). This example, and the story of the second translation into English of *O Físico Prodigioso*, both reveal that, despite the apparent orderliness of the publisher's choices when placed in a circuit-type model, the reality of how a given work comes to be published in translation is heavily reliant on the affective relationships between readers and the texts that circulate between them. The network model that sees the work of literature as only or principally an item of capital does not, and cannot, account for such chance decisions, encounters and conversations. Consequently, to describe the world as it really is, we must cast off ordering principles and neat structures and grapple with the uncertainties about the relationships between individual actors/people in a given chain or network, and the objects with which they interact (Latour, 2005, 22–25).

Describing reality as it is has particular importance for the literatures of nations perceived as small, because the superimposition of a neat, orderly model on what is in reality messy and disorderly has the effect of presenting narratives differently and reconstructing them in a way that favours the marginalization or peripheralization of certain literatures and the centralization and hegemony of others, leading to production figures about literatures in translation that inordinately privilege literature translated from French, German and Spanish, which accounts for more than 40 per cent of all literature published in translation in the UK (Donahaye, 2012). By ignoring the chance encounters, conversations and decisions – the human relationships – that lead to works being published in translation, it also makes invisible (and thus unproblematic) the way in which some writers, languages, nations and literatures may be favoured over others.

While connections and networks are obviously crucial to the decisions that are made about the translations of literatures, those of us working on the literatures of nations perceived as small may have some advantages in an alternative academic model that favours the slow unpicking of the connections between actors in a network: perhaps we have greater engagement with the various mechanisms, people and organizations who form part of the process by which literature comes to be produced in translation because it is often easier to access people in a relatively small field, and because we often desire to promote our language areas and their literatures. Scholars working in and on the literatures and cultures of nations perceived as small may rely more heavily on translations for our published work, as well as for promoting the cultures of the areas that we work on, because far fewer people read 'our' language. For example, if we take the statistics produced by Literature across Frontiers (Donahaye, 2012), around 2.2 per cent of all publications, and 4.4 per cent of literature published in the UK is translated from another language (an improvement on the 3 per cent so frequently cited). For languages perceived as small, such as Portuguese, the picture is far worse: around 0.01 per cent of all literature published in the UK, and around 2 per cent of all literature in translation that is published in the UK is a translation from Portuguese. Compared with literature translated from French, which accounts for around 20 per cent of all translated literature, and 0.9 per cent of all literature published in the UK, there is an obvious imbalance in linguistic and cultural power. The situation is still more concerning in terms of the representation of people who speak those languages: Portuguese is the sixth most widely spoken language in the world, three times more widely spoken as an L1 language than French, yet it is far less widely taught in the UK. This imbalance has an obvious detrimental impact on education and knowledge about the regions where those languages are spoken, especially in university courses on comparative and world literatures, where teaching

Does Size Matter? Questioning Methods for the Study of 'Small'

staff are reliant on what is available in translation. Studying the translations of literatures of nations perceived as small thus opens an opportunity for resisting the increasingly dominant academic models that reduce literature to a commodity within market capitalism and overlook or hide the outrageous imbalances in power between cultures and between people (Álvarez and Vidal, 1996, 4).

Reading Between the Lines: Telling Stories of Discrimination

Tejaswini Niranjana (1992, 172) proposes that reading and translating against the grain may provide an opportunity for acts of resistance against the hegemonic order, and the same can be said for the potential of our theoretical approach to the study of how translations come about. While Venuti (1998, 124) may well be broadly right to say that publishers' approaches to the translation and editing of foreign texts are largely commercial and imperialistic, it is the scholar's task to identify and analyse that relationship in specific cases and, as a result of that analysis, propose or suggest measures that may be taken to counter dominant imbalances with regard to what comes to be published in translation. We need, therefore, to develop methodologies that account for statistics as part of the story of how texts circulate, and that create the scope for a deep exploration of the mediating function of texts, and indeed social relationships, in terms of what comes to be translated and published.

Statistics provide crucial information about what comes to be available for sale in translation, and an analysis of statistics can provide leads to discovering how many people – and perhaps even who – may have read a given work. But we must be mindful that statistics and communication circuits are not the full story; they will never be able to account for gifts and recommendations, the circulation of texts borrowed from lending libraries, or translations produced purely for the love of the text and which never come to exist in a bound, formally published format. These much less quantifiable forms of translation may nonetheless provide significant textual pleasure, may contribute to deepening our understanding of the world, or may even lead to other, more formal translations being produced and entering new epistemic domains (perhaps even entering the 'centre' of anglo-francophone scholarship and thus becoming measurable as objects of knowledge). As well as travelling along a pathway that leads solely to publication, translation may be used to strengthen literary, academic and professional bonds between like-minded colleagues, such as Lesley Saunders' reading of her translations of poems by Portuguese women at the research colloquium (19 December 2015), which concluded the 'Contar um Conto/ Storytelling' research project led by Ana Raquel Fernandes and celebrated the long research and teaching career of the much-admired mentor of many scholars of Portuguese literature, Patricia Odber de Baubeta.

Translations of individual items of short fiction (rather than novels or single-author collections) are more likely to fall under the radar of the statistical search for texts in translation because the titles of the individual texts contained in an anthology are less visible in the quick search mechanisms that we use (see Baubeta, 2007, 27–32). Given that short fiction in Portuguese is genre-coded as feminine and favoured by female authors (Fernandes, 2013, 362–63), this lack of visibility in anthologies raises questions about the visibility of women in (translated) literature more generally, as I will discuss below. Additionally, there are translations that are produced but never come to see formal publication because of obstacles within the circuit of communication around that particular text. Such is the case of Nicholas G. Round's skilful English translation of *Felizmente Há Luar!* (1961) by Luís de Sttau Monteiro (1926–93), which exists in electronic format but cannot be published because of a lack of sufficient funding to cover the high cost of permissions. For every translation that comes to be published, several more may come to exist verbally or textually but never appear in paid-for print. The qualitative approach commenced here, therefore, highlights that we must take statistics about published translations with more than a pinch of salt; we must remind ourselves of the probability that there exist many more translations of which we may never become aware, published in anthologies and journals, perhaps, or circulated or performed among friends and colleagues, teachers and their students (see, for example, Fernandes, 2013, 367). Bearing this in mind, we may further begin to ask searching questions about how some choices seemingly come to be made repeatedly, with the effect that certain voices are promoted and privileged and others excluded and silenced.

Statistics-based, quantitative approaches can nevertheless be used to make visible and open to critique the reality of what comes to be available in paid-for print (and therefore available to a wider audience, thus complementing the personal relationships that drive the circulation of texts as epistemic items). Postcolonial, feminist and postmodern theory have all established the selectivity and imperialism of the grand narratives that we construct to describe the world, such as the privileging of Western forms of

Does Size Matter? Questioning Methods for the Study of 'Small'

science, knowledge and culture in global terms (e.g. Harding, 2002; Sousa Santos, 2014b, 227–29; Spivak, 1993, 66); the tendency to a form of periodization that excludes that which does not coincide with Western norms (e.g. Friedman, 2002; Apter, 2013, 58–69); the unequal importance given to men's roles in historical narratives resulting in a broad failure to recognize women's presence and participation in events and indeed, in literature (Beauvoir, 2010, 656–57; Spender, 1989, 31; Klobucka, 2008, 17); and the ignoring of colonized and oppressed peoples in Western narratives, along with other identity markers such as language, class and ethnicity (e.g. Said, 1994, 24; Matumona, 2011, 39; Marx and Engels, 2004, 30). But what has this to do with the translation of the literatures of 'small' European nations?

If we impose a neat, grand narrative of how literature circulates, then not only do we exclude the qualitative from the story, but in doing so we also fail to realize the potential that the discipline of translation studies holds to expose the pathways that create the movement of ideas and literary form (Simon, 1996, 136). Those grand narratives are easily and frequently extended to cover the content of literary texts, meaning that what are in fact (for example) male-gendered, colonial or imperial, hegemonic perspectives from the so-called centre come to be rebranded as broad 'universal' qualities, or values that must be reproduced by the literatures of the so-called peripheries if they are to be understood as 'relevant' and familiar enough to enter the centre, the site from which statistics are counted and the location from where their circulation at all becomes visible and accountable within the dominant critical framework (such as that of Damrosch, 2003, 135).

Other stories that may be told from the margins allow for a crystallization of the radical effects of notions of the universal and the reliance on statistics within literary studies. Using the sex of the author as an indicator, the statistics demonstrate not only how infrequently Portuguese literature is translated in many countries (even in countries where there is a high number of Portuguese migrants, like France, Germany, the USA or Luxembourg), but also, of those works that are translated, how few of them are by women. Table 3 summarizes detailed information taken from the Camões Institute website (the government agency responsible for the promotion of Portuguese language and culture overseas):[1]

---

[1] The countries selected for comparison show a range of 'large' and 'small' countries, some sharing the same language, and some having a large Portuguese immigrant population. The scope of this study does not allow for a fuller exploration of all the countries listed on the Camões website.

Rhian Atkin

Table 3 Literary works translated from Portuguese in selected countries

Country	Total no. of literary works translated from Portuguese	Total no. of literary works by women translated	Literary works by women as % of all literary works translated	Total number of different literary authors translated	Total number of female literary authors translated	Female authors as % of all different authors translated
Germany	257	32	12.5%	73	33	45.2%
Austria	11	0	0%	7	0	0%
Belgium	50	2	4%	21	2	9.5%
Croatia	43	5	11.6%	12	4	33.3%
Spain	666	25	3.8%	86	17	19.8%
UK	165	5	3%	24	2	8.3%
Czech Republic	54	6	11.1%	32	5	15.6%
Sweden	53	2	3.8%	20	2	10%
Norway	21	0	0%	8	0	0%
Luxembourg	2	0	0%	2	0	0%
France	530	26	4.9%	76	14	18.4%
USA	98	1	1%	25	1	4%

Even the briefest of observations notes that women are significantly less likely to be translated into another language, and that gender inequality remains firmly entrenched in the selection, production and publication of translations from Portuguese (as do other inequalities, if we consider the prevalence of specific authors within that group). This view is supported by data amassed in UNESCO's Index Translationum (online): in this database, which does not distinguish between the world variants of the Portuguese language of 424 works (both literary and non-literary) originally written in Portuguese and published in English translation in the UK since 1979, around 12.2 per cent are by women (of which one-quarter are by just two Brazilian authors, Clarice Lispector (1920–77) and Patrícia Melo (b.1962)).

Germany is by far the most gender-equal of the countries that I examined, at least in terms of the numbers of different authors translated, but significant inequality persists in the number of works translated. Again, Index Translationum data supports this finding: of 1,089 literary and non-literary works published in Germany since 1979, 18 per cent are by women (and of these works, 18 are by Lispector, and perhaps somewhat surprisingly, 12 are translations of the single epistolary work attributed to Mariana Alcoforado (1640–1723), a Portuguese nun). Yet while an analysis of the statistics clearly reveals that women are overwhelmingly less likely to enter the world of international letters by means of the publication of their work in paid-for translations, the statistics do not reveal at which stages of the process gender inequality needs to be checked in order to achieve greater numbers of translations of works by women. Furthermore, and although we might notice with surprise the apparent exacerbation of inequality in countries often noted for their equalities legislation and practice, only a very close, qualitative analysis of the whole process would begin to be able to reveal where and how this apparently anomalous inequality emerges in Scandinavian countries, for example. In other words, the statistics on their own reveal that we must continue to fight for greater equality in the representation of women as producers of literature in other countries, and in the way that we represent other cultures through translation. However, the statistics do not reveal where we may best focus our efforts to achieve lasting change.

We must not follow Damrosch (2003, 158) in simply asserting that 'some literary works [...] may be so closely dependent on detailed, culture-specific knowledge that they can only be meaningful to members of the originating culture', because to do so is to conflate the foreign with that which cannot be understood. Feminist scholars of language and translation have pointed out how the language that we use – including the language we use to talk about translation – is both gender-coded and draws on a vocabulary of sexism and colonial domination (Irigaray, 1994, 48; Simon, 1996, 1; Niranjana, 1992, 2); while Sousa Santos (among others) observes that our critical language maintains an intellectual colonialism (2014a, 33–34). Simon (1996, 18–19) has further illustrated that language and concepts, even in English, are marked by metaphorical gender distinctions that are an 'extension of the binary, oppositional structure that pervades all our thinking' in the West. As Luce Irigaray (2004, 8) has so forcefully argued, even when we talk about supposedly neutral or universal qualities, the implied subject of such discourses is conventionally male. Seen in this light, Damrosch's assumption that literature exists within some kind of neutral cultural meritocracy in which the best or most 'universally' accessible will somehow float to the surface is understood as rooted in his privileged position as an Anglo-American, white, male scholar at Harvard. To talk about the 'universal', in this context, is to ignore the myriad reasons why the literary works of particular countries, or indeed, particular people or groups of people, may not be selected for published translation at all (and the historico-political contexts in which that peripheralization has come about).

There are numerous problematic issues of adaptation to a dominant-culture audience, which may mean that the 'information load' of a text is perceived to be too high for it to be worthwhile producing and publishing a translation (Tymoczko, 1995, 12–13). The 'universalist' view implicitly rejects any responsibility on the part of the dominant culture to seek to understand the other, refusing in the process the pleasure that arises from learning about other worlds. Whether we are talking about a nation, a language, a sex or a social class (or one of many other things), if we believe in equality we must contest the idea that some works simply deserve to be translated more than others, or that some works have an inherent or essential quality that enables them to be read, while others do not. If we do take a universalist line, then we really must also acknowledge that in practice this will always mean a continuation of the privilege and cultural power that specific languages, cultures and social groups have enjoyed for centuries. In effect, the authority of what we call knowledge will continue to be codified, variously and in its totality, as white, anglo-franco, hetero-normative and male. That claim to authority will continue to permit or disallow the movement of knowledges, positions and perspectives across cultures, nations and languages. Alternatively, if we focus on readership – on the agency of readers and translators, of the relationship that arises between texts and their readers, between authors and translators and readers – then we are more able to understand the material and intellectual *effects* of texts, rather than simply the number of them that circulate; and in doing so, we will be able to hear more of the voices and perspectives of the other (whoever that other might be in a given context), and we will be able to challenge the exclusionary order of the production, promotion and scholarship of literature in translation.

The Agency of the Text: New Portuguese Letters

The case of the translation (or not) and reading (or not) of the seminal Portuguese feminist text *Novas Cartas Portuguesas* (1972) is significant in this discussion about textual agency because of the way in which feminists internationally rallied in support of its authors, Maria Isabel Barreno (1939–2016), Maria Teresa Horta (1937–) and Maria Velho da Costa (1938–), who were imprisoned after it was published because the deeply conservative dictatorship deemed the book an offence to public morality. As Ana Margarida Dias Martins (2012, 28–29) tells us, the authors sent a copy of the untranslated Portuguese text to the prominent French feminist, Christiane Rochefort. It was opened by her Peruvian neighbour, Carmen – a Spanish speaker able to read Portuguese – and the text (and knowledge of it and its authors' situation) was subsequently circulated through discussions, verbal translations and performance (see also Klobucka, 2015, 107–08). This meant that the text was read fragmentarily at best, if indeed it was read at all. In the first two years after the book's publication in Portugal, *Novas Cartas Portuguesas* achieved widespread international popularity due to the feminist solidarity movement that mobilized around it. Yet when it appeared in translation in France (1974), the UK and USA (1975), Germany (1976) and Italy (1977), its reception was lukewarm (Martins, 2012, 29; Klobucka, 2015, 110–12). By this time, the Portuguese Revolution of 25 April 1974 had brought an end to both the dictatorship and, not long thereafter, the Three Marias' imprisonment. So how might we measure the book's international success when, as Martins (2012, 25) notes, 'it failed to enter the feminist canon of theory texts in Europe and the US'? The book did not become a bestseller in translation, and indeed, even in Portugal, it remained out of print for much of the 1980s and 1990s, although new editions were published in 1998 and 2010 (Owen and Pazos Alonso, 2011, 22). Yet the success of this work is both widespread and persistent: the informal translation and circulation of the text and fragments of it served to bring together and inspire women across the world to fight collectively for justice for these authors, and for women's emancipation in general. Even if *Novas Cartas Portuguesas* was later to be overlooked as a theoretical text by some of the very women who fought for its authors' release from prison (Martins, 2012), the history of its circulation attests to its mediating function and the material agency emerging from the relationship between readers (or potential readers) and the text. This story illustrates that it would, of course, be near impossible to map neatly the precise ways in which a text circulates or is communicated.

Rhian Atkin

The structuring principles of order and of how we understand literary success are codified as white, male, capitalist and imperialist (Ingold, 2007, 152–53). If the way that we talk about the world not only reflects that world (Moi, 2002, 157), but also helps to structure and create it, then the phallogocentric principles contained within the notions of order and capital success are therefore bound to be reflected in the way that the chaotic array of data that are available to us is assessed. For this reason, a focus on the complexities of reality is necessary in order to degender academic discourse about networks, moving away from the dominance of masculine-coded notions of linearity to allow for the coexistence of multiple narratives, and to create a space of discourse where the rational ceases to be coded as masculine, rather than being removed altogether (Moi, 2002, 159).

The gendered order of scholarship is further reinforced in reality in terms of what is translated, and, as a result, who has access to which texts from what 'peripheries'. In Portugal, it continues to be the case that more men are published, and that men are more firmly inscribed in literary histories and canons, despite a significant rise in women writers publishing their literature since the 1974 Revolution (Owen and Pazos Alonso, 2011, 13). Proportionately, even more works by men are selected for translation (as shown by the data in Table 3), meaning that the image presented of the literatures of 'smaller' nations such as Portugal is even more male-coded than that of 'central' nations such as the UK. Added to this inequality, the privileging of the novel for translations elides the significant number of women authors writing and winning prizes in the short fiction and poetry genres (Fernandes, 2013, 366). While there are always anomalies, then (*Novas Cartas Portuguesas*, despite its lack of commercial success, has been translated into several other languages), it is generally clear that women are less likely to be translated, and their works are less likely than men's to be circulated widely (Fernandes, 2013, 368).

The privileging of male authors that is established in the publication of literature in translation is then amplified once more through the academic disciplines of world literature and transnational or comparative literary studies, where there is a heavy reliance on the translation of literatures perceived as small or minor, into languages perceived as major. If male authors are overwhelmingly more likely to be selected for publication in translation, then the case studies available within both translation studies and world literature studies are overwhelmingly dominated by men. Wittingly or unwittingly, we as scholars and teachers reproduce and perpetuate a structural system of inequality, against which feminist and postcolonial scholars have been fighting for several decades. Furthermore, if we take an intersectional approach to this type of exploration and include multiple factors such as race or skin colour, ethnicity and place, we see emerging within both the market for the production of translated literature, and the academic fields of translation studies and world literature studies, a geopolitics of knowledge that re-establishes and sustains a widely discriminatory epistemology. A case in point might be the literature of Mozambique, where white male writers are more likely to be translated into English than black women writers, despite the fact that there are far fewer white men than women of colour living in the country. The implications of identifying and describing the individual stories of the processes by which literatures of small nations come to be translated are positive, because the knowledge that comes from this type of approach provides the tools for us to contest and destabilize the phallogocentric order, and to improve the practice of selection and production of literatures in translation, and the scholarship of those literatures, which may both represent and in turn contribute to producing a more equal world.

Conclusion

This chapter in many ways raises more questions than it answers, because it highlights how much we do not know, and cannot know. The answers that I propose rely on a valorization of the qualitative along with the quantitative. By understanding more thoroughly the complex, affective relationship between readers and texts, we may be able to add more of the messy feminine to the orderly grand narrative of the economic model for understanding how texts come to be translated and published. Second, if we understand the emergence of the literature-as-commodity model as basically capitalist, phallogocentric and imperialist, we must recognize and critique the concomitant revelation of how far we have not come. There have been serious and important attempts by scholars like Simon, Tymoczko and Niranjana to contest patriarchal and imperialist approaches within translation studies, and I would add that we need also to contest the very foundations of the knowledge that we have, and that means going against the orderly grain of scholarship as such. Attempts to discuss and map what translations do and how they circulate do not reveal the whole story; they cannot reveal the imbalance of power in terms of who has access to the networks and epistemic traditions that maintain both the flow and the status quo of knowledge of the literatures of the 'other'. Even

Rhian Atkin

knowing how many texts come to be translated and how many of those are by women, black or brown or white people, from large or small nations, does not give us the tools to understand why and how those texts come to be selected. Whether we look at this problem in relation to nations, or in relation to the sex of the authors translated, to really understand the power structures at play (and to really reveal the overwhelming cultural dominance of what is coded as heterosexual, white, imperialist and masculine in the translation industry), we must accept and acknowledge that we can never know the whole story; and we must be conscious that as long as parts of the story are missing from our knowledge, then we need to make every effort to look at as much detail as possible. This is a mode of scholarship that is and needs to be slow, careful and nit-picking; that is less reliant on uncontested, neo-liberal notions of the book as commodity and that celebrates the material agency of literature and its potential to change, as well as represent, the way that we see and construct the world.

Bibliography

Online Data Sources
Instituto Camões Website: works translated from Portuguese: www.instituto-camoes.pt/obras-traduzidas/root/cultura-externa/edicao/obras-traduzidas [accessed 15 September 2016].
UNESCO Index Translationum – World Bibliography of Translation: www.unesco.org/xtrans/bsform.aspx [accessed 15 September 2016].

Works Cited
Álvarez, Román, and M. Cármen-África Vidal. 1996. Translating: A Political Act. In Álvarez, Román and M. Cármen-África Vidal (eds). *Translation, Power, Subversion* (Clevedon: Multilingual Matters), 1–9.
Apter, Emily. 2013. *Against World Literature: On the Politics of Untranslatability* (London: Verso).
Barreno, Maria Isabel, Maria Teresa, and Maria Velho da Costa. 1994. *New Portuguese Letters*. Trans. Helen R. Lane (London: Readers International).
Baubeta, Patricia Anne Odber de. 2007. *The Anthology in Portugal: A New Approach to the History of Portuguese Literature in the Twentieth Century* (Bern: Peter Lang).
Casanova, Pascale. 2004. *The World Republic of Letters*, trans. M.B. DeBevoise (Cambridge, MA: Harvard University Press).
Chitnis, Rajendra, Jakob Stougaard-Nielsen, Rhian Atkin and Zoran

Milutinović. 2017. Translating the Literatures of Smaller European Nations: A Picture from the UK, 2014–16. Available from: https://www.bristol.ac.uk/media-library/sites/arts/research/translating-lits-of-small-nations/Translating%20Smaller%20European%20Literatures%20Report(3).pdf [accessed 18 January 2018].

Damrosch, David. 2004. *What is World Literature?* (Princeton: Princeton University Press).

Darnton, Robert. 1982. What is the History of Books? *Daedalus*, 111 (3), 65–83.

De Beauvoir, Simone. 2010. *The Second Sex.* Trans. Constance Borde and Sheila Maloney-Chevalier (London: Vintage Books).

Donahaye, Jasmine. 2012. *Three Percent? Publishing Data and Statistics on Translated Literature in the United Kingdom and Ireland* (Making Literature Travel series, Literature across Frontiers). Available from: www.lit-across-frontiers.org/wp-content/uploads/2013/03/Publishing-Data-and-Statistics-on-Translated-Literature-in-the-United-Kingdom-and-Ireland-A-LAF-research-report-March-2013-final.pdf [accessed 11 August 2016].

Even-Zohar, Itamar. 1990. The Position of Translated Literature within the Literary Polysystem. *Poetics Today*, 11 (1), 45–51.

Fernandes, Ana Raquel. 2013. Women Authors in (Ex)Change: Short Fiction in Portugal and the United Kingdom (1980–2012). *Comparative Critical Studies*, 10 (3), 355–76.

Friedman, Susan Stanford. 2006. Periodizing Modernism: Postcolonial Modernities and the Space/Time Borders of Modernist Studies. *Modernism/Modernity*, 13 (3), 425–43.

Harding, Sandra. 2002. Must the Advance of Science Advance Global Inequality? *International Studies Review*, 4 (3), 87–105.

Harland, Mike. 2006. 'Modern Portuguese Literature'. In France, Peter (ed.). *The Oxford Guide to Literature in Translation* (Oxford: Oxford University Press). Available from: www.oxfordreference.com/view/10.1093/acref/9780198183594.001.0001/acref-9780198183594-e-107&gt [accessed 23 August 2016].

Ingold, Tim. 2007. *Lines: A Brief History* (Abingdon: Routledge).

Irigaray, Luce. 1994. *Thinking the Difference: For a Peaceful Revolution*, trans. Karin Montin (London: Athlone Press).

Irigaray, Luce. 2004. *An Ethics of Sexual Difference*, trans. Carolyn Burke and Gillian C. Gill (London: Continuum).

Klobucka, Anna. 2008. Sobre a hipótese de uma *herstory* da literatura portuguesa. *Veredas*, 10, 13–25.

Klobucka, Anna. 2015. New Portuguese Letters in the United States. In Amaral, Ana Luísa, Ana Paula Ferreira and Marinela Freitas (eds). *'New Portuguese Letters' to the World* (Oxford: Peter Lang), 97–119.

Latour, Bruno. 2005. *Reassembling the Social: An Introduction to Actor-Network Theory* (Oxford: Oxford University Press).
Martins, Ana Margarida Dias. 2012. *Novas Cartas Portuguesas*: The Making of a Reputation. *Journal of Feminist Scholarship*, 2, 24–39.
Marx, Karl and Friedrich Engels. 2004. *The Communist Manifesto*. Trans. Samuel Moore (London: Penguin).
Matumona, Muanamosi. 2011. *Filosofia Africana na Linha do Tempo: Implicações Epistemológicas, Pedagógicas e Ptráticas de uma Ciencia Moderna* (Lisbon: Esfera do Caos).
Moi, Toril. 2002. *Sexual/Textual Politics*, 2nd edn (London: Routledge).
Niranjana, Tejaswini. 1992. *Siting Translation: History, Post-Structuralism and the Colonial Context* (Berkeley, CA: University of California Press).
Owen, Hilary and Cláudia Pazos Alonso. 2011. *Antigone's Daughters? Gender, Genealogy and the politics of Authorship in 20th-Century Women's Writing* (Lewisburg, PA: Bucknell University Press).
Said, Edward W. 1994. *Culture and Imperialism* (London: Vintage).
Said, Edward W. 2003. *Orientalism* (London: Penguin).
Santos, Boaventura de Sousa. 2014a. *Epistemologies of the South: Justice against Epistemicide* (Boulder, CO: Paradigm).
Santos, Boaventura de Sousa. 2014b. 'From the Postmodern to the Postcolonial and Beyond'. In Rodriquez, Encarnación Gutiérrez et al. (eds). *Decolonizing European Sociology* (London: Ashgate), 225–42.
Scott, Joan W. 1991. The Evidence of Experience. *Critical Inquiry*, 17 (4), 773–97.
Sena, Jorge de. 1986. *The Wondrous Physician*. Trans. Mary Fitton (London: Dent).
Sena, Jorge de. 2016. *The Prodigious Physician*. Trans. Margaret Jull Costa (Sawtry: Dedalus).
Simon, Sherry. 1996. *Gender in Translation: Cultural Identity and the Politics of Transmission* (London: Routledge).
Spender, Dale. 1989. 'Women and Literary History'. In Belsey, Catherine and Jane Moore (eds). *The Feminist Reader: Essays in Gender and the Politics of Literary Criticism* (Basingstoke: Macmillan), 21–33.
Spivak, Gayatri. 1993. 'Can the Subaltern Speak?' In Williams, Patrick and Laura Chisman (eds). *Colonial Discourse and Postcolonial Theory: A Reader* (New York: Harvester Wheatsheaf), 66–111.
Tymoczko, Maria. 1995. The Metonymics of Translating Marginalized Texts. *Comparative Literature*, 47 (1), 11–24.
Venuti, Lawrence. 1998. *The Scandals of Translation: Towards an Ethics of Difference* (London: Routledge).

Coda:
When Small is Big and Big is Small

Svend Erik Larsen
(Aarhus University/Sichuan University)

Size matters, so the saying goes. And yet. I happen to be visiting professor in Chengdu for a three-year period, and it came as a shock for my students at Sichuan University when I told them that the number of my fellow Danes only amounts to one-third of the population of their home city, which holds around 16 million people. And for China as a whole – well, to compare the number of my compatriots with the entire population of China exceeds my mathematical skills. 'But Hans Christian Andersen, Isak Dinesen, crime fiction, some Danish movies and TV series have more readers and viewers in China than any Chinese writer has across the world!', they exclaim. Which is true, but this truth also disrupts our immediate and apparently self-evident understanding of what is small and what is not.

This should come as no surprise. Since the story of David and Goliath, it has been common knowledge that maybe small is small, but also that this platitude does not tell us anything about the importance, strength and resilience of the small guy compared to the big bloke. Small is big and big is small. The area of literature is no exception from this observation, for which this collection of articles offers amply evidence with examples from books, writers, films and TV series from less dominant European languages and from concerted efforts to successfully promote translations to reach an international audience.

This book is the outcome of an AHRC-funded research project called 'Translating Literatures of Smaller European Nations'. As all research worth its name, this project does more than proving the relevance of its subject and providing us with new knowledge. It also pushes us, readers and researchers alike, to ask basic questions anew in a more nuanced and maybe more profound way. Thus, having read the book one might ask: will the use of the term 'nations' in 'small *nations*' (euphemistically called 'smaller') serve as the best key term to bring our reflections further? Apparently not. Examples from Catalan, among other languages, and the ambiguous relationship between Serbian and Croatian suggest otherwise. Despite debates on possible independence, Catalonia is not, at time of writing, a nation state; before Serbia and Croatia seceded from Yugoslavia, each now with a national language, Serbo-Croatian was regarded as one language with internal differentiations. Gaelic, Manse, Inuit, Sami, Basque, Breton and other minority languages could have been added to show that quantitative criteria like 'small' or 'smaller' are not sufficient to capture the process of cultural self-assertion through translation independent of the size and of the national location.

Moreover, certain languages, like Estonian, Lithuanian, Latvian, Slovak or Slovenian, have been minority languages at one point, and national languages at another. Other languages again, like Faroese, were listed as dialects before being recognized as separate languages. To take a last example, within Europe, Portuguese is the official language of only one, relatively small, nation, but if we look at language usage worldwide, it cannot be considered a 'small' language, and with regard to literature and culture, arguably attracts more attention internationally through its use in Brazilian, African and other Lusophone contexts. So, to add nations to small is not necessarily helpful. If, at this point, you are not confused, the complexity of smallness has escaped you.

What about 'small *languages*' then? This term may offer better assistance to our deliberations than 'small nations', given the fact that language is the media of both literature and translation in a somewhat narrow definition of translation, though highly relevant in a literary context. Taking 'small languages' as our guiding term may lead to the following question concerning the shadow existence of literatures in certain languages: what to do about it? The answer is translation and cultural promotion, as demonstrated in the preceding pages. The same question would have been a trickier one under the headline of 'small nations'. Then, the question could either spur a belligerent attitude, as in the Middle East, or an inward-looking self-centredness: 'Denmark First' (you can change this nationality with other nations, some with insular proclivities). Neither of the two positions would work for literature whether written in small languages or not. It is in the DNA of languages and literatures that they travel, mix and mingle in an ongoing cross-cultural exchange of words, terms, themes, metaphors, myths, stories and meanings. In fact, the exclusive national containment of literature is only an ideological confinement in a particular historical European context.

Coda: When Small is Big and Big is Small

Languages, small and big, are by nature both receptive and expansive and translation is an integral part of this dynamics. So, if smallness is the issue, 'small languages' is a better catchphrase than 'small nations'.

Following the same line of thought, the International Comparative Literature Association has, over a period of more than fifty years, published and still publishes volumes in the series 'Comparative Histories of Literatures in European Languages'. This enterprise only takes into account where those languages have been and continue to be active across the world, including encounters with other languages, but does not pay much attention to which nations might be regarded as their true home turf. However, this series cannot avoid running into the problem of power relations. The dissemination of European languages goes hand in hand with colonization, and language policies in the postcolonial period still reflect this historical fact.

Power relations also affect the role of small European languages. The status of many linguistic and ethnic minorities inside European nations on today's map of nation states is the outcome of internal colonization within former empires and national configurations: Icelandic, Faroese and Inuit in the bygone Danish empire, to take but one example. Bilingual countries like Belgium and Finland reflect the problem of linguistic dominance in different ways. In Belgium two languages, French and Flemish, are of equal domestic importance, although apparently with an increasing dominance of Flemish. Yet seen from a European perspective, French is a big language, Flemish is not. The situation is different in Finland, but against a similar background of two main languages, Finnish and Swedish. Swedish is a minority language in Finland, while it is the dominant official language of neighbouring Sweden; both languages, however, belong to the smaller languages of Europe. When I see such power relations as the result of internal European colonization and de-colonization, it is because they follow the same pattern as European colonization did around the globe in the encounter with indigenous languages.

At times, terms like 'minor languages' and 'minority languages' have been used to catch this power-laden situation in political rather than cultural terms. However, 'minor' and 'minority' change their meaning if we expand them to also embrace literature. 'Minor literature' might indicate literature which then, if only indirectly, is regarded as being of lesser value rather than of lesser dissemination. If instead we take 'minor literature' as a term used to characterize writers like Kafka, who used a big language within the context of a small language, it becomes a very particular term within a certain literary theory. This is not what the articles in this book are interested in. 'Minority literature' is broader and more precise, but relates to specific non-national

Svend Erik Larsen

communities where recognition of their rights to use their languages as well as other legal rights as minorities are at stake. Precise or not, this term cannot capture the whole literary field of literature, translation and dissemination as this book tries to do under the heading of 'small'.

I would suggest another term that both reflects size and power and, at the same time, points to a dynamics resulting from human enterprise and a cultural vision. My experience in China is a case in point. My Chinese students and colleagues take Chinese literature to be neither small nor minor, and rightly so; they also do not find such labels helpful to characterize the status of Chinese language. The term I find most useful is 'underrepresented' languages and 'underrepresented' literatures, taking 'nations' out of the equation. Chinese literature is clearly underrepresented on the global scene on the background of its history, the amount of literary production and the status of China in world.

For the Chinese themselves, overcoming this situation is, to a large extent, a matter of global visibility alone, almost independent of content, as also seems to be the case in some of the examples in this book. For the rest of us, its increased representation would mean access to an improved cultural exchange with strong imaginative and aesthetic appeal beyond contemporary politics and economy. Clearly, some of the literatures discussed in this volume are overrepresented in relation to any quantitative measurement. Yet cultural appeal does not depend on size, but on the human effort to reach out, thus following the innate potential of any language and literature. The bottom line is that 'representation', whether over- or under-, is the result of human initiative and activity, size is not.

From this perspective, size of language or literature reveals a productive paradox, related to phenomena like indirect translation and also to a certain extent to self-translation, both of which are also commented upon in this volume. The first Danish translations of Chinese Nobel Prize winner Mo Yan (b.1955) were made from English; when his fame grew and more Danes graduated in Chinese, translations – and highly improved translations, one has to add – were published directly from Chinese, along with other writers. This situation is well known in the long literary history of European literature and written literatures from other continents.

What are the implications? At least one of them is that a global language like English is often used to make other literatures visible. Here, 'big' works to the benefit of the 'small', or, better, overrepresented languages may contribute to redress the imbalance of global representation of other literatures and cultures, a paradoxical fact that is hard to articulate through the isolated

Coda: When Small is Big and Big is Small

dichotomy of small and big. Under- and over-representation of literature is, as everything of value in cultural exchange, a matter of complex negotiations between languages independent of national location. With the growing group of bilingual or plurilingual writers emerging from migration, self-translation becomes more common than before and works in the same direction as indirect translation: breaking up bipolar oppositions between big and small.

Another important implication is the potential self-defeating effect of being a big language. In the first centuries CE, Latin branched out in 'small', 'minor' and maybe 'minority' languages, now the Romance languages, and turned Latin into a dead language. Likewise, English as a contemporary global language also escapes the control of its native speakers as it proliferates in various Englishes (just look at the spellcheck on any computer). Consequently, but to the dismay of many Brits, the Booker Prize now includes literatures in English from any part of the world. There is more than one native English standard across the world, there are pidgin languages that work like official languages, and there are professional broken Englishes used extensively across the globe, by myself to take one example near at hand.

This process involves power, but not institutionalized power as was the case in the former colonies. Chinua Achebe (1920–2013) (1965, 30) stated once that the English he would return to its native speakers after having used it to place African literature on the world map would not be the same he received from them. They may even not recognize it. We are dealing with cultural power embedded in cultural exchanges via languages, literatures and translations, a power that is constantly negotiated with regard to its ability to represent meanings and values beyond its primary linguistic and cultural boundaries. The book you have just read is a contribution to this negotiation.

Bibliography

Achebe, Chinua. 1965. English and the African Writer. *Transition*, 18, 27–30.

Index

Editors' Note: Because of the high number of literary texts mentioned in the chapters (often only once), their titles have not been included in this index, except where the author's name is not known. Please search for such texts through the author's name.

Aberdeen Press & Journal 80
Aboulela, L. 236, 244
Abrams, D.S. 131
Achibe, C. 234, 241, 271
Actes Sud (French publisher) 193
Adichie, C. 228, 244
Adler-Olsen, J. 188
Afghanistan 188
African literature 199, 229, 234, 271
Afzelius, N. 149, 161
agencies (for the promotion of literature) 59, 60, 64, 113–20, 250
agents, literary 49, 50, 52, 53, 58, 61, 80–82, 84, 131, 134, 190, 192 197–98, 250, 251
Agger, G. 198, 201
Akbatur, A. 60, 65
Albania 173
Alcoforado, M. 259
Alexandria 166, 171

Alghero 127
Ali, R. 30, 44
Allen & Unwin 74, 77, 84
Alma Books 135
Alonso, C. Pazos 261, 262, 266
Álvarez, R. 251, 264
Alvetegen, K. 191
ambassadors for national literatures 27, 28, 30, 42, 43, 88
American, United States of America 16, 17, 56, 63, 69, 119, 121, 126, 132, 145, 149, 151, 152, 154, 160, 173, 185, 188, 191, 199, 213, 214, 257, 258, 261
Amsterdam 95, 101
Anderson, B. 209, 224
Anderson, C. 138–41, 42
Andorra 127
Anglo-Catalan Society 131
Anvil Press 41
Apter, E. 257, 264
Arab 33, 63

273

Index

Arabic 228
Aragon 127
Arber, E. 99
Archilochus 173
Ardenne-Diephuis, E. Van 95, 96, 104, 108
Argentina 188
Arion, G. 184
Armenian 2
Arnautović, M. 30, 44
Arts Council England 251, 252
Aschehoug (Norwegian publisher) 194
Asian literature 199
Athens 166, 168, 170
Atterbom, P.D.A. 147, 149, 150, 161
Auden, W.H. 167, 169, 170, 173–74, 175, 177, 181
Auředníčková, A. 76, 89
Austen, J. 15, 146
Australia 173
Austria 110, 155, 258
Austrian (Austro-Hungarian) Empire 21, 37, 79, 80, 82, 85, 86, 114, 115, 154, 155
Aventinum (Czech publisher) 87
Azzopardi, P. 240, 244

Baggesen, J.I. 152
Baker, M. 27, 44, 110, 124, 227, 244
Bakhtin, M. 243, 244
Balduinus 99
Balearic Islands 127, 128
Balkans, The 5, 27–29, 30, 38, 119, 123
Balmer, J. 176, 181
Balzac, H. de 76
Balzamo, E. 54, 65
Banac, I. 33, 44
Bandia, P.F. 67, 234, 244
Barcelona 131

Bargallo, J. 129, 142
Barnouw, A. 99
Barnstone, A. 169, 170–71
Barnstone, W. 171
Barreno, M.I. 261, 264
Barthes, R. 240, 244
Bartol, V. 116
Basque 136, 206, 268
Bass, E. 78
Bassnett, S. 186, 201, 234, 244
Bassnett-McGuire, S. 231, 234, 236, 237, 241, 242, 244, 245
Baubeta, P.O. de 256, 264
Baumgartner, W. 49, 65
Beauvoir, S. de 257, 265
Beckett, S. 232–33
Beer, J. 103
Beets, N. 96
Beganović, D. 31, 45
Behrendt, S.C. 161
Belarusian 2
Belgium 55, 58, 103, 154, 258, 269
Belgrade 14, 19
Bell, H. et al. 230, 245
Bellman, C.M. 152
Beneš, E. 70, 75
Benson, A.B. 152
Berengarten, R. 179
Berg, R.G. 151, 161
Berglund, K. 190, 197, 198, 201
Bergman, K. 187, 188, 201
Berlin 69, 208
Berne Convention for the Protection of Literary and Artistic Works 139
Bernières, L. de 175–76, 182
Beskow, B. von 149
Besmusca, B. 105
Bessis, S. 208
Bethune, J.E.D. 149
Bhabha, H. 205, 224, 232, 234, 237, 245

Bibliotheca Flandrica (*Belgica*)
  94–95
Bibliotheca Neerlandica 59, 91, 92,
  94–106
Bibo, I. 207
Biedermeier 149
Bingley, C. 102, 107
Birch, A. 102–04
Birmingham 104
Bjork, R.E. 149, 161
Blackwood's Edinburgh Magazine
  149
Blair, T. 80
Blasim, H. 137
Blätter für literarische Unterhaltung
  151
Bleja, D. 221, 225
Boas, E. 153, 161
Bödeker, B. 151
Bodelson, A. 187
Bolderen, Trish van 230, 245
Bondy, F. 156
Bonnier (Swedish publisher) 194
Book Crossing 186
Booker Prize 135, 271
Borgström, E. 147, 161
Bosnia 12, 13, 16, 28, 29, 30, 31, 32,
  33–44
Bougarel, X. 31, 32, 41, 45
Bourdieu, P. 110, 124, 126, 140,
  142
Bouwman, A. 105
Branagh, K. 199
Branchadell, A. 207, 225
Brazil 259
Bredero, G.A. 106
Bremer, F. 152, 153
Brems, E. 93, 107
Breton 268
Březina, O. 83
Bridge Project, The 58, 62
Brincat, J. 228, 229, 245

Bristol 191
British, Britain 69, 72–75, 77, 78,
  82, 83, 84, 85, 88, 104, 121, 126,
  128, 132, 135, 136, 137, 138, 139,
  142, 148, 151, 152, 153, 154, 157,
  160, 168, 176, 189, 191, 199, 207,
  209, 217, 227, 232, 234, 235, 254,
  258, 261, 271
British Empire 150
Brockhaus, F.A. 149, 151, 153
Brockway, J. 100
Brod, M. 79, 89
Broomans, P. 146
Broomé, A. 198, 201
Brotherton, A. 100
Browning, R. 171
Brumble, D.H. III 105
Brun, F. 152
Bruns, A. 49, 65
Büchler, A. 2, 7, 126, 142
Buck, P. 77
Budapest 208
Bugge, P. 71, 89
Bulgaria 58
Bunin, I. 77
Burg, S.L. 41, 45
Bush, P.R. 132–34, 142, 234, 244
Butter, O. 85
Buturović, A. 39–40, 45

Callimachus 166, 171, 178
Callus, I. 228–29, 245
Cambridge 20, 99
Camilleri, A. 184
Camoes Institute 257
canon formation 6, 23, 24, 57, 95,
  96, 151, 159, 187
Čapek, J. 74, 78
Čapek, K. 71, 73, 74, 75–79, 82, 83,
  84, 85, 86, 88, 89, 90
Carmichael, C. 116, 124
Casablanca (film) 212

275

Index

Casanova, P. 1, 3, 4, 7, 10, 13–16, 17, 18, 23, 25, 92, 101, 107, 110, 123, 124, 140, 146, 160, 161, 185, 201, 248, 264
Cassar, A. 233, 234–39, 240, 245
Castilian Spanish 127
Catalan 5, 113, 126–44, 206, 268
Cavafy, C.P. 165–83
Cavafy, J. 168
Caxton, W. 99
CD Project RED 206, 218, 224
Celtic-language literature 6
censorship 56
Center za slovensko književnost 113, 115, 116–17, 124
Central Europe 63, 85, 118, 119, 123, 160, 205, 206, 208, 213, 214, 217, 219, 221
Central European Observer 76, 86
Cervantes, M. de 80
Chamberlain, N. 73, 89
Chambers Edinburgh Journal 152, 153
Chandler, R. 184
Chatto & Windus 97
Chengdu 267
Chesterman, A. 232, 245
Chesterton, G.K. 74
Child, L. 205
children's literature 105, 118, 130
China, Chinese 69, 185, 187, 267, 270
Chitnis, R. 2, 7, 53, 54, 55, 153, 253, 264
Chmielarz, A. 221
Christianity 34, 36
Christie, A. 184
Clark, N. 106
Clarke, M. 191

Clegg, N.
Coelho, P. 137
Coenen, F. 98, 106
Coëtlogon, L.-C.-E. 152
Coetzee, J.M. 104
Cold War 69, 88
Coleridge, S. Taylor 152
Colie, R. 98, 101, 107
Colledge, E. 99, 106
Collins 102
Collison, R. 150
Comics 213, 214
Comma Books 137
Committee for the Protection of Freedom of Thought and Literary Expression 115
Communist Party of Yugoslavia 14
Conolly, D. 165, 182
Conrad, J. 15
Coquille, F. 162
Cordon, W. 95
Cortest, Luis 173
Ćosić, Dobrica 41
cosmopolitanism 29, 31, 41, 42
Costa, M. Jull 251, 252
Costa, M.V. de 261
Cottin, S. 148
Couperus, L.M.-A. 98, 105, 106
Craig, C. 4–5, 7, 185, 201
Craighill, S. 199, 200, 201
Creative Europe 60, 65
creative writing 6, 234
crime fiction 141, 184–201
Crime Writers Association Daggers Awards 190–91, 201
Criterion, The 168
Croatian, Croatia 13, 16, 17, 19, 20, 28, 29, 32, 33, 35, 37, 38, 39, 258, 268
Cronin, M. 110, 111, 123, 124, 227, 245

Index

cultural agreements 55, 56
cultural diplomacy 6, 54–57, 63, 69–72, 76, 77, 82, 87, 88, 92, 93
Cussler, C. 205
Cyrillic alphabet 17
Czech 52, 53, 70–88, 153, 155, 156, 187, 207, 217, 258
Czechoslovakia, Czech Republic 54, 55, 56, 58, 70–88

D'Haen, T. 96, 107
Dahl, A. 188
Dalkey Archive 119, 120, 139, 143
Dalven, R. 167, 169, 170, 174
Damrosch, D. 4, 7, 10, 16, 18, 25, 250, 257, 259, 260, 265
Danish 2, 136, 149, 152, 154, 187, 188, 191, 195, 196
Dante 171
Darnton, R. 250, 252, 253, 265
Daskalopoulos, D. 178, 181, 182
Davis, J. 172
Dayton peace negotiations 13
De Spiegel der Letteren 96
Dedalus Books 251, 252
Dejmek, J. 73, 89
Deken, A. 96
Deleuze, G. 4
Delić, R. 33
Deming, H.C. 158, 159, 162
den Doolaard, A. 59
Denmark 58, 160, 187, 190, 194, 195, 196, 197, 198, 267, 268, 270
Dent, J.M. & Sons 251
Diaz, J. 239
Dickens, C. 76, 154, 155
Diederich Verlag 94
digital culture 205–06, 210–23
digital technologies 138, 210
Dimaras, C. 169

Direcção-Geral do Livro e das Bibliotecas 251
Dizdar, M. 29, 30, 39, 40, 41, 45
Döblin, A. 81
Dols Salas, N. 127, 143
Donahaye, J. 254, 265
Donfried, M. 69, 70, 71, 82, 88, 89
Doyle, A. Conan 184
Drewniak, P. 185, 217, 225, 249
Drieu La Rochelle, P. 87
Društvo slovenskih pisateljev 113, 114, 115, 118, 119, 120, 124
Duarte, J.F. 48, 65
Dukes, A. 77, 89
Dumas, A. 154, 155
Durrell, L. 174, 177, 182
Durych, J. 74, 79, 80–81, 86, 89
Dutch 2, 59, 60, 91–108, 136, 140, 155, 157, 214, 230
Dvořák, A. 85
Dyseegaard, C. 199–200
Džaja, S.M. 37, 45

Eagleton, T. 15, 25
Eaude, M. 134, 143
Eco, U. 212
Economist, The 134, 143
Economou, G. 172, 173
Edwards, R. 98, 100
Ehrenström, M. von 149, 162
Eisner, Paul 80–81
Ekdawi, S. 168, 169, 182
El Hachmi, N. 134
Eliot, G. 15, 146
Eliot, T.S. 168, 171
Elsschot, W. 94, 96, 98, 106
Elytis, O. 166, 167
Emants, M. 104
Emmerich, K. 172, 182
Engels, F. 257, 266

277

Index

English (language) 1, 15, 18, 20, 60, 62, 72, 97, 100, 119, 177–79, 180, 184, 186, 187, 190, 192, 194, 195, 205, 215, 219, 221, 222, 227, 231, 232, 235, 236, 237–38, 240, 241, 242, 243, 247, 248, 259, 270, 271
   translation into 2, 14, 16, 17, 34–40, 55, 74–75, 82, 91–92, 94–95, 99, 103, 105, 109–10, 111, 118, 119, 122, 123, 126, 129–34, 136, 137–38, 140, 142, 148, 154, 157, 158, 165, 166–73, 178–79, 180, 186, 188–92, 200, 205, 206, 207, 217, 218–19, 239–43, 258, 263
English, J.F. 190, 202
Enlightenment 21
Erben, K.J. 85–86
Essmann, H. 148, 162
Estonian 187, 268
ethics of translation 27, 42
ethnonationalism *see* nationalism
Euphrosyne *see* Nyberg, J.
Europe Centrale, L' 76
European Network for Literary Translation 62
European Union 60, 127, 206, 208
Even-Zohar, I. 2, 7, 250, 265
Evropský literární klub (ELK) (Czechoslovak publisher) 58
Eyre & Spottiswoode 97

Faber & Faber 74
fan fiction 154
fan translation 211, 213, 217, 218, 219–20, 223
fantasy 205, 206, 212, 215, 216, 220, 222, 223
Faroese 268, 269
Farrar, Straus & Giroux 199
feminism 248, 256, 259, 261–63

Fenoulhet, J. 93, 105, 106, 107
Fernandes, A.R. 256, 262, 265
Ferrante, E. 137, 140
Ferré, R. 227, 229, 230, 245
festivals, literary 118–20
Feylbrief, J. 98
Filandra, S. 33, 45
Filipović, M. 39, 45
film and television 3, 188, 199, 211, 214, 218
Fine, J. 38, 45
Finland, Finnish 58, 60, 148, 269
Finn, H. 63, 65
Firmat, G. Pérez 232, 233, 243, 246
First World War 54, 69, 77, 79
Fischer, O. 75
Fitton, M. 251
Flaubert, G. 15
Flemish 60, 95, 96, 269
Flines, G. de 101, 102, 103, 107
Flygare-Carlén, E. 50, 52, 53, 54, 145, 146, 148, 153, 154–60, 161
Foreign Review 149
Forshaw, B. 188, 191, 198, 202
Forster, E.M. 168, 182
France 55, 58, 63, 69, 88, 127, 128, 149, 191, 207, 210, 220, 227, 235, 257, 258, 261
France, P. 148, 162
Franco, F. 127
Frank, A.P. 148, 162
Frankfurt Book Fair 63
Franssen, T. 59, 64, 65, 130, 134, 140, 143
French 18, 20, 54, 87, 95, 102, 136, 152, 214, 217, 227, 230, 232, 235, 248, 254, 269
   translation into 2, 14, 53, 54, 60, 61, 62, 94, 154, 155, 158, 167, 169, 187, 193, 199, 258
French, D. 217, 218, 219
Friedman, S.S. 257, 265

278

Index

Fronius, H. 160, 162
Fulińska, A. 218

Gaelic 268
Galba, M.J. de 132
Galician 136
Gallenzi, A. 135
Galsworthy, J. 74, 77
Game of Thrones 205
Gant, R. 100
gatekeepers 6, 27, 28, 30, 40, 42, 43, 55, 77, 88, 132–34
Gedin, D. et al. 54, 65
Geherin, D. 188, 190, 202
Geijer, E.G. 149, 152
gender 6, 95, 145, 146, 147, 149, 151, 152, 153, 159, 247, 258, 259, 262
genre 6, 141, 145, 146, 186, 189, 198, 201, 205, 216, 222
Gentikow, B. 49, 65
Gentzler, E. 110
Geoffrey Bles 74, 85, 86
Georganta, K. 173, 182
Georgian 2
German (language) 2, 21, 49, 58, 62, 70, 71, 73, 75, 79, 81, 82, 99, 105, 135, 136, 148, 149, 151, 152, 153, 154, 155, 156, 159, 160, 196, 198, 199, 214, 233, 254
    translation into 53, 54, 63, 76, 80–81, 94, 109–10, 135, 136, 148–50, 151, 152, 154–55, 156, 187, 217
German Book Prize 135
Germany 56, 58, 63, 73, 77, 79, 83, 149, 150, 155, 257, 258, 259, 261
Gibbs, M. 220
Gienow-Hecht, J. 69, 70, 71, 82, 88, 89
Gies, A. 221, 225
Ginsburgh, V. et al. 130, 143
Glas, F. de 126, 143

Glassheim, E. 80, 89
globalization 2, 5, 11, 53, 62, 64, 106, 110, 111, 184, 185, 186, 188, 192–97, 212–13
Goebbels, J. 56
Goethe, J.W. von 1, 3, 15
Goldsmid, E. 99
Gollancz 217, 220
Google Books 149, 186
Gouanvic, J.-M. 205, 220, 225
Gow, J. 116, 124
Granta 228
Grasset, Editions 87
Graves, R. 177
Greek, Greece 165–80, 188
Greenblatt, S. 12–13, 23, 25
Grosjean, F. 237, 245
Grutman, R. 230, 245
Guardian, The 75, 134
Guatemala 188
Guattari, F. 4
Guenon, R. 33, 34
Guttfeld, D. 225
Gyldendal (Danish publisher) 194

HaCohen, R. 60, 65
Hadewijch of Brabant 95, 99
Haigh, A. 55, 65
Halbe, H.-G. et al. 148, 162
Hálek, V. 85
Hammersköld, L. 150
Hanč, J. 86
Hansen, C.J. 148, 162
Harding, S. 248, 250, 257, 265
Harland, M. 251, 265
Harper 158
Harrison, N. 133, 143
Harry Potter 212
Harsent, D. 180, 182
Hart-Davis 102
Harvard University Press 170
Hašek, J. 74, 79–80, 88

Index

Hass, R. 166, 183
Hathi Trust 149
Havel, V. 88
Haviaras, S. 170, 179
Hawkesworth, C. 162
Hayden, R.M. 41, 45
Haynes, K. 148, 162
Heaney, S. 170, 177, 182
Hebbe, G.C. 158, 159, 162
Hebrew 60, 187
hegemony, cultural 2, 3, 10, 247–48, 254, 257
Heilbron, J. 52, 59, 100, 107, 202, 206, 225
Heinemann 97, 100, 101, 102, 103, 104
Hellewell, O. 231
Hellstrom, B. 191
Helvig, A. von 148, 150, 162
Henriksson, K. 199
Herbst, P. 154
Herder, J.G. von 152, 210
Heritage Films 214
Hermans, T. 97
Hermans, W.F. 97
Hermansson, G. 53, 54, 79, 145
Hermes 151
Het Kouter 96
heterolingual text 229, 230, 234, 235, 236, 237–38, 239, 240, 243, 244
Hildebrand 96
Hill, A. 102, 107
Hirst, A. 170
historical novel 74, 80
Hitler, A. 73
Hjort, M. 3, 4, 7, 200, 202
Hodder & Stoughton 102
Høeg, P. 186, 188, 199, 200
Høier, A. 200, 202
Holmquist, I. 147, 162
Holt, A. 186

Homer 102, 171
Horta, M.T. 261
Howitt, M. 148, 150, 151, 162
Howitt, W. 148, 150, 151, 162
Hrabal, B. 88
Hudson, L.A. 81–82
Hulbert, D. 106, 107
Hungarian 70, 82, 209, 215
Hungary 56, 58, 155, 156, 207, 215
Hutcheon, L. 10–13, 16, 18, 19, 25
Hutchinson 81, 84, 97
Hyde, L. 84
Hyde, P. 119, 124

Ibsen, H. 49, 50
Icelandic, Iceland 58, 148, 149, 190, 269
Igbo 242
Independent Foreign Fiction Prize, The 135, 137
Independent, The 134
Index Translationum 56, 109, 110, 130, 131, 195, 258, 259, 264
IndexC19 149
Indonesia 93
Indriðason, A. 186, 190, 191
inequality 1, 2, 3, 4, 5, 18, 123, 247–48, 255, 258, 259, 262
Ingold, T. 253, 262, 265
Institució de les Lletres Catalanes 135
Institut Roman Llull 128, 129–31, 142, 143
institutions, cultural 6, 16, 52, 54, 57, 58, 61, 109, 110, 111, 113, 114, 116, 117, 118, 120, 121, 122, 123, 128, 129, 135, 217
Instituut voor Vertaalkunde 100
International Comparative Literature Association 269
Inuit 268, 269
Iran 33, 188

Index

Irigaray, L. 259, 265
Irish, Ireland 173, 209
Islamist 33
Israel, D. 199–200
Istria 111
Italian 2, 21, 61, 82, 102, 121, 136, 155, 157, 214, 235, 236
  translation into 95, 154, 158
Italy 56, 111, 128, 156, 188, 228, 235, 236, 261
Izetbegović, A. 29, 30, 31, 32, 33, 45

Jacquemond, R. 63, 66, 209, 225
Jahić, A. 32
James, H. 15
Janda, B. 58, 59
Janion, M. 207–08, 210, 215, 225
Jantar Publishing 86
Japanese, Japan 57, 93, 184, 187, 213
Javna agencija za knjigo 113, 114, 115, 117, 118, 119
Jeffreys, P. 168, 183
Jenkins, H. 210–11, 212, 225
Jensen, K. 6
Jensen, P. Majbritt 188, 202
Jewish 34, 79, 81, 83
Joensuu, M. 186
Johnson, S. 235
Jonasson, J. 137, 140
Jones, E. 176, 182
Jones, F.R. 27–30, 31, 34, 39–42, 44, 45, 46
Jornet, K. 134
Jović, D. 41, 46
Joy, T. 102, 107
Joyce, J. 171
Judah, T. 41, 46
Jungersen, C. 191
Jupan, D. 56
Jury 189
Jusdanis, G. 167, 183

Kaczar, K. 215, 225
Kafka, F. 4, 269
Kager, M. 232–33, 245
Kandel, M. 215, 219, 221, 225
Kapsalis, D. 178
Karásek, J. z Lvovic 80
Kärrholm, S. 191, 192, 202
Kasten, T. 80, 89
Katope, C.G. 174, 183
Keats, J. 152, 168
Keeley, E. 169, 183
Kellgren, J.H. 149, 152
Kennedy, W.J. 235, 245
Khartoum 236
Khomeini, Imam 31
King, F. 177
Kingdom of Serbs, Croats and Slovenes 111
Kings College London 82
Kirino, N. 184
Kiš, D. 13–14, 17–24
Klastrup, L. 211, 213, 225
Klauberová, O. 77, 89
Klíma, I. 88
Klimkiewicz, A. 231, 240, 245
Klobucka, A. 257, 261, 265
Knausgaard, K.O. 136, 137
Knight, S. 191
Knorring, S. von 153
Knowlson, J. 232, 245
Kondos, Y. 165
Konrád, E. 74
Konůpek, J. 86
Korean 187
Körkö, H.-N. 63, 66
Körner, C.T. 152
Kosmopoulos, D. 178
Kosovo 10
Kovač, M. 1, 7, 189, 193, 202
Kovtun, G. 74, 89
Kranj 111
Kras 111

281

Index

Krátká, P. 75, 90
Krause, A.L. 162
Krispyn, E. 104
Kristeva, J. 215
Kruczkowska, J. 175, 183
Kudělka, V. 76, 90
Kuipers, G. 64, 65, 130, 134, 140, 143
Kundera, M. 1, 7, 68

Läckberg, C. 188
Lagerlöf, S. 153
Lahiri, Jhumpa 236, 246
Lamartine, A. de 151
Lancelot und Sanderein 95
Lane, M. 251
Lane, T. 251
Larsen, S.E. 3
Larsson, A. 191
Larsson, S. 186, 188, 189, 191, 192, 193, 194, 197, 198
Latić, D. 29, 30, 31, 41
Latin 17, 171–72, 243, 271
Latin American literature 229
Latour, B. 253, 265
Latvian, Latvia 2, 113, 268
Laugesen, A. 63
Lauret, M. 233, 246
Lawler, S. 112, 124
Lazarus, N. 208, 225
League of Nations 55, 57, 70, 72
Leavis, F.R. 15, 26
Lefèbvre, E. 94
Lefevere, A. 51, 66, 121, 124, 234, 236, 237, 242, 245
Leffler, Y. 53, 54, 66, 79, 145, 155, 156, 162
Left Bank Pictures 199
legitimacy 9, 12, 15, 24, 92
Leiden 101
Leipzig 156, 160
Lenngren, A.M. 148, 151

Leonhardt and Høier (literary agency) 200
Leopard Vörlag 199
Leppihalme, R. 122, 123, 124
Lermavner, D. 114, 124
Levec, F. 114, 124
Library of Netherlandic Literature 104
Liddell, R. 169, 183
Lifschultz, L. 30, 44
Lindqvist, Y. 195, 196, 202
Linn, S. 63, 66
Lionnet, F. 4, 7
Literární noviny 76
literary history 10–12, 15, 19–20, 21, 22, 23
Literature Across Frontiers 2, 126, 136, 254
Lithuanian, Lithuania 2, 209, 217, 268
Little, A. 41, 46
Little Entente 56, 57, 72
Liverpool 168
Ljubljana 110, 114, 116, 117, 118, 120
Logenbach, J. 171–72, 183
Lokhorst, E. van 94
London 69, 74, 75, 79, 81, 82, 83, 85, 86, 97, 131, 132, 154, 155, 157, 168, 208
London House and Maxwell 101
London Magazine 104
'long tail' 138–42
Longfellow, H.W. 151, 152
López, I. Herrero et al. 156, 162
Lovrenović, D. 38, 46
Low Countries 5
Lowell, J.R. 152
Lower Carniola 111
Lower Styria 111
Lundqvist, A. 149, 162
Luxembourg 257, 258

Index

Maanen, W.G. van 97
Maatschappij der Nederlandsche Letterkunde te Leiden 96
Maatschappij der Nederlandse Letterkunde 91
Macedonian, Macedonia 2, 209
Machar, J.S. 74
MacInnes, M. 175, 182
Mackridge, P. 170
MacLehose, C. 200
Macmillan 74, 102
Madoc maecte, W. Die 99, 106
Mahmutćehajić, R. 29, 30, 33–39, 41, 46
Mahon, D. 175, 182
Maj, K. 211, 225
Majkowski, T. 216, 226
Majorca 124
Malanos, T. 168, 169, 178, 183
Malcolm, N. 41
Maloney, E.J. 239, 246
Maltese, Malta 5, 122, 227, 228, 234–44
Mamo, J. 122, 236, 246
Mankell, H. 186, 188, 189, 190, 192, 198–200
Manse 268
Mansell, R.M. 113, 127, 143
Mapelli, C. 158, 163
Margaris, I. 178
Mariken von Nieumeghen 95, 96, 99
marketing 135–38, 141
Marklund, L. 188, 190
Marten, M. 80
Martins, A.M. Dias 261, 266
Martinus Nijhoff Prize 100
Martorell, J. 132
Marx, K. 257, 266
Masaryk, J. 77, 83
Masaryk, T.G. 70, 71, 73, 75, 76, 77, 78, 80, 82, 84, 85
Massot, J. 137, 143

Matis, H. 63, 66
Matrix, The 211
Mattos, A. Teixeira de 98
Matumona, M. 257, 266
Mavrogordato, J. 169
Mazzini, M. 120–22, 231
McMartin, J. 60, 63, 66, 67
Mediterranean 4, 228
Meek, K. 191
Meijer, R. 96, 102, 105
Melantrich (Czech publisher) 81
Melo, P. 259
Mendelssohn, D. 169, 171, 172
Mendoza, E. 184
Merrill, J. 175, 177, 182
Messent, P. 202
Mexico 184
Meyer, D. 184
Meylaerts, R. 4, 6, 8
Michael Joseph 74
Mickiewicz, A. 219
Milan 158
Milton, J. (translation studies scholar) 63, 67
Milutinović, Z. 14, 26
Minderaa, P. 94, 95, 96, 104
Minsk 208
mobility studies 11
Mody, J. 106
Moe, M.Z. et al. 124
Mohnike, T. 149, 163
Moi, T. 262, 266
Moliner, E. 134
Mondadori (Italian publisher) 61
Monteiro, L. de Sttau 256
Montenegro 16
Monthly Religious Magazine, The 153
Monzó, Q. 134
Moore, D. Chioni 208
Moretti, F. 3, 7, 146, 157, 160, 163, 185, 202

Index

Mozambique 188, 263
Mozetič, B. 116, 117
Mulisch, H. 96, 97
Muller, J.W. 99
Multatuli 96, 97, 98, 102, 105, 106, 107
multiculturalism 29, 40, 42, 228
multilingualism 227, 229, 230, 241
Munch-Petersen, E. 154, 163
Munich 80, Munich Accord 73, 88
Muñoz, B. Gómez 143
Murphy, C. 7, 8
Muslim, Islam 12, 30, 31, 32, 33, 34, 35, 36
Musschoot, A.M. 94, 107

Nahuijs, A. 98
Národní listy 153
Nation and Athenaeum, The 168
National Fonds voor Letterkunde 94
national identity 6, 13, 110, 111, 112, 113, 116, 120, 122, 149, 206–10, 221–22
nationalism 16, 17, 29, 30, 31, 37, 39, 40, 41, 42, 70–71, 73, 75, 79, 80, 81, 85, 88, 112
Naughton, J.D. 73, 90
Nazareth, B. van 95
Nazism 56, 81, 207
Nederlands Genootschap van Vertalers 100
Nederlandsche Uitgeversband 91
Neff, V. 78
Nesbø, J. 136, 140, 186, 188, 191
Nesser, H. 191
Netflix 141
Netherlands, The 58, 59, 60, 91, 92, 93, 100, 104, 105, 148, 173
Neumann, S.K. 76, 79
Neupokoyeva, I. 3, 8
New Amsterdam Books 105
New Testament 111

New York 79, 81, 119, 131, 132, 154, 157, 158
New York Times, The 188, 200, 205, 223
New Zealand 173, 188
Nicander, K.A. 150
Nicolosi, R. 36, 46
Nielsen BookScan 126, 136, 137
Nikolaou, P. 178, 182, 183
Nilsson, L. et al. 186, 203
Niranjana, T. 227, 255, 259, 263, 266
Nobel Prize for Literature 77, 137, 166, 270
Noppen, L.C. van 106
Nordic Council Literature Prize 195
Nordic *see* Scandinavia
Norris, D. 4, 41
Norstedts (Swedish publisher) 193
Northern Ireland 175
Norway, Norwegian 2, 58, 60, 136, 149, 187, 188, 191, 196, 197, 258
Novák, A. 76, 79
Nyberg, J. 145, 146, 147–55, 159–60

O'Neill, E. 77
O'Shiel, E. 133
Obama, B. 205
Observer, The 74
Occitan 206
Oceanic languages 60
Ohnesorg, K. 156
Olbracht, I. 78
Òmnium 135
Orbis (Czechoslovak publisher) 84–85, 86
Order of the White Lion 77
Oriental languages 60
Orthodox Christianity 37
Orzoff, A. 70, 71, 87, 90
Oslo 58
Ossian 147, 149

Ottoman Empire 32, 37, 40
Oudshoorn, J. van 98, 106
Oversteegen, J.J. 97, 99, 100, 101, 104, 107
Owen, H. 261, 262, 266
Oxford University Press 74
Oxford World's Classics 170
Oziewicz, M. 226

Palavestra, P. 20, 26
Palmblad, V.F. 149, 151
Papoutsakis, G. 169
Pares, B. 86
Paris 69, 87, 139, 208
Parrott, C. 80
Parthenis, A. 178
Paterson, D. 177, 182
Pavić, M. 16–17
Peereboom, J. 97 108
Pekař, J. 80
PEN Club
   Netherlands 91
   Prague 74, 75, 82
   Slovenia 113, 115
Penguin Books 101, 102, 105, 137, 171, 253
Penninc 99
Pepper, A. 184, 203
Perce, E. 158, 163
Perica, V. 31, 32, 41, 46
Peridis, M. 183
peripheral literatures 2, 3, 4, 5, 10, 60, 61, 62, 140, 184, 185, 186, 192, 201, 206, 210, 247, 248, 253, 254, 257, 260
Person, L.S. 152, 163
Perucho, J. 132
Peter Davies 102
Petersens, H. 149, 163
Petrona Award 191
Petrović, S. 19, 22, 23, 24, 26
Phosphorists 147, 150, 151

Pinchin, J.L. 174, 183
Pine, R. 174, 183
Pinsky, R. 169
Pirandello, L. 77
Pittsburgh 85
Pla, J. 134
Plassman, J.O. 94–95
Plato 35
Playfair, N. 74
Plomer, W. 173, 177, 182
Poe, E.A. 151, 152, 163, 184, 187
poetry 30, 85, 145, 147–53, 159, 165–80, 230, 232, 233, 234–39, 256
Poland, Polish 5, 55, 58, 70, 136, 155, 156, 205–23
Polish Book Institute 217, 218, 219
Polygon 221
Popa, V. 30, 46
Popović, A. 230
Popović, P. 19, 20, 22, 24, 25, 26
popular culture 212, 222
Portuguese 2, 5, 136–37, 249, 251, 252, 254, 256, 257–58, 261, 268
post-colonial 11, 209, 227–28, 231, 234, 241, 248, 256, 263, 269
post-Soviet 208, 216
Pound, E. 171
Powage, W. 223, 224
Prague 58, 71, 73, 74, 77, 79, 80, 81, 82, 86, 87, 156, 208
Pratt, M.L. 232, 239, 246
Pregl, S. 118–20, 123
Premi Internacional Ramon Llull 135
Priestman, M. 191
Primo de Rivera, M. 127
Prix Formentor 126
prizes, literary 118, 135, 137, 187, 189–92, 262
propaganda 70, 73, 87
Prose, F. 230, 246

Index

Protestantism 80, 111, 116
publishing 1, 2, 44, 49–50, 51, 52, 58, 59, 61, 62, 64, 74, 76, 77, 78, 81, 84, 85, 86, 87, 97, 101, 102, 106, 115, 117, 120–21, 128, 129, 133, 135, 139, 141, 154, 156, 157, 160, 191, 192–97, 199, 217, 250, 255
Puerto Rico 227
Pym, A. 42, 43, 46
Pytlík, R. 79, 90

Quercus 193

Rabelais, F. 80
Radziwon, M. 207, 226
readers 53, 122, 133, 135, 141, 146, 153, 167, 168, 169, 170, 185, 187, 210, 211, 236, 237–38, 239, 249, 250, 255, 260, 261, 263
reception 49, 147, 150, 153, 159, 191
Reformation 21
Reid, C. 177, 182
Reinink, H.J. 91, 100
Renaissance 21
Research Assessment Exercise 133
Reve, G.K. van het 96, 97
Reynolds, S. 86
Ribnikar, V. 16, 26
Richard Bentley 155
Richard, L. 219, 226
Rieu, E.V. 102
Riga 208
Ritso, Y., 179, 182
Rochefort, C. 261
Rodereda, M. 132, 133, 134
Rohde-Gaur, S. 151
Roig Sanz, D. 4, 6, 8, 60, 67
Roman Catholic 37, 75, 80, 114, 208, 209

Romance languages 136, 154, 228
Romani, G. 163
Romania 56, 57, 58, 72, 155, 173, 184, 253
Romanticism 127, 145, 147, 149, 151, 215, 219
Rønning, H. 187, 194, 203
Rosenthal, D.H. 130, 131, 133
Roslund, A. 191
Round, D. 84
Round, N.G. 256
Round Table Talks (Poland) 216
Rowling, J.K. 214
Roxen, G. 223
Roy, O. 35, 46
Rühling, L. 150, 163
Rundle, C. 61, 67
Rupel, M. 125
Rushdie, S. 31, 231, 234, 246
Russian, Russia 2, 79, 136, 187, 208, 217
Ruthenia 71
Ryan, M.-L. 211, 226

Sachperoglou, E. 170
Said, E. 207, 257, 266
Šalda, F.X. 87, 90
Sales, J. 130, 134
Salomonsson Agency 198
Sami 268
Sánchez Piñol, A. 133
Sant Jordi Prize 135
Sant, A. 239–43, 246
Santos, B. de Sousa 250, 257, 259, 266
Sapiro, G. 52, 93, 105, 108, 140, 144
Sapkowski, A. 206, 213–23, 224
Sarajevo 12, 29, 30, 31
Saramago, J. 137, 252
Sardinia 127, 136
Saunders, F.S. 63, 67

Index

Saunders, L. 256
Saunders, W.H. 149
Savidis, M. 170, 179
Scaggs, J. 191
Scandinavia 5, 49, 53, 72, 141, 148, 155, 157, 159, 184–201, 259
Scandi-noir 137, 141, 188
Schein, E. 94, 108
Schendel, Arthur van 106
Schindler, J.R. 31, 33, 46
Schlegel, D. 148
Schmid, D. 184, 203
School of Slavonic Studies 82, 86
Schreiber, P. 219, 226
Schwartz, M.S. 50, 54
Scotland 236
Scott, J.W. 248, 266
Secher, M. 198, 203
Second World War 22, 33, 55, 57, 58, 63, 93, 100
Seferis, G. 166, 167, 178, 179, 183
Segura, A. 127–28, 144
self-translation 122, 227, 229, 230–44, 271
Selver, P. 73, 74, 79, 82–84, 86, 90
Semitic 228
Sena, J. de 250–53, 266
Serbian, Serbia 9, 10, 12, 13, 16–22, 28, 29, 30, 31, 32, 33, 35, 37, 38, 39, 41, 214, 268
Serefas, S. 182
Serés, F. 134
Seton-Watson, R.W. 73
Sfinx (Czechoslovak publisher) 58
Shakespeare, W. 15, 168, 171
Sharon, A. 171
Shaw, G.B. 74
Sheffield 131
Shelley, P.B. 152, 168
Sherard, P. 169
Shin, S.-M. 4–7
Shoup, P.S. 41, 45

Sicily 184
Siebenhaar, J. 97
Sigurdsdottir, Y. 186
Sijthoff (Dutch publisher) 101
Silber, L. 41, 46
Šimáček (Czech publisher)
Simon, S. 234, 241, 246, 257, 259, 263, 266
Siskind, M. 160, 163
Sjöwall, M. 187, 189, 191
Skerlić, J. 19, 22, 26
Sklad Vladimirja Bartola 116
Skogen, T. 63, 67
Skopje 209
Škvorecký, J. 88
Slaatta, T. 187, 194, 203
Šlancarová, J. 74, 90
Slauerhoff, J. 97
Slovak 2, 71, 268
Slovene, Slovenia 2, 20, 21, 109–25, 214, 231, 268
small national literatures 1, 2, 3, 4, 5, 6–7, 9–10, 11, 12, 13, 15, 18, 19, 23, 24, 25, 44, 53, 55, 56, 58, 59, 87, 92, 109, 110, 112, 113, 115, 119, 120, 121, 122, 123, 126, 127, 138, 140, 145, 146, 153, 154, 165, 179, 186, 198, 206–10, 223, 227–30, 247–48, 253, 254–55, 257, 262, 267–71
social media 141
Socialist Alliance of Working People of Yugoslavia 15
Socialist Realism 14
Söderlund, P. 147, 163
Sohár, A. 209, 215, 226
Solana, T. 134
Somerwil, J. 103
Somoza, J.C. 190
Søndberg, O. 199
South Africa 184
Soviet Union 14, 88

Index

Spain 56, 127, 128, 136, 258
Spanish 2, 128, 135–36, 142, 154, 172, 187, 227, 233, 235, 254
Spanish Civil War 133
Spanish Economic & Commercial Office (ICEX) 136
Spencer, S.-A. 144
Spender, D. 257, 266
Špirk, J. 48, 67
Spivak, G. 257, 266
Squires, C. 2, 8, 190, 192, 193, 197, 203
Srebrenica Report 32, 33, 46
  Hussein, Saddam 33
St John, J. 104, 108
St Martin's Theatre 74
Staël, Mme. de 147
Stagnelius, E.G. 149, 150
Stalin, J. 14, 88
Stalinism 207
Stanovnik, M. 113, 125
Star Wars 211
state funding for literary translation and promotion 60, 69, 74, 75, 91, 93, 113, 114, 117, 121, 128, 129, 195, 217
Steed, H. Wickham 73
Steiner A. 186, 193, 194–95, 203
Stern, G. 171, 172
Stichting tot Bevordering van de Vertaling van Nederlands Letterkundig Werk 91, 92, 93, 97, 100, 102, 103, 105
Štih, P. et al. 114, 115, 125
Stohler, U. 153
Stok, D. 217, 219, 220
Stougaard-Nielsen, J. 141, 145, 185, 187, 188, 203
Strindberg, A. 53, 54
Sturzenbecker, O.P. 151, 163
Stuttgart 160
Štybr, J. 85

Sue, E. 154, 155
Sulek, M. Malek 86
Sundance Film Festival 138
Sundhausen, H. 34, 47
supply-driven translation 48, 51, 52, 53, 54, 57, 58, 59, 60, 61, 62, 63, 223
Süssmann 62, 67
Svedjedal, J. 145, 163, 188, 203
Swan, G.N. 164
Sweden 58, 173, 187, 188, 189, 193, 194, 196, 197, 198, 258
Swedish 2, 52, 53, 54, 56, 136, 145–64, 186, 187, 188, 191, 196, 197, 269
Switzerland 58, 155

Tadzhikistan 188
Taiwan 188, 220
Tanoukhi, N. 228, 246
Tau, M. 50, 59
Tegnér, E. 149, 150, 152, 153
Teirlinck, H. 96, 106
Tennyson, A. 152, 168
Texas 106
Theoharis, T.C. 170
Theorin, J. 191
Thompson, J.B. 53, 67, 197, 203
Thoms, W.J. 99
Thornton, R. 177
Tihanov, G. 5, 186, 201, 204
Times Literary Supplement, The 97
Tito, J.B. 14
Tkacz, M. 215, 226
Tolkien, J.R.R. 211, 214
Tolstoy, L. 76
Tomlinson, J. 201, 204
Tonkin, B. 135
Tosca, S. 211, 213, 225
Toury, G. 48–49, 50, 51, 52, 67, 222, 226
Traduki Project 62

Index

translation 1, 2, 5, 6, 14, 17, 25, 27–28, 42–44, 48–64, 72, 84, 86, 92–93, 95, 100, 105, 109–13, 114, 117, 120–22, 123, 126, 128, 129–42, 145, 147, 148, 151, 154–59, 160, 165, 173, 177, 184, 185, 186, 194–96, 197, 199, 200, 205–06, 209, 213, 216–20, 222–23, 227, 229–30, 234, 243–44, 248, 254–56, 258, 263, 270–71
   and impartiality 27, 28, 37, 40, 43
translation studies 100, 109, 112, 123, 222, 229, 231, 232, 234, 244
translators 27–30, 40–44, 64, 77–78, 80, 81, 83, 84, 88, 92, 98, 99, 100–01, 106, 114, 120, 121, 129, 130, 132–34, 139, 140, 142, 148, 154, 158, 172, 178, 191, 217, 218, 219–20, 230, 231, 236, 237, 239, 244, 252, 260
Translator's Charter 139
translingualism 6, 227, 229, 230, 232, 234, 235, 236–39
transmedia 205–06, 201–23
Tree, M. 128, 144
Trentacosti, G. 2, 7, 8, 126, 142
Trevelyan, R. 97
Trivedi, H. 231, 245
Trstenjak, D. 114
Trubar, P. 111
Trubarjev sklad 113, 115, 116, 123
Tsirkas, S. 169, 183
Turkish, Turkey 60, 173, 187, 188, 208
Twayne 104, 105
Twisted Spoon (Prague publisher) 86
Tymoczko, M. 27, 47, 110, 260, 263, 266
Tzalopolou-Barnstone, E. 171

Uhland, L. 152
Ukrainian 2, 217
Undset, S. 59
Union of Yugoslav Writers 115
United Kingdom *see* British, Britain
United States of America *see* American
University College London 82
Unwin, S. 77, 78, 83, 84, 90
U.S.S.R. 14, 69
Ustaša 33

Valassopoulo, G. 168
Valencia 127, 128
Van Gorcum (Dutch publisher) 97
Vančura, V. 78
Vanderauwera, R. 98, 104, 108
Vargas, F. 191
Vayenas, N. 167, 182, 183
Velickovic, V. 209, 226
Venuti, L. 1, 8, 110, 112, 125, 126, 139, 144, 187, 193, 204, 205, 226, 247, 248, 255, 266
Vereniging von Letterkundigen 91
Verhaus, B. 101
Vestidjk, S. 97, 100, 105, 106
Vidal, G. 170
Vidal, M. C.-A. 251, 264
video game 206, 213, 214, 217
Vienna 156, 208
Vilenica 118–19
Vilnius 209
Vimr, O. 48, 54, 56, 67, 68, 69, 71, 87, 90, 97, 115, 193, 222
Virago 133
Vitalis (Erik Sjöberg) 149
Vivó, E. Torrents 144
Vlaamse Academie 95
Vočadlo, O. 74, 82–84, 86, 90
Vondel, J. van den 106
Vostaert, P. 99

Index

Voulis, Y. 178
Vriesland, V. van 94

Waade, A.M. 201
Wahlöö, P. 187, 189, 191
Walschap, G. 94, 96, 98, 106
Warsaw 208
Warsaw Uprising 216
Wassifiri 228
Watts, S. 249
Wawn, A. 149, 164
Weatherall, M. 77, 78, 81, 84
Weatherall, R. 77, 84
Weidenfeld, G. 126
Wells, H.G. 74
White, R.S. 235, 246
White, T.H. 251
Winchester, J. 158
Winder, S. 253
Wired 138
Wirten, E. Hemmungs 192, 204
Wischenbart, R. 189, 193, 197, 202, 204
Witcher, The 205–06, 210–33
Witt-Bratström, E. 155, 162
Woestijne, K. van de 94

Wolff, B. 96
Wolters, I. 53, 59
women writers 86, 145–60, 189, 256, 258, 259, 261–62
Woodward, S.L. 41, 47
World Fantasy Lifetime Achievement Award 222
world literature 1, 3, 11, 16, 50, 73, 134, 178, 184–85, 192, 248, 250, 254, 262, 263
WorldCat 149

Yan, M. 270
Yellow Bird 199
Yourcenar, M. 169
Yugoslav Writers' Association 115
Yugoslav, Yugoslavia 9–25, 27, 33, 41, 56, 58, 72, 111, 115, 268

Zabus, C. 232, 234, 241, 246
Zanello-Kunovsky, N. 87, 90
Zauberga, I. 111, 113, 115, 121, 125
Zedinjena Slovenija 114
Zeman, M. 80
Zernack, J. 49, 68

Printed and bound by CPI Group (UK) Ltd, Croydon, CR0 4YY
11/12/2022

CW01192830